*Also by Mike Ripley*

*Margery Allingham's Albert Campion*

MR CAMPION'S FAREWELL *
MR CAMPION'S FOX *
MR CAMPION'S FAULT *
MR CAMPION'S ABDICATION *
MR CAMPION'S WAR *
MR CAMPION'S VISIT *
MR CAMPION'S SÉANCE *
MR CAMPION'S COVEN *
MR CAMPION'S WINGS *

*The Fitzroy Maclean Angel series*

LIGHTS, CAMERA, ANGEL
ANGEL UNDERGROUND
ANGEL ON THE INSIDE
ANGEL IN THE HOUSE
ANGEL'S SHARE
ANGELS UNAWARE
Etc.

*Other titles*

DOUBLE TAKE
BOUDICA AND THE LOST ROMAN
THE LEGEND OF HEREWARD

*Non-fiction*

SURVIVING A STROKE
KISS KISS, BANG BANG

* *available from Severn House*

# MR CAMPION'S MOSAIC

## Mike Ripley

**SEVERN
HOUSE**

First world edition published in Great Britain and the USA in 2022
by Severn House, an imprint of Canongate Books Ltd,
14 High Street, Edinburgh EH1 1TE.

Trade paperback edition first published in Great Britain and the USA in 2023
by Severn House, an imprint of Canongate Books Ltd.

severnhouse.com

*British Library Cataloguing-in-Publication Data*
A CIP catalogue record for this title is available from the British Library.

ISBN-13: 978-0-7278-5098-0 (cased)
ISBN-13: 978-1-4483-0783-8 (trade paper)
ISBN-13: 978-1-4483-0782-1 (e-book)

*All Severn House titles are printed on acid-free paper.*

MIX
Paper from
responsible sources
FSC
www.fsc.org   FSC® C013056

Typeset by Palimpsest Book Production Ltd.,
Falkirk, Stirlingshire, Scotland.
Printed and bound in Great Britain by
TJ Books, Padstow, Cornwall.

# A Note on Evadne Childe

The crime writer Evadne Childe (1890–1965), whose novels featuring the amateur sleuth and archaeologist Rex Troughton are now long out of print, was one of the most popular writers in the 'Golden Age' of British detective fiction. Her association with Mr Albert Campion during her lifetime is detailed in the 2020 novel *Mr Campion's Séance* which, remarkably, is still in print, and which provides the only accurate bibliography of Evadne Childe titles.

*Mr Campion's Mosaic* is set in 1972, seven years after Evadne Childe's death, just as television begins to take an interest in her famous detective.

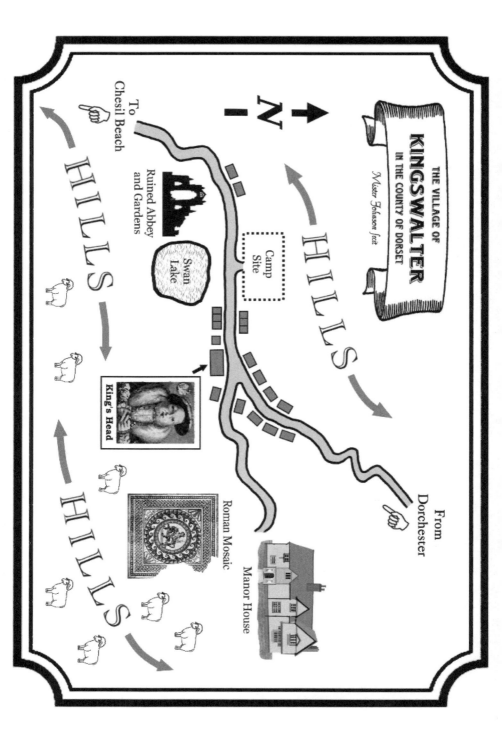

# ONE
## Poor Substitute

'Our formal business concluded and our lunch well and truly consumed,' announced Eric Rudd, 'we move to the informal, and I am sure far more entertaining part of today's agenda.'

Standing at the microphone and concentrating intently on the few notes scribbled in pencil on a postcard held at waist height, Mr Rudd failed to hear the whispered comment of the person seated next to him at the long top table.

*'Nobody said it had to be entertaining . . .'*

'But first, I must thank the committee and staff of the Concert Artistes Association for allowing us to use their splendid hall and the Jesters Bar and for looking after us so well.' Mr Rudd paused for the customary round of applause from the gathering. 'But before we turn, with anticipation and great pleasure to our guest speaker . . .'

*'. . . or pleasurable.'*

'. . . I would ask him to perform the ceremonial cutting of the birthday cake, in honour of what would have been Evadne Childe's eighty-second birthday. Ladies and gentlemen, I call upon our special guest, a man with more experience of long-bladed weapons than any of us here . . .' (polite laughter) '. . . to do the honours: Mr Albert Campion.'

The shining, pearl-handled carving knife presented to Mr Campion did indeed resemble a dangerous weapon, especially as it was offered to him the way a disinterested second would present a sabre across his forearm to a doomed duellist. Grinning foolishly towards his audience and resisting the temptation to take up a fencer's *en garde* stance, Mr Campion squared up to the birthday cake, which had been stealthily placed on the table before him by one of the ladies of the committee.

He paused, the knife blade quivering like a highly polished

mirror over the cake, but it was not for dramatic effect. Behind his large, round spectacles, his eyes blinked rapidly three times as he focused on the white icing covering the cake on which had been piped, in pink icing, the dedication *Happy Birthday Evadne Child.*

'Oh dear,' he said, making a first tentative cut, 'there seems to have been a spelling mistake, and so I insist on claiming the slice which should have had the "e" that is missing from the end of Childe.'

There were a few nervous giggles and suppressed clearings of throats around the room.

'It's the outside caterers' fault,' explained Eric Rudd, tight-lipped. 'The cake was only delivered this morning and we had no time to get it corrected.'

'Not to worry,' said Mr Campion, 'I don't think Evadne would have wanted a fuss made.' He slid the knife blade into the cake, exerting some force to crack through the ice-hard icing. 'In fact, it reminds me of the story of the religious Yorkshireman who ordered a headstone for his late lamented wife. He wanted a simple epitaph to display his wife's faith and devotion to God and told the stonemason to carve the words "She Was Thine". Unfortunately, as today, the "e" went missing and the headstone arrived saying, "She Was Thin". Furious, the Yorkshireman complained that the mason had forgotten the "e" and demanded the stone be redone. When the second version came back, it read "E She Was Thin".'

A trickle of restrained laughter rippled around the room, but Eric Rudd's face remained as blank as the wood panelling.

'I think you have to be northern to fully appreciate that,' said Campion sheepishly.

'Apparently so,' said Mr Rudd, waving over a waitress to remove the cake and oversee its butchering into individual portions before moving the microphone stand towards Campion and saying, 'The floor is yours.'

'*And may it open up and swallow me if I try any more jokes like that.*'

'Mr Chairman, ladies and gentlemen,' he began. 'I come before you as a poor substitute, as I cannot hope to match the erudition of last year's guest speaker at your inaugural birthday lunch, that distinguished crime writer and reviewer for *The Times*, Harry Keating, who has forgotten more detective stories than I will ever read.

'I cannot, and will not attempt to, make a case, as he so eloquently did, for Evadne Childe's place in the pantheon of *grandes dames* of purveyors of fictional murder and mayhem. For that, you really need my wife, who has been a lifelong fan of Evadne's novels and who sings their praises at every opportunity.

'I can, however, claim a small distinction, which neither my wife nor Harry Keating can match, in that Evadne and I shared a godmother. This rather tenuous connection was a useful bargaining chip when I begged her to autograph one of her novels at my wife's request. That was during the war, and we had certain dealings for some years after that, as I am sure you are all, as aficionados of her work, well aware. Her last novel, *Cozenage*, sadly published posthumously, was dedicated to me, unworthy as I am of such an honour.'

His audience were hoping for more and Mr Campion knew that, particularly his involvement – widely rumoured but never publicly acknowledged – in the Evadne Childe novel *Pearls Before Swine*, which appeared to critical acclaim and commercial success in 1963. It had been Evadne's last detective novel published in her lifetime, and Campion could, at the very least, have reminded them that a bright, shiny paperback edition was now widely available for the very reasonable price of three shillings and sixpence.

Instead, he chose to lead them down a safer, less sensational path; more *Woman's Own* than *News of the World*.

'I first met Evadne in 1940, in the early days of the war. She was already a successful writer of detective stories and, sadly, already a widow, as her husband, and the love of her life, Edmund Walker-Pyne, had been a fatality in what is now rather callously called the Phoney War, though at the time I seem to remember we called it the Bore War.' Mr Campion surveyed the room, his face stonily serious. 'I do not think I need remind anyone here that those early months of war were neither phoney nor boring for those serving, as Edmund was, at sea in the navy.'

Gentle nods of approval and pursed lips showed that he had estimated the average age of his audience accurately.

'The death of her husband hit Evadne hard. Edmund was not

only her true love and liege-man, but he was the inspiration for her archaeologist detective hero Rex Troughton. And what a hero he was; indeed still is, for as long as the novels of Evadne Childe remain in print, we will enjoy his adventures and, as I can see that a representative of her long-time publisher, J.P. Gilpin & Co., is present with us today, I am sure we can rely on that. If not, then we should make it clear that we are willing to take the Gilpin's representative hostage here and now and feed her only on birthday cake until the publisher accedes to our demands.'

There was an outbreak of restrained giggling around the table, and even the representative of J.P. Gilpin & Co., the stately Miss Prim, joined in the jest by fanning her face with the palms of her hands to ward off a mock fainting fit.

'At that first meeting, Evadne and I were on a pistol shooting range in the basement of a police station in Piccadilly. I will say no more about that particular conclave, other than it convinced me never to challenge Evadne to a duel . . .'

He had more stories about Evadne Childe, few of which would have been new or revelatory to a dedicated fan, but to which, Campion felt, he could give a personal imprimatur. He stressed Evadne's dedication to her mother and her strong links with her publisher without going into too much gruesome detail, and her generosity in taking in displaced persons during the war, about which he was intentionally vague, and he touched on her passion for spiritualism and séances, though he was even more vague on that score.

His audience were left with the impression that here was someone who had known the object of their affection and clearly shared in their admiration of Evadne the author, but who was too much of a gentleman to reveal anything salacious about Evadne the woman. Perhaps there was nothing salacious to report though, if there was, surely Albert Campion would be the one to know. A confidant of the hierarchy of Scotland Yard, as well as, it was whispered, a crime-solving collaborator with Evadne in real life, later portrayed, albeit obscurely, in her fiction, he surely must be able to dangle some morsel of gossip before the eager faces of the members of the Evadne Childe Society. After all, Evadne had dedicated her final novel *Cozenage* – the book the Society rarely spoke of, as it described the death of her hero Rex Troughton – to Albert Campion, and therein must lie a story for which the world, or at least the Society, was now more than ready.

But Mr Campion was turning over no stones, breaking no oaths, betraying no secrets, not that day. His lecture was nothing less than a spotless eulogy of Evadne Childe the woman and Evadne Childe the author – and no one was more grateful for that than the presiding chairman of the luncheon and the Evadne Childe Society, Mr Eric Rudd.

Indeed, it was an obviously relieved Eric Rudd who got to his feet and pulled the microphone and its stand to what was clearly its rightful position in front of him, in order to propose the formal vote of thanks.

'I speak for all of us,' he announced, brooking no argument, 'when I express my sincere thanks to Mr Campion . . .'

Campion braced himself for an outpouring of praise for his erudition, insight and eloquence, looking down humbly at the white tablecloth before him and being politely surprised and delighted when a waitress slid a plate bearing a large slice of cake into the space.

'. . . for filling in at such short notice. I know many of us were disappointed at the last-minute change of speaker, but I am sure we all found Mr Campion a worthy substitute, who has proved excellent value for his honorary membership of the Society.'

Mr Campion gave a slight nod in humble recognition of an honour he had not sought and then smiled benignly as applause flowed, if not thundered, around the room.

'And now may we have the coffee to go with the cake?' said Mr Rudd, addressing the waiting staff.

He sat back down in his seat and exhaled loudly, but whether it was in relief that Mr Campion's oration was over, or in anticipation of his cake and coffee, was unclear. As the table microphone was removed and cups and plates clattered down and spoons rattled, he turned to his left to lean into the shoulder of the guest of honour, only to find that said guest had been distracted by the person to his left, an elderly lady in a fur coat and blue cloche hat who was wafting a sheet of lilac notepaper in Campion's bemused face.

'I realize it might be an imposition,' she was saying in clipped tones which brooked no dissention, 'but could I trouble you for your autograph? I have a niece who collects them.'

'Only if I am allowed to use my real name, which I am obliged to do when I am out in civilized company,' said Campion, straight-faced, as the woman rooted around a capacious handbag, finally extracting a fountain pen.

'Oh, but of course,' his admirer agreed enthusiastically, 'I quite understand the delicacy of the situation and that a gentleman in your position has to observe certain . . . conventions.'

'You are most understanding, my dear lady. The name Campion has served me well for many a year, but the Inland Revenue can be particularly severe when it is enshrined in writing.'

'Oh yes, they can be very strict,' gushed the autograph hunter.

By the time she had recovered a pair of glasses from her handbag and examined the flowing signature in still-wet ink of 'J. Mornington Dodds', Mr Campion had turned away, summoned by Mr Rudd.

'Campion, a word if you please. Bring your coffee and cake into the bar. Miss Prim will join us there.'

Although Mr Campion knew Miss Prim of old, as the formidable gatekeeper of J.P. Gilpin & Co., the publishers of the novels of Evadne Childe, he had not seen her since the funeral of Gilpin's most profitable author, nor had he been given the chance to greet her before luncheon had been called, having been monopolized by the chairman, as all guests of honour were, it seemed. Patiently he allowed Mr Rudd to make the formal introductions, then warmly shook Miss Prim's hand.

'How nice to see you, Miss Prim. Are you here represent-ing Gilpin's the publishers or the Gilpin family? I thought Jeremy Gilpin was our president. In fact, I'm sure of it, as it says so on the Society's letterhead.'

'Mr Jeremy is proud to support the Society,' said Miss Prim, 'but sadly found that today's event clashed with a previous engagement in his diary.'

'Ah, yes, the Test Match at Lords.'

'I wouldn't know about that,' answered the woman, raising her eyebrows while Mr Rudd coughed in a belated attempt to distract from a sensitive topic, 'but Mr Gilpin missed an excellent talk, especially one given at such short notice.'

'So everyone keeps saying. Tell me, Eric, why was I summoned at three days' notice?'

Mr Rudd almost choked on a forkful of cake at being asked such a direct question.

'The speaker we had pencilled in dropped out due to illness,' he recovered with only a small explosion of crumbs. 'It was very sudden.'

'Well, I hope I wasn't too much of a disappointment.'

'Not at all, old man, not at all. You did splendidly.'

'One or two of the ladies of the committee were slightly disappointed,' said Miss Prim, 'but only slightly. They thought your diction was wonderfully clear.'

'I shall take that as a compliment, but do tell me who I replaced. Eric here has been very secretive on that score.'

'We had hoped for a talk from Peyton Spruce.'

'The film star? Good heavens, I really was a poor substitute. Still, that explains the autographs.'

Although he had not been a regular cinemagoer in recent years, in the late 1940s, the heyday of cinema attendance in an austere and war-damaged Britain, he had sat in his fair share of darkened Odeons and ABCs, seeking an hour or two of escapist entertainment while trying not to disturb the courting couples. Few of the films he had seen then had lodged in his memory. In truth, he had often taken more interest in the newsreels which accompanied them, but occasionally a performance, or a name, had stuck, and one such was Peyton Spruce.

It was a name unusual enough to stick in any circumstances, especially as Campion had read somewhere that it was the actor's real name rather than a stage name. He was personally aware of the protocols of the acting profession, and its union Equity, when it came to names, as he had a son and a daughter-in-law who counted themselves proud to be thespians. He had shared several soul-searching hours with son Rupert as he agonized over whether he should change his name, as there already was an actor called Gerald Campion, who also ran a snug little club in Soho (of which Mr Campion could not resist becoming a member). Rupert's wife Perdita had finally opted for the expedient of her maiden name, Browning, for theatrical purposes, on the grounds that two Campions in Equity were quite enough. Mr Campion had smiled ruefully at their agonizing, for the name Albert Campion – although he preferred to call it a *nom de guerre* rather than a stage name – had served him well for more than fifty years.

'You remember Peyton Spruce?' asked Eric Rudd.

'Of course I do,' said Campion. 'I am of that era. I believe I saw him on stage first, rather than screen, in a completely unmemorable production of *Macbeth* before the war.' He flung a hand up to his mouth. 'Oh dear, am I allowed to mention the Scottish play here?'

'This is a club for variety artistes,' said Mr Rudd rather severely, pronouncing it 'arteests', 'not the RSC.'

'Then I think we're safe, but in any case, that's by the by. Peyton Spruce would have been absolutely the ideal choice as a speaker for the Evadne Childe Society as he was the only actor to portray Evadne's dashing archaeologist sleuth Rex Troughton on the silver screen.'

'Until now,' said Miss Prim.

'Really? What have I missed? I admit I do not keep up with the popular arts, unless they manage to elbow their way on to the goggle box on a Sunday evening, and it must be twenty years since I saw the film of *The Moving Mosaic*. That was the only one of Evadne's books which got filmed, wasn't it?'

'It was,' said Mr Rudd, 'and it was not Evadne's finest hour.'

'Nor was it Peyton Spruce's from what I recall.'

Mr Rudd rankled.

'I happen to think Peyton Spruce gave a fine performance. He was a handsome chap, upright and clean-cut. Just the sort to play Rex Troughton.'

'I'm afraid "was" might be the appropriate word here. Spruce was simply too old for the role. Rex Troughton, if memory serves, was a dashing *young* man, based on Edmund Walker-Pyne, her late husband, whom she adored. He was in his twenties when Evadne fell in love with him and, like most fictional detectives, he never got old. Sadly, because of the war, neither did Edmund.'

'We must agree to disagree, Campion, though I maintain that Spruce did a first-rate acting job in a third-rate film, which should have remained true to its source material instead of diverting into a pathetic romantic comedy.'

'Yes, we can agree on that,' said Campion. 'I know my wife, the avid fan, was terribly disappointed with the film.'

'So were the critics,' said Miss Prim, 'and no doubt the producers when they saw the box office returns, as were Gilpin's, who had invested money producing a paperback edition of the book with Peyton Spruce as Rex Troughton on the cover.'

'And Evadne Childe was positively furious with the way the film people had treated her book. She swore blind she would not let any other of her books be filmed.'

Campion stared intently into Mr Rudd's face, which was beginning to colour slightly.

'May I ask how you know that?'

'From her letters,' Rudd said haltingly. 'You see, I was a dedicated fan of Evadne's work. One even had the pleasure of briefly meeting her at a book signing event. I began to write to her . . .'

'Fan mail.'

'I suppose you could call it that.' Mr Rudd's cheeks were glowing pink. 'Always care of her publisher, all quite proper, and she always replied – handwritten, very polite letters which I still treasure.' The pink domes of his cheeks now shone red. 'We corresponded from 1949 up to 1962. I wrote to congratulate her on *Pearls Before Swine* which came out that year, but she never replied. I understand now that she had suffered something of a shock that year.'

'She certainly had,' said Campion, looking at Miss Prim as if requesting permission to elucidate.

The formidable Miss Prim took charge.

'Her editor and friend, Veronica Hatherall, had been murdered and it was nothing personal, Eric; she stopped answering all her fan mail. I composed a pro forma "Thank you for your interest" letter, with a facsimile of her signature, which Gilpin's send out to this day. Veronica's death hit her hard, and after *Pearls* there was, as you know, only one more novel, and that was published posthumously.'

'And no more films,' said Campion.

'Until now,' said Eric Rudd, mutating from devoted Evadne fan to curator of her legend, 'which is why the Society needs your help, Campion; in fact, is prepared to employ you.'

Mr Campion's eyes widened behind his large, round, tortoise-shell spectacles.

'Me? I am not a film producer.'

'It's more of a legal matter.'

Mr Campion breathed a loud sigh of relief.

'And I am certainly not a lawyer. Come to think of it, I find being called a film producer the less offensive.'

'But you used to be some sort of a private detective, didn't you? Because that's exactly what we need right now.'

Mr Campion was taken aback, though not totally surprised, by the disdain that Rudd had injected into the words 'private detective'. For many years, his long-time associate, Mr Magersfontein Lugg, a reformed cat burglar – well, not so much reformed but now at least house-trained – had maintained long and loud that 'private narking' was 'common', and beneath a proper gentleman and even a 'gent's gent', as he sometimes styled himself if pressed for a job description. While Campion had never claimed to be a private detective, it was widely known in certain circles, both police and private, that he had undertaken the occasional 'commission' for financial reward, and indeed had once had a visiting card printed which declared that deserving cases were preferred and that anything 'sordid, vulgar or plebeian' would be ignored.

On more than one occasion, these 'commissions' had earned him the gratitude of Scotland Yard (and other, less public, mechanisms of the realm) rather than financial reward, but those days – he insisted to anyone who would listen – were behind him. Those who knew him well, however, were not convinced. As he was now seventy-two years old, although, he would insist, still as fit as a Stradivarius, Mr Campion maintained publicly that he was ready for a quiet life of retirement out of the public eye. Even those who knew him only by reputation found this difficult to believe. Friends, colleagues and enemies alike simply could not envisage a time when Mr Campion settled for a pipe-and-slippers, by-the-fire existence and, in his heart of hearts, neither could Albert Campion.

'I cannot envisage why the Evadne Childe Society should be in need of a detective, but I understand the Metropolitan Police employ quite a few, and they can't all be busy chasing bank robbers or raiding grubby bookshops in Soho. I do know some very helpful policemen at Scotland Yard; would you like me to ask if they can spare one?'

'It is not a matter for the police—'

'Not yet, perhaps,' Miss Prim interrupted him.

'Or lawyers, but certainly some discreet inquiries are necessary.'

'You had better come clean, Eric,' said Campion, 'if you wish to retain my attention; otherwise I have a cup of coffee going cold and a slice of cake positively wilting.'

'Mr Rudd really ought to have briefed you before he asked you to be our speaker today,' said Miss Prim.

Campion turned to her, offering Rudd his right shoulder. 'Why don't *you* brief me, Miss Prim? I take it that whatever this is, it involves your publishing firm.'

'In the long run,' she answered, 'it certainly does, but our immediate problem concerns the man you had to replace as our guest speaker at such short notice.'

'Star of stage and screen, though not for some time, Peyton Spruce.'

'Exactly. The man who played Rex Troughton on film in 1952 and who was supposed to revive the role in a new version of *The Moving Mosaic* for television – on the BBC!' Her voice began to quiver with excitement and Mr Campion made a play of looking suitably impressed. 'Only . . .'

'Only?' Campion prompted.

'Three days ago, someone tried to murder him.'

'Murder an actor *before* a performance? That is unusual.'

Eric Rudd snorted in disgust, propelling cake crumbs into the air. 'Pah! If only it was just a matter of damage to an old actor, that would be simple. No, Campion, the situation is altogether far more serious than that.'

# TWO

## Scene Setting

Partly to defuse Mr Rudd's blood pressure and partly to alleviate the mist of confusion settling on Mr Campion's head like an unwanted laurel wreath, Miss Prim showed Rudd the palm of her right hand in a fair imitation of policeman ordering traffic to STOP!

'Eric, please allow me,' she said and, without waiting for permission, turned her back to him and her face to Campion.

'Peyton Spruce was indeed involved in some sort of incident which resulted in him being injured badly enough so that he was unable to attend the Society's birthday lunch today, though we are still unclear as to the details. You very kindly stepped into the breach, but that is only a minor symptom of the overall problem.'

'I don't mind being a symptom,' said Campion cheerfully. 'There's far less responsibility involved than if one is expected to be a cure. But what on earth is the malaise which affects you? It must have something to do with dear old Evadne, you being her publisher and Eric her cheerleader.'

'It does, or rather it involves the rights to Evadne's works. You are well aware that Evadne felt somewhat responsible for the murder of Veronica Hatherall back in 1962.'

'Yes, I was, though there was no guilt on her part whatsoever.'

'Be that as it may, Evadne took it upon herself to look after Veronica's mother Pauline, who was confined to a care home near Brighton. In her will, Evadne assigned the royalties from her last book, *Cozenage*, to Mrs Hatherall, to help pay the costs of her care, which they did comfortably until Pauline Hatherall passed away two months ago.'

'Oh, I am sorry,' said Campion, 'I had no idea.'

'The problem was that Evadne also left her the film rights to her Rex Troughton books.'

'Really? Are those not quite valuable?'

'Well, they might be if anyone wanted to buy them.'

Campion looked at Eric Rudd, who was holding his tongue with some difficulty.

'Which they now do?'

'Let me come to that,' resumed Miss Prim with a deep breath.

'Gilpin & Co. are an old-fashioned publisher; one might even say behind the times. They see their role as providing good-quality hardback books from authors they can trust. They were always suspicious of paperbacks, licensing them to other houses, and never paid any attention to film or television or even radio rights. If those were negotiated, it was something an author did for themselves, or their agent did for them.'

'I wasn't aware that Evadne Childe had an agent.'

'She didn't. Veronica Hatherall, as her editor, negotiated the sale of *The Moving Mosaic* to the film's producers. I remember her being very excited about it at the time because it was her favourite Rex Troughton title and it was set in Dorset where she used to go on holiday as a child. Unfortunately, she was rather naive and agreed to a deal which involved a percentage of the profits from the film. Of course, there were none because the film was pretty awful.'

'That may be your opinion,' Eric Rudd growled.

'Well, the critics thought so, as did the distributors, and when it did get a showing, the cinema-going public stayed away in droves,' countered Miss Prim. 'Most importantly, Evadne Childe thought it was terrible, and she was terribly hurt when Sir Mortimer Wheeler, the archaeologist, called it a "desecration" on the radio. She wrote to Gilpin's to say she didn't blame Veronica, but she never wanted any other of her books to be mangled in the same way.

'The film company which made it folded within the year, and Evadne bought back the rights for a nominal sum. They were in the bundle of rights which she assigned to Pauline Hatherall, any income to go towards her care and comfort in her final years, though as it turns out Mrs Hatherall outlived Evadne.'

'And became the first honorary member of the Society,' said Eric Rudd proudly, ignoring the warning glare from Miss Prim.

'An honour,' continued Miss Prim with narrowed eyes, 'which Mrs Hatherall repaid by leaving the rights, both assigned and unassigned, to the Society in her will.'

Mr Campion smiled.

'By Jove, I think I'm following all this and, if I'm right, my crystal ball tells me the Evadne Childe Society could be due a bit of a windfall, courtesy of the late Evadne Childe, via the late Mrs Hatherall.'

He realized that by flippantly citing the deaths of two elderly and probably blameless ladies, he was pushing the boundaries of good taste, but given Evadne's long interest and firm belief in spiritualism, the thought appealed to him that her ghost might be somewhere directing the moves on this particular chessboard; or should that be a Ouija board?

'There is a problem,' said Miss Prim.

'I thought there might be.'

'When the BBC began to take an interest in the Rex Troughton books, we at Gilpin's had to refer them to Pauline Hatherall as the rights' holder, even though she was well into her seventies' – Mr Campion coughed discreetly at that – 'and quite ill, not to say rather frail, though her nursing home seemed to be doing a very good job of looking after her. I mean, she was all there, up here.' Miss Prim tapped her temple with a forefinger.

'You mean all her faculties were present and correct?'

'They certainly were. Gilpin's offered to advise her on any negotiations with the BBC, but she would have none of it. Said she had access to the best advice possible and it was going to be done her way.'

'Her way being . . .?'

'That the first book the BBC adapted was *The Moving Mosaic*, because it had been her daughter's favourite and because she, like Eric here, had rather liked the 1952 film version, particularly Peyton Spruce's performance as Rex Troughton. In fact, she liked that so much that she insisted that Spruce be given a starring role, and had a clause to that effect written into the option.'

'But Spruce must be nearly as old as I am,' said Campion, hoping that his voice did not sound desperate.

'Actors rarely play their real age,' said Eric Rudd, perhaps conscious that he was now himself into his seventh decade, 'and they stay active for a long time. Take Gielgud and Richardson, for instance: they're both still strong performers.'

'I somehow doubt they are in contention for the role of the dashingly handsome, two-fisted man of action, which was how Evadne envisaged Rex Troughton. All that running and jumping over archaeological digs – as well as shooting or biffing the bad guys – sounds quite exhausting to me. Surely, Peyton Spruce must have retired by now.'

Mr Rudd coughed diplomatically. 'He has opted for a life outside the footlights in recent years.'

'You mean he's *resting*, which is how the acting profession pronounces the word *unemployed*. You forget, Eric, I have a son in the business – occasionally.'

'Mr Spruce lives quietly, with some other theatricals, in Ealing. It's not a care home, like the one Mrs Hatherall was in, but I suppose you could call it a retirement home of sorts.' Miss Prim clenched her hands together, as if in prayer or at confession, though it was not clear to whom she was appealing. 'Certainly, his appearances on stage or screen have been rather . . . sporadic in the last decade.'

'I'll say,' said Campion. 'Oh, I'm sorry if that came out rather viciously. I really meant to say that I can't recall seeing Spruce in anything since *The Moving Mosaic*.'

'Perhaps that's for the best. He went to live in France for several years,' Mr Rudd did not attempt to disguise his disdain for that country, 'and appeared in some *French* films' – now disdain had turned to disgust – 'always playing a stupid English stooge with a bowler hat and umbrella, most often caught in some sex scandal. Not even ITV would employ him after that.'

'I tried to inform him of Evadne's funeral, but we never got a reply from the address we had in France,' said Miss Prim. 'Then Eric had the idea of setting up the Society, and it was he who tracked down Peyton to Ealing and made him an honorary member. Sadly, it was not in time to invite him to be our guest speaker last year, but Mr Keating did an excellent job.'

'And this year you got little old me, instead of the film star you all wanted.'

'Oh, but you did splendidly, Mr Campion, and at such short notice.'

'Now about that,' said Campion seriously, 'it's not the short notice I mind, but I am curious as to the reason for it. Did you really mean it when you said someone tried to murder him?'

'Running someone over in a car is certainly attempted murder in my book!' Mr Rudd blustered, but Miss Prim took a more Christian view.

'It could have been an accident, Eric, we must not jump to conclusions, and Peyton was not actually murdered, just injured. It may have prevented him coming here today, but it shouldn't prevent the new production from going ahead.'

'Is that likely?'

'There is a possibility, given all the other strange things which have happened.'

'What strange things?'

'That's exactly why we need a detective,' said Mr Rudd, rather smugly. 'That's why we need you.'

Mr Campion took a circuitous route from the Concert Artistes club back to his Bottle Street flat in order to ponder and evaluate what he had been told, what he knew and what he might do.

From Bedford Street he headed towards Leicester Square, then diverted along the Charing Cross Road (resisting the temptation of the second-hand bookshops) and threaded his way through Chinatown, revelling in the scent of exotic herbs and spices and trying not to be distracted by the strange and wonderful array of items animal, vegetable and mineral on sale.

By the time he was striding down Piccadilly, he was confident he had assembled the relevant facts, if not necessarily in a logical order, and although he had a large number of questions, he knew he had fewer answers.

The three main characters in the drama in which he had been invited to participate were Evadne Childe, Mrs Pauline Hatherall and Rex Troughton, which was unfortunate as two of them were dead and one was fictional. The problem seemed to be how the fictional Rex Troughton was to be brought to life in a new BBC film version of *The Moving Mosaic*, and that meant that Peyton Spruce had to be considered as a person of some interest.

As far as Campion could ascertain, Gilpin's – Evadne's publisher and beneficiary of any increased sales of her books thanks to television exposure – must, logically, support the project. Their emissary, Miss Prim, had been honest and forthright and was one of the least duplicitous persons Campion could recall encountering in a long career of mingling with recidivists, cut-purses, thieves both petty and international, spies, traitors and general n'er-do-wells.

Eric Rudd, an obvious, if solitary, fan of Spruce's less than spectacular original interpretation of Rex Troughton, would surely be on side and bring the full weight of the Evadne Childe Society along with him. They were a force not to be trifled with as, even on brief acquaintance, Campion had put them down as vociferous and regular complainers to whoever was supposed to be in charge of standards at the BBC. Most seemed to be ladies of a certain age, an age which could certainly have encompassed an infatuation with a younger Peyton Spruce when he was in his matinee idol heyday, and Campion counted himself fortunate that they had not greeted his role as substitute speaker with a barrage of bread rolls.

He had learned that Eric Rudd had first proposed the idea of an Evadne Childe Society in 1960, and although Gilpin's had been quite keen on the idea (as they had not been asked for funding), Evadne herself had not supported such idolization during her lifetime.

Quite clearly, Mr Rudd and the Society would be vocal champions for a new version of *The Moving Mosaic*, even if confined to the small rather than large screen. As, he assumed, the late Mrs Pauline Hatherall must have been, for she had sold the BBC the rights to make it, or rather an option to do so.

Miss Prim had explained the intricacies of the rights contract signed by Mrs Hatherall. As with all such contracts, it seemed, what the BBC had bought was an 'option' to film the Rex Troughton stories, as Evadne had written them as a series of television dramas, the payment for that option being ten per cent of the total purchase price. The remaining ninety per cent of the contract would be due – and Campion found this a wonderfully arcane phrase – 'the day principal shooting commences', as was customary in the film and television industries.

What Mr Campion found intriguing, along with Eric Rudd's clumsy attempts to play the matter down, was the destination of that ninety per cent, which no one was vulgar enough to put a figure to, but must surely be in the thousands of pounds. Mrs Hatherall had received the ten per cent option fee but had died before 'principal shooting' commenced and a larger payday ensued. In her will, Mrs Hatherall had left the bulk of her cash to the nursing home where she saw out her days, but the film rights to the Evadne Childe Society, which would now benefit from a consider-able inheritance when – and if – principal shooting did commence.

So the Society not only had a noble motive for supporting the new film, to honour and promote the work of Evadne Childe, but a rather more base one: financial gain. Gilpin's, Evadne's publishers, were in an identical situation, dedicated to promoting the legacy of their star author and very aware, as even Campion was, that exposure on television, no matter how badly done, guaranteed a boost in sales. Not having been able to publish a new Rex Troughton novel for five years, irrespective of the fact that the character had been killed off in Evadne's last book, would certainly have made a dent in Gilpin's balance sheet.

Which left Rex Troughton himself, or rather Rex Troughton as portrayed by Peyton Spruce.

Campion could not think of a single reason why an ageing actor whose career, with the best will in the world, had faded into obscurity would not be positively chomping at the bit at the prospect of a chance to perform to an audience and, thanks to television, perhaps the biggest audience of his career. Who was it that said old actors never die, they just quiver in the wings awaiting a cue?

Spruce must surely be in favour of the remaking of *The Moving Mosaic*, and was probably of the old school of acting who still remembered his lines twenty years on. He would see it as a return to stardom; not that his star had ever risen very highly in the firmament of British theatre or film, and certainly not in television.

Since his performance in *The Moving Mosaic*, Campion could not recall seeing Spruce in anything other than in a black-and-white newspaper and magazine advertising campaign for Brylcreem, where he still cut a dash for a man of his age, with all his hair, black and shining, firmly in place. There again, he was no fan of French cinema – and he could hear Lugg in his head saying, 'Who is?' – and for all he knew, Spruce's time living in France may have seen him achieve cult status in the *Nouvelle Vague*.

There would undoubtedly be publicity value in having Spruce reprise his role twenty years on, even if the original version had not exactly set the silver screen alight – hardly singed it, in fact – and the BBC would be happy with that, added to which it seemed to have been their idea to adapt the Rex Troughton books in the first place, and they had already put up some of the money. Thus, they were the least likely to have an interest in sabotaging the production.

For that's what appeared to be going on, once additional information had been extracted from Mr Rudd and Miss Prim.

It had been squeezed out of them only after a firm prompting from Mr Campion.

'I wasn't invited here today just as a last-minute replacement speaker, was I?'

'Well, you were, but you seemed a perfect choice given the circumstances. You are a member of the Society; you knew Evadne and her work, and you have some experience of . . . investigations.' Mr Rudd's voice trailed off in embarrassment. 'We didn't think you would refuse and, once here, you could be persuaded to help us get to the bottom of things.'

'Then tell me which things I am expected to get to the bottom of. I suspect there's more to this than an injury to your first-choice speaker.'

'You are quite right, Mr Campion, we have not given you the full picture,' confessed Miss Prim. 'Peyton Spruce's accident—'

'If it was an accident!' spluttered Eric Rudd, before being silenced by a piercing feminine glare.

'Whatever happened to Peyton, it was only the latest in a series of . . . incidents . . . which have dogged the pre-production of the new version of *The Moving Mosaic*.'

'Pre-production?'

'The period of preparation before filming begins; everything from casting, writing the script, finding locations, rehearsing the actors, hiring a film crew, designing the costumes, building the sets and keeping the budget on track.'

'It sounds positively exhausting,' said Campion.

'I'm told it is. A good producer has to be not only a good general but a ruthless one. Do you remember the film *The Longest Day* from about ten years ago?'

'About the invasion of Normandy, the one with just about every film star who could fit into a uniform? Of course.'

'They say that producing that film was only *slightly* less complicated than organizing the real D-Day.'

'I can believe it,' said Campion innocently. 'Having to deal with all those actors must have been a nightmare.'

'My point is that there are so many aspects to pre-production that lots of things can go wrong, and if too many things do go wrong, people lose confidence in the project and the project gets abandoned. Do you have any idea how many films and television shows never get beyond pre-production?'

'I haven't a clue, my dear lady.'

'Neither have I, actually,' admitted Miss Prim, 'but I think it's a lot. I do know that of the modern popular fiction we publish at Gilpin's, at least half have film and television options taken out on them, but none ever seems to get exercised.'

'You mean they never get to the day of principal shooting? So what happens to them?'

'The rights go into a sort of limbo until the period of the option expires. A film company might try to sell the option on to another producer – that's called "turnaround" or "being in development hell" – but usually things just fizzle out, leaving everyone disappointed after getting their hopes up.'

'Are you suggesting that something similar might happen with *The Moving Mosaic*?' Campion asked gently, his face a picture of serious concern.

Eric Rudd could contain himself no longer: 'Dammit all, we are only three weeks away from principal shooting, they can't call it off now!'

'Why should they?'

'Because all concerned are getting very nervous,' said Miss Prim, remaining calm, 'and that includes Gilpin's and the Society as well as the producers, and probably the actors.'

'Let me guess,' said Mr Campion, 'Peyton Spruce's little accident was not the first misfortune to shake confidence in the project.'

'What have you heard?' snapped Eric Rudd.

'Nothing, other than what you have told me, which is, dare I say so, less than the whole picture. What else has happened?'

'There were photographs,' Miss Prim began, ignoring a vicious glare from Eric Rudd, 'which were sent to both Jeremy Gilpin and to Eric as president and chairman of the Society, respectively. They showed Peyton Spruce and a young female in a rather compromising position.'

'A very young female, not much more than a girl . . .' Mr Rudd had clearly decided to elaborate in detail now that the secret had been revealed, '. . . not half his age, and they were on a beach *and* damn' near naked.'

'A beach is usually quite a convincing alibi for being nearly naked,' said Campion smoothly. 'Unless one is in Scotland in winter, where it is simply not credible, or at Frinton-on-Sea where it is probably still illegal. Could they not have been innocent holiday snaps?'

'Nothing innocent about them. Man of his age . . . Quite disgusting.'

'The photographs had a message on the back,' said Miss Prim. 'It said, "Do you want this man as your hero?" on all of them, both the set sent to Gilpin's and the ones Eric received.'

'Any idea when they were taken?'

'We think about fifteen years ago, when Peyton was in his mid-fifties.'

'And the girl?'

'No more than nineteen.'

'A daughter perhaps?'

For a moment Campion thought Mr Rudd might explode.

'You don't treat a daughter like that, and certainly not on a public beach! Anyway, Spruce doesn't have any children.'

'So we don't know who the female in question is?'

'We have no idea,' said Miss Prim, 'and she is not really the point. What worries Jeremy Gilpin is the implied threat that if Peyton Spruce makes a career comeback, the photographs will be released to the press and there will be damage to the reputations of Rex Troughton, Evadne Childe, and Gilpin's as her publisher.'

'Not to mention the poor old BBC, who are coming under pressure from the Festival of Light people and their clean-up TV crusade,' Campion added, not entirely helpfully.

'Even worse,' said Rudd, 'just the threat might make them pull the plug on the whole thing, given what else has happened.'

Mr Campion sighed loudly. 'There has to be more, so why not just tell me? My days of squeezing blood from stones are so far behind me – I've quite forgotten how to do it.'

'There have been other incidents,' Miss Prim said in a rush, as if making up for lost time. 'The BBC producer in charge of *The Moving Mosaic* has received a series of vicious poison pen letters; one of their location scouts down in Dorset was rushed to hospital with severe food poisoning, a man called Don Chapman; and then the chap they appointed to direct the film was attacked in Soho two nights ago and his arm broken. Plus the owner of the location where they planned to film is threatening to revoke permission because his land has been overrun by hippies.'

'Oh,' said a blithe Mr Campion, 'is that all?'

On the back of a discarded agenda paper from the Society's annual general meeting, Campion had made a note of the two addresses he had extracted from Eric Rudd and promised 'to look into things'. He had abandoned a cold cup of coffee and a barely nibbled slice of cake on the counter of the Jesters Bar, noting that Peyton Spruce's image on the actors' standard ten-by-eight publicity picture was not among those gracing the walls.

'Is Spruce a member here?' he asked Rudd.

'No, he never regarded himself as a concert artiste, probably thought he was too serious an actor to mingle with the music hall tradition. They can be terribly snobby, actors.'

'Indeed they can, but they are usually very good for gossip.'

'You won't find anyone here who would gossip about Peyton Spruce.'

'Oh don't worry about that.' Campion smiled. 'I have a personal and very reliable source of gossip when it comes to the acting profession.'

'What sort of source?'

'Another actor.'

Whenever Campion gave advance warning of a visit to London, his long-time companion Magersfontein Lugg – part major-domo, part *éminence grise* – always insisted on giving the Bottle Street flat 'a proper airing' and ensuring that it was stocked with essential supplies. If Campion was visiting alone, these invariably comprised whisky, gin, tonic and soda waters, half a pound of back bacon and two eggs. Should Lady Amanda be accompanying him, Lugg's shopping list extended to include Ryvita crispbreads, grapefruit, plain yoghurt and a basket of fruit, and a bunch of flowers for decoration.

Absenting himself from his official responsibilities as the beadle of Brewers' Hall in the City never posed a problem for him and from the way he floated around the flat with a feather duster, whistling tunelessly (or so Mr Campion liked to imagine), his domestic duties seemed more of a relaxation than a chore, though he had been known, when provoked, to declaim that 'Some of us have jobs to go to!'

At first subdued and clearly sulking, ostensibly because Campion had not brought him back a slice of birthday cake but really because he had not been invited to the celebrations at the Concert Artistes Association ('one of the nicest little clubs I ain't a member of'), Lugg cheered up immensely when Campion telephoned his son Rupert and asked if he was free to join them for 'a boys' night out on the town'.

As Rupert's wife Perdita was otherwise engaged in an evening performance of a rather dour modern play in a studio theatre in Islington, and Rupert himself was 'resting' he was therefore, to Lugg's delight, both footloose and fancy-free.

'We'll go somewhere where we can get a good steak, or a Barnsley chop,' Campion had said after cutting the connection with a finger but keeping the receiver to his ear. 'His mother thinks he needs feeding up.'

Lugg patted his enormous stomach.

'Couldn't agree with her more,' said the fat man, eyeing Campion suspiciously, 'and you're up to something, ain't yer?'

Mr Campion smiled benignly, a forefinger poised over the dial of the telephone. 'You wouldn't happen to know the number of the Ealing Broadway police station off the top of your head, would you?'

# THREE

## Longitude Zero

T he two Campions and Lugg dined well, but fairly abstemiously, in a small Italian restaurant off the north side of Oxford Street, which did the best steak tartare outside France, according to Mr Campion. Lugg, who preferred his beef 'dead and roasted', settled for a large sirloin well done, and Rupert, being a resting actor whose wife was working that evening – and every other evening bar Sunday with matinees on Thursdays and

Saturdays – announced that anything would be a pleasant change
from beans on toast.

Mr Campion briefed his fellow diners over their meal and a
bottle of Valpolicella Ripasso, suffering the well-meaning interjec-
tions of Lugg, who had shared some of his connections with the
late Evadne Childe, a woman – Lugg ruminated fondly – who was
'a rum old bird' if ever there was one.

When he announced that he would be taking the train to Brighton
the next day, Lugg perked up and demanded to know if he should
pack his bucket and spade.

'You're not invited, old fruit,' said Campion. 'I'm visiting a
residential care home and after one look at you, they might not
let you out.'

Trying his best to look offended, Lugg smoothed down the
slightly stained white napkin he had tucked into his collar.

'Just as well, as I have a previous h'engagement – an official
function at the hall.'

'Meeting of the local Temperance Society, perchance?'

'Annual luncheon of the Northern Home Counties Brewers'
Association h'actually. They always have jugged hare on the menu
and bring Charlie Wells's beer up from the country. I'm partial to
both, so'd be a shame to miss them.'

'It would indeed, so you enjoy yourself, just remember to check
the local press for any reports of a hit and run accident in the
Ealing area earlier this week. It might be worth ringing the nearest
hospitals, see if they treated any film stars lately.'

'Peyton Spruce?' Lugg's eyes widened. 'You reckon anyone
remembers him? He could rob a bank without a stocking on 'is
'ead and not be fingered in a line-out.'

'One little old lady in a care home on the south coast remembered him and I'd like to know why. Meanwhile, you Rupert—'

'I've never heard of him,' said Campion's son, tucking into a
multicoloured cassata ice cream.

'Then you start with a blank sheet of paper – or almost blank.'
Campion slid a piece of notepaper across the table. 'That's his
current address, I'm told. Don't go there, but find out what you
can about Peyton Spruce. Your agent, Maxim, might be a good
place to start, and see what gossip you can dig up on this BBC
remake of *The Moving Mosaic*.'

'This new film,' Rupert said hopefully, his spoon poised in mid-air, 'would there be a part in it for me?'

The next morning, Mr Campion's train deposited him in Brighton on time, but it was not his final destination, though he quickly found a taxi to take him the few miles along the coast to the cliff-top town of Peacehaven, a place famous for having the Greenwich Meridian run through it. Mr Campion took a perverse satisfaction in knowing that he was fifty-something degrees north in terms of latitude, but he was *exactly* nought degrees either west or east in longitude. It was a small crumb of comfort in an uncertain world.

His driver found the White Horses care home without difficulty. As he climbed out of the taxi, Campion, peering out to sea and into the wind, could see how the home had got its name, as it offered an unrestricted view of squadrons of white-horse waves rolling across the Channel. It was a vista which could take the observer's mind (especially an elderly and infirm observer) away from the fact that they were on a clifftop, and that the journey to the beach below could be swift but fatal if due precautions were not taken and the warning signs ignored.

The management of White Horses seemed to have taken this into consideration, and the home, a large white modern villa, had been built with a surrounding wall high enough to deter both intruders and sleepwalking escapees. It also boasted a solid, studded front door – strong enough to thwart the raids of Saxon pirates who had once sailed on those very white horses out to sea – which yielded to Mr Campion with no more violence than a finger on a bellpush.

Campion removed his fedora and introduced himself to a shiny-faced young woman in a nurse's uniform who invited him in and informed him that Sister Mary was expecting him. Slightly hesitantly he entered the office of White Horses' manager Mary Graham, unsure as to whether he was meeting a chief executive or a mother superior.

'Don't worry, Mr Campion,' said Mary Graham, rising from behind an impressive oak desk and casually fastening the middle jacket button of a dark blue corduroy trouser suit, 'I am not a nun.' She tugged gently at the frilly cuffs of a white blouse, fluffing them out of her jacket sleeves like a Georgian dandy. 'Though I used to be – in a previous life – and my staff don't like me to forget it.'

'I was not . . .'

'You were thinking it; all my visitors do, especially the men. It seems to unnerve them.'

'That could prove useful,' said Campion.

'It often does.'

'May one enquire what made you turn, if I may put it this way, from the public to the private sector when it comes to caring for people?'

Mary Graham released Mr Campion from a firm, business-like handshake. She was a middle-aged woman with close-cropped brown hair, who wore no make-up, her face showing more lines than it deserved.

'If God gave me a skill,' she said, 'and I firmly believe there is a God, and he did – it was to ease the passing of others from this life and as a nurse, or what you might call a sister of mercy, I have done just that for most of my adult life, half of it in holy orders.'

'Until . . .?' prompted Mr Campion. 'You had an epiphany of some sort? I am sorry, that sounded terribly rude.'

'It did, but you are right, I did have an epiphany of a sort. I became disillusioned with my church – not my God – and their attitude to end-of-life care. Confessions became more important than care and, not to put too fine a point on it, dying was regarded as a terribly serious business.'

'I think I would agree with that. At my age I have little choice.'

Mary Graham wagged a forefinger as if to admonish him. 'Of course it is, but there is no reason we should wear sackcloth and ashes *before* the inevitable event. Let those whose time has come enjoy what pleasures God's world can offer whilst they can. If they want a sea view, to have their dog with them at the end, or champagne with their dinner, why not? I saw too many kind and generous souls locked away in dark isolation and forgotten about. Out of sight and out of mind. I cannot believe that any merciful God would approve of that.'

'I suspect you are a supporter of the hospice movement.'

'I am indeed, though here at White Horses we are a residential nursing home and all the staff are medically trained.' Mary Graham smiled a slightly wicked smile. 'Some of our residents actually recover and are discharged. There are those, of course, without families to support them, for whom this is the last stop on their life's journey, and so we try to make their passing as comfortable, and as happy, as possible. Pauline Hatherall was one of those, and I can assure you her last days here were very happy. That is why you are here, isn't it?'

She motioned for Campion to take a seat and then settled herself back in her chair behind her impressive desk. It was a long time since Campion had felt he was back in the headmaster's study having to explain himself.

'You do not seem terribly surprised, Miss Graham.'

'It's Mrs Graham, actually – another reason why I am no longer a nun. The late Commander Graham was a naval man who built this house so he could gaze out to sea on the off-chance that something interesting might happen beyond the windows, though it never did. He called the house Longitude Zero, insisting that the Greenwich Meridian ran through it, and he was out there on the cliff edge messing about with a sextant when he fell over the edge, so perhaps something interesting did happen beyond the windows once, which is probably the reason very little surprises me these days.'

'I am so sorry.'

'Please do not pity me. The commander was not the marrying kind – and neither was I. When I found myself with this house, which is far too big for a lonely widow, I put it to good use. After changing the name, of course. Longitude Zero sounds terribly *fatal* somehow.'

It certainly had done for the late commander, thought Campion, who was in no doubt that he was dealing with a strong-willed and resourceful woman.

'Let me get straight to the point, Mrs Graham,' he said. 'I am indeed here about the late Mrs Hatherall although, to be perfectly honest, I have no legal and very little moral authority to ask you questions about her.'

'But that won't stop Albert Campion,' said Mrs Graham with a fleeting smile. 'Oh yes, I know who you are. Pauline Hatherall told me all about you, years ago, when she moved in with us. She had lost her only daughter, and no parent should have to bury their child, especially a daughter who was murdered.'

'Poor Veronica.' Campion sighed. 'It was an awful tragedy.'

'Pauline did not blame you; she praised you as the man who brought her daughter's killer to justice.'

'A sort of justice. I regret immensely that I did not make the time to visit Mrs Hatherall and explain things.'

'Mrs Walker-Pyne did, on several occasions, and we all had to pretend we did not know she was the famous Evadne Childe.' Mrs Graham allowed herself a ghost of a smile at the memory. 'She and the daughter had been very close, I believe.'

'They were. I am told that a genuine friendship between an author and their editor can be highly productive, though it is rare. I take it Mrs Hatherall was a fan of Evadne's Rex Troughton books?'

'A very big fan. She had a collection of signed first editions, which she left to White Horses in her will. I keep them in the lounge where we have a little library for residents and visitors.'

'Would you know if she had a particular favourite?'

'She certainly did.' Mrs Graham, elbows on the desk, made a tent of her fingertips. 'It was *The Moving Mosaic*; and that's why you're here, isn't it?'

At the same time, almost ninety miles north (and less than one degree of longitude west, had anyone calculated it), Rupert Campion was discussing the same topic with his agent Maxim Berlins in a cramped corner of the main bar of The York Minster in Dean Street, Soho, better known to those who regularly squeezed into its confines as The French House.

'Of course I've heard of *The Moving Mosaic*,' Mr Berlins said, balancing a glass of Ricard on the narrow shelf which ran the length of the bar at just the right height to make it uncomfortable to rest an elbow on. 'The BBC are very excited about it. High hopes for it ushering in a new era of crime dramas on television; going to be quite radical, they say. Mind you, I got that from one of their press officers, so it's probably not reliable.'

Rupert took a sip from his half-pint of bitter, having lost a considerable quantity through being jostled by the early lunchtime crowd and, due to the throng, found himself physically closer to his agent than he had ever been before, and conscious of the fact that it would not be a good career move were he to spill beer down Maxim's Italian-cut brown mohair suit.

'So it's a big production number, is it?'

'From what I hear on the grapevine it is – and the answer is no.'

'No what?'

'No, there isn't a part in it for you, not that I'm aware of. They are keeping the casting close to their chest – for good reason, according to the rumours.'

'Do you know who the producer is?'

'Not one of the usual suspects, that's for sure.' Maxim sipped his Ricard for dramatic effect. 'It's a woman.'

'A woman?'

'I know. Who would have thought Aunty Beeb was so courageous? A bright young thing called Tamara Reams apparently. Oxford – of course – and a high-flyer tipped for big things, but perhaps not quite so soon, the sort who wants to rock the boat to see where the apples fall.'

Rupert was not sure he followed the metaphor, but it probably made sense in one of the many mid-European languages which Maxim spoke.

'In what way? I thought it was a detective story, there's nothing new in them, they're very popular. Good Lord, *The Mousetrap* has been running for twenty years.'

'And before you say anything, I can't get you a part in that either.'

'That wasn't a hint,' said Rupert, though in fact it had been. 'I was just curious as to how this Tamara Reams was planning to shake up the traditional, rather stodgy, detective story.'

'Well now, according to the gossip . . .' Maxim nuzzled his drink and leaned in to his client as though passing state secrets, '. . . she has some radical ideas. For a start, she's using film and location shooting to show off the best of the British countryside, which is sure to go down well overseas, especially America, when the BBC sells the series into foreign markets.'

'You mean the quaint roses-round-the-door Cotswold image you get on biscuit tins and tea towels?'

'Exactly so. The Americans love it, the Canadians and the Australians think they miss it. Foreign sales, you see, it's a growing market for the BBC. They might even sell it to France. Have you ever *seen* French television?'

'Well, that doesn't sound too radical to me,' said Rupert, raising his empty glass to Maxim's eyeline. It was a hint rather than an offer and it was stoutly ignored.

'No thank you, Rupert, I have lunch with a client,' said Maxim politely before checking his wristwatch, 'which fortunately is just down the street at Quo Vadis. I cannot be late, so I will be brief.'

Maxim quaffed his drink and smacked his lips before continuing.

'The radical idea this Tamara Reams has produced is the format. She wants to make a series of films – "Rex Troughton Investigates", or something like that – each of which are two hours long. That's longer than most of the films you would get at the cinema, unless it's an epic with an intermission so you can buy a choc ice.'

'That sounds ambitious, and expensive,' said Rupert, genuinely impressed.

'It is both, and that's why there is a lot riding on it. If it takes off, it could usher in a whole new era of television drama.'

'There are certainly plenty of Rex Troughton books to have a go at,' said Rupert, to prove he had done his preparation on the works of Evadne Childe. 'Twenty or twenty-one, I think.'

'Twenty-three,' said Maxim, showing he too had done his research, 'and of course they can hire some jobbing writers to do original scripts, maybe bring the stories up to date. Quite a few were written in the Thirties, and you can't really see the viewing public putting up with two hours of a whodunit set back then, can you?'

'Oh, I don't know. The period flavour might play well in America.'

Maxim snorted into his Ricard.

'The Americans would think it *was* contemporary England! Still, country houses and the murder of an aristocrat or two might sell it. If it ever gets off the ground that is, given the bad voodoo dogging the production.'

'Bad voodoo? Do tell.'

'It's all Green Room gossip, of course.'

'The best kind.'

'And I cannot reveal my sources,' Maxim said with a wink and an impish smile, indicating that he would if pushed, 'but the whole project seems to be dogged with bad luck. One of the directors up for the first film got beaten up on the way back from an awards ceremony; there are poison pen letters flying about all over the place; some rather explicit photographs have been sent to the governors of the BBC, anonymously of course, and there's chaos down in Dorset on the main filming location. Not only have some of the location scouts gone down with suspected food poisoning, there's also some sort of dispute with the local landowner; and one of the key locations – the one with the Roman mosaic that's supposed to go missing in the plot – has been occupied by a gang of protestors, or possibly gypsies, or perhaps hippies having a Love-In. Do they still have those?'

Maxim fastened the middle button of his suit jacket and judged the distance to the door to Dean Street.

'Anyway, I wouldn't touch the programme with a borrowed bargepole. If ever there was a *Titanic* desperately seeking an iceberg, then *The Moving Mosaic* sounds like it, and they haven't even started shooting.'

'It sounds like a nightmare,' agreed Rupert as Maxim turned to leave. 'Are you sure there isn't a part in it for me?'

'It was Mrs Hatherall's favourite Rex Troughton story,' said Mary Graham.

'And also her daughter's, I believe.'

'Well, that's perfectly understandable. You have read it, I presume?'

'Almost certainly,' said Mr Campion vaguely, 'but a long time ago.'

'Then you might remember that the action takes place in a village in Dorset.'

Campion nodded enthusiastically, even though he had been momentarily distracted by a seagull flying on an almost kamikaze course towards the picture window of Mrs Graham's office.

'In the book, the village is called Blackcombe, but it is based very closely on the real village of Kingswalter, which has a manor house, a ruined abbey and the remains of a Roman villa.'

'And a traditional country pub with roses round the door.' Campion spoke with conviction, even though he was guessing.

'Naturally,' confirmed Mary Graham. 'It also had a campsite for tents and caravans, and that's where the Hatheralls spent many a summer holiday when Veronica was a child. The late Mrs Hatherall always maintained that it was Veronica who persuaded Evadne Childe to visit Kingswalter, which she did just after the war. She was clearly inspired by the place and *The Moving Mosaic* was the result.'

'They made a film of it, as I recall.'

'They certainly did, and that was Mrs Hatherall's favourite film of all time. Veronica took her to a screening of the film before it came out. It wasn't a red-carpet premiere or anything grand like that, but for Pauline it was pure Hollywood glamour. I think that was when she fell in love with the star.'

'Peyton Spruce?'

'So you've seen the film?'

'When it came out, which must be twenty years ago now. I honestly don't remember that much about it, other than the fact that Evadne Childe hated it.'

Mary Graham raised an eyebrow. 'Don't all authors loathe what cinema and television does to their books?'

'It's almost expected of them, but I think the sensible ones keep quiet, take the money and run. Evadne Childe never cared about the money and didn't want any more of her books filmed in her lifetime. Quite why she bequeathed the rights to Mrs Hatherall, I really don't know, other than her misplaced guilt about the death of her daughter.'

'Perhaps she did not need the money and thought Mrs Hatherall might.'

'Certainly Evadne was concerned that Mrs Hatherall was taken care of, and of course the rights were not worth anything until somebody bought them. Now they have, it seems that White Horses here will be the ultimate beneficiary.'

Mary Graham interlocked her fingers and rested her chin on them, fixing Campion with a glassy stare. 'White Horses received a very generous cash bequest in Pauline's will,' she said coldly, 'the bulk of which came from the initial option on the rights. The rights themselves went to the Evadne Childe Society. Mrs Hatherall had no surviving family, the will was not contested and whether the new film gets made or not, White Horses' connection with it is at an end. Quite frankly, after all the meetings over the last year or so, I can't say I'm sorry about that.'

'Meetings . . .?' prompted Campion.

'Oh my sweet Lord, we had lawyers, producers and directors from the BBC, researchers, the Childe Society, accountants, copyright lawyers and goodness knows who, though no journalists. I draw the line at journalists.'

'Very wise.'

'Mrs Hatherall was getting so many visitors that the other residents were getting quite jealous. Mind you, they were all delighted whenever Peyton Spruce and his friends turned up; they always brightened up the place.'

'Spruce visited Mrs Hatherall?'

'Several times. She'd been writing to him for years and he would send her signed photographs, but when he came to see her in person she was absolutely over the moon. I told you, she was in love with him, or perhaps she was in love with Rex Troughton and Peyton Spruce *was* Troughton to her, given all the memories she must have had of the book, the Kingswalter setting and, of course, her daughter.'

'I think,' said Mr Campion deliberately, 'it would be useful if you could give me a list of Mrs Hatherall's visitors. *All* of them.'

# FOUR

## The Clapham Cossack

Having allowed the morning rush hour to subside, Mr Campion took a District Line tube to Ealing Broadway and then strode into West Ealing with impunity along the Uxbridge Road, musing, as he passed the town hall, that it displayed, in Kentish ragstone, all the exuberance of Victorian taste for the mock gothic with, he feared, all the concomitant crudities. In comparison, the fire station and then the municipal

offices were drab and functionally angular, clearly hoping to go
unnoticed and happy to let the town hall take whatever architectural
glory was going.

Mr Campion's destination, Broughton Road, also displayed
along its relatively short length some rather brutal concrete, where
blocks of flats had replaced the houses destroyed by a parachute
mine in December 1940, claiming fourteen lives in the process.
Yet many Edwardian semi-detached houses had survived unscathed;
solid family houses with bay windows upstairs and down and small
front gardens protected by thigh-high brick walls.

The address Campion was seeking was one of the few detached
Edwardian mansions in the street and was known not by a number
but by the name Curtains. It was one of the addresses he had been
given at the Evadne Childe Society, along with that of White
Horses in Peacehaven, and he wondered, rather immaturely, if it
too could be the name of a residential care home, one specifically
for ageing actors. If it was, it was a joke of the darkest hue.

Rupert's research had mined few details about the address, other
than that it was a place where 'forgotten theatricals lived with
their memories'. The house known as Curtains was owned by a
'legend' of London's shadow theatrical world; that is, the world
of music hall, which never got nearer to the West End than the
Aldwych and was, as far as Campion was concerned, a lost world.
The property owner was a woman grandly named Anastasia
Tempest, who as an actress had appeared in several silent films
but had failed to make the transition to 'talkies'. Rupert was at
first surprised that his father did not recognize the name as they
were surely 'of the same vintage' and then was confused as to
why Campion *père* was giving him such a filthy look.

Anastasia Tempest might not have set the stage or the cinema
screen alight, but she had proved herself a shrewd businesswoman,
acquiring the Broughton Road house in 1944 at a time when a
second Blitz – with flying bombs rather than parachute mines –
had conveniently lowered property prices. As to what sort of house
or home it was, Rupert had been able to discover only that it was
not registered as any sort of care or retirement home, but he had
shown some initiative by making a flying visit to an Ealing post
office where he had consulted both the telephone directory and
the electoral roll and discovered two things.

There was no telephone listing for a Miss, or Mrs, Anastasia Tempest on Broughton Road, but the house Curtains was listed in the electoral roll and within it, registered to vote, was a Miss Alice Dubbs. Checking back in the phone book, Rupert found Miss Alice Dubbs and her Ealing telephone number listed for Curtains. Interestingly, the electoral roll showed there were four other residents of Curtains eligible to vote: Peyton Spruce, Thomas Alfred Taylor, Sheila Kaye and Brogan Bates, though none of them had an entry in the phone book.

Campion had received Rupert's report by telephone on his return from the south coast, although he was no clearer in his mind as to what sort of a residence Curtains could be, other than it was unlikely to be a hideout for fugitives from the law, as few of them take the trouble to exercise their democratic prerogatives.

It was Lugg of all people who was able to shed some light on the matter, having called round to the Bottle Street flat, replete from his regional brewers' annual lunch, on the off-chance that Mr Campion might join him for a 'nightcap', it being after six and the pubs being open. Protesting exhaustion from a surfeit of sea air, Campion had declined the offer, but to placate the big man, had presented him with a stick of brightly coloured Brighton rock as a souvenir. Before an astonished Lugg could offer either thanks or a vicious retort, the telephone had rung and, when Campion had greeted his son, Lugg had placed an elephantine ear next to the receiver that Campion held against his.

By the end of the call on which he had so shamelessly eavesdropped, Lugg's face had crumpled into a moonscape of smug conspiracy.

'Never 'eard of Anastasia Tempest?' he said, nose in the air and sniffing loudly in haughty derision. 'Blimey! Either yer memory's going wiv old age or you wasted yer bachelor years.'

'In deference to my darling wife, I must agree that my *bachelor* years, pre-Amanda, were certainly wasted, but fail to see how familiarity with this Anastasia Tempest would have rescued them; and before you enlighten me, make sure your mind has not taken a smutty path or byway.'

Lugg waved his ham-hock hands to disperse the suggestion. 'I'm not talking dirty, I'm talking a legend of the 'alls: the Clapham

Cossack she was. Well, that's what she was known as when she did her act.'

Mr Campion adopted his most vacant expression.

'Are you saying that Alice Dubbs of Broughton Road Ealing was in fact the subject of admiration in your misspent youth?'

'I never knew that was her real moniker, she took that *rooshian* name 'cos of her act – it was a Cossack dance, you know, high kicks from a crouched position and whirling like a dervish. She always did it to fast music, the Sabre Dance f'r instance. Many a time the pit orchestra couldn't keep up with her. Dead athletic she was – she was a blur when she twizzled and turned in them footlights.'

'Let me hazard a guess,' said Campion, 'that her popular appeal was due to a skimpy costume.'

'Apart from the shiny black boots,' Lugg reminisced with a smile, his eyes half closed, 'her costume was all fur, but it was skimpy. Yeah, skimpy's the word.'

As Campion approached the front door of Curtains, along a path of crazy paving flanked by regimented rectangles of small flowers, he tried to dispel the image not of an energetic burlesque performer, but of Lugg's face remembering her in full furry flight. Yet that high-kicking object of Lugg's youthful lust must surely be as old as Lugg now, or indeed, himself, and unlikely to be still in show business. He had, however, looked up the native term for a traditional Cossack dance – the Ukrainian word *hopak* – in case he needed to break the ice, though with the stage name of the Clapham Cossack, the odds were that her knowledge of life on horseback on the Russian steppes was limited.

Fortunately, the slim, white-haired woman who eventually answered the doorbell seemed in no danger of demanding a band to be struck up, nor did she show any desire to converse in Ukrainian.

'Can I help you?'

'Good morning,' said Campion, raising his fedora, 'my name is Albert Campion and I was hoping to have a word with Peyton Spruce.'

'You don't look like you're from the BBC – far too respectable.'

'Why, thank you. I'm not, though our interests may coincide on this occasion.'

'Peyton's not here just now, he's out shopping. I am Alice Dubbs and this is my house. You are welcome to come in and wait for his return. In fact, I insist you come in and tell me all about it. Everyone here tells me everything; those are the house rules.'

Campion followed his hostess down a wide hallway with doors to each side, which ended in an impressive dark oak staircase. The lady of the house – he was trying desperately not to think of the title 'Clapham Cossack' in case it slipped out inadvertently – opened the third door on the left and bid him enter.

She was certainly of a similar age to Campion and, in her smart, bright red high heels, came up to his shoulders. She wore a light-weight tailored suit and a white blouse pinned at the throat with a large silver brooch in the shape of a star with a central orb of flecked amber.

Following the advice of Agatha Christie, Campion made a point of noticing the woman's hands, the backs of which were always supposed to betray a woman's age, despite the many adjustments she could make to other aspects. Mr Campion drew no firm conclusions from his observations, but he did note that Miss Dubbs had a thing for finger rings with semi-precious stones, as only her thumbs remained unadorned.

'So what is your particular interest in Peyton, Mr Campion?' she asked after guiding her visitor to one of several mismatched armchairs in what was clearly her private sitting room, which Campion suspected she referred to as her 'parlour'. It was a very feminine room, with patterned throws over the armchairs, crocheted doilies on every flat surface, an eclectic collection of pottery dogs on the mantelpiece guarding a three-bar electric fire and framed prints of famous pastoral scenes on the wall, mostly the work of Constable and Stubbs, familiar to the patrons of thousands of British public houses. It boasted French windows leading out on to an impressively long back garden, where a thin stick of a man was leaning on a hoe tending one of the many flower beds, separated by large geometrically shaped stone planters. A yard-wide strip of manicured lawn bisected the beds and the pot plants like a runway, ending in a single tree and a small garden shed, its planking pock-marked with algae.

'My interest is primarily to see how he is, as I understand he was involved in a road accident recently,' said Campion, 'and to pass on the best wishes of some of his fans. He was unable to make a speaking engagement the other day and I was a poor substitute, I'm afraid, so we do have a connection, albeit a tenuous one.'

'But you don't know Peyton?'

'Not personally, but I know of him, and his career.' Campion paused and studied the thin face of the woman in the chair opposite, 'and I have just remembered where I have seen *you* before.'

'And where was that?' Miss Dubbs's thin face showed no emotion, but her shoulders hunched as she leaned forward in her seat.

'In a photograph, hanging above the Jesters Bar in the Concert Artistes club. It was a very attractive head-and-shoulders studio portrait of a beautiful woman.'

'It would not be polite to suggest that you check the prescription in those glasses of yours, Mr Campion, but there again, if you managed to recognize this little old lady from that ancient picture, your optician must be a good one.'

'You are too modest.'

'Nonsense! I am – was – an *artiste* in a world where modesty is either unknown or a handicap. It is rarely a strength. I am pleased that picture of me still hangs there, of course, though not out of vanity, but because it replaced, at my insistence, an earlier one taken in a more flamboyant part of my career.'

'As the Clapham Cossack?'

'You are not the innocent you try to portray, are you, Mr Campion?' Miss Dubbs's face now lit up with amusement and sheer devilment. 'It's a good act you've got there, but it doesn't fool an old trouper. You knew who I used to be before you crossed the threshold.'

'A friend of mine was a fan of your act.'

'A friend, of course it was a friend; it's always a friend or a friend of a friend.'

'Your beauty made quite an impression on him, an impression which has lasted for some considerable time.'

'It was not my beauty he remembers.'

To Campion's surprise, and trepidation, Miss Dubbs stood up out of her chair, reached down with both arms and grasped the hem of her skirt, which she proceeded to raise to two inches above the knee before performing a half-turn in a brief genuflection.

'It was these your friend remembers. My legs were my fame and fortune.'

'Clearly a valuable asset,' said Campion nervously, wondering what one of Mrs Christie's detectives might deduce from such a sight.

Miss Dubbs allowed her skirt to slide back into decency and resumed her seat.

'My Cossack dance got me noticed – in more ways than one – and I was quite an attraction on the halls, especially among the boys in uniform. And then the Bolsheviks killed the Tsar and frolicking Russians went out of fashion.'

'But that wasn't the end of your theatrical career, was it?'

'Far from it. Are you familiar with the term "chorine"?'

'As in a dancer in a chorus line?'

'I was not just *a* dancer in the chorus, but *the* dancer. Once I moved into the more legitimate musical theatre, I quickly realized I was so much better than the average hoofer in the line, and if the other girls couldn't keep up, that was their look-out. I would be the one who stood out, the one the audience remembered, and they did. You see, I didn't have the voice for a leading role – truth is I can't sing for toffee – but I could *dance*, and so I made sure that I was the chorine who made a bigger impression than the star of the show.'

Campion wondered how popular Miss Dubbs had made herself with the rest of the chorus line, but doubted that any such concern had crossed her mind.

'It got me noticed by some people with interests in the film business. They were silent movies, so my voice didn't matter, and I let my legs do my singing. Unfortunately, my legs could not act and straight parts eluded me, though I did audition for a young Mr Hitchcock once, but I wasn't blonde enough. When talkies came in, I knew not to push my luck, so I did some choreography and ran rehearsals for some West End shows, but stayed out of the limelight and settled down to the only career open to a chorine of a certain age.'

She paused for Campion's response, studying his owlish face.

'Which was? The career, I mean, not your age, of course.'

Miss Dubbs smiled and nodded as if acknowledging chivalry.

'I found myself a sugar daddy . . . Does that shock you?'

'I will try not to let it,' said Campion without conviction.

'He was a kindly gentleman, much older than me, and fortunately well-off enough to support a wife and family down in Sussex as well as me. He'd seen my Clapham Cossack act during the war – the first war, that is – and never forgotten it.'

'Perfectly understandable,' agreed Campion.

'He was a bit of a stage-door johnny, and was hanging around one of the theatres waiting for some actress or other when I turned up to put the chorus line through their paces. He recognized me and we . . . well, we hit it off. We had to be discreet because he had quite a public position in the legal profession, though I have no intention of telling you his name even though he is no longer with us.'

'I have no wish to know it, but would I be right in thinking your gentleman friend established you in this house?'

'Oh, *please*! There's no need to be coy; he was my *lover* and a very considerate one. And don't look at me like that or I will tell you in great detail of the private performances the Clapham Cossack gave!'

Campion held up his hands in surrender.

'But you are quite right. He bought this house outright for me during the second war and visited me regularly for several years, even establishing a bank account for me to pay the bills because to leave cash on the mantelpiece would have been vulgar. It was an arrangement we kept secret, because he could not acknowledge me, and overall it was a very happy arrangement until he died.'

Her voice dropped and, with her hands in her lap, she began to fiddle nervously with her rings.

'I had no idea he had died – that he was even ill – until I read his obituary in the papers,' she said quietly, 'and I didn't dare go to the funeral; but that, I suppose, is the price paid for being a kept woman.'

'But you stayed on in the house.'

'I had nowhere else to go and, anyway, I like it here. My savings kept me going for a year or two but then . . .'

'You began to take in lodgers.'

Campion was struck by the fact that he had encountered, over two days, two strong, resourceful women with completely different backgrounds and life experience, who had acquired property and used it to bolster their independence. Mary Graham, down in Peacehaven, had opened White Horses and attracted residents. Alice Dubbs had used the legacy of her Clapham Cossack days to attract – he thought he was safe in saying – paying lodgers.

'Oh, they're not lodgers! We are housemates in a sort of commune; the house is mine, of course, but we share all the bills and we all have specific tasks and responsibilities.' She pointed a bejewelled forefinger at the French windows and the tall, thin man tending the flower beds. 'Thomas, for instance, has green fingers, and so naturally became our gardener. He keeps us in soft fruit and makes jam every year but has no interest in vegetables. His main interest is in flowers, which are pretty, but not as nourishing as a crop of potatoes or carrots. Still, he does his best.'

'A well-kept garden can only add to the value of the property,' said Campion.

'Very true, though I have no intention of selling. Curtains will see me out, and then my housemates will have to fend for themselves somehow.' Miss Dubbs spoke with a lilt in her voice and a smile, leaving no doubt that such an eventuality was a long way off.

'How did Peyton Spruce come to join your little community, if I may ask?'

'You may, because Peyton's why you came and here am I boring you with my little journey through life.'

'I distracted you, but it has sounded a frightfully interesting voyage so far. When did Mr Spruce join the expedition here at Curtains?'

'Nearly ten years ago now. He and Brogan had been living in France . . .'

'Brogan?'

'Oh, it was nothing like *that*. Peyton and Brogan go back a long way, and when Peyton thought he'd found a career in French cinema, it conveniently coincided with Brogan's ambition to own his own vineyard, so they bought a farm together.

'Peyton got some film work but then it dried up. Brogan got to press grapes for a few years and drank whatever profit they made. Eventually they had to sell up and move back to Blighty, their funds considerable reduced.'

'And you took them in.'

'Well, they had to audition first.'

'Audition?'

'This is a theatrical establishment, Mr Campion, we don't want just anyone as a housemate, only those who have trodden the boards in some form or another. That way we get on because we know each other's foibles and follies.'

'Did they have to actually perform their . . . act?'

'No, no, merely assure us – well, me mainly – of their theatrical credentials. Peyton came with an advantage as Sheila, one of our happy band of "Curtain Callers", as we label ourselves, had worked with him in the past and Thomas out there' – she pointed towards the garden again – 'turned out to be his biggest fan, and had even appeared in a film with him – as an extra, of course.'

'So Peyton was voted in unanimously?'

'If we were a democracy, he would have been, but I remind you, this is my house. I never had any qualms about Peyton; after all, he's a charming and very handsome man, very *active* for his age.'

Mr Campion suppressed a wince at the emphasis Miss Dubbs put on the word, hinting that her Anastasia Tempest personality was not far below the surface.

'Of course, Peyton insisted on bringing Brogan with him and, at first, I had my doubts, but Brogan came with a car. It's a bit of a banger and it is French, but it has proved very useful as neither I, nor Peyton for that matter, can drive. Goodness knows why the neighbours don't complain about the thing littering up the street.'

Campion felt he knew exactly why any neighbours of the formidable Miss Dubbs would be reluctant to complain.

'It's a quite ghastly machine,' she went on. 'The steering wheel is on the wrong side; it's the most garish yellow colour, and it looks like a dustbin on wheels. I refuse to ride in it myself, but it is useful for doing the shopping and running errands.'

'I can't say I noticed any such monstrosity on my way here.'

'Brogan has taken Peyton to do the grocery shopping. He does the driving and Peyton makes sure he comes back with something other than nasty Algerian red wine in plastic bottles.'

'How is Peyton? I understand he was in a road accident recently and, really, that's why I'm here, to see how he is.'

'Oh, don't worry about Peyton,' said Miss Dubbs, flapping away any concern with her hands. 'He may look like a Savile Row tailor's dummy but he's as tough as old boots.'

'What happened?'

'He got clipped by a drunk driver as he was crossing the Uxbridge Road late one night when he was out walking the dog. Don't worry, he doesn't actually have a dog, he just likes a stretch of the legs before bedtime, and we call it his dog-walk hour.'

'I wasn't worried about any canines, real or imaginary,' said Campion tersely, 'just about Peyton.'

'I would have blamed Brogan had he not been here watching television with me when it happened, but Peyton wasn't badly hurt. He had a sore hip and leg, though most of the damage was when he fell on his face in the road. He had spectacular bruising and what we used to call a "pearler" of a black eye. A day's bed rest and some tender ministrations from Sheila and he was good as new. You see, Mr Campion, we look after each other here at Curtains.'

'It wasn't necessary to send him to hospital?'

'Good Lord, no. Actors are tough, Mr Campion, they have to be, given the amount of slings and arrows thrown at them during their careers.'

'But some of them seem to have enjoyed the outrageous fortune of finding a refuge here at Curtains.'

Miss Dubbs considered Mr Campion's remark, as if weighing the value of a response.

'Actually, Peyton is the only what you might call serious actor among us, in that he came from the legitimate theatre and then films. The rest of us had backgrounds in the profession but were not straight actors. We are a motley crew and that's for the best. Can you imagine what a house full of resting actors must be like?'

'I can,' said Campion with a sigh. 'I have a very vivid imagination.'

'*There can be no room for ego in acting,*' quoted Miss Dubbs dreamily. 'Do you know who said that?'

'No.'

'An idiot no one remembers.'

Campion laughed and filed away the quote to use on Rupert. Miss Dubbs, satisfied with her little homily, cocked her head to one side and then looked out of the French windows to where the spectral gardener had frozen in mid-hoe and was clearly listening to something.

'Brogan's car has a distinctive sound,' Miss Dubbs explained, 'and it sounds as if the shopping expedition has returned. It's always a relief to find that machine has made its way back in one piece. Shall we go and greet the rest of the gang?'

Campion followed her out into the hall, where he could hear the over-revving of an engine and the harsh mechanical screech of a handbrake being pulled on with excessive force from outside on the street. Then he registered the slamming of a car door, some muffled voices, a clump of footsteps, and then the doorbell was pressed, and then pressed again.

'The postman always rings twice,' Miss Dubbs said with an enigmatic smile, 'at least when he's forgotten his keys.'

For a moment, Campion was bemused at the reference, but when the Clapham Cossack stretched her long legs down the hall to reach the door and pull it open, he allowed himself a brief, 'Oh, I see . . .'

Parked in the street, at the bottom of the garden path, was a bright yellow Renault 4L van which had seen better days, the days in question being in a former life as a French post office van. A crude respraying had failed completely to obliterate the words *La Poste* on the side, or the initials *PTT* on the driver's door.

'Sorry, Alice, forgot my keys again,' said the stocky, bearded figure standing on the path in a deep, fruity voice. He wore a naval duffel coat and had a shopping bag dangling from each hand. Behind him, walking towards the house, was a taller, immaculately dressed man in blazer and flannels, also weighed down with shopping bags and behind him, at the kerbside by the yellow van, its rear door open, a woman with long white hair constantly having to be brushed away from her face was hauling yet more bags out of the van's interior.

'We have a visitor, Brogan,' Miss Dubbs said to the bearded man.

'How very splendid!' The man lowered his bags to the ground, which they hit with a loud clinking noise, and offered a hand. 'Brogan Bates.'

'Mr Campion is here to see Peyton.'

'Of course he is,' said the man, his voice now pure gravel. 'Let me introduce them.'

He indicated that Campion should step out of the house and on to the path and, as he stepped by her, Campion heard Miss Dubbs say, 'Oh, no' quietly to herself.

The man who had introduced himself as Brogan Bates took Campion's arm and led him before his victim, who put down his shopping bags and stood before the visitor in polite expectation.

'Allow me to introduce my very good friend.' As Bates began to orate in a deep, fruity voice, he mimed the scattering of rose petals in front of his victim. 'That well-known stalwart of stage and screen . . .'

'Brogan, *please* . . .' said Peyton Spruce out of the corner of his mouth.

'The *international* film star, famed for his acting prowess in two languages . . .'

'Stop it!'

'That renowned thespian, worshipped by millions of adoring fans, famed across the globe . . .'

'Brogan, now you're being really embarrassing.'

The bearded man turned away from Campion and stood face-to-face with Peyton Spruce, but did not lower his voice.

'Look! I never said you were any bloody good, but you are well known!'

# FIVE

## The Curtain Callers

'That was Brogan's party piece,' said Peyton Spruce as he shook Campion's hand. 'He's been doing it for years and I have to react as if I'm shocked and horrified every time.'

'You gave a very convincing performance,' said Campion, 'proving, as my son is always telling me, that acting is really all about *re-acting*.'

'Your son is in the profession?'

'He would very much like to be, but at the moment is resting between engagements. I think that's the technical term, is it not?'

'An all too familiar one. Now, let me do my chores and get all this shopping put away, then I'm all yours. Can we use the Green Room, Alice?'

'Of course, darling,' said Miss Dubbs, but her eyes were on Brogan Bates who was halfway down the hall, a shopping bag in each hand. 'Brogan will no doubt want the bar open, but I'll make a pot of coffee for the more abstemious among us.'

Spruce winked at Campion as he bent to pick up his share of the shopping. 'Alice doesn't approve of Brogan,' he whispered.

'Hardly anyone does,' said the woman following him up the path, swaying under the weight of not two, but three shopping bags. 'I'm Sheila, but don't mind me.'

'Here, let me lighten your load,' offered Campion, prising the handles of two bags from her clenched fist. 'Let me take these indoors while you close up the van.'

Out on Broughton Road, the bright yellow Renault's back door yawned fully open as if waiting to receive any passing French mailbags. It dawned on Campion that Sheila must have been travelling with the groceries in the back of the two-seater vehicle.

'Brogan will see to the van eventually,' she said, 'but with a bit of luck not before somebody steals the ghastly thing.'

'I think that unlikely,' said Campion. 'It wouldn't make a good getaway vehicle unless you were robbing a post office in the Dordogne.'

They exchanged smiles and then he followed her inside to the kitchen, where the shopping was piled on to a scrubbed wooden table.

'Peyton, take Mr Campion through to the Green Room. Sheila and I will put this lot away and bring the coffee,' ordered Miss Dubbs.

Spruce gave her a mock salute and indicated that Campion follow him into the front room of the house, which had at one time been an Edwardian family's parlour, probably reserved for special visitors or perhaps the laying-out of a deceased loved one. No respectable Edwardian patriarch would have recognized it without a sharp Pooter-esque intake of breath, not least because hardly a sliver of wallpaper was visible thanks to the collage of theatrical posters, programmes, faded black-and-white photographs and yellowing reviews cut from newspapers which covered the walls from skirting board to dado rail. An added surprise would have come from the fact that a miniature public house seemed to have been created in one corner of the room, and the bar was being enthusiastically restocked by Brogan Bates.

The room, apart from two matching high bar stools, was full of random wooden furniture which could have been salvaged from a bankrupt (or bomb-damaged) pub some time in the Fifties, or borrowed from a contemporary theatre Green Room, which is exactly what it emulated with the addition of a full bar.

'Don't mind Brogan,' said Spruce, 'he's heard it all before.'

'I made most of it up!' scoffed Bates, without turning round from his task of screwing an optic into a new bottle of gin.

'I'm sorry,' said Campion, 'heard all what before?'

For the first time, Mr Campion managed to study his prey closely – if 'prey' was appropriate, and Campion was not sure of that yet. Spruce was without doubt a handsome fellow, and it was easy to see why the ladies had – and still did – found him attractive, even at his age. And at that, Campion mentally rebuked himself, for he and Spruce must be the same age near enough, even if the actor looked ten years younger, so could it be nothing short of pure envy which made him look very closely for tell-tale signs of artificial youthfulness?

It was cold comfort that he found them. The thick wavy hair, parted on the left, looked real enough, but its black, shiny lustre had been enhanced, if not created, by chemical hairdressing products, the proof being clear for anyone near enough to see in several faded brown spots on his shirt collar. On careful examination, it was clear that Spruce was wearing skilfully applied make-up, which Campion put down to either him being an actor *per se*, or some clever cosmetic work to cover bruises and cuts around the cheekbones as, after all, the poor man had recently been involved in a road accident, hadn't he?

'Heard all the gruesome details of my less than fabulous career,' Spruce was saying, breaking into Campion's reverie. 'I assume that's why you're here. You are a journalist, aren't you?'

'Most certainly I am not,' said Campion, adjusting his spectacles,

as though his dignity had been assaulted. 'I was told that Miss
Dubbs does not allow journalists on the premises.'

'Christ! You're not a rozzer, are you?' Brogan Bates exclaimed,
jumping and turning – with the skills of the Clapham Cossack?
– until his back was to the bar, his arms outstretched in an over-
dramatic attempt to shield it from official prying eyes.

'No, I'm not a policeman. Were you expecting one?'

'Not at all. I'm sorry,' Spruce exuded charm, 'please forgive an
actor's vanity. I just assumed you were here to interview me.'

'About *The Moving Mosaic*?'

'Well, yes.'

'I would certainly like to talk to you about that, if I may.'

'Oh, hell's teeth!' boomed Brogan Bates, in a voice which began
to ring faint bells with Campion. 'What's happened now?'

'Has something happened since the accident?' Campion asked
innocently. 'That was really my main concern, or rather the concern
of the Evadne Childe Society, who were hoping to hear some
details of *The Moving Mosaic* at their Annual General Meeting.'

'Ah, yes,' said Spruce, his eyes dropping. 'I'm sorry I missed
that because the Society has been very loyal to me. I hope they
weren't too disappointed.'

'Oh, but they were, but only in the quality of the speaker who
replaced you. I was despatched to discover how you were.'

'As you can see, I am still alive. I was shaken rather than stirred,
as they say, but apart from a few cuts and bruises, I'm fit as a
fiddle and ready for my close-up, Mr DeMille.'

'As long as Mr DeMille doesn't look *too* closely . . .' Brogan
Bates had lowered the volume, but his voice was still a rich, deep
bass and slightly menacing, not to mention, thought Campion,
irritatingly familiar.

'Brogan is referring to my wearing make-up, which I normally
do only when on stage or before a camera.' Spruce turned his head
so that Campion got the benefit of his left profile. 'The exception
today, if you'll forgive an old actor's vanity, is to conceal a couple
of nasty bruises.'

'It was applied with skill,' Campion conceded. 'I can't see a
thing. It was a hit-and-run incident, was it?'

'Yes, it was, though I wasn't the one doing the running after-
wards. Still, no serious damage done.'

'Did you get a good look at the car or the driver?'

'I'm afraid not.'

Campion would have believed him implicitly, even knowing he was a professional actor, had it not been for the sly darting flash of his eyes in the direction of Brogan Bates, who said nothing, but tugged at his beard then turned back to busying himself on the bar.

'So, you're looking forward to doing *The Moving Mosaic* for a second time?'

Spruce laughed politely. 'It's a wonderful opportunity for an actor.'

'To get it right, this time?' muttered Bates loudly.

'Don't mind Brogan,' said Spruce, reaching out to pat Campion's knee, 'his role is to keep me on my toes.'

'And what of your role?'

'Excuse me?'

'Your role in the remake of Evadne Childe's book.'

'Well, it's not exactly a remake of the old film. It will be in colour, for one thing, and it will be the first of a series starring Rex Troughton.'

'Presumably he will have aged, as we all have, since you last played him.'

The polite smile flickered away from Spruce's face but almost instantly returned.

'I'm afraid I cannot discuss casting or scripting matters outside of the production; my contract is very definite about that.'

Mr Campion paused as if trying to remember something important.

'I believe Pauline Hatherall had very definite views on the matter.'

Now Peyton Spruce paused, as if for dramatic effect. 'You knew Mrs Hatherall?'

'No, only her daughter. I regret not visiting her down in Peacehaven, but I understand you did.' He looked over to Bates, who was straining to draw an obstinate cork from a bottle which declared itself to contain Bull's Blood. 'You both did.'

Bates shrugged his shoulders.

'Somebody has to drive the star of the show to meet his fans,' he said, his voice again low and menacing, as if he was narrating a ghost story, and with that, Campion placed him.

'I've just recognized you,' he said gleefully, 'though I should
have done so straight away – well, not you as such, but your voice.'

'His most photogenic feature, according to one of his wives,'
Spruce added with a sly grin, confirming to Campion that he was
in the presence of a long-standing double act, in life if not on stage.

'*All* my wives!' roared Bates, rolling his eyes.

'They must have been brave women to marry the voice behind
*Just a Scream at Twilight.*'

'There's a turn-up for Curtains – a fan of mine coming to call.'

Campion would be the last to say he was a fan, but he did
remember the BBC's radio show, broadcast late on Saturday nights,
which showcased horror stories from all over the world. The
programme had begun in the late 1940s – long enough after
the war for the real horrors to be forgotten – and had run for several
years, each episode introduced by the graveyard bass of Brogan
Bates and sometimes narrated by him, but always ending with his
chillingly famous sign-off: *Goodnight, listeners, and remember to
turn the lights off as you go up to bed . . . If you dare!* He remembered agreeing with Amanda that Rupert listening to such
programmes would not be allowed until he was at least twelve, to
avoid nightmares, and that some of the stories had even disturbed
his own usually carefree slumbers. There was one, about Mother
Nature reclaiming the land around a former concentration camp in
Germany, which he could still remember thanks to Brogan Bates's
sepulchral delivery, even though its title and author were long
forgotten.

'Whatever happened to *Just a Scream at Twilight*?' Campion
asked him. 'I thought it was very popular.'

'It was, but bloody Hammer Films came along and cornered
the market. Nobody wanted to listen to ghost stories on the radio
when they could comfort their frightened girlfriends in the
one-and-nines in the dark of the local Roxy.'

'That's a pity, they were rather good; you had just the voice
for them.'

'Just the voice for threatening young girls in dark places,'
said Spruce with a sly smile, clearly enjoying the chance to score
off Bates.

Campion turned his attention back to Spruce, hopeful of catching
him distracted and off-guard.

'May I ask what you discussed on your visits with Mrs Hatherall?'

'Fan stuff,' he replied, 'if you'll spare my blushes. Pauline was a big fan of mine and she'd been writing fan letters for years. I always reply to my fans, send them photographs, autographs, things like that, even a lock of hair to the most ardent ones.'

'That's why the *really* popular film stars go bald before their time,' Bates interjected waspishly.

'I understand Mrs Hatherall was a fan of the film of *The Moving Mosaic*, but that was twenty years ago,' Campion persisted. 'You only began to visit her after she had inherited the film rights from Evadne Childe and the BBC had started to take an interest in them.'

Spruce's expression alternated rapidly between hurt innocence and indignation, something Campion felt would not be a strain for an actor.

'She wrote to me to tell me the news that a producer was sniffing around the rights, but until then I had no idea she had been left them. She was excited about it and so was I, I don't mind admitting it.'

'Were you present when she met with the BBC producers?'

Now a third expression clicked into place: surprise. 'Good Lord, no; that would have been totally inappropriate. I did not represent her in any way, except as a friend, and am neither an agent nor a contracts lawyer.'

'But you stood to benefit from the sale of the rights.'

'Indirectly, perhaps I will, but not financially if that is what you're suggesting.'

'I think your visitor is suggesting rather a lot, Peyton,' growled Brogan Bates, raising a full-to-the-brim glass of red wine to his lips. 'And I don't see why you should put up with it.'

Spruce looked at Campion with a spaniel's countenance of despair, but Campion was spared any further demonstration of the contents of Spruce's acting locker by the door being flung open. Alice Dubbs entered bearing a tea tray rattling with crockery.

'Elevenses!' she trilled. 'I see you've started without us, Brogan, and it's not even noon.'

Bates flourished his left wrist and made a play of consulting his wristwatch. 'It is somewhere.'

'It always is for you,' echoed a new voice.

Behind Alice Dubbs came the small, mousey woman Campion had helped with the groceries, who was holding another tray, and behind her the echo: the thin, gaunt man he had seen in the garden through the French windows, still wearing a thick pair of gardening gloves.

'The gang's all here now,' Alice Dubbs addressed Campion directly, 'so let me introduce the rest of the Curtain Callers. Albert Campion, this is Sheila Kaye, who helps me keep these unruly men in order, and this is Tommy Taylor, whose sole purpose in life is to keep us amused.'

Mr Campion presumed that the Clapham Cossack had a nice sideline in irony, as the horse-faced Tommy Taylor looked the most miserable man he had ever seen. He was the sort of character Lugg would have described as a man who had lost a five-pound note down a drain and, in looking for it, dropped his wallet into an open sewer and then, reaching for it, had toppled in after. Perhaps, Campion thought, there was such a thing as a naturally sad-faced clown.

'I know of the career of Anastasia Tempest of course,' said Campion, 'and that of Peyton Spruce, and I have recognized the dulcet tones of Mr Bates from his radio broadcasts which dared me to turn the lights out when I went to bed, but I'm afraid Miss Kaye's fame eludes me, which is clearly my loss.'

'I assure you it isn't, Mr Campion,' said the woman in a squeaky voice, which matched her mouse-like demeanour. 'There is absolutely no reason why you should have heard of me – I was always behind the scenes. I'm a make-up artist.'

'One of the best,' said Spruce.

'You should know, ducky,' Bates guffawed. 'She knocks ten years off you!'

Although he deplored Brogan's rudeness, Mr Campion conceded that the bearded imbiber did have a point: even allowing for additional work needed to mask his injuries from the hit-and-run, Spruce did look a good ten years younger than his birth certificate might suggest.

'And you, Mr Taylor?' asked Campion, ignoring Bates, 'May I ask what your talent is?'

But Brogan Bates was not to be ignored.

'*Is?* Don't you mean *was*? Good God, man, if you're old enough to remember Peyton and foolish enough to remember me, then how come you don't recall that famous comedian Tommy Tuppence? For Mr Taylor is none other than he, the funny man who tickled ribs from Cleethorpes to Clacton and made housewives from Salford to Sheffield wet themselves!'

'Brogan, really!' Miss Dubbs admonished him.

Bates calmly poured himself a second glass of wine.

'*In vino* I speak only the *veritas*.'

'It is a rare and unusual talent,' said the man introduced as Tommy Tuppence, 'to be equally obnoxious whether drunk or sober.'

'Now boys, behave yourselves. We have company,' said Miss Dubbs severely.

Tommy 'Tuppence' Taylor glared daggers at Brogan Bates, but a man with such a long, horsey face could not maintain concentrated malignance for long, and his eyes dropped to his feet, on which he wore sandals over white socks and not, as Campion flippantly hoped, elongated clowns' shoes.

Slowly, as if it was terribly heavy, he raised his head and looked at Campion, though he addressed the room rather than the visitor.

'Mr Campion neither knows nor cares who I am,' he said in an oddly high-pitched voice which Campion, normally good on regional accents, could not place as anything more specific than generally northern, 'as I seriously doubt he has ever been to a holiday camp or paid to see an end-of-the-pier show. He's here to see the star of the show, not someone like Tommy Tuppence, who used to come lower down the bill than the juggling act or the Punch & Judy man.'

'I suspect you do yourself an injustice,' Campion said. 'Making people laugh to forget their worries is an ancient and honourable calling. I take it Tommy Tuppence was your professional name?'

Before Taylor could answer, Bates could not resist another interruption.

'They called him Tuppence because tuppence was the most they could charge for a seat at his shows!'

'Brogan, that's enough!' snapped Spruce with genuine anger. 'Leave Tommy alone.'

The anger sparked, flashed and was gone in an instant, and

Spruce had turned back to Campion, not a hair out of place, as the confident, relaxed film star acknowledged one of his legion of fans.

'Tommy acquired the name because of his catchphrase – *Give you tuppence for 'em, missus*,' he explained, as Tommy himself once again concentrated on his feet, 'and though some may label his act old-fashioned, I predict there will be a re-evaluation of our veteran comedians. And not to spare his blushes, Tommy also once appeared in a film with me.'

'As an extra,' mumbled Taylor, though he made no attempt to stop the eulogy.

'Let me guess,' said Campion, 'it was in the original film of *The Moving Mosaic*.'

Spruce looked, or at least feigned, surprise.

'Why, yes, it was, back in 1952. We actually met on location down in Dorset. Tommy sort of adopted me, even though I was supposed to be the film star and he was the total novice. He kept the autograph hunters at bay and protected me from manic directors and crazy continuity girls.'

'And the acting?' Campion addressed Taylor, who allowed Spruce to answer for him, despite a loud snort of derision from Brogan Bates.

'Tommy executed his part perfectly.'

'Executed is right,' muttered Bates from behind his wine glass.

'It was a non-speaking role,' said Taylor almost apologetically, 'as a barman in The King's Head – that's the pub in Blackcombe. All I really had to do was watch the customers get drunk and misbehave.'

Campion noticed that both Miss Dubbs and Sheila Kaye glanced automatically towards Brogan Bates, anticipating a waspish comeback, but it was Taylor who stung first.

'Since then, of course, I have been lucky enough to experience a masterclass of method acting in just such a scenario, so today I could play the part much better, but I realized back then that film acting wasn't for me.'

'You preferred to feed off your audience,' said Campion. 'That's what all the great comedians say, isn't it?'

'Partly. Audiences can love you or hate you and you know instantly. With the film camera you can never tell unless you have an instinct for it.' As he spoke the Green Room fell strangely quiet; perhaps it was unused to humbleness. 'Or if the camera loves you. Sometimes it does, you can see that with some of the Hollywood screen idols – the camera is just drawn to them. The camera was never drawn to me, not like it was to Peyton. I soon realized acting wasn't for me.'

Tommy Taylor's voice trailed off, leaving an almost church-like silence, which Campion could not decide was a reaction to his self-deprecation or his honesty, both emotions being, he suspected, rarely displayed at Curtains.

'You called the filming location Blackcombe, which is the name of the village in Evadne Childe's book . . .' Campion prompted gently.

'It was a village called Kingswalter, as I remember,' said Spruce. 'Quite picturesque. There was a manor house where they'd found the remains of a Roman villa in the grounds, and a ruined abbey or monastery or something, and a pub, of course. The locals treated us like visiting royalty, all except the lord of the manor, who really wasn't very happy at all that we were there. Thought it all a terrible imposition.'

'Can you recall his name?'

'Ward something . . . a double-barrelled name . . . Ward-Tetley, that was it. Ex-army and he certainly let you know it. He complained that the film crew frightened his sheep more than the Germans had during the war!'

'Did you know that Kingswalter was a favourite holiday destination for Mrs Hatherall and her daughter when she was young?'

Spruce seemed surprised at the question. 'She may have mentioned it . . .'

'Oh, she did,' said Tommy Taylor. 'It was one of the reasons she started writing fan letters to you. She loved the book so much because it was set there.'

'That's right,' said Spruce, recovering, 'she did talk about Kingswalter and holidays there with . . .'

'Veronica,' Campion filled the gap.

'I never met the daughter, I'm afraid.'

'Your loss,' said Campion. 'She was a lovely girl, and what happened to her was tragic. It was Veronica who negotiated the rights for that original film on behalf of Evadne Childe and her publisher, so it clearly meant a lot to the Hatherall family, even if Evadne Childe was not enamoured with the outcome.'

'Then it's a good thing she's dead and out of the picture!' Brogan Bates's voice boomed out in suitably graveyard tones.

'Brogan, don't be a pig!' shouted Alice Dubbs. 'Imagine if we wished that on you!'

'We have,' Campion heard Tommy Taylor say under his breath.

Bates sprang to his own defence, pouring himself more wine as he did. 'All I meant was that the BBC now have the chance to do the story and the character justice, and it could be a big break for Peyton. Nobody here would begrudge him that, would they?'

As silence greeted this remark, Campion assumed nobody did, but he thought it worth pressing the point.

'May I ask just how much Mrs Hatherall was behind this new version of *The Moving Mosaic*?'

'You may ask,' said Spruce, 'but I cannot answer, because details of the production are under wraps and I am contracted not to talk to the press.'

'But I am not a journalist,' said Campion.

'Then why are you here asking questions?'

Somewhat to Campion's surprise, the accusation – which he had been expecting – came from Tommy Taylor.

'Essentially to see how Mr Spruce was recovering from his hit-and-run accident.' He paused for dramatic effect, thinking that the audience in front of him would appreciate it. 'And to ask why nobody in this household bothered to report the incident to the police.'

# SIX

## This Temple of Arts and Muses

Mr Campion took the Central Line eastwards to Holborn, from where he wandered into Bloomsbury and the offices of J.P. Gilpin & Co., still the proud publishers of the works of Evadne Childe.

There had been a time when Miss Prim had patrolled the entrance hall, as implacable as a Gorgon, protecting the directors and the editors from both fawning readers and furious writers. Now, surely nearing retirement – though in Campion's view retirement ages in publishing were a flexible feast – she had been granted the title of office manager and given a small office to go with it. Although not much bigger than a cloakroom, which it probably had been when the Gilpin's office had been a private town house, Miss Prim was inordinately proud of it, and delighted to welcome her visitor into it, despite his arrival without an appointment, something which raised several eyebrows among the receptionists who manned the front desk and the switchboard.

'Apologies for dropping in on you without warning,' said Campion, 'but I thought you might want to know that I have come hotfoot from the wild west of Ealing to report that Peyton Spruce is alive and well and distraught that he could not attend the lunch at the Childe Society.'

'I will pass on the news to Mr Rudd,' said Miss Prim. 'And *The Moving Mosaic*? Is it going ahead?'

'As far as I can tell. Peyton was not exactly forthcoming on the subject. I gather that the BBC has issued some sort of D-notice on the programme, and no one is supposed to talk about it. However, I have an idea about that . . . somebody who may be able to give me some juicy details.'

'Mr Campion, I would hate this to become an imposition.'

'Nonsense. My wife would never forgive me if I did not do my utmost to protect the reputation of Evadne Childe. She was always her biggest fan, and in later years became her friend, but to return to juicy details . . . you mentioned some rather indelicate photographs which had been sent to the Gilpin directors here.'

Miss Prim opened a drawer in her desk – a desk which occupied fifty per cent of the floor space she had been allocated – and pulled out a large brown envelope, which she handed to Campion as if it was diseased or, at best, on fire.

'They arrived at weekly intervals, and Eric Rudd at the Society received exactly the same.'

Campion upended the envelope and three eight-by-ten black-and-white photographs slid out on to the desk. There was no indication of the order in which they had been received – or taken

– but the first one Campion picked up and examined showed a younger, bare-chested Peyton Spruce, wearing swimming trunks, kneeling on a beach with his arm around the shoulders of a bikini-clad young girl with long dark hair. Both were in focus and smiling at the camera. The other two shots had been taken from much further away but were frighteningly more intimate.

They showed a man and a woman in swimming costumes lying on an otherwise deserted beach, their arms around each other in a clinch that was obviously amorous. Footprints in the sand led up to the couple, to the right the remains of a wave crept towards their bare feet, and beyond them loomed the black shadow of a cliff. Only the approach of the sea seemed to differ in the two shots, suggesting that an incoming tide was the last thing on the couple's minds.

Campion held up the first print, leaving the other two on the desk. 'This is clearly Peyton Spruce. Do we know who the girl is?'

'No idea,' said Miss Prim, 'but she looks very young.'

'She does indeed, but are we sure it's the same girl in longshot, and if that is indeed Peyton, who is, I suspect, not administering mouth-to-mouth resuscitation?'

'Look on the back,' advised Miss Prim.

Campion turned over the photographs. On the reverse of each one, printed in block capitals, was the caption: DO YOU WANT THIS MAN AS YOUR HERO?

Back at the Bottle Street flat, before he did anything else, Mr Campion treated himself to a long, hot bath and a change of clothing. On the tube journey from Ealing, he had been forced into one of the smoking carriages, where he could at least get a seat and not have to suffer the indignity of a woman clipping a child around the ear and saying, 'Stand up and let the elderly gentleman sit down', as was happening more and more these days.

Cleansed of London grime and clinging tobacco smoke, which he noticed with the Puritanical distaste only a former smoker could, he sat down at the telephone and summoned Lugg and his son Rupert to a 'brains trust' that evening, securing their attendance by promising to supply the required victualling.

He then settled down to a long call to his wife to offer his

apologies for not returning home as planned, but safe in the knowledge that Amanda, a dedicated fan of Evadne Childe's books,
would allow him considerable freedom from domestic duties if he
was protecting the reputations of her hero Rex Troughton and his
creator. She did, but with her usual caveat.

'You have to remember, darling, that unlike me, you are not
getting any younger, so please don't go tearing around the fleshpots
of London stirring up trouble.'

'I never stir up trouble,' Campion had said. 'At best I stand
back and watch it simmer. And the only fleshpot I intend to visit
is the BBC, but for that I need your help. I need you to ring your
ardent admirer and ask him to meet with me tomorrow.'

Amanda had left a delicate silence hang down the line before
saying, 'Which particular admirer would that be?'

'I know it must be difficult to keep track of them all, my dear,
but I was thinking of the amorous Welshman.'

'Would that be Alun Gwyn Williamson by any chance?'

'Just how many governors of the BBC are currently infatuated
with you?'

'I'm admitting only to Alun,' said Amanda coyly. 'I suppose
it's about Evadne and *The Moving Mosaic*?'

'It is.'

'Then make sure you ask him if there's a part for Rupert.'

Campion was pouring tea for Rupert when they heard Lugg
puffing up the stairs to the flat. Only when the fat man was served
and settled with cup and saucer did he begin his report on his
visit to the Curtain Callers.

'They sound a rum lot,' said Lugg, waving an empty cup in
demand of a refill, 'but then actors always did.'

'No offence taken,' said Rupert rather primly.

'Some intended,' muttered Lugg. 'What did they say about not
reporting the 'it-an'-run to the local cop shop?'

'That was useful research on your part, by the way; it rather
floored them, and they exchanged shifty looks and then said they
hadn't wanted to attract publicity.'

''Ardly likely to make the front page of the *News of the World*,
was it? This Spruce, who doo 'e think 'e is? Now, if it had been
the Clapham Cossack, that would have been a different matter. I
bet there's more remembers her than can recall Peyton Spruce.'

'I rather doubt that,' said Campion, 'and Miss Dubbs seems as sprightly to me as she was when she was Anastasia Tempest. She would have no trouble dodging a speeding car.'

'Showing a fair proportion of leg in the process.' Lugg grinned.

Mr Campion quickly changed the subject.

'But you're right, they were – are – a rum lot out at Curtains, a veritable Ealing Comedy, you might say.'

'And they're all old actors, living in some sort of retirement home?' asked Rupert.

'Oh, it's not a retirement home, it's more like a student house-share, though they are all elderly and probably retired, except for Peyton Spruce, who it seems is coming out of retirement. And Peyton seems to be the only proper actor there. Miss Dubbs, or Anastasia Tempest, was a dancer. Brogan Bates was what I think was known as a "voice artist" and, as the old joke goes, has the perfect face for radio. The other female there, Sheila Kaye, was a make-up artist, and quite a good one, judging by the work she still does on Peyton Spruce. Not only did she cover up his bruises from the hit-and-run, but she makes him look ten years younger.'

'Think she could do that for me?' Lugg leaned forward, gurning horribly.

'She lives in Ealing, not Lourdes,' retorted Campion. 'And then there was Thomas Taylor, or Tommy Tuppence, the most miserable-looking comedian I have ever laid eyes on.'

'Not the "*Give you tuppence for 'em, missus*" chap?' Lugg exclaimed. 'That was his catchphrase when he did his *schtick* as a rag-and-bone man, pretending to knock on the doors of lonely housewives. Saw him in summer season on the pier at Southend or Clacton, years ago. What's 'e doin' now?'

'Gardening from what I saw. A strange man, long, lugubrious face, something of the undertaker about him. Not very friendly, kept his gardening gloves on indoors.'

'Clearly a wrong 'un, then,' said Lugg with heavy sarcasm.

'Well, he wasn't exactly the life and soul of the party; I think Brogan Bates has taken that role for himself. He certainly has an established repartee going with Peyton Spruce.' He turned to his son. 'Rupert, see if you can dig up any gossip on Bates – when he last worked, for instance.'

'I'll do my best,' said Rupert, 'but if his career was mostly in radio, it might mean a visit to the BBC archives.'

'Don't do that just yet, as I'm going to Broadcasting House tomorrow.'

Rupert's eyes lit up. 'Are you going to see any producers?'

'No, just a friend of your mother's.'

Mr Campion had teased his wife mercilessly about her 'secret admirer' ever since Lady Amanda had appeared as an expert witness at a Parliamentary Select Committee on defence procurement, where an ambitious Welsh Tory MP (something of a rare breed) called Alun Gwyn Williamson was attempting to make a name for himself. It quickly transpired that Mr Williamson MP, a man righteously indignant about the noise generated by RAF jets on training flights over the Brecon Beacons, knew absolutely nothing about modern fighter jets, the RAF's need for them or their cost.

Everyone agreed, and even Hansard hinted at it, that Amanda had answered Mr Williamson's rather naive questions with patience and good grace and, in the cold light of the next day, Amanda had received a bouquet of roses and a handwritten note on House of Commons stationery begging her forgiveness for asking 'such stupidities' and thanking her for not making him look like a 'total idiot'. To which Amanda had replied, perhaps too promptly, that she had been happy to present the views of an aeronautical engineer in the service of her country and could always be called upon if needed in future to serve at the pleasure of the Minister of Defence, a post to which Alun Gwyn Williamson was clearly destined.

Sadly, or perhaps fortunately, no one else thought this, and his political career continued on the back benches, although he kept in touch with Lady Amanda over the years by means of Christmas cards and invitations to government cocktail parties, where he could show her off with toe-curling introductions along the lines of: here is a female who works in aeroplanes but doesn't push a trolley or serve drinks.

In such situations, Amanda was more than capable of looking after herself and, because Williamson had introduced her to some interesting people over the years, she politely suffered his social ham-fistedness because it was always useful to know an MP or two, at least until they lost their seats. As did Alun Williamson in

1966, when an ungrateful electorate robbed him of his special status as that rarest of beasts, a Tory MP in Wales.

Although not destined for high political office, Alun did have certain attributes which worked to his advantage when he suddenly found himself looking for a new career. He was relatively young, not yet fifty, an accomplished public speaker, had an unblemished political record, due to never having rocked a political boat, and a formidable military history which lacked only medals for conspicuous gallantry in the field. A born staff officer, he had been captain at the end of World War II, serving in India, a major during the Malayan insurgency and a lieutenant colonel on his retirement shortly after hostilities ceased in Korea, not that Alun in any of those theatres of conflict actually experienced any hostilities personally.

He tried his hand in the City and quickly realized he was not suited to the battlefield of Stock Exchange trading, but at least he did not lose anyone their family fortune and he was astute enough when it came to his own investments, as well as quick to accept non-executive directorships with numerous companies.

His greatest assets, however, were that he had served in a famous Welsh regiment, been an MP for a Welsh constituency (albeit as a Tory), had a country house in Wales and actually spoke Welsh. In short, he was Welsh, and thus a suitable candidate for prominent roles in charities and academic institutions supporting or protecting Welshness. Consequently, when the BBC's Board of Governors was looking for a safe pair of Welsh hands to represent the wishes of the principality, Alun was an obvious choice despite the fact, much trumpeted by the popular press, that he had never owned a television set.

Amanda had no scruples in telephoning Alun Gwyn Williamson and asking for a favour, as he was a man who enjoyed being needed, and appreciated, by anyone whom he might himself need in the future. After all, he assumed it was in a good cause and – even though he admitted he had never heard of Evadne Childe – he did promise to brief himself on *The Moving Mosaic* before his promised meeting with Mr Campion.

Campion was escorted with great solemnity by a uniformed attendant from the entrance hall to the oak-panelled boardroom, where Alun Gwyn Williamson waited for him in splendid isolation, leaning up against the stone fire-surround, checking his wristwatch against the art deco clock hanging above it.

'Awfully good of you to see me,' said Campion, looking around as he shook the offered hand, 'and here in the holy of holies, at the heart of the empire.'

'The room was free this morning and, as mere governors, we do not have offices, so we are allowed to bring visitors here. It was not meant to intimidate you, that only works on BBC staff.' Williamson spoke with a smile, his voice displaying a natural musicality. The man had charm, thought Campion, plenty of it; certainly enough to compensate for deficiencies in intellect.

'If not intimidated, I am impressed,' said Campion, 'and again, thank you for allowing me to pester you. You must be busy enough, as I understand from the posters down in the lobby that it is the BBC's fiftieth birthday.'

He thought it diplomatic not to mention that he had spotted the delightful graffito added to one of the posters which declared: *The BBC has always been fifty years old.*

'Never too busy to do a favour for Lady Amanda, though the production side of television drama is not exactly my field of expertise. Still, anything for Amanda, so I mugged up on this *Moving Mosaic* thing.'

'I apologize if my wife made you do homework, and I appreciate the fact that this isn't exactly in your remit here, as there is no, as far as I am aware, obvious Welsh connection.'

'They didn't appoint me just to keep the chapelgoers and their hellfire preachers happy in the valleys, or to make sure the Eisteddfod gets full coverage, you know. It's just that the governors don't usually get involved in programme making. Conflict of interests and all that; stops friends and acquaintances sliding up and asking if there's a part in such-and-such for their daughter.'

Or son, thought Campion.

'But as it happens, I do have a connection to this project, though it's nothing to do with Wales.'

'You're a fan of the Rex Troughton books?'

'Who? Oh, I get it. No, I've never read any of Miss Childe's books. Do I have to? She'll probably hate what we do with her book, writers usually do, though goodness knows we help them sell more copies.'

'Evadne Childe passed away seven years ago,' said Campion, trying not to sound reproachful, 'so her opinion is moot; perhaps for the best as she hated the film they made of it back in 1952.'

Williamson's face shone with boyish enthusiasm. 'That's another thing I know about it! The chap who played the hero – the archaeologist – in that old film is going to be in the new version. Meat and drink to the publicity department that is.' His brow furrowed. 'Can't actually remember his name, though.'

'Peyton Spruce.'

'That's it. Oh, wait a minute, I do know that name because there's been a spot of bother over some letters, anonymous letters. What d'you call them? Poison pen letters, that's it.'

'Have you seen them?'

'No, but the personnel department assures me that we get hundreds a day – many bearing Sussex or Surrey postmarks – which are much worse.'

'So that's not your connection to *The Moving Mosaic*?'

'Good Lord, no, that goes back to my army days.'

'I'm sorry, I don't follow.'

'Well, of course you don't, how could you?' Williamson spoke with the air of an MP patronizing an irate constituent, a skill no doubt useful at the BBC. 'It has to do with Kingswalter Manor.'

Mr Campion peered over the tops of his spectacles, indicating that he was expecting enlightenment.

'Ward-Tetley,' said Williamson, as if it explained everything.

Mr Campion inclined his head slightly and waited patiently.

'I served under Brigadier Ward-Tetley out in India at the end of the war, then he left the army and retired to be lord of the manor down in Dorset at his family home, Kingswalter Manor. It was the brigadier who opened up those Roman ruins to the public and let the film crew in to make *The Moving Mosaic* in 1952, and that's where our new version is to be filmed.'

'And your connection with the brigadier is thought to be useful in smoothing the way for the new production?'

'It would have been if the old boy hadn't pegged out on us five years ago and left the whole shooting match to his wayward son. Pity, really, because the brigadier was a gentleman and very easy to deal with; a nice old buffer, if you know what I mean.'

'I do; I've known some splendid old buffers in my time,' said

Campion, 'but from your tone I would guess that the son is less approachable.'

'You can say that again, boyo.' For the first time Campion detected a Welsh heritage. 'Ranald, not Ronald, Ward-Tetley is a waster, probably a scoundrel and a layabout, if you know what I mean.'

'I think I do: we call them "lie-abouts" in Suffolk.'

'Oh, you live in Suffolk?'

'Norfolk actually, which would be Suffolk if it could. Is the son and heir to Kingswalter Manor causing the corporation problems?'

'I think it is Ranald's mission in life to cause everyone problems. I know he was always a burden to his father.'

'Bit of a black sheep?'

'Black as a whole flock of them. His mother died when he was a lad and he got expelled from every boarding school the brigadier found for him, until it got so the good schools wouldn't touch him. Even Rugby threw him out.'

Mr Campion let that one pass over him, wondering if the slight was coincidental or whether he should be impressed that Williamson had researched the fact that he was an Old Rugbeian.

'We all thought National Service would straighten him out, but they went and abolished it, just at the right time for young Ranald, so it was straight off to Oxford, which isn't the same thing at all.'

'I hear it used to be quite similar, though.'

'You would, but then you're a Cambridge man.' So, Alun Gwyn had been doing his research. 'But Oxford didn't last, and Ranald got sent down after the first year.'

'What were his crimes, or should that be vices?'

'Just the one vice, the same one at all those schools: gambling. The boy is a compulsive gambler and got expelled from one school for running a roulette wheel in the dorm, from another for setting up a line of credit for the boys with a local bookie. Same sort of thing at Oxford, where he ran up massive debts and tried selling off books from the Bodleian to pay them off. He's a classic example of the problem gambler.'

'The problem being that he wasn't very good at it.'

'He was bloody awful at it, and it worried the brigadier into an early grave, I reckon, as Ranald was an only child and bound to inherit Kingswalter Manor. That is why he had a clause put in his will stating that Ranald could inherit the income from the estate if he lived there in the big house, but could not sell off any portion of it until the year 2000. If he chose not to live there, the house and land would go to the National Trust.'

'The end of the millennium is far too far away for me to contemplate,' said Campion, 'and my wife will probably have turned *me* over to the National Trust by then. How did Ranald take it?'

'Not well. He's still a young man – thirty-two, I think – though he has gone through two wives already, and he has no discernible skills when it comes to estate management. The only thing he's got going for him down there is that he owns the local pub and has the remains of a Roman villa in his grounds.'

'Hence, the mosaic featured in book, film and now on television.'

'Possibly. Nothing's certain yet. As I said, there have been problems, one of which is young Ranald demanding more money for us to film on his property, having decided that his original "location disruption" fee was not good enough. He's virtually holding the production to ransom before it's started. Some would call it blackmail.'

'Tricky,' admitted Campion, 'doing a film about a mosaic if you can't actually show the mosaic. I take it that the budget for the programme is not . . . shall we say . . . flexible enough to accommodate him?'

'Don't talk to me about the budget for this thing! I certainly can't talk about it publicly, but I will say that, if it comes off, this will be seen as a prestige production and possibly trail-blazing in many ways.'

Williamson said 'trail-blazing' as if they were words from a foreign language, or at least foreign to the BBC.

'In what ways?'

'I'm not sure I should be telling you this,' said Alun Gwyn, looking at Campion with hopeful, spaniel eyes, 'but if I can't trust Amanda . . .'

'Who controls her husband with an iron will,' Campion said, grinning foolishly, which seemed to convince Williamson.

'Very well, then. There is an awful lot riding on *The Moving*

*Mosaic*. It not only has a female producer, which hasn't gone down well in some quarters, but it is also going for a new format, running for two hours per episode, which is quite revolutionary and only something the BBC would risk. I mean, could you imagine an ITV audience sitting through two hours of drama?'

Campion ignored the question but noted the fact that Williamson had clearly nailed his colours to the BBC corporate mast. 'Is there anything I might usefully do? I have something of a moral obligation to see that the work of Evadne Childe continues to prosper and, of course, I would be more than happy to support the BBC. Perhaps there's a role for an honest broker if various parties are in conflict and I have time on my hands these days. A brief holiday in Dorset wouldn't come amiss.'

'Well, if you could knock some sense into Ranald Ward-Tetley, we would certainly appreciate it, although it would have to be done totally unofficially. The BBC could not sanction anything you did.'

'I do understand the concept of what our American cousins called plausible deniability.'

Williamson seemed impressed. 'The CIA use that phrase,' he said with relish. 'You're a dark horse, Campion. Amanda always said you were deeper than you looked. Have you had dealings with them?'

'I couldn't possible say.'

'Of course not, but I think we understand each other and, yes, it might be useful for you to have a word with young Ranald.'

'Could you arrange an introduction?'

'Oh, I doubt that.' Williamson's face fell. 'Relations seem to be at an impasse. The producer, a woman called Tamara Reams, is down there trying to sort out various problems, of which Ranald is only one, and I'm told things are somewhat strained. I could certainly clear a path for you to visit the talented Miss Reams and get you access to the location film unit, though I warn you, she prefers the term "Ms", which I'd never heard before.'

'Dorset is beautiful at this time of year,' said Campion casually.

'It most certainly is, though not a patch on Wales of course. Still, if you fancy a trip down there, there's a pub in Kingswalter which does accommodation.'

'The King's Head!' said Campion so suddenly that Williamson recoiled.

'You know it?'

'I've never been there, though I must have seen it in the old film of *The Moving Mosaic*, but the village in that was called Blackcombe and the pub had a different name.' Campion shook his head slowly in despair. 'I must be getting old as I never put two and two together when they said Kingswalter . . . The King's Head at Kingswalter . . . now I remember where I heard the name.'

'Where was that?'

Campion drew a deep breath before answering. 'In America, actually, at the court martial following the massacre.'

# SEVEN

## The Kingswalter Massacre

It was common knowledge that Mr Albert Campion had seen active service during World War II on two continents, though rarely had he been called upon to wear a uniform, and such was the nature of that service that it was never reported publicly nor even mentioned in despatches other than extremely secret ones unlikely to be read for fifty years or more.

In the autumn of 1944, he was ordered to transfer his talents from Europe to the United States, the specific mission he was given being of such a highly confidential and sensitive nature that he was, as he felt, forbidden to talk about it even in his sleep.

Based initially in Washington, a further demand on Mr Campion's time was made by the military attaché at the British Embassy. His presence was requested as an observer at an American military trial at Fort Bragg in North Carolina and, though technically representing the British Crown, it was stressed he was to be an observer only and had no plenipotentiary powers whatsoever.

He was to attend the court as a silent presence, there only to see that justice was done to British interests – though they were never clearly explained to him – and to ensure that the memory of the late Mrs Ivy Trimble, landlady of The King's Head, Kingswalter, Dorset, was honoured, or at least respected.

Unsure of exactly what was expected of him, a situation he was very familiar with, Mr Campion was treated courteously and offered every comfort by the US Army, who even provided a comprehensive brief on the proceedings he was to witness, along with the assurance that the trial would not be a long one as the verdict was already cut and dried.

To service the Allied invasion of Normandy in June 1944, vast areas of southern England had been turned into staging camps and depots for thousands of troops and the vast amount of equipment and supplies they required. Many were retained as re-supply depots after the invasion, one such being in the grounds of Kingswalter Manor, which also doubled as a temporary base for a company of non-combatant soldiers, in this case, soldiers of colour, whose duties were primarily transport, services and supplies.

Mr Campion had seen the films made during the war by the American military with the Ministry of Information, including *Welcome to Britain* presented by the actor Burgess Meredith, which advised American soldiers arriving in England that they might find the treatment of people of colour somewhat different to what they were familiar with back home in Alabama or Georgia.

It was a warning which should have been taken to heart in the incident at Kingswalter, an incident which would have made for sensational headlines had either the British or American press been allowed a whiff of the story at the time. It being wartime, the lid had been kept firmly on, the deceased had been buried dutifully but very, very privately and, in one case, an undisclosed amount of compensation paid.

On a dank, wet evening in October, in one of the temporary barrack huts in the grounds of Kingswalter Manor, a game of dice being played by six soldiers of colour gradually got out of hand when two of the gamblers decided they were losing more than their fair share, their irritation fuelled by copious amounts of hard liquor which had been illicitly distilled by one of the cooks in the mess hall kitchen.

The two losing dice-throwers, convinced that the gods of chance had deserted them, stormed out of the game and the barracks and decided to walk into the village of Kingswalter and to The King's

Head public house, where they were confident of a warm welcome from the landlord and landlady, George and Ivy Trimble. Security at the camp being lax, no one challenged the two soldiers as they made their way unsteadily through the dark night, nor did anyone remind them that they were breaking camp curfew and did not have passes to do so.

No one at the camp would have cautioned them about visiting The King's Head as such, for the pub was known to welcome the soldiers of colour from the supply depot and serve them without a qualm, and the dozen or so locals huddled around the fireplace or the skittle table, sipping pints of mild ale, would probably have appreciated their presence, as smiling faces, American cigarettes and chocolate bars – it was generally agreed – all made the pub a more interesting place after five years of wartime restrictions and the same old moans from the all-too-familiar local customers. Ivy Trimble would have insisted they received a warm welcome from her 'regulars', as she had ever since the manor had become a supply depot and, until that October night, there had never been any trouble at the pub involving the military (apart from an unfortunate incident in 1941 when a Polish army dispatch rider, who had lost his way, was mistaken for a German paratrooper and detained by the village's two Home Guardsmen in the cellar of The King's Head, where he developed a taste for the pub's limited supply of bottled stout).

Unfortunately, Mrs Trimble never got to welcome the two soldiers, whom Campion was instructed to refer to only as Private A and Private B, that night, or any other night.

The two soldiers, angry and already drunk, had chosen the one evening, and the exact time, when their spontaneous visit to The King's Head coincided with a random patrol by two American military policemen intent on checking the passes they did not have. Barring the entrance to the pub with their physical bulk and menacing 'night sticks' the MPs, both white, confronted the two privates of colour and ordered them back to their barracks. There was no independent report of this verbal altercation, other than by statements from villagers present inside the pub, who confirmed that 'voices were raised', but the angry American accents had proved impossible to follow.

Rebuffed and, they felt, abused – although they subsequently freely admitted they were out of bounds and drunk – the two privates stormed off into the night, their anger growing with every step as they hurried back to Kingswalter Manor. There, they were reunited with their dice-rolling friends, now even more drunk on barrack-room hooch, who were incensed at their treatment.

It was never clear exactly whose idea it was to break into the camp's armoury, which itself required little skill other than the ability to break a padlock off the door of one of the manor's requisitioned stables, nor who suggested stealing one of the unit's jeeps, but when blood runs hot, such details rarely matter.

In short order, the stolen jeep, overflowing with six soldiers of colour, the two privates seeking retribution now armed with Thompson submachine guns, was barrelling its way down the narrow lanes into Kingswalter, pulling up in a screech of brakes and the shouting of obscenities outside The King's Head. The commotion almost immediately resulted in the front door of the pub opening and the two MPs – who had been enjoying a half-pint of mild each at the bar – bursting out through the blackout curtain.

They were greeted with a hail of bullets, which not only peppered them, but also the wall, door and windows of the pub. The two MPs were killed outright on the doorstep. Two local customers who had been slow to throw themselves to the floor suffered flesh wounds, one in the hand and one in the right buttock. Mrs Ivy Trimble, drying a washed glass behind the bar, took a bullet in the throat and died before her husband could get to her.

'So what happened to them – the soldiers?' asked Rupert as he dropped a gear and accelerated so the Jaguar could overtake a slow-moving Ford Cortina towing a caravan.

'They were arrested within the hour, flown back to the States next day and put on trial the following week. The two shooters were sentenced to death, their four friends to life imprisonment. They all pleaded guilty, and all expressed great remorse about the death of Ivy Trimble, the pub's landlady, who they said had always treated them fairly. It was all rather tragic and terribly sad.'

'And you were involved in the court-martial?'

'No, not involved, merely an observer. I just happened to be in America at the time on . . . other business . . . and I was asked to witness that justice had been done for Mrs Trimble and to make sure there were no wandering journalists around who might pick up on the story. The incident was thoroughly hushed up over here, of course, and to this day still is. I've certainly never heard it mentioned, and I probably should not have told you. If you breathe a word, I will be forced to slap a D-notice on you.'

'A D-notice?'

'D for Disinherited, my boy, though – to be perfectly honest – I cannot really see the harm in people knowing about the Kingswalter Massacre after all this time; it was one cruel horror among so many others, and Ivy Trimble, whose death was totally unintended, deserves to be remembered.'

'Perhaps she is,' said Rupert, straining his head to see whether it was safe to overtake yet another caravan. 'Maybe the local darts team plays for the Ivy Trimble trophy or something. The pub is still going, I take it?'

'It certainly is, though of course it's under new management. We'll be staying there, so best not to mention the demise of a previous landlady until we get the lie of the land. It might also be advisable to profess ignorance of the impending filming.'

'Why?'

'Because when I rang The King's Head to book our rooms, the landlord, who is called Higgins by the way, said in no uncertain terms that we would not be welcome if we were anything to do with those so-and-so's from the BBC, except he didn't say so-and-so.'

'What's that all about?'

'I have no idea. I thought the landlord of the only pub in the village would have welcomed the extra trade.'

'I suppose there was no chance of bed and breakfast at the manor house then? The BBC lot will have nabbed that.'

'Hoping to locate their casting couch, were you? Hard luck. I'm told the advance units of the film crew are based in Dorchester, and that relations with the current lord of Kingswalter Manor – I use the term figuratively; he's not titled – are rather strained at the moment.'

'But the manor house is integral to the plot of the book. That's where the mosaic is,' said Rupert then, catching his father's surprised look, 'and yes, I've read it – or rather, I'm halfway through it – and before you say anything, I wasn't looking for a part I could play . . . well, not specifically.'

'I'm sure you could play any part going, Rupert, but you know such things are not in my remit. All I can offer is temporary employment as my chauffeur, and in that role, you are doing splendidly.'

'Mother insisted I drive. She said Dorset was too far and the roads too narrow for you these days.'

'At my advanced age?'

'She didn't say that, merely implied it. What exactly is your remit anyway?'

Campion concentrated on the view through the windscreen of the busy road ahead, where every other vehicle seemed to be towing a caravan or was a high-sided lorry travelling at speed, belching black exhaust fumes, and he was glad Rupert was doing the driving. 'I think I am expected to play the diplomat,' he said.

'And not the detective? I thought that was always your role of choice.'

'I have never pretended to be a policeman, I simply don't have the gait for it,' said Mr Campion with a sly smile, 'and you know what Lugg thinks about "private narking"; dead common, he calls it. So the role for which I am best suited, I feel, is the one I am best known for – indeed should have won an Oscar for, if there was any justice: that of kindly old uncle who listens patiently to the concerns of all parties without fear or favour.'

'Resolving everything in a civilized and diplomatic manner?'

'Good heavens, no! Usually someone gets biffed or at least rapped across the knuckles with a ruler if they've been naughty.'

'And somebody has?'

'Most certainly, though I cannot think who or, more importantly, *why*. This new version of *The Moving Mosaic* seems to be jinxed before it has started, or rather somebody is trying to jinx it, though I just cannot see who would benefit from putting a spanner in the camera, so to speak.'

'Is there money involved?' Rupert asked. 'There usually is.'

'Well, the Evadne Childe Society stands to inherit a tidy sum once the rights left to them by Mrs Hatherall are exercised on the first day of filming proper, so it clearly isn't in their interest to wreck things. The BBC seems to be backing the project with a large budget, probably with an eye on next year's BAFTA awards,

so they would want things to go smoothly. Which leaves us with
Peyton Spruce, who has the best reason of all for wanting the film
to go ahead, as it's a chance of a comeback, a revival of a career
he thought was long over.'

'Could it be personal? About Peyton Spruce, I mean.'

'It certainly could, or it's being made to look as if it is. There
have been poison pen letters to the BBC and some very suggestive
photographs to Evadne Childe's publishers, and then the road
accident near his home, if it was an accident.'

'Whether it was or it wasn't, why didn't he report it?'

'Good question. I suspect he simply did not want to draw too
much attention to the incident. If somebody deliberately tried
to run him over, they might try again, which might make it
risky to employ him. If it was an accident, he might be wary of
someone thinking he's just a doddery old fool who is not safe
out in traffic.'

Campion studied his son's profile as Rupert concentrated on his
driving. 'Did your mother say something similar when she told
you to drive me down to Dorset?' he said after a pregnant pause.

Rupert remained silent, but his cheeks blushed pink.

The Jaguar purred across Hampshire, nipped a corner off
Wiltshire and crossed the Dorset border in time for Mr Campion
to suggest a pub lunch in Blandford Forum, where Rupert could
try a pint of Badger Bitter from the local brewery, or, as he was
driving, watch his father enjoying one.

As he did so, sipping mournfully on a tomato juice, Rupert
asked if The King's Head in Kingswalter had played a part in the
plot of *The Moving Mosaic*.

'Not really,' Campion told him, 'though of course in the book
the village was Blackcombe and the village pub was called something really strange . . . The Swan and Cemetery, that was it.'

'What a ridiculous name for a pub!'

'Strange, I'll admit, but there is probably a good reason why
Evadne came up with it – there usually was in her books – and
it's not unique. There is actually a pub called that in Burnley or
Blackburn . . . one of those towns up in the north-west which
begins with a "B".'

'How on earth do you know that?'

'I don't, but Lugg swears to it and, where pubs are concerned,

Lugg's word is his bond, and you can take it to the bank as long as you don't mind stepping into a backroom for a serious third-degree from the manager. But to answer your original question, the pub is only mentioned as the local watering-hole for the archaeologists digging up the Roman villa. Evadne couldn't have known about the massacre at the pub, or she would surely have incorporated it in her book; she couldn't have resisted. You know what those crime writers are like: they are positively magpies the way they pick up odds and sods and use them.'

'But she did visit Kingswalter, didn't she?'

'Oh yes. I'm told she stayed at the manor as a guest of the owner who must have been a fan.'

'The manor where those soldiers came from during the war?'

'Yes, but it would have been four or five years after the war when Evadne visited, and the owner was a military man who would have obeyed the orders to keep quiet about it. Perhaps the village just wanted to forget; people did, you know. Unless you were writing memoirs, most of us didn't want to talk about the war. We were sick and so very tired of it.'

'And there's a problem with the manor, as far as the filming goes?'

'So I understand. The new management there is proving rather difficult, and I think I'm expected to spread oodles of my natural charm to soothe troubled waters, if that's not murdering a metaphor, which it is.'

'But if it's the mosaic that's the nub of the plot – though I'm not sure why anyone would want to *move* a mosaic floor—'

Mr Campion wagged a finger. 'A-ha, no spoilers, you'll have to read the book.'

'But if the mosaic is crucial, and the mosaic is in the grounds of the manor, I would have thought the owner would be quids-in and could charge the BBC for filming there. The alternative would be for the producers to build a film set somewhere and fake it, which wouldn't be as good. Plus the fact that once it's been on the telly, the tourists will turn up by the coachload, happy to fork out twenty-five pence for a look at the real thing.'

'I'm told a location fee was agreed but now, as principal filming day approaches, the new lord of the manor wants to renegotiate his fee – upwards, naturally.'

'He sounds an utter sod,' said Rupert quietly as a waitress delivered their ploughman's lunches.

'Everything I hear about young Mr Ward-Tetley makes me agree with you, but I always hold to the maxim that one shouldn't be truly rude about someone until you have met them at least once, or, at a pinch, seen them from the top of a Number Eighty-Eight bus.'

'Did you say Ward-Tetley?'

'I believe I did.'

'Ranald Ward-Tetley?'

'You know him?'

'We were at Rugby together, briefly.'

'I thought he was expelled.'

'Oh yes, he was, for gambling. Which reminds me, he still owes me money.'

Circumnavigating Dorchester, Mr Campion pointed out the looming mound of Maiden Castle, and made sure his chauffeur appreciated that it wasn't the sort of castle which had a drawbridge and a portcullis, but rather an Iron Age hill fort where the local tribes congregated during troubled times.

Now it provided a happy hunting ground for archaeologists, as indeed did the whole county, and was alleged to be the site of a last great stand against the invading Roman legions – but then archaeologists did tend to draw the maximum drama out of the most minimal of evidence. It was certainly true that unlike the Ancient British tribes of modern-day Kent and Sussex, who welcomed the idea of living in a unified Europe-wide empire, the locals in Dorset, the Durotriges, were far more belligerent, and a legion under the command of Vespasian was dispatched to teach them the benefits of life under Rome. If no one else did, Vespasian certainly enjoyed those benefits, eventually becoming the emperor.

One of the archaeologists who excavated at Maiden Castle, he added, had been the famous Sir Mortimer Wheeler, Britain's most famous archaeologist, who was almost certainly a model for Evadne Childe's hero Rex Troughton, even down to the trademark trilby which Wheeler often wore when digging a site, something Peyton Spruce had adopted in the original film version.

'And speaking of our favourite film star,' Campion had said, 'did you manage to turn up anything on his other half in the double act, Brogan Bates?'

Rupert, concentrating on not missing the turn-off to Kingswalter and the coast, took his time answering.

'Probably nothing you don't already know. He used to be a big voice in radio, but that was years ago, though some of the' – he risked a look at his father – 'older generation of listeners remember him presenting late-night ghost stories. I couldn't find anyone who remembered him doing any straight acting, either theatre or film, though you might have thought he had a career in voice-overs for adverts when commercials came in with ITV.'

'I think he would have been living in France by then,' said Campion, 'with Peyton Spruce.'

'Well, they were inseparable, or so everyone says, which is remarkable considering.'

'Considering what?'

'Considering that Bates ran off with Spruce's wife.'

'Did he now? Come on, my boy, details, details . . .'

'Well, it's all old gossip.'

'Not if you haven't heard it before, so crack on, dish the dirt before we get to Kingswalter.'

'Very well, and with the caveat that my sources may not be totally dependable, it seems that Brogan, who was best man at Peyton's wedding during the war, then performed the function of co-respondent in the couple's divorce a couple of years later and married the woman himself. By all accounts Peyton was quite relieved to be shot of her, as it wasn't the first time Tania – that was her name by the way – had strayed. It wasn't to be her last either, as Brogan found out, and *they* were divorced after six months.'

'So Spruce and Bates shared a wife, how very modern. This Tania, was she an actress by any chance?'

'I would remind you, dear Papa, that your daughter-in-law is an actress,' said Rupert, arching an eyebrow, 'but yes, I think she was.'

'I don't suppose Peyton returned the favour and acted as best man at Brogan's wedding to Tania, did he?'

'I don't think so.'

'No, that would have been too much to ask, but it seems they remained friends and went off to live in France together.'

'Perhaps the experience brought them closer together. What is it you always say? *A trouble shared . . .*'

'*Is two people worrying unnecessarily.* Perhaps here was the exception to the rule,' said Campion. 'Any clues to Brogan's love life when he was in France? I ask not out of salacious curiosity, but because I have been shown evidence of Peyton's familiarity with the opposite sex there.'

'I couldn't dig up anything much on Brogan in France, but there was a rumour that he scraped a living doing voice-over trailers for forthcoming films, as his French is quite good. You know the sort of thing, when you go to the pictures and after the adverts and before the main feature, a deep voice announces the "coming soon to a theatre near you" film. Peyton, of course, made a few films over there, but they were French films, so nobody here's ever seen them.'

Rupert raised a forefinger from the steering wheel to indicate that the Jaguar was about to pass a whitewashed stone kerbside cairn which informed them that they were approaching Kingswalter.

'I did hear one story about Brogan, though it's not about his sex life. When he failed in his wine-making efforts, he tried to get more radio work at the BBC, but the word is that he repeatedly turned up drunk for auditions, including one for a spot on *The Goon Show*, but was replaced by Valentine Dyall, whoever he was.'

Mr Campion sighed at the callowness of youth and began to take note of the scenery.

'When you were a small child,' he said, 'this is where we would play the first-to-see-the-sea game, which your mother insisted we always let you win. I don't think we can do this here because Kingswalter is not actually on the coast, though Chesil Beach must be just over those hills.'

The approach to Kingswalter was via a long slow bend downhill to where the village nestled in a fold between the hills. Halfway through their descent, the topography of the settlement became clearer. If Rupert had been expecting the ruins of a Roman villa, a sort of small-scale Pompeii but without the volcanic ash, then he was disappointed, but in the distance there was a ruin, and it was an impressive one – that of the medieval Kingswalter Abbey. Next to it was a circular body of shining water, surely too large for a village pond, which butted against the road but, before that, a cluster of stone-built houses and what might just be a village pub, though still too far away to confirm it as the notorious King's Head.

Rupert braked gently, for the descent was deceptively steep, and as the car followed another bend, the area to the right of the road as it ran through Kingswalter became visible.

Opposite what Rupert had already mentally christened the duck pond was a field in which sheep might have been expected to safely graze. Instead, it was occupied by a collection of cars, vans and campervans. Some had awnings attached to them and some had tents next to them, making it more an encampment than a mere car park, but at that distance it was impossible to make out any actual campers.

'It looks like the tourist season's started,' said Rupert.

'I don't think they're tourists,' said Mr Campion. 'It looks more like an invading army to me.'

# EIGHT

# No Tinkers, No Hawkers, No Ghosts

It was easy to see why the small valley in which Kingswalter nestled, as if in the folds of a badly made bed, had attracted human habitation from the time ancient man (and no doubt woman) had decided that green grass, fresh water and two lines of small, rolling hills protecting it from seaborne storms to the south, and hiding it from landward invaders to the north, were the optimum conditions for settlement. Before the road through it, along which the modern village had clustered, it would have been impossible to see into the small valley until actually descending into it. Clearly this had not hidden the place from all intruders, as at least one rich Roman had built a villa there and decorated it with a mosaic floor. Then, centuries later, it had been deemed a sufficiently peaceful and remote site for monks to establish an abbey. It was not, however, remote enough to escape the attention of Henry VIII's eagle-eyed decommissioners of monasteries, and so the abbey, its medicinal gardens, its tithe barns and its impressive freshwater fish pond had been left to be ransacked for building materials or to be reclaimed by nature, until it found favour with visiting Victorian artists who took to painting the few arches still standing and the gravestones of the senior monks from a Gothic perspective, emphasizing dark shadows and trees bent in the wind. On a summer's day, this image did the ruined abbey no favours as, although somewhat overgrown by lush green vegetation, the abbey did not look threatening, only sad at becoming, since the discovery of the Roman mosaic, Kingswalter's second most popular tourist attraction.

Not that the mosaic – which had enjoyed notoriety in fiction, on film and soon on television – was immediately obvious to the curious visitor, having been successfully hidden for seventeen hundred years or more until uncovered by archaeologists. Today's visitors, clutching their entrance fees, if such were needed, would have to know that they should descend into the village and take the first left turn (the only available turn), just before The King's Head, into a twisty lane which curved back up the hill to Kingswalter Manor. They would have to do this on trust unless they had an Ordnance Survey map to hand, as the turning was not signposted nor the lane named, but it would eventually lead the intrepid tourist to a double dip in the roll of the hills which hid the manor and its antiquities from prying eyes, except those who had the price of admission.

Mr Campion had, naturally, consulted a map before setting out and so knew, roughly, the lie of the land, but he suggested that Rupert drive the length of the village before they quartered themselves in The King's Head. Rupert agreed in the hope that the road out of the village might rise high enough for him to have a view over the rolling hills forming the southern flank of the valley, and he would be able to gleefully declare that he could see the sea.

Keeping well within the thirty mph speed limit, which only a fool would ignore given the narrowness of the road and the steepness of the decline into and the incline out of the village, Rupert concentrated on steering the Jaguar dead centre down the middle of the street, straddling a white line nobody had bothered to paint. The stone cottages, most with grey slate roofs, though more than one boasting a fine example of the Dorset thatcher's art, had clearly been built along a street designed to take a horse and cart, and not more than one at a time, with little opportunity for overtaking. To make the nervous driver even more nervous, most of the houses were set back from the road but protected by very solid stone walls and, in many cases, stone mounting blocks, which may have been convenient for the local horse riders but were a nightmare for the modern motorist who valued his vehicle's paintwork.

Rupert mentally crossed his fingers and hoped that he did not meet any traffic coming the other way, nervously imagining his reaction should a tractor or, even worse, a bus (did they have a bus service out here?) suddenly confront him.

None did, but he only half heard his father's running commentary as they passed The King's Head, vaguely registering that the inn sign it displayed depicted the head of King Henry VIII, a remark-able, or perhaps very pragmatic, honour for the very monarch who had dissolved the abbey that had once been Kingswalter's main claim to fame and the hub of the local economy. It would almost certainly have been the main source of the beer drunk in the village, for pre-Reformation monks (and many since) had proved to be master brewers, and if anything of the abbey gardens survived, it would certainly still show signs of bog myrtle, which was widely used in brewing before the introduction of hops.

There was little suggestion, from the inside of a passing car, that the sturdy, whitewashed pub had been the scene of a bloody massacre. It had all the chocolate-box charm of an ideal English country hostelry, the sign proclaiming its loyalty to a monarch whose portrait embodied a fondness for ale and roast beef, swinging from an iron frame above the door. Perhaps the window boxes with their multicoloured displays of flowers concealed the odd bullet hole, but otherwise the pub seemed a perfectly normal example of the institution, apart from a large home-made sign attached to the dark oak front door.

On what appeared to be flattened cardboard box had been painted, in large, angry capital letters in red paint, the words:

NO TINKERS

NO HAWKERS
NO GHOSTS

As Rupert was driving slowly, still half expecting to meet a tractor or hay cart head-on, his passenger was able to read the warning notice aloud, which he did without comment other than 'Well, well' and a slight chuckle.

Indeed, Mr Campion seemed more interested in the large pond that now appeared on their left, which they had seen from the top of the hill and which had, presumably, served as a larder of fresh fish for the monks of Kingswalter Abbey, coming in particularly useful on Fridays, though the only activity in or around it today was a single solitary swan floating majestically in the middle of the greenish water, its head regularly dipping nervously below the surface more in hope than expectation.

Beyond the pond lay the abbey – or what was left of it, with one broken arch and three outcrops of stone walls visible above ground, poking through the vegetation which blanketed the ruins. From the road it was impossible to get any real sense of the layout or size of the abbey as it would have been in its prime, and no attempt seemed to have been made to explain its history to the casual visitor. It was almost as if the abbey had resigned itself to being usurped by the discovery of a Roman villa and its mosaic floor, and had pulled a blanket of brambles, nettles and long grasses over its skeletal remains to make sure it was out of sight as well as mind.

Apart from two or three cottages, the abbey ruins marked the end of Kingswalter, and Rupert dropped a gear as the Jaguar began its climb up the road which would lead over the next roll of hills and, hopefully, give him a childhood win in the first-to-see-the-sea game.

It was not to be, as halfway up the slope Mr Campion spotted a lay-by which had been strategically placed to allow traffic toiling upwards to get out of the way of traffic hurtling downwards. It was big enough for the Jaguar to use as a turning circle, and Rupert performed the manoeuvre fluidly, claiming only a moral victory, and began the return run into Kingswalter.

From this line of approach, the abbey, the pond and, in the distance, The King's Head, were visible to the right of the road, the only feature of interest to the left being the field opposite the abbey fish pond, which had clearly been set up as a campsite. Mr Campion, for reasons he did not explain, instructed Rupert to drive slowly by it as he wanted 'a good look' at the current residents, which he concluded vaguely were 'a mixed bunch'. When Rupert suggested it might be a gypsy encampment, Mr Campion shook his head, adding that neither was it an overnight campsite for families of holidaymakers as there was no sign of any children present.

If he did draw any firm conclusions, Mr Campion kept them to himself, and directed Rupert to pull over on to the forecourt of the pub. Rupert did so, hoping that he might be able to park under a bullet hole or two. Instead, he positioned the Jaguar under the expressionless gaze of a badly painted Henry VIII, a portrait which would have shamed even the most inept Holbein copyist, facing the firmly closed door with its home-made warning.

'Do we wait for opening time?' Rupert asked.

Campion consulted his wristwatch, though he knew they were in the middle of what Lugg called 'No-Man's Land', those empty afternoon hours when the British pub was closed by law in order to boost ordnance production for a war which ended in 1918.

'No, we're residents and as we are neither tinkers nor hawkers, and certainly not ghosts, we have every right to disturb their afternoon nap.'

Roy and Tessa Higgins had had quite enough and were almost at the end of their tethers, yet their reaction to their latest visitors was polite and professional, though only after a short, aggressive interrogation.

'You ain't anything to do with those BBC buggers, are you?'

'Absolutely nothing,' said Mr Campion smoothly, though Rupert, who had experienced a brief surge of hope that he had been recognized from one of his equally brief appearances on television, looked disappointed. 'We have reserved rooms in the name of Campion.'

'Gentlemen from London . . . o'course you have.'

'As I said on the phone, I am happy to pay in advance.'

'So you did, so you did.'

Roy Higgins – for that was the name on the 'Licensed to sell' sign on the lintel above the door – contorted his face into a smile of resignation; a smile which indicated that his afternoon was

being disturbed, but it would be worth it for a cash customer. It
was a signal for his wife Tessa to step in front of him and present
a more welcoming face of hospitality.

'Let me show you your rooms, gents. I'm sure you'll find them
comfortable, and they're at the back so you won't be disturbed by
the traffic.' She paused and shook her head as if to clear it. 'What
am I saying? If you gents is from London, you won't notice a few
tractors going by after all that hustle and bustle in the big city.'

'Do I take it you don't like London, Mrs Higgins?' Campion
asked through his most charming smile.

'No, I do not, sir, you can keep it. Not that I've ever been there,
nor am I likely to ever go. Bridport's quite big enough for me,
Dorchester for a posh day out.'

'You know, I think I envy you, Mrs Higgins, and I'm sure you
will look after us quite splendidly.'

'Please call me Tessa, and just shout if there's anything me or
Roy can do for you. How long will you be with us?'

'Well, that's a moveable feast as I'm afraid we are unsure of
our movements. Two or three days perhaps? If that's acceptable
to you, of course.'

'Perfectly fine by me, so long as you give me due warning if
you want to take your meals here. The breakfast comes with the
bed, of course.'

'Hence the expression Bed and Breakfast, a splendid
institution.'

'So you'll definitely be taking breakfast?' Mrs Higgins asked
rather sharply.

'But of course, why ever wouldn't we?'

'I just wondered if you heard something about us,' the woman
said airily, holding open a door to the staircase leading up to their
rooms.

Behind the Campions, Mr Higgins growled a warning.
'Tessa . . .'

Mrs Higgins took her cue, said, 'Follow me please, gentlemen',
and set off up the stairs as if it was a race.

Keeping up a fast pace to stay ahead of her guests, Tessa Higgins
pushed open the doors to two perfectly adequate, really quite cosy,
bedrooms and only paused at the end of the first-floor corridor in
front of a door bearing an enamel sign saying 'WC'.

Without opening the door, probably to avoid embarrassing the 'gentlemen', Mrs Higgins explained proudly, 'The facilities are all in here, along with your towels. You have the bathroom privately to yourselves, as you're our only guests this week.'

'That's most acceptable,' said Mr Campion, 'but I can't believe we're your only residents. The village seems to have been invaded, judging by the number of cars parked down near the abbey fish pond.'

Mrs Higgins, clearly happy to have got the introductions to the 'facilities' out of the way, was more than willing to enlighten her guests.

'Them's not proper visitors, they're gawkers pure and simple,' she gushed. 'Most of them are loplollies with nothing better to do. They come and they go and they have their meetings and there's always a few hanging round all evening in the public bar. We don't interfere with them, and as long as they pay for their drinks we let them use the toilets down in the bar.'

Mr Campion noted the distinction between residents having 'facilities' while the great unwashed in the public bar had 'toilets'.

'If they are not proper visitors, what are they?' he asked.

'People with no sense and too much time on their hands if you ask me. They sleep in their cars and their tents most of the day and then they hang around the village all night, well after closing time, snooping around with their torches and cameras and thermometers.'

'Thermometers?' Rupert blurted in surprise.

'They are not amateur naturalists, are they?' Campion suggested. 'Out on a quest to spot some nocturnal animal? Do you have a rare breed of badger living around here?'

Mrs Higgins choked back a laugh.

'They ain't after animals, they're here to hunt ghosts! Call themselves The Prophetics, would you believe, and they go wherever they think there will be a ghost. It's their hobby, would you credit it?'

'Have these ghost-hunters had any luck in Kingswalter?'

'Don't be ridiculous! Oh, sorry, sir, I didn't mean to be rude, but there are no ghosts in Kingswalter, and just wanting one won't conjure one up. My husband calls them the ghost-botherers, but I just call them daft.'

'It seems to be a popular village,' said Campion casually, 'and I gather from your husband that he's expecting a visit from the BBC.'

'Oh, don't get him started on them, they've been and gone and we were glad to see the back of them, though I don't see why Roy should get all het up, it was me who did the cooking.'

'The cooking? I'm sorry, I don't quite follow . . .'

'It was me in the kitchen, wasn't it, when one of them got ill and they said it was food poisoning, though me and Roy had the same supper that night and we were fine.'

'So a BBC man was taken ill here and he blamed food poisoning?'

'Well, he didn't; he was in no fit state to say anything. It was the ambulance man who thought it was something he'd eaten – and the doctors in the hospital.'

'Hospital?'

'In Dorchester – the chap might still be in there for all I know. We even had the police round about it, and a health inspector, but they couldn't find anything wrong with my kitchen. Still, not the sort of thing you want hanging over you when you go up for your licence. If you want to keep on the right side of Mr Higgins, I wouldn't mention ghosts and certainly not the BBC.'

'That seems sound advice,' agreed Mr Campion.

To prove they had complete faith in Tessa Higgins's cooking, the Campions said they would certainly take dinner in the pub that evening, and were immediately promised 'a nice table away from our regulars', which rather disappointed Mr Campion who had hoped to pick up on the local gossip.

Having settled their overnight bags in their rooms, father and son agreed that they should stretch their legs after their long drive, and Mr Higgins had his siesta disturbed again in order to unlock the front door and let them out into the late afternoon sunshine.

'You take the high road and I'll take the low,' announced Mr Campion on the forecourt of the pub.

Rupert seemed not to hear, had turned his back on his father and was staring intently at the frontage of The King's Head, his gaze slowly sweeping every square foot of the white plasterwork.

'Looking for bullet holes?' asked Mr Campion.

'Out of morbid curiosity, yes. Can't see any though.'

Campion took off his spectacles and pointedly offered them to his son.

'Right-hand window, about two inches above the top of the frame, dead centre. It's painted over, but there's an indentation there that suggests ricochet to me. I spotted it as soon as we arrived. The bullets which did the random damage would have gone through the glass, and the blackout curtains.'

'So the landlady, the one back then who was killed . . .'

'Ivy Trimble.'

'She was "random damage", was she?'

'I did not mean to sound callous, but Mrs Trimble was in effect an innocent bystander, in the wrong place at the wrong time. She was not the target of the shooting; the American military policemen were. Her death was a tragic accident.'

'Surely that would make her a perfect vengeful ghost, wouldn't it? Someone from whom life was cruelly ripped.'

'A good point, and nicely put, but our present landlady didn't actually say the pub was haunted. In fact, she said there were no ghosts in Kingswalter at all, so what are our ghost-hunters hunting? There's a ruined abbey, so there could be a chance of phantom monks and the remains of a Roman villa, so they may be hoping for a spectral, toga-wearing figure wanting to show off his mosaic flooring.'

'Surely the Kingswalter Massacre is the most likely source of a haunting, if a-haunting you must go,' said Rupert, making his father smile.

'Except that the story of the shooting has been kept secret ever since the war. The locals may well remember it, but it's not public knowledge. I'm curious to know what these Prophetics are looking for.'

'Does it have anything to do with *The Moving Mosaic* or the BBC's film?'

'I have no idea, but it seems odd that so much is going on in and around Kingswalter at the moment.'

'So you are taking the low road down to that campsite to snoop around?'

Campion drew himself to his full height and sniffed the air as if offended. 'I am an English gentleman out for an afternoon stroll, taking in the fine country air and a passing interest in local antiquities. Perhaps I will meet someone in my meanderings around Kingswalter Abbey and a conversation may ensue; who knows?'

'And what's the high road I'm supposed to take?'

'That little lane up there to the right. I believe it leads to Kingswalter Manor and a mosaic floor of some notoriety. If the owner's at home, you can ask him for the money he owes you.'

The lone swan was still on duty, patrolling the village pond, checking out the overhanging willows and snooping through the rushes growing around the edge, on the lookout for intruders or possibly just a quick snack. Campion knew that over the hill and along Chesil Beach was a well-known gathering ground for swans; it would be only a few flaps of an impressive wingspan away. Perhaps the Kingswalter swan had been unlucky in love, for there was no sign of a mate, or had he been cast out from the breeding grounds for some unspecified offence? Whatever the cause of his seclusion, he cut a lonely figure and Campion felt a pang of sympathy for him, though he was far from sure whether the swan was a cob or a pen.

Even though he appeared to be fascinated by the plight of Kingswalter's sole swan, Campion's gaze flicked regularly to the field across the road which mentally he thought of as a campsite. He counted seven vehicles parked haphazardly in the field – and it must be *somebody's* field – and as it was un-gated, more could join them at any time.

One of the vehicles was a Dormobile camper van and one clearly a reconditioned ice-cream van, the rest a mixture of family saloons of varying ages. A couple of tents or awnings had been erected to provide an element of privacy, and although there were signs that campfires had been lit, the site was pleasingly unblighted by litter. The only thing missing from the campsite was any sign of the happy campers themselves. Perhaps, like Roy Higgins at the pub, they took an afternoon nap, or that his wife was correct in her assertion that they were nocturnal and only came out after dark.

The permanent residents of Kingswalter seemed equally as elusive, as few felt the need for afternoon exercise, and the sheep scattered over the hills on either side of the village were quite content to graze without the supervision of a shepherd.

There was also little traffic and Campion felt safe enough walking down the middle of the road – though as there was no pavement he had little option – until he came level with the remains of Kingswalter Abbey and began looking for a way into the ruin among the tangle of bushes and brambles.

He was drawn to a narrow gap in the foliage by a distinct rustling in the underbrush, too clumsy a presence to be an animal unless, of course, the lovelorn swan from the pond had been trained in jungle warfare and saw him as an intruder on his or her historic territory. Campion felt sure that the monks of the abbey would have kept swans, and perhaps this was a descendant, many eggs removed, of one of those.

'Ow! Bloody things!'

There again, swans did not usually swear, and Campion deduced that the shaking of a nearby bramble was a result of very human intervention.

'Damn, damn, damnit!'

'Hello there,' Campion called out as he eased aside a branch of laurel. 'Is everything all right?'

There was more shaking of foliage as a figure jerked upright from a crouched position. It was a female figure dressed entirely in black, with long black unruly hair. By contrast, her face was deathly pale and half hidden by the palm of her right hand pressed against her mouth.

'Bloody blackberries,' she said, sucking the heel of her hand. 'Why do they have to be so prickly? Now I've dropped the flamin' lot.'

She bent down and picked up a large, wide-brimmed floppy yellow hat covered in dark red stains, having clearly been used as a receptacle for her harvest.

'The monks here would have called them God's bounty,' said Campion, 'the first fruits of the harvest.'

'I call 'em free food,' said the woman, and Campion detected the twang of a London accent.

'I did not mean to disturb you; I was only trying to get a better view of the ruins. It's rather confusing, isn't it? It looked much clearer from the top of the hill.'

'Keep your eyes on the ground or you'll trip over them. There are bloody big stones just left lying around so you could turn your ankle easy as pie. Whole place is a mess, can't work out where anything went, apart from the old garden, which is still clear enough, but the cemetery's disappeared completely.'

'Cemetery?' Campion asked, genuinely curious.

'They would have buried the monks somewhere, but I can't tell where.'

The woman scowled to show her irritation at the unfairness of it all, flipped the last two renegade blackberries from her hat and plonked it on her head, blackberry juice, stains and all. It was the act of a truculent child, and to Campion she appeared as a truculent teenager, although this was no girl, but a woman in her thirties. Still, to Mr Campion, that was the flower of youth, and there was something strangely familiar about the woman, or a younger version of her. Could it be that they had met before or, he thought, repressing the urge to giggle, in a previous life?

'Are you particularly interested in cemeteries?' he asked her. 'Are you sure there was one? Surely there would be a sign or something.'

Careful of his footing, Campion stepped closer to the woman, who was idly picking blackberries and eating them, as if in revenge against the brambles which had stabbed her. He noticed that her fingers were stained with dark red juice, suggesting that her battle with the brambles had not been totally one-sided.

'Of course there was one once. The pub in the village was called The Swan and Cemetery but changed its name to The King's Head.'

'I don't think that's totally accurate,' said Campion.

'Wothcha mean by that exactly?'

And there it is, thought Campion, South – or *Sarf* – London, unless he was very much mistaken.

'I happen to know that the pub called The Swan and Cemetery was a pure fiction.'

'A what?'

'A made-up name. It may have been based on the local hostelry, but that name only appeared in a book where the village was called Blackcombe, though it was certainly inspired by Kingswalter.'

'But I was told by one of the locals . . .'

With her lower lip quivering, the woman looked more than ever like a young girl – one whose favourite toy, or best dress, had just been taken from her.

'They were probably pulling your leg, it's what locals do to visitors, but I assure you, the name Swan and Cemetery was the name of a pub in a book, and also a film, from twenty years ago, and I know this because I knew the author, a wonderful lady called Evadne Childe.'

'Bloody hell!'

It was not the reaction Campion had been expecting and the woman's next exclamation surprised him even more.

'You're 'im, the geezer wot hired me to do the séance for Evadne Childe in that posh house in Fitzroy Square. You're ten years older but you still talk funny.'

'I think I will take that as a compliment,' said Campion uncertainly, 'but you have me at a disadvantage . . .'

And then, suddenly, fickle memory woke up and Campion remembered. 'Good grief! I know you, don't I?'

'And I know you,' she answered.

# NINE
## Lord of the Manor

Rupert took the high road. If it could not compare with anything offered by the Highlands of Scotland, the lane leading to Kingswalter Manor was certainly an incline, and it twisted and turned up the south side of the valley as steeply as the road down the north edge had. Near the village there were trees and patches of dry stone wall, but higher up the hill there was gorse and then grass and the occasional white starburst of exposed chalk, populated only by itinerant sheep. From the summit, Rupert felt sure he would be able, at last, to see the sea, but he was again denied, for his objective suddenly appeared without warning on his left through a strand of trees, as the lane ended abruptly at a set of iron gates leaning drunkenly open, though a footpath continued on up the slope for the more adventurous.

Rupert paused to catch his breath and surveyed the short drive up to the manor house itself. He recalled his father's fondness for incessantly quoting a well-known author – Rupert forgot exactly who – in whose opinion, *No English country house is worthy of its name if it is not breathtaking at half past six on a June evening.*

It was an admirable phrase, but in all honesty could not be applied to Kingswalter Manor, whatever the time was, as it was far from breathtaking. As he approached up the short drive, which seemed made of equal parts of shingle and weeds, the front aspect reminded him of a child's drawing of a farmhouse: a central front door with two large sash windows on either side and three above on the first floor. The only embellishments were a wooden porch guarding the front door, giving it a church-like air, and a smaller sixth window cut centrally in the tiled roof. Its construction was of grey-brown Portland stone, which had scabs of ivy and the stumps of a climbing rose bearing witness to some vicious and inept pruning.

There was no sign of the remains of a Roman villa and no sign pointing tourists to its mosaic, which Rupert assumed must be hidden in the trees that surrounded the house, as the upper slopes of the hill beyond were clearly devoid of human activity past or present.

In fact, on his walk up to the manor, Rupert had not encountered a living soul, nor, as far as he was aware, any ghosts, proving Tessa Higgins's assertion that the village was ghost-free. Still, it was deadly quiet standing there alone in front of that stern stone house and realizing that – given the lie of the land – he could not actually see any of the village and only the very tops of the hills where the road ran down and into it and then up and out.

It struck him as an odd site for a villa built by a wealthy Roman, or more likely a Romano-Briton keen to adopt the luxuries of the invader, but then he realized that a view of Kingswalter would have been neither desirable nor possible, as the village had probably not existed other than as a temporary encampment for the builders and painters – and mosaic-makers – employed to construct it. Once complete, the villa would have functioned as a self-contained entity, growing its own food and importing wine from Gaul, no doubt via Poole harbour along the coast.

Which was just about all Rupert could remember from his

schooldays, but then he remembered that his schooldays were why he was here and, his opening line rehearsed in his head, he reached for the old-fashioned bell pull hanging in the porch over the front door.

His action set off a muffled jangle of bells deep within the house, which Rupert thought were being studiously ignored, until he heard the snap of a bolt being drawn and a key turning in a sturdy iron lock.

The door creaked inwards and the first thing Rupert noticed was that it was opening over a carpet of unopened letters and circulars, several in ominous brown envelopes. Then his attention switched to a pair of remarkable grubby feet encased in a pair of threadbare leather sandals, seemingly content to trample the layer of abandoned mail deeper into the carpet.

He raised his gaze, taking in a pair of thin legs in faded blue jeans and an untucked white cotton shirt smeared grey where cigarette ash had landed and been carelessly wiped away, until he was looking directly into the face of a man with long, unkempt hair and moist, puppy-dog eyes.

'Yes?'

'Ranald?' Rupert was sure it was, but was in no doubt that the years had not been kind to the current lord of Kingswalter Manor.

'Perhaps,' said the man, now puzzled. 'Who wants to know?'

'Rupert Campion. We were at school together. You owe me seventeen-and-six.'

'Backgammon or poker dice?'

'Whist, actually.'

'Rupert! How good to see you!' Ranald Ward-Tetley pulled the door fully open, and as he did so wafted a distinct herbal scent towards his guest. 'Do come in, old chap, haven't seen you in years.'

But as Rupert stepped over the threshold, his host put the palm of his right hand on his chest, as though barring entry.

'Tell you the truth, Rupert, I don't really remember you at all, but if you say I owe you seventeen-and-six, I believe you, and if we were playing whist at school, that must have been Rugby, because that was the last time I played that stupid game. In fact, I've given up cards altogether these days, unless, of course, you'd like to go double or quits on a hand of pontoon . . .'

Rupert declined the offer of a chance to double his schoolboy winnings with a polite mumble, even though, from what he remembered, Ranald had been spectacularly unlucky at cards and so his seventeen-and-six stake had a good chance of becoming £1.76.

In a kitchen which did not seem to have been modernized since 1930, and where the washing up had not been done since 1970, Ranald offered his visitor a cup of tea as he was sure he had 'the makings' somewhere, though the milk might be slightly off as the milkman had not been.

'I wouldn't fancy being a milkman if I had to struggle up that hill from the village every morning,' said Rupert innocently.

'Our milkman has a pony and trap,' said his host. 'It's quite picturesque really. The problem is not the steepness of the slope, but the anticipation of payment once a month, something of which he has been disappointed of late.'

'Oh, I see.'

'I hope you do, old boy, because your seventeen-and-six, plus whatever interest may have accrued in the intervening years, is in the wind, I'm afraid. In the wind and far away.'

'I didn't really seek you out about a card game fifteen years ago . . .'

'Just as well,' Ward-Tetley put his hands in the pockets of his jeans and pulled out the linings to emphasize his point, 'because I am completely *brassic*, though I have really no idea where that expression comes from.'

'It's a corruption of "boracic" as in boracic lint, a sort of medical dressing for wounds, which in turn is Cockney rhyming slang: boracic lint – skint.'

Ranald's eyes widened as he spooned tea leaves from a tin which had once held shortbread into a bulbous brown teapot.

'Wow! I clearly should have stuck it out at school. Where did a nice boy like you learn things like that?'

'An old family retainer,' said Rupert, who had long ago given up trying to explain Lugg to strangers, an exercise his wife Perdita once claimed was like trying to describe a spiral staircase without using one's hands.

'Wait a minute . . .' Ranald wrestled with the cable of an electric kettle, plugged it into a socket and flicked a switch. He waited, as if checking that the electricity was still connected, before finishing his thought. 'I think I've placed you, young Rupert. Your mother turned up to collect you at the end of term and the school ran out the red carpet for her because she was Lady something-or-other. Turned up in a flash sports car and had us all drooling – the car, I mean, not your mother Campion . . . Lady . . . No, it wasn't Campion.'

'Lady Amanda Fitton.'

'That's it, you're right!'

'I know I am; she's my mother.'

'Well, she made quite an impression among some of the lower sixth, I can tell you. I suppose that tall string bean of a chap, who looked like a vicar permanently out of his depth, was your father?'

'Albert Campion,' Rupert admitted.

'Do I know him?'

Ranald unplugged the steaming kettle and held it aloft. He glanced around, trying to locate the teapot, appearing pleasantly surprised when he did.

'I don't think so,' said Rupert, 'but you and he have a mutual interest.'

'We do?'

'Evadne Childe.'

'Who? Never heard of her.'

Rupert thought he disguised his reaction rather well. He was an actor, after all.

'The woman who wrote *The Moving Mosaic*, the book about *your* mosaic which the BBC are about to film.'

Ranald's eyes widened and he beamed in delight. 'So you've brought the cheque! Oh goody! Forget the tea, I have whisky . . . somewhere.'

'Steady on, old chap. I do not come bearing cheques.'

'But you bring *news* of a cheque?' Ranald's face had fallen, and the enthusiasm in his voice was instantly replaced by a piteous whine.

Rupert held out his arms as if submitting to a search.

'I'm afraid I bring no cheques nor carry tidings of any. Were you expecting one?' Rupert asked, knowing that the question was redundant.

'I certainly am, a big one from the BBC, and between you and me, it can't come too soon.'

Rupert surveyed the chaos of the kitchen and its empty shelves and the threadbare state of his host's jeans. 'Milkman problems?'

Ranald nodded and sighed loudly. 'Milkman, butcher, wine merchant, baker, candlestick-maker if I used one, electricity board, council rates, another wine merchant, every turf accountant from Dorchester to Bournemouth, two ex-wives and a gamekeeper-cum-gardener who is totally useless except for the odd rabbit he shoots for the pot and the occasional sheep which commits suicide under the wheels of his tractor. I'd starve to death without them.'

Mr Campion had briefed his son on the terms of Brigadier Ward-Tetley's will as regards Kingswalter Manor, but Rupert thought it only polite to feign ignorance.

'Oh come off it, chum, things can't be that bad. You're lord of the manor, aren't you? The estate must come with a living, doesn't it?'

'Don't confuse me with a bishop!' spluttered Ranald. 'The estate is supposed to provide an income, but it's nowhere near what I need to cover my outgoings.'

*Ah, the Micawber Principle*, thought Rupert, remembering his Dickens.

'You mean cover your debts,' he said.

'Yes, my outgoings. I may have an impressive address, and I admit that is always useful, but to maintain it I need cash, and I simply can't generate enough from the estate and I'm not allowed to sell anything.'

'Not even the sheep on the hill above us? They are yours, I assume?'

Ranald had to consider this for a moment. 'Probably, and we do sell the odd one or two now and then, but if I got rid of the whole herd, that's my only collateral gone for a Burton and no bank would give me the time of day.'

'Are things really that bad? Have you no other source of income?'

'Only the pub.'

'What? The King's Head? We're staying there.'

'Good, please put lots of cash over the bar.'

'We'll certainly try, but surely, if you own a pub . . .'

'You'd think so, wouldn't you? Oh, the Higginses are good tenants, couldn't ask for better, but thanks to the whim of my late father, their rent is fixed until they decide to retire. They pay it every quarter on the dot but, frankly, the current quarter's was spent before it was paid, and so is the next quarter's, and the one after that come to think of it. You see,' he paused to draw breath, 'I had considerable debts and I just can't keep up with them.'

Rupert balked at the idea of suggesting Ranald look for a 'proper job' for, as a 'resting' actor, it had been put to him many times.

'Could you . . . economize?' he asked without conviction.

'Goodness knows, I've cut things to the bone. I got rid of my television because I couldn't afford the licence, I had the telephone disconnected and I sold my car; well, it was repossessed actually. And if you want to check the larder here, you'll find I'm living off iron rations.'

'I believe you,' said Rupert, slightly worried at what he might find if he started rummaging through kitchen cupboards, 'but there must be something you could do with this house . . . the pub . . . the land. What about that campsite down in the village near the pond?'

'Swan Lake.'

'I'm sorry?'

'My father named it Swan Lake, swan singular, as a bit of a joke. There was only ever one swan living there. Hundreds fly overhead each year, heading down to Chesil Beach, but only one ever bothered to visit Kingswalter.'

'There seem to be plenty of visitors in that campsite across the road. If that's part of the estate, you should be down there charging for car parking at least.'

'Maybe I could have if my father hadn't opened that field up as common land during the war, so the locals could graze their animals. Now every Tom, Dick and Harriet can roll up and pitch a tent there. When this latest bunch turned up, somebody rang the local fuzz, and they came and looked and scratched their heads and said there was nothing they could do unless somebody took them to court. Do I look as if I have the cash to go to a solicitor? Anyway, Roy Higgins asked me not to as they might be a pain, but they bought their beer and sandwiches in The King's Head and they do have some other advantages.'

'What exactly are they doing here? Mrs Higgins at the pub told us they were some sort of ghost-hunting club.'

'I have absolutely no idea – they seem obsessed with the pub

and with this house. They come lurking around every night and
have even asked if they can set up cameras and thermometers in
here. 'Course I told them to bugger off unless they were prepared
to offer some compensation, which they weren't.'

'Is the manor supposed to be haunted then?'

Ranald shrugged his shoulders. 'Not that I've ever heard or
noticed. The only rumblings in the night round here come from
my stomach.'

'Mrs Higgins said the pub wasn't haunted either, so what are
these ghost-hunters doing?'

'Wasting their time and making my life difficult. I had a sweet
deal with the BBC for their filming, but having that bunch of
loonies hanging around is giving them cold feet. Them, and all
the other things that have been going wrong. The producer lady
is on the verge of a nervous breakdown if you ask me.'

'The ghost-hunters are interested in your Roman mosaic?'

'No, just in the house and the pub, which they insist on calling
The Swan and Cemetery, even though I told them that was just a
joke name thought up by my father.'

'Which he shared with Evadne Childe.'

'Who's she? Oh, yes, the woman who wrote the book, you did
say. I never got round to reading it.'

'But you know it's about, or at least based on, the mosaic floor
in your Roman villa.' Rupert, worried by the confusion floating
across Ranald's face, thought he should make sure. 'You do have
a mosaic, don't you?'

Ranald shook his head as if to clear it. 'Of course, come on,
I'll show you. And if you or your papa can reassure the BBC that
everything is hunky-dory so they can release some funds, I'd very
much appreciate it.'

'I'd love to see the mosaic,' said Rupert, 'but getting the BBC
to loosen their purse strings may be beyond us.'

'I'm sure you'll do what you can for an old school chum.'

'To be honest, Ranald, we weren't that close at school.'

'We weren't? Good, then I don't feel so bad about not remembering you. Still, if you won't do it for old times' sake, do it on
the off-chance you'll get your seventeen-and-six back. Now, let's
have that tea. Can you see any clean cups anywhere?'

Rupert was not unworldly enough to judge a person purely on

dress sense or financial circumstance, or indeed on hygiene, but Ranald Ward-Tetley's frequent lapses of memory, confusion and downright oddness bothered him. One thing, he felt, might explain things when, over mismatched, cracked (and not entirely clean) mugs of perfectly foul tea without milk, Ranald produced a rectangular Golden Virginia tobacco tin from the back pocket of his jeans and prised off the lid. From it he took a green packet of cigarette papers, extracted two, and with impressive dexterity licked a gummed strip and spliced the two together, then crumbled something into the shreds of tobacco and began to roll a cigarette.

'Can I tempt you?' he asked Rupert optimistically.

'I don't smoke,' said Rupert, hoping he did not sound too prudish.

'Good. More for me.'

He lit his home-made cigarette with the yellow Cricket lighter which lived in the tin, inhaled deeply, then exhaled a cloud of fragrant smoke which he immediately tried to waft away.

'Better take this outside,' said Ranald, grinning foolishly. 'Let's go play archaeologists.'

'Like Rex Troughton.' Rupert got to his feet with indecent haste.

'Who?'

'He's the hero of *The Moving Mosaic*.'

'I really must read the book – or maybe the script Tamara left me. Would that be easier?'

Rupert clenched his fists; his heels rose slightly off the floor and his spine tingled – all natural reactions of an actor in the proximity of an unfilmed script – and he spoke with a dry mouth.

'You have the BBC script?'

'She left me one on condition I didn't show it to anyone. I thought it might make good bedtime reading so I took it upstairs but then forgot which bedroom I put it in. There are nine you know, which is ridiculous really with only me here, so I . . . alternate. Suppose I'd better dig it out.'

'You said "she" gave it to you. Tamara?'

'Tamara Reams, the producer. Odd job for a girl, don't you think? Bossing all those film people about. Still, she's the one with the BBC's chequebook, so got to keep her sweet. I sort of hoped she'd be popping round to sign off our deal, but she does have a lot on her mind.'

'Is she staying locally?' Rupert asked casually.

'The BBC mob are staying at The Junction Hotel in Dorchester, but she's probably pining at the County Hospital.'

'Pining?'

'One of her chaps, a set designer I think she called him, went down with a bad case of food poisoning after eating at the pub. Almost died, according to Tamara, though I think she's being a bit of a drama queen because the chap is clearly her boyfriend, and you know what these arty-farty theatrical types are like.'

'I can imagine.'

The lord of Kingswalter Manor led his guest out of the house down the short drive almost to the iron gates, and then on to a footpath through the trees to the right which Rupert had missed entirely on his arrival. Once in the trees, Rupert lost all sense of direction, but the disorientation did not last long as he entered a clearing, almost a perfect coppiced square, which had, unlike the driveway to the house, been cleared of grass, weeds and brambles. It was no more than twenty yards from the front door of the manor, but totally camouflaged from both it and the lane leading up from or down to the village. As they entered the clearing, Ranald pulled the cigarette tin from his jeans, ground his cigarette out on the lid and then added the stub to the contents. It was either his contribution to the Keep Britain Tidy campaign, thought Rupert, or he was concealing evidence.

Suddenly – so suddenly he almost fell in – he was looking down into a rectangular depression in the ground, perhaps a foot deep, at the bottom of which was the central roundel, or what was left of it, of a mosaic floor some twenty feet in diameter. The edges had been nibbled away by natural agents of erosion, but the central design of a series of concentric circles each decorated with a running motif was remarkably intact. It was not as bright as Rupert had expected and, probably due to time and weather, the colours had faded to dark greens and yellowy browns, yet the central design – the figure depicted in the centre circle – remained as impressive as it had been intended to be when the floor was laid. It had not, however, impressed Ranald's hill-roaming sheep, which had visited it often and left numerous calling cards.

'Crazy, isn't it?' said Ward-Tetley. 'That it's survived so long. If the villa hadn't been built on this slope, it would almost certainly have been destroyed by ploughing a thousand years ago.'

'But where's the villa?'

'According to the archaeologists who did a report for my father, the manor was built on top of most of it and so what's left will only be excavated when the house falls down, which could be soon if the BBC don't come up with some funds. For some reason, this piece of flooring survived; the walls, roof tiles and beams didn't. Them falling in on top of it probably protected it from the elements.'

'But you don't leave it exposed like this, do you?'

Ranald squirmed and pushed his hands deep into the front pockets of his jeans. 'Father had this system of covering the site with bales of hay during the winter. Used to get them from a farmer over in Puncknowle, but we had a bit of a disagreement about delivery costs. Anyway, the BBC wanted it open and they said they would pay to have old Pertinax protected.'

'Pertinax?'

'The smug-looking chap in the centre with the capital P on his head. Pertinax was the only Roman emperor I could think of beginning with P.'

The centre circle of the mosaic did indeed depict the chest and head of a male figure, and clearly a Roman one, with the folds of a toga over one shoulder, though Rupert thought his expression rather kindly, not smug. There was indeed a large P above his head and crossed lines behind it, and to either side a large fruit, now a faded orange, as if picked straight from the tree.

'It's not Pertinax, it's not any emperor,' said Rupert. 'You wouldn't ask your guests to walk across the face of the emperor. Showing disrespect like that could get you into trouble. The P, and those crossed lines which form an X, are the first two letters of "Christ" in the Greek alphabet. It's the Chi-Rho symbol of early Christianity.'

'Blimey! So that's Jesus Christ?'

'Hardly. If you wouldn't walk on the face of the emperor, you'd hardly walk on the face of Christ. It was probably a portrait of the owner of the villa, showing that he was a Christian.'

'The Romans were Christians?'

Rupert shook his head in despair. 'What did you read at Oxford?'

'Mathematics, but I wasn't there for long,' said Ranald, unconcerned. 'So why has the chap got oranges either side of his head? Was he a fruit farmer?'

'I think they are meant to be pomegranates, signifying immortality.'

'How do you know all this stuff?'

'It's all in Evadne Childe's book. It's exactly how she described the mosaic found by Rex Troughton and his team of trusty archaeologists. Clearly she saw it for herself when she was researching the book, and I'm pretty sure she stayed at the manor as a guest of your father. That would have been around 1949.'

'I was just a kid then doing the rounds of the schools,' Rupert noted the plural of 'schools', 'so not surprisingly I don't remember her. Do you think there's any added value in her having stayed here?'

'You mean as in putting up a plaque?'

'I was thinking of it as a visitor attraction. I mean if the mosaic is going to be on telly, people might be willing to pay to stay here and see the real thing.'

'They may well, and the Evadne Childe Society would certainly be interested, but wouldn't you have to spend quite a lot renovating the place?'

'Which makes the fee from the BBC all the more vital. This film, this *Moving Mosaic*, is it going to be any good?'

'Well, it's a thriller with a charismatic detective hero, and they're always popular. But you've got a script, you tell me.'

'Oh, I couldn't get on with it,' Ranald admitted, shaking his head as if to expel the very thought. 'It wasn't like a book; it was all typed out like a play with stage directions, and trying to read it was like being back at school. I just couldn't be bothered. One thing puzzled me though.'

'Only one?'

'The title really. The mosaic goes missing and a detective is involved, right?'

'In a nutshell, yes,' Rupert said wearily, having decided it was pointless to waste good sarcasm on Ranald.

'So somebody steals the mosaic . . . Why in God's name would anyone steal a Roman mosaic floor?'

Rupert beamed. 'That's the twist and it's a good one, but you have to read the book to find out.'

# TEN
## The Ghost-Botherers

M r Campion's connections to the late Evadne Childe
extended over six decades, although he only actually knew
her for twenty-five years. The discrepancy, he would
cheerfully explain to anyone remotely interested, was that he and
Evadne happened to share a godmother, the Countess of Costigan
and Dorn, though neither was aware that they were 'godsiblings'
until well beyond the age where they might reasonably expect a
birthday postal order, even if the countess, a leading socialite,
had been able to remember the birthdays of the dozens of children
to whom she was godmother.

Evadne's career as a bestselling author of crime fiction had
crossed paths with several real crimes, which had resulted in
interventions by both Amanda Campion, as a long-term fan of
Evadne's Rex Troughton novels, and her husband in his role as
'a professional busybody'. One of those interventions had been
necessary due to Evadne's firm belief in spiritualism, brought
on by the loss of a much-loved husband who had the unfortunate
distinction of being one of the first British fatalities of World
War II. For reasons so convoluted they could have featured in
the plot of a detective story (which in fact they did), Amanda
had arranged a series of séances to impress Evadne Childe
and had hired, on what she thought was good authority, a
professional clairvoyant. Sadly, but not surprisingly, no contact
with the spirit world had been made on that occasion, the
medium in question being unable to place a trunk call to
the other side on her Ouija board.

Mr Campion remembered that medium, who had dressed as a
female 'Teddy boy', but had not seen her for ten years, and yet
here she was, in the grounds of a ruined abbey in darkest Dorset,
picking blackberries. The wide-lapel drape jacket, bootlace tie
and drainpipe trousers had been replaced, mercifully, with a

long-sleeved dress of flimsy black material, equally incongruous when hacking one's way through a thick bramble bush. Yet Campion could see her, in that gothic setting, being a perfect subject for a painting; a thin, spectral figure in a wafting black dress. Only the bright yellow floppy hat spoiled the image, as if a mischievous Turner had wandered by and pressed a thumb full of Naples Yellow on to the canvas above the model's head.

Her black hair was longer than he remembered and her face not quite so youthful, but it was definitely the same woman. If only he could recall her name to prove that old age had not yet claimed his most valuable remaining asset, his memory.

'Sally!' he exclaimed with such joy that the woman facing him recoiled. 'Sally DeLuca of the Spiritualist Alliance.'

'Not any more.'

'Have you abandoned your attempts to contact the spirit world and hung up your Ouija board?'

'Well, I don't sit around a table waiting for them to come to me, that's for sure.' Miss DeLuca adopted an expression that Campion could only think of as haughty. 'Nowadays I go hunting them.'

In the last heat of the afternoon sun, Mr Campion did the gentlemanly thing and helped Miss DeLuca refill her floppy hat with blackberries. He had no intention of offering his favourite fedora as an additional collecting bowl, but he was willing to brave a battery of thorns as he lifted the lower branches of the brambles to reveal the juiciest berries, which always remained hidden from the casual forager.

With Campion carefully holding the thorny twigs out of harm's way, Miss DeLuca's darting hands had soon plundered the bush enough to have a hat full again, though many a blackberry failed to make it to the hat, as evidenced by the red stain around her lips. When some imaginary quota had been filled, the woman thanked him for his help and began to force her way through the underbrush towards the road, making no objection as Campion followed in her wake.

'Are you staying in the village?' he asked.

'Over there.' She pointed across the road to the field being used as a car park or a squatters' campsite, depending on one's point of view. 'Mine's the camper van. The others come and go as they please. Some stay all night and leave first thing in the morning; some don't arrive until after dark.'

'Others? Is this a group excursion?'

'Sort of. We are an informal network and we're known as The Prophetics.'

'That sounds awfully momentous,' said Campion, 'and please don't take this the wrong way, but is it a religious organization?'

'Only for those who believe that there is something after death.'

She made the statement as a matter of fact, but to Campion it still seemed a strange thing to hear on a quiet, sunny afternoon on a deserted road in the middle of the deepest, greenest English countryside, with only a single swan floating on its private lake to bear witness.

'So all of you go looking for ghosts?'

'We identify – we predict – where spirits *will* appear after a suitably traumatic death event.'

'Given that death is usually a traumatic event for somebody, how do you narrow down your . . . search area, so to speak?'

'Well, the more violent the death, the better,' said Miss DeLuca, as though commenting on the weather.

Campion resisted the urge to glance around and check they were not being overheard, but the road and the surrounding hills were devoid of wagging ears. If the sheep grazing on the slopes above them had noticed the two humans at all, they would have thought only that there was a young woman helping an elderly gentleman across the road while exchanging pleasant chit-chat, not deep in discussion about violent death.

'And was Kingswalter Abbey the scene of some violence in the past?' Campion asked innocently. 'It wouldn't surprise me if it was. I mean, those monks Henry VIII put out on the street in 1539 or whenever it was, might not have gone quietly and been made to suffer.'

Sally DeLuca looked at Campion, then at the hat full of blackberries, then back at Campion.

'No, we didn't come here for the abbey, it's just that I like blackberries. It's the pub and the manor house which ought to be haunted. Those are the places connected to a violent death.'

'You sound awfully sure, but both are quite old buildings and surely, over time, people must have died there, some of them not peacefully . . .'

'But there was one death in particular which was violent and shocking, leaving an innocent soul in torment because the events surrounding her death have been kept secret – covered up by the government. Only by being revealed to those who can see, will that spirit find rest.'

Mr Campion controlled his facial muscles into an expression of innocent curiosity, although he was sure he was in the presence of a true believer. Miss DeLuca had, over the ten years since he had first encountered her, progressed from being a medium for hire ('Have Ouija Board, Will Travel'), who could have earned a living with a travelling fair or on a seaside pier, to a woman with the self-confidence of a fanatic. And from the number of vehicles parked near her camper van, she was of that most dangerous strain of fanatic, the one with followers.

'And these,' Campion pointed across the road to the parked vehicles, 'are of a like mind?'

Sally nodded enthusiastically. 'We are of varied psychic abilities, but all of us together hope to welcome a wandering spirit into existence so that they may find resolution.'

'I am not sure I quite understand,' said Campion. 'You are attempting to conjure a ghost where no one has ever reported one . . .'

'We do not *conjure!*' she snapped. 'We investigate locations where spirits are likely to be waiting in limbo, straining to be recognized, and we help them appear. Once they appear, they are free.'

'And your research has brought you all to Kingswalter? How?'

'As a group The Prophetics have members nationwide. Some have driven hundreds of miles to be here, taking time off work. Once I put the call out about Kingswalter . . .'

'The call?' Campion immediately imagined Miss DeLuca in a trance, head bowed over a candle on a table, communing telepathically with her followers from Cardiff to Camden.

'I wrote about the case in our newsletter,' she explained, 'and the response was immediate.'

'What case?'

'The case of Ivy Trimble, of course.'

'Who is? Or should that be who was?' Campion feigned ignorance. It was something he thought he did rather well.

'Ivy Trimble was the landlady of the village pub during the war. One night in 1944, drunken American soldiers based at the manor house stormed the pub with machine guns and shot her to death. The government hushed it all up, of course, and Ivy Trimble's story has never been allowed to be told. If her ghost will appear to us, then she can rest.'

'What a terrible story, I had no idea such things could happen,' lied Campion, 'but if the government hushed it up all those years ago, how did you find out about Mrs Trimble?'

'A whistle-blower.'

'Excuse me?'

'Someone who knew of the cover-up of the crime and thought the truth should come out.'

'How? By producing a ghost to testify in court?'

The woman looked at him pityingly and casually popped another blackberry into her mouth with red-stained fingers.

'Of course not, but the appearance of Ivy Trimble's spirit will make headlines and *then* the truth will come out. But that is not our concern.'

'It's not?'

'Our interest is provoking the appearance of the spirit while it is restless and seeking justice, for that is when spirits are at their most active, knocking on the door of this world.'

'So The Prophetics identify a place where there ought to be a ghost and then act as a sort of doorman, or gatekeeper, to invite them into our mortal realm?'

'In a way, yes,' she said suspiciously, 'and I can tell from your face what you think about us.'

'Ah, my face; my most vulnerable spot,' said Campion. 'I have no views of any import on your group, but as I am currently staying at The King's Head, I was merely wondering if my beauty sleep was likely to be disturbed by spectral apparitions and things that go bump in the night.'

Miss DeLuca clutched her yellow hat closer to her bosom, squashing the remaining fruit so that juice seeped through like a bloodstain. 'All right, I get it, you're a sceptic. Most people who don't have the calling are. Scoff all you like.'

'My dear lady, I did not mean to scoff and I am genuinely interested in the violence which robbed a fine country pub of its landlady. What exactly happened?'

'It was during the war.' The woman's mood switched as if controlled by a light switch, moving from the frustration of dealing with a non-believer, to the frisson of sharing a secret. 'There were American soldiers based at the manor house here and they used The King's Head, but one night things got out of hand and Ivy Trimble refused to serve a couple of GIs who were drunk and abusive. She barred them from the pub but they came back later that night with machine guns, burst into the bar and riddled poor Ivy with bullets.'

'Good heavens, how terrible! What happened to the soldiers?'

'Nobody knows,' she lowered her voice conspiratorially, 'because it was all covered up, by the army, by the government, by the police. I hope they were caught and hanged, but if they were that was hushed up too and Ivy was effectively written out of existence.'

Mr Campion took off his glasses, produced a white handkerchief like a conjuror and concentrated on polishing the large round lenses.

'A fascinating story, but if the murder of Ivy Trimble was so successfully hushed up, as you put it, and has remained a secret for nearly thirty years, how do you come to know about it?'

'It was written up as an article for The Prophetics' newsletter, complete with details of how to get to Kingswalter and even the name of the man who lives at the manor, though he wasn't exactly pleased to see us.' She paused and, Campion thought, treated herself to a brief smile. 'At least not at first.'

'Why is the manor of interest? The pub – the scene of the crime – I can understand, but the manor?'

Miss DeLuca again regarded Campion as if he was at best a child, at worst, just rather slow.

'The soldiers who killed Ivy were based at the manor. If – when – she returns, it may be at the pub or at the manor to confront her killers.'

'Let us hope she is not a vengeful ghost, but tell me more about this newsletter article.'

'What's to tell? I can give you . . . sell you a copy at members' rates if you step by my van. It came to me, as editor, through the post. It was neatly typed and ideal copy for us, just the sort of thing we cover.'

'And the author was a member of The Prophetics?'

'I have no idea; the article was anonymous. It came with a note simply asking if we might find this useful and no fee was necessary. We don't get many contributions, so that last bit rather clinched it.'

'It usually does,' agreed Mr Campion.


'Did you know there were three Popes in Dorchester?' Campion asked Rupert as they settled down to dinner accompanied by pints of ale served by Tessa Higgins.

'Aren't you thinking of Avignon in the Middle Ages?'

'No, Dorchester, and you are currently enjoying their beer. The local brewery, Eldridge Pope, has three of the Pope family, perhaps even more, at the helm. They do a barley wine named after Thomas Hardy; another local boy made good.'

'The *Far from the Madding Crowd* chap? I have to say, that's a bit like how I felt this afternoon up the hill with the present lord of the manor.' Rupert leaned over his plate of steak pie and chips and continued in a whisper. 'Did you know that Ward-Tetley actually owns this pub and yet he's flat broke?'

Campion waited until Mrs Higgins had taken her place at her husband's side behind the bar, then did an obvious head-turning look around the bar.

'Well, it's not exactly packed with holidaymakers, is it?'

'Or locals,' observed Rupert.

Campion nodded to the far corner of the bar, indicating two elderly men, both with walking sticks hooked over their chairs, playing dominoes at a table in the window and, sitting alone near the fireplace on a three-legged stool, a weather-beaten character of about sixty puffing on a short pipe virtually concealed by the peak of a tweed flat cap.

'Those must be the locals Mrs Higgins promised to keep at a safe distance while we ate, but when we've finished I don't see why we should not mingle with the natives. For the price of a round of drinks, we may learn something to our advantage, but in the meantime, fill me in on your meeting with young Ranald and do not spare his blushes, but do keep your voice down. These walls may not contain a ghost but, in a village this size, they probably have ears.'

Rupert's report on his meeting with Ranald Ward-Tetley lasted for the entire main course; only once did he pause to allow Mrs Higgins to skip from behind the bar to clear their plates as soon as they released their knives and forks.

His general opinion was that Ranald was a sad case, prone to wallowing in self-pity and no doubt lonely, rattling around in that shell of a manor house which, as far as he was concerned, had no ghosts, more's the pity, as a good haunting might have brought in a few visitors. He was clearly strapped for cash and thus very reliant on the fee he was expecting from the BBC for allowing them to film his mosaic, which seemed his only interest in *The Moving Mosaic*. He had not read the book or, as far as Rupert could tell, seen the original film, and had never heard of Evadne Childe. He wasn't even sure of what the mosaic he had inherited depicted, or why anyone should be interested in it.

'Well, he did go to Oxford,' said Campion with a twinkle in his eye. 'Did he say anything about the invasion of The Prophetics?'

'He was rather ambivalent about them. I got the impression that he thought they were a pest at first, but has now rather warmed to them. He said they had their uses.'

'Mmm, interesting,' said Campion, then looked up and smiled broadly as Mrs Higgins arrived with dessert, a shiny metal bowl containing two large balls of white ice cream, each with a round, brown biscuit pushed into them like crashed flying saucers.

'Clotted cream ice cream from Devon,' she announced, ''but the biscuits are Dorset gingers.'

'That's good to know, thank you,' said Mr Campion, who smiled until she had retreated out of earshot.

'But young Ranald is all in favour of the BBC doing their film, correct?'

'Absolutely desperate, I'd say. He's not remotely interested in the film itself, only in the location fee he will get. You know he has a script of the production and he hasn't even opened it, can you believe it?'

'That would certainly rankle with an actor looking for a part, should there be one in the vicinity . . .'

Rupert pulled a face, a mixture of surprise and indignation. 'I didn't stoop to asking Ward-Tetley for a part if that's what you're thinking. I know when not to waste my breath, but I would have liked a look at the script . . . out of professional curiosity.'

'Of course. There was no one from the BBC at the manor?'

'Not a soul. I told you, Ranald lives far from the madding crowd, in fact far from any crowd; or perhaps he's run out of crowds who will put up with him. I got the impression that he'd offered the manor to the film crew as a base, but they took one look and wisely chose a hotel in Dorchester.'

'You know which one?'

'Yes, The Junction. It's convenient for the hospital where one of their number has . . .' Rupert glanced towards the bar and finished the sentence silently, miming the words, '. . . food poisoning.'

Campion nodded his approval at his son's delicacy. 'So Ranald is clearly in the "Pro" camp when it comes to the filming, as he stands to profit from it, and profit is always a good motive.'

'What about The Prophetics? Did your afternoon ramble bear fruit?'

'In more ways than one, if you like blackberries.'

Mr Campion smiled at the thought, sampled his Devonshire ice cream, which was good, and snapped a Dorset biscuit in half. Only when his taste buds had approved the excellent combination did he present his own report, beginning with his surprise reacquaintance with Sally DeLuca.

Unlike Ranald Ward-Tetley, Miss DeLuca was well aware of Evadne Childe, indeed had met her, albeit ten years ago and not exactly in the most sociable of circumstances. But her presence in Kingswalter as the leader of The Prophetics seemed to have nothing directly to do with *The Moving Mosaic*. The ghost-hunters were there to hunt ghosts, to flush them out where they had never appeared before, presumably by a concentration of psychic energy which would, somehow, will them into existence and yes, Campion agreed with his son, it sounded completely bonkers.

The particular ghost they were hunting was the former landlady of The King's Head, Mrs Ivy Trimble, who had died so tragically back in 1944, as she had been identified as a suitably angry spirit, whose death had been successfully covered up by cruel authority. Despite the blanket of official secrecy thrown over her death, the newsletter of The Prophetics – for which Mr Campion had paid five pounds, though that did include a year's associate membership of the organization – had somehow acquired an account of Mrs Trimble's tragic history.

Mr Campion was, however, in the privileged position of knowing that the account published, and presumably believed, by The Prophetics was far from accurate. There was no mention of the fact that the rogue American soldiers were men of colour and that their quarrel was with two almost certainly over-officious white military policemen, the real target of their gunfire. Mrs Trimble had been in the wrong place at very much the wrong time, but was portrayed as the sole intended victim.

'The interesting thing,' said Campion, 'was not that they got only half the story, but they got the story at all. What sort of journalist is it who discovers a government cover-up and gives it free, without even a by-line, to the newsletter of a bunch of ghost-botherers?'

'One who couldn't sell the story anywhere else?' Rupert suggested.

'I doubt that,' scoffed his father. 'I can think of several Sunday papers that could make a sensational meal out of it, not to mention a couple of left-wing journals which would love to highlight another example of America's unhappy history of race relations. No, this isn't amateur journalism, this is mischief.'

'To what end?'

'I don't know, unless it's an attempt to muddy the waters, sow confusion and create chaos so the BBC cannot film in peace.'

'But you said The Prophetics were not interested in *The Moving Mosaic*.'

'I don't think they are, though if they do flush out a ghost, having a BBC film crew on hand would do wonders for the reputation of The Prophetics.'

'That's a bit of a stretch, isn't it? Could it be just coincidence that The Prophetics and the BBC descend on Kingswalter at exactly the same time?'

'I distrust coincidence when it results in innocent pleasantries; when it produces chaos and confusion, I suspect a malevolent hand at work.'

'But how does disrupting the BBC's filming benefit The Prophetics?'

'I don't see how it can, but it might somehow benefit whoever sent in that article about the Kingswalter massacre, flawed though it was. The thing is, how did our journalist friend come across the story in the first place? That's the trouble with state secrets, one never knows who knows them.'

Mr Campion finished his ice cream and glanced towards the bar, hoping to catch the landlady's eye. 'I wonder if they run to coffee here?'

Mrs Higgins signalled that she would attend their every need presently but, before she could lift the hatch and escape from behind the bar, the front door of the pub burst open and the until-now silent pipe smoker by the window growled: 'Watch out! It's rush hour!'

Campion was not surprised that the incoming crowd comprised The Prophetics, led by Sally DeLuca, as it would have been unusual for villagers to enter thus *en masse* and he had not heard a charabanc carrying a Mothers' Union outing draw up outside, though he was unclear as to why he had thought the Mothers' Union should be out on a pub crawl at this time of night.

The crowd, if six people constituted a crowd, were overwhelmingly female, and all followed Miss DeLuca's fashion sense, wearing black, gauzy, ankle-length dresses, their individuality marked by scarves and in one case a headband, in bright yellow, possibly small homage to their leader's bright yellow floppy hat. The sole male among them showed no such flashes of colour, being dressed in a rather shiny grey suit, which gave him the air of a confused vicar unsure of whether he was at a wedding or a funeral, the image not helped by the fact that he was struggling to keep hold of a double armful of empty beer and cider bottles.

With a cursory nod acknowledging Mr Campion, Sally DeLuca made a beeline for the bar, where she began to negotiate with Roy Higgins about the deposit refund due on the bottles they were returning, which would offset the cost of the replacements they were demanding. As bottles of stout and cider were passed over the bar and money changed hands, The Prophetics remained standing, whispering among themselves rather than socializing with the customers. Campion noticed that at any one time two or three of the group would close their eyes and their lips would move as if in silent prayer. Perhaps they were tasting the psychic atmosphere.

Having armed themselves with full bottles and at least half a dozen packets of crisps, The Prophetics began to troop out, Miss DeLuca politely thanking the Higginses and wishing them good night. Both landlord and landlady had kept them under strict observation at all times, clearly indicating that the group was expected to be on their best behaviour. The Prophetics had complied, caused no disturbance, and had paid cash, obviously aware of the unwritten law of the house.

Only when the door had closed behind the last one of them did the pipe-smoker by the fireplace turn on his stool to face the Campions.

'Don't worry about them,' he said in a deep, throaty chuckle. 'They don't bother the living, only the dead.'

# ELEVEN

## The Unbothered Ghost of Ivy Trimble

M r Campion ordered coffees for himself and Rupert and 'a pint of whatever that young man by the fire is drinking', at which Tessa Higgins blew air over quivering lips and shook her head in despair.

'You need to change your glasses if you think that's a young man. That's Joe Lunn.'

'My good lady, at my age, everyone is young, and I do hope Mr Lunn will join us.'

'For a free pint he will,' said Mrs Higgins, 'just keep one hand on your wallet.'

'Your wallet's safe enough,' said the man, who was suddenly pulling up a chair to their table, 'but my name is Joe Lunn, she was right about that.'

Campion introduced himself and Rupert as two coffees and a pint of bitter landed on their table with little ceremony. The speed with which Mrs Higgins turned on her heels and retreated to the bar merely confirmed her disapproval of this mingling with the locals.

'From the way you described them,' said Mr Campion, 'I take it you have come across our rather odd fellow travellers before.'

'Well, they ain't local, that's f'sure. Thought they was some of those hippies with their California dreaming when they first rolled up,' said Joe Lunn, taking the pipe from his lips to make room for the rim of his glass.

'Their rather sombre fashion sense would suggest otherwise. They seem dressed for a funeral rather than a love-in, if such things still exist.'

'You've got that spot on. They're more interested in ghosts and ghoulies.' He paused as if a thought had just struck him. 'I ain't seen you before,' he said to Campion, then turned on Rupert, 'but I saw you up at the manor this a'ternoon.'

'I didn't see you,' Rupert said defensively.

'Weren't supposed to. Wouldn't be much good at my job if you had. I'm the gamekeeper up there.'

From behind the bar Roy Higgins, displaying his acute hearing, interjected loudly with: 'Gardener more like it!'

'He's not wrong,' admitted Lunn, 'and gardener is one up from rat-catcher, which is what I mostly do to earn my corn, not that young Mr Ranald is generous with the corn.' He put down his pint pot long enough to extend a gnarled finger at Rupert. 'I saw the two of you by that blasted mosaic an' I hope you was bringing good news which would benefit his bank balance.'

'I'm afraid not,' said Rupert, thinking it unwise to bring up an old seventeen-and-six debt, 'though I do hope things work out for Ranald – we were at school together . . . briefly.'

Joe Lunn nodded sagely. 'He could have done with a bit more education, but then couldn't we all?'

'To return to the recent arrivals in the village,' said Campion, 'who have just departed, if that's not too funereal a way of putting it; you sounded as if you knew of their rather strange hobby.'

'You mean hunting for ghosts? Good luck to 'em. They'll not bother Ivy Trimble.'

'Ivy Trimble? Who's that?' Campion asked, studiously avoiding his son's widening eyes.

Joe Lunn failed to notice Rupert's creased brow, took another gulp of beer and leaned into the table, clearly pleased to have an audience.

'Ivy was the landlady here, 'fore the war. You won't hear her name mentioned much round here due to how she met her end. There's not many left who know that terrible story.'

'But you do?' Mr Campion made a mental wager with himself as to how many more pints of ale it would take to get the complete narrative.

'I'm the nearest thing to an eyewitness you'll find these days.'

'Witness to what?'

'Ivy Trimble's violent death, right here in this very bar.' He paused for dramatic effect. 'Machine-gunned she was, cut down like a Chicago gangster by people who were supposed to be our allies, our comrades-in-arms.'

'How absolutely shocking,' said Mr Campion, suitably shocked, 'and you witnessed this?'

Joe Lunn raised a forefinger. 'I said I was the *nearest* thing to an eyewitness you'll get these days. Didn't say I saw it myself, but my dad did, he was here in the bar the night it happened and told me all about it when I got demobbed from the army. He said he didn't want to see another uniform as long as he lived. He's gone now, of course, but peaceable. Not like poor Ivy.'

'Who . . .?' Campion prompted.

'There were Yanks stationed up at the manor back then. It would have been 1944, a while after D-Day. I know that because my lot were well into Belgium by then. Anyhow, a bunch of them Yanks, hopped up on booze and pills no doubt, took it into their heads to visit the good old King's Head, but they were in such a state, Ivy refused to serve them. They went and got their Tommy guns, came back and opened up, bullets everywhere, and my dear old dad crawling on the floor to keep out of the way of all that flying lead. Ivy Trimble wasn't so lucky. They got her dead to rights.'

'An unfortunate but probably accurate turn of phrase, Mr Lunn. Was anyone apprehended for Mrs Trimble's murder?'

Joe Lunn drained his pint mug before answering, and was delighted to see Mr Campion signalling to the bar for a refill before the glass hit the table. 'It was all hushed up, of course, what with the war still being on and the Yanks supposed to be on our side. Ivy's husband left Kingswalter for good, some say with a handy slice of compensation from the American army, but then some folk will say anything.'

'They will indeed, and frequently do,' said Campion. 'I presume it's the ghost of Ivy Trimble which The Prophetics are pursuing.'

'Well, good luck to them, I say. There ain't never been no word of a ghost here, let alone up at the manor, though them ghost-botherers are convinced if Ivy don't appear here it'll be up there where her killers were based. Pure daft if you ask me; don't know where they get their ideas from.'

'Neither do I, Mr Lunn, but you raise a good point. If the authorities slapped a D-notice on the incident, which was quite likely in wartime, how did our friends camping down by the old abbey hear about Ivy Trimble?'

Joe Lunn sipped his second pint, smacked his lips in approval and began the ritual of relighting his pipe. When he shrugged his shoulders, a small Roman candle of sparks erupted from the bowl.

'Beats me, but they already knew about Ivy before they got here. They tried asking around for more juicy details' – he nodded in the direction of the two old-timers playing dominoes – 'but nobody in the village would ever say anything to incomers, even if they knew the story. Besides, the subject is *verboten* in here if you want to keep on getting served.'

This time he jerked his head towards the current landlady.

'The only spirits allowed in here are those behind the bar. She can't stomach talk of ghoulies and ghosties – won't have any of it. I reckon it's a religious thing; still, it's her pub and the only one in the village.'

'So who could have told The Prophetics that The King's Head might be a happy hunting ground for them?'

'Like I said, beats me. There's few who know the story.'

'But you do.'

'Yes, from my dad, but I don't go broadcasting it.'

'Forgive me, but that's exactly what you've been doing for the last two pints. Could I ask if you've told anyone else the saga of Ivy Trimble's murder?'

Rupert, who had remained silent throughout these exchanges, had in fact been closely studying the facial expressions of Joe Lunn, with a view to adding them to his repertoire as an actor.

Should he ever be called upon to take the role of 'scheming country yokel', he felt totally prepared.

'I've been telling you the tale,' Joe Lunn said defensively, 'not any Tom, Dick or Harry who drops by, because you was here when they came in. I saw the way that woman in black – dresses a bit like a witch, she does – looked at you. You're not one of them, but you know who they are. Then I saw him' – an accusing finger was aimed at Rupert – 'up at the manor this afternoon, an' I reckoned you might be interested, like your colleague was.'

'Our colleague?'

'From the BBC. About two months ago. Nice chap, he was scouting out locations for this film they're making.'

In that instant Joe Lunn gave Rupert another shot in his acting armoury: the expression of a man who thinks he has said too much but doesn't know how or why, but has clearly seen the prospect of another free drink disappearing over the horizon.

'And you told him the story of Ivy Trimble?'

'Well, he seemed interested in "local colour", as he called it, and he was on expenses.' Lunn studied the level of the remaining liquid in his pint pot. '*Generous* expenses.'

'Have you told anyone else the story of Mrs Trimble?' asked Campion.

'Not a living soul,' said Joe Lunn and then, with a fiendish grin, added: 'Nor a dead one.'

It was agreed by all concerned that it was a fine night for 'ghost-bothering' and so, after Joe Lunn's glass had been refilled yet again, and medicinal brandies ordered for themselves, the Campions agreed to accompany him up the hill to the manor where, he said, The Prophetics were sure to have gathered to drink their bottled beers and conjure spirits, or whatever it was they did after dark.

Putting themselves in the hands of their gamekeeper guide, the Campions were somewhat disconcerted when, prior to departure, Joe Lunn said he couldn't leave without his gun, which Roy Higgins produced, with a scowl of disdain, from behind the bar. It was a small-bore single-barrelled folding shotgun, a .410 if Mr Campion's eyes did not deceive him, which, with the skeleton stock folded under the octagonal barrel could be carried unobtrusively under a long overcoat, making it a perfect poacher's weapon as long as the rabbits being poached were less than thirty-five yards away.

They were not exactly put at their ease when Joe Lunn volunteered the information that he had been made to lodge the gun behind the bar ever since 'the incident' during a darts match some time ago. Campion nodded quietly, accepting that this appeared a sound policy on the part of the landlord, while making sure that the gun was not loaded as it disappeared under the folds of Lunn's coat.

Mr Campion dismissed Rupert's suggestion that they should drive up to the manor, preferring the element of surprise, but did insist on taking a torch from the boot of the Jaguar to help guide his way. Not that it was needed immediately, for a bright moon illuminated the lane up to the manor, so bright that Joe Lunn, his countryman's instincts taking over, gravitated towards the trees and bushes to the side of the lane, occasionally disappearing completely, and silently, to re-emerge on to the lane a few yards ahead of them.

Rupert was somewhat disconcerted by Lunn's disappearing and reappearing act, and his need to concentrate on keeping up with his father's long stride added to his frustration of being the youngest of the trio but being outpaced by a tipsy gamekeeper and a seventy-two-year-old gentleman who might have been strolling down Pall Mall.

The iron gates loomed up in front of them and, down the short drive, the dark silhouette of the manor house.

'The mosaic is in the trees somewhere here to the left,' said Rupert, but was instantly shushed by his father, who had stopped dead in his tracks and was straining to locate the source of a faint murmur floating through the night air.

Joe Lunn signalled for the Campions to leave the drive and join him in the trees to the right, and in single file they picked their way through the underbrush until they had a clear view of the front of the house.

The Prophetics were seated on the ground in a semi-circle near the front door and were clearly the source of the indistinct murmuring as well as the faint whiff of cigarette smoke. Some of them held small hand torches, their beams pointed at the ground; two of them had lit candles crammed into beer bottles and they could have been mistaken for some strange prayer group, yet they were not praying or incanting, they were quietly chatting. The occasional 'pop' as a bottle was opened, the scrape of a match and the shaking of a bag of crisps indicated that this was more a picnic than a religious service, but it was definitely a vigil of sorts.

'Is this what they do?' Campion whispered to Joe Lunn.

'Most nights if it ain't raining,' Lunn whispered back on a gust of beer fumes.

'They seem quite well-behaved.'

'And they take their litter with them. Strange way to pass the time though. Hey up! There's movement.'

One of the group got to her feet and, although it was dark and she was wearing black, Campion was sure it was Sally DeLuca. The others fell silent, their attention focused on the door of the house.

They heard the metallic snap of a bolt being withdrawn and the door creaked open, allowing a tongue of pale orange light to escape. For the first time the watchers in the trees could see the faces of The Prophetics in profile, all locked in adoration towards the source of the light.

'If they're expecting Ivy Trimble, they'll be disappointed,' hissed Lunn.

As the door opened wider, The Prophetics who, apart from their leader, Sally DeLuca, had not moved, might have been disappointed, but they did not seem surprised to see Ranald Ward-Tetley holding an ancient oil lamp at head height. It was almost a Christmas scene: the Victorian householder answering the door to a group of small children singing carols, except they were adults seated or kneeling on the ground and there was no snow in evidence.

Yet the householder seemed set on playing his part to the full as Ranald had stepped forward, raised his lantern, and was clearly offering Miss DeLuca money dredged deep from a trouser pocket. In return, the woman reached into a bag slung over one shoulder, took out something small enough to fit in her fist and in turn offered it to the lord of the manor. No one spoke during the exchange and Ranald and his light withdrew into the house, leaving The Prophetics in the dark, Miss DeLuca resuming her place in the semi-circle.

Mr Campion tapped his companions on the shoulder and mimed

that they should withdraw down the drive. Only when they were back near the gates did he speak.

'Well, that was strange, wasn't it?'

'He uses them oil lamps when they cut the electric off,' said Joe Lunn.

'I didn't mean that. Ranald was buying something from them.'

'Well, where else is he going to get his whacky baccy in a place like Kingswalter?' said Rupert, and fortunately the night was dark enough to protect him from his father's look of pure scorn.

Rupert still felt a distinct chill in the air and hastened to make amends. 'The mosaic is just through the trees if you want to see it while we're here, but you'll need your torch. I don't think they'll see it from the house.'

'Not once you're in the trees,' agreed Lunn, 'it's well hidden and maybe it should stay that way.'

'It could be the making of young Ranald's fortune,' said Mr Campion, pushing his way through the lower branches and aiming the beam of his torch downwards.

'Then the bookmakers are in for a good time,' muttered Joe Lunn.

Campion ignored the comment as Rupert had parted the greenery in front of him and Campion's torchlight was being reflected a thousand tiny times by the shards of the mosaic, which lay before them as naturally as a rug thrown on the floor.

'It's just as Evadne described it,' Campion said quietly.

'I know,' said Rupert, 'and its survival is remarkable. What baffles me is that if the story is the *moving* mosaic, how is it actually moved?'

Once again the darkness spared Rupert his father's disapproval.

'You haven't read the book, have you?'

'I haven't *finished* it, but I am reading it.'

Mr Campion sighed.

'I will explain all over a nightcap back at The King's Head.'

'Sounds like a good idea,' said Lunn.

'I'm sorry, Mr Lunn,' said Campion, shining his torch beam into the gamekeeper's face, 'but it will be closing time when we get back and therefore residents only as far as the licensing law is concerned. I'd hate to get you into trouble with the only pub in the village.'

Lunn made a grunting noise and was still muttering to himself as they threaded their way through the vegetation to the iron gates. Once on the lane and heading down the slope back to Kingswalter, Lunn produced the shotgun from his coat and unfolded it, then took a cartridge from his pocket, loaded the gun and cocked the hammer.

Watched by a nervous Rupert and a remarkably calm Mr Campion, he aimed the barrel up into the night sky and pulled the trigger. The resulting bang produced a series of distant squeals and screams from the direction of the manor.

Deftly, Lunn folded the shotgun on its skeleton stock and tucked it back under his coat.

He had a crazed grin on his face as he answered Campion's unasked question.

'Something to keep them ghost-botherers happy,' he said. 'They like things that go bump in the night.'

In The King's Head, now officially closed to both non-residents and ghosts, the Campions were offered the run of the Higginses' private lounge, just off the public bar, to enjoy the generous brandy nightcaps Mrs Higgins was delighted to serve them before she and her husband retired for the night. They further endeared themselves to their hostess when Mr Campion asked if there was an 'honesty book' where they could write down any further drinks they might help themselves to from the bar, with a view to settling up in the morning, and she was visibly impressed when Rupert got up from his chair to wish her a formal 'Good night.' So impressed that, as she and her husband climbed the stairs to their bedroom, she declared, 'Lovely manners! I told you they was gentlemen an' not at all like that lot from the BBC.'

The Campions exchanged knowing smiles when they heard that, then they settled themselves in the strategically placed armchairs from which Roy and Tessa watched television in their off-duty hours.

'So what do you make of our new-found friend Mr Lunn?'

'Bit of a character,' said Rupert. 'I suspect he decided on the role of rural rogue from an early age and has been refining his act for years for the entertainment of tourists willing to buy him beer. Every village should have one.'

'I think you've pegged him correctly, but his version of the

Kingswalter Massacre was intriguing, to say the least, and certainly worth the price of admission.'

'It was?'

'Unfortunately for Joe Lunn, he chose to tell his version to someone who knew the real story – me. He made it sound as if Ivy Trimble had had an altercation with the American soldiers who shot her. There was no mention of the military policemen, who probably provoked the incident through their crass treatment of the soldiers of colour and were the prime target of their anger. As far as I recall, the unfortunate Mrs Trimble was popular among the GIs stationed at the manor, and at their trial the gunmen showed genuine remorse that she had been caught in the crossfire.'

'Well, he didn't have your ringside seat of proceedings, did he? In fact, he got the story second-hand from his father, who may not have been the most reliable of witnesses, or the story got lost in translation or Chinese whispers every time he told it.'

'That's the first interesting thing,' said Mr Campion, sipping his brandy. 'Lunn said he had only ever told one other person, a chap from the BBC a couple of months ago.'

'And you believe him?'

'Yes, I do. If he'd told all and sundry in the hope of getting free beer, then surely the story would have got out and reached the press by now. Joe Lunn might have been tempted to tell the Sunday newspapers himself, but clearly he took the threat of being barred from the one pub in the village by Mrs Higgins very seriously, so I do believe he's only told one person before now.'

'Why a BBC man?'

'Who knows? Perhaps to ingratiate himself with the production team, offer his services as a local guide and go-between. Perhaps he was short of funds and sniffed out an expense account with his poacher's instincts. It might be worth having a word with mine host here tomorrow, see if he remembers the encounter, or we could ask the BBC.'

'We could?' Rupert's eyes lit up, and not under the influence of the brandy.

'I think we should pay the production team a visit in Dorchester, now we know where they are lodging.'

'That's a first-rate idea,' Rupert enthused. 'We could go straight after breakfast.'

'I'd like to take a look at that mosaic in daylight first,' said Campion, 'then we could pop over to Chesil Beach or visit some of the interesting museums in Dorchester, have a nice lunch somewhere . . .'

Mr Campion decided he had teased his son enough. 'Oh, very well, breakfast, then the mosaic, then Dorchester.'

'Will we get to see Tamara Reams?'

'I hope so as she is the main producer, so I'm told, though I suspect she probably feels under siege what with all the mishaps dogging the film.' He pointed his brandy at his son. 'We're there to help if we can, not add to her problems, so keep that sad puppy-dog face in your locker and don't you dare ask if . . .'

'I won't, I won't, but if I do get to meet her and make an impression, and then my agent rings her next week and tells her I'm an available actor . . .'

'I thought all actors were available. Always. However, if that curbs your overenthusiasm, I cannot object.'

'You don't look too happy about it.'

'No, it's not that, I'm sure you'll behave yourself. I was thinking about Joe Lunn's story of the massacre.'

'So he got the details wrong. What's the problem?'

Mr Campion raised his spectacles on to his forehead and gently massaged the bridge of his nose with thumb and forefinger. 'The thing is,' he said, 'Joe Lunn's rather partial, not to say sketchy, version of events back in 1944 may have been given in complete innocence, but what is interesting is that his was the version of events which found their way into the newsletter of The Prophetics.'

'You mean that whoever Joe Lunn told, then told The Prophetics, turning them loose on Kingswalter?'

'Precisely, though I have no idea why.'

Breakfast at The King's Head confirmed Mr Campion's suspicion that Tessa Higgins firmly believed it to be the most important meal of the day, if not the week.

Only when she saw that her guests were doggedly scaling the mountains of sausages, bacon and eggs she had placed before them did she concede to answering Mr Campion's questions.

'We don't keep a Visitors' Book – perhaps we should – but I think I know the chap you mean. About two months ago, you said? That'd be right. Said he was scouting locations for the BBC for a film they were planning. A real hail-fellow-well-met chap, got on with everyone, especially Joe Lunn. In fact, they got thick as thieves, those two.'

She raised a hand to her mouth in the universal drinking motion. 'If you know what I mean. Joe took him up to the manor and to the abbey, to show him the monks' garden, which he was very interested in and, to be fair, Joe knows his stuff when it comes to the local flora and fauna. Not that I approve of Joe Lunn scrounging free drinks from visitors, but the chap didn't seem to mind at all. He came back with the others.'

'Came back?' asked Mr Campion.

'Earlier this month, with other BBC people.' She dropped her voice. 'Only stayed for one night; well, they all did, because that's when we had the *incident*'– she mouthed the word, but then clarified – 'the *accusation* of food poisoning. Of course, that did it for Mr Higgins. He threw them all out and now won't have anything to do with BBC people.'

'Can you remember his name?' Rupert asked. 'The BBC man?'

'Sorry, whatever it was, it didn't stick in my flea brain, but I do remember he drove a very shoddy, very noisy little van.'

Mr Campion picked at his breakfast, while Rupert devoured his with gusto on the principle shared by soldiers and thespians that one never knows where the next fry-up is coming from.

'Slight change of plan,' he said as Rupert chewed. 'Rather than see the mosaic this morning, I'd like to visit the abbey ruins.'

# TWELVE

## In a Monastery Garden

Mr Campion had maintained that a brisk walk before the sun had burned off the morning dew was a vital pre-requisite for a clear head when serious thinking had to be done, plus, after the breakfast they had enjoyed, it was a necessity for the waistline.

'I had something of a love/hate relationship with Latin as a schoolboy,' he said as he and Rupert set out down the single street.

'That is not surprising,' said Rupert, even though his father's opening gambit was. 'Most schoolboys do, unless they are complete swots.'

'You asked me last night how somebody could move a mosaic floor and so I will tell you as we stroll, though you could have saved yourself a lecture had you finished Evadne's book.'

'I tried another chapter in bed,' Rupert said weakly, 'but I'm not used to brandy late at night and just couldn't keep my eyes open.'

'Then you must listen and learn, my boy, for you never know when the technique might come in useful, though I admit such circumstances may be rare, unless you change professions and go to work for the British Museum.'

'It may come to that if a decent part doesn't come along soon.'

Mr Campion ignored his son's glumness.

'As I was saying, Latin grammar was a bit of a struggle for me, requiring far too much concentration, but I found the Romans and their history and skulduggery quite fascinating. In fact, they went up in my estimation when I learned that the most important ones probably spoke Greek rather than Latin.

'I remember being give a speech by Cicero to translate for an exam. It was a legal plea, a defence, and very much an "oration". Did you know that Cicero took drama coaching from an actor called Roscius Gallus, whom he had once defended? Typical lawyer, playing to the gallery. I'm not boring you, am I?'

'Not yet,' said Rupert.

'Good, because I intend to come to the point any day now. The thing is, the grammar of this legal speech didn't interest me at all, but he had given the speech at the trial of a chap called Milo, who might have been an ex-gladiator with political ambitions and had been accused of killing a rival, and that *did* interest me, so I forgot to translate old Cicero's dramatic prose and instead read around the subject, becoming quite fascinated with the last years of the Roman Republic.

'I can't, at this distance, remember where I read it, though Evadne Childe probably consulted the same source, but I came across the story of how a rich Roman merchant had taken a fancy to a mosaic pavement he'd spotted in Utica, which I'm sure you know was a Carthaginian city in Tunisia.'

'Not the one in upstate New York?'

'Don't be facetious and please save questions and votes-of-thanks for the end of the lecture. Anyhow, this mosaic was already two hundred years old and had been brought to Utica – the one in Tunisia – from Alexandria, and that's the one in Egypt, not the one in Scotland, nor, before you ask, the one in Virginia.'

'Carthage . . . Tunisia . . . got it,' conceded Rupert.

'So our rich Roman took a liking to this mosaic floor and thought it would make a splendid present for his mistress, whom he was keeping in luxurious isolation at his villa near Naples. But how to get it across the Mediterranean in one piece?'

'The same way it had got to Utica from Alexandria?'

'Good, you are paying attention – there may be questions at the end. First, our resourceful Roman glued papyrus to the surface of the mosaic tiles, then a layer of linen; well, he probably had slaves to do it for him. When that was done, he had them dig trenches down the sides of the floor to expose the layer of lime mortar which glued the floor to its foundations. Once he could get at all four sides of the rectangle, he had his loyal and enthusiastic staff use long, fine-toothed saws to cut through – horizontally – that layer of mortar, until the mosaic pavement was free of its earthly bonds with a flexible layer of papyrus and linen protecting its intricate surface design.

'All that remained to do was roll the floor up around a wooden cylinder until it was the size and shape of a large barrel – a hogshead, say.'

'A hogshead – that's fifty-four gallons of beer, right?' offered Rupert.

'Very good. Did you learn that at school?'

'No, from Lugg.'

'So he does have his uses. Anyway, to conclude, the barrel-shaped mosaic could now be loaded on to a ship and transported to Naples where, to the delight of his mistress, it just had to be unrolled and stuck down again. And that's how you move a mosaic. Here endeth the lesson, to tumultuous applause.'

'You've remembered that story from your schooldays?' Rupert hoped he did not sound too incredulous at the length of time involved in that question.

'I was reminded of it when I read Evadne's novel the first time around, but of course they glossed over it in the first film. Probably too expensive to stage.'

'That answers the "how" question, but what about the one Ranald Ward-Tetley asked me. *Why* would anyone want to steal a mosaic floor?'

'I hope you told him to read the book.'

'I did.'

'Good, and you'll have to finish it to find out – I'm not spoiling the ending for you.'

They reached the large village pond, which Rupert said had been named Swan Lake by Ranald's father, and, sure enough, there was the single swan on lonely patrol. Even so, there was more activity on the pond than in the field across the road, where the parked vehicles of The Prophetics, including Sally DeLuca's camper van, were static and silent.

'I think ghost-botherers are having a lie-in,' said Campion, 'after their vigil at the manor.'

'How long before they get bored and go home?'

'Who knows the staying power of the fanatic? I suspect reports of a poltergeist in Peterborough could draw them away at any moment.'

'Could you arrange that?'

Mr Campion affected a look of shocked indignation at the suggestion.

'Why spoil their fun? As far as I can see, they are harmless. Eccentric, I admit, but harmless, and they have no interest in the filming of *The Moving Mosaic* one way or the other, though the person who pointed them towards Kingswalter certainly seems to have.'

Mr Campion had never professed to be a gardener, though in the days since his so-called retirement, he had taken an interest in the kitchen garden and orchard which served the Campions' country home. The more formal, floral garden was very much the empire of Lady Amanda, who allowed her husband's presence whenever heavy lifting or serious wheelbarrowing was required, a stricture Campion was happy to obey, preferring to apply his green fingers to things he could harvest rather than admire.

Rupert, who was far more comfortable with foliage painted on scenery than the real thing, followed his father through the brambles and into the abbey ruins without question, but was confused as to where they would find a garden in among this jungle of weeds, thorns and fallen stonework. He was not even sure they would find an abbey in there, or what was left of one after more than four centuries of abandonment, though he soon learned from constant tripping and toe-stubbing that what was left of the fabric of the abbey was underfoot and determined to inflict a twisted ankle on careless trespassers.

He realized that the way to make progress was to follow his father's footsteps, as Mr Campion seemed to have a mountain goat's ability to negotiate the uneven terrain and the thickest tangle of bramble, whilst also keeping his hands at a height which avoided the waving nettles trying to nuzzle them.

Beyond the remaining ghostly standing arch, which might have been part of the cloister, Mr Campion paused and studiously examined the ground before him.

'What exactly are we looking for?' Rupert asked, sucking his wrist to ease a nettle sting.

'The physic garden – all monasteries had them, usually next to the vegetable garden,' replied Campion, peering downwards. 'Monks were great gardeners, you know, as it kept them busy. Idleness was the devil's workshop, so work in the gardens was good for the soul, as well as the stomach and their general health, as the physic garden grew the plants they used as medicine: sage, betony, comfrey, garlic, hyssop, poppies and so on. I think we're roughly in the right place.'

'How on earth can you tell, Pop? These are just weeds.'

'Most of them are, but there is one here which could be a clue that we're in the physic garden. There.'

He pointed to a plant among the nettles which had shiny, pale green oval-shaped leaves.

'Bog myrtle,' he declared, 'or sweet gale. Not much appreciated these days, but once very popular in the brewing of beer, before the introduction of hops from Flanders, that is. Henry VIII hated his ale brewed with hops; thought it a terrible piece of European interference in something quintessentially English. And the monasteries were big centres of brewing, not that that had anything to do with him taking against them, at least I don't think it did.'

'Is that what we were looking for?'

'Not really, I was hoping to find wolfsbane or even foxgloves or something equally nasty, but I can't spot anything particularly dangerous.'

'So we were really looking for flowers, like deadly nightshade?'

'Foxgloves – *Digitalis purpurea* – would have been more likely, but that was the general idea.'

'And what prompted your sudden interest in horticulture?'

Mr Campion looked at his son, blinked twice and sighed. 'I would have thought it obvious. A stranger visits The King's Head and talks to local son-of-the-soil Joe Lunn about gardens. Suddenly, there's an outbreak of food poisoning there and a BBC man is put in hospital. Or is it just my suspicious mind?'

Mr Campion declared there would be another change of plan, or perhaps just an extension to the plan he had changed earlier. Once again, his visit to the Kingswalter mosaic in daylight was to be postponed, in favour of a trip into Dorchester, following detailed directions from Roy Higgins ('don't ever ask the wife for directions') at the pub, where they collected the Jaguar.

Rupert, sensing they were en route to a meeting with the BBC personnel entrusted with the filming of *The Moving Mosaic* – and any meeting with *anyone* from the BBC was surely an opportunity to further his career – asked if he had time to change and spruce himself up. His father, however, was of the opinion that his appearance, while casual for an audition, was perfectly respectable for visiting an invalid in hospital.

'Don't look so glum,' said Mr Campion, 'it might prove a useful contact for you, as I believe the patient in question is a location scout for the BBC.'

Realization dawned on Rupert's face. 'The chap who went down with food poisoning.'

'His name is Don Chapman, or so Miss Prim at Gilpin's told me. I could have checked with Mr Higgins at the pub, but I suspect it is a very sensitive subject there. He was suspicious enough when I asked for directions to the County Hospital.'

Somewhat cheered, Rupert settled himself behind the Jaguar's steering wheel; by the time the car was purring up the hill out of Kingswalter, he was smiling because the thought had occurred to him that if the location scout for *The Moving Mosaic* was incapacitated and hospitalized, then the film's producers might be looking for a replacement; at short notice, and preferably someone already on location . . .

They found the hospital and the patient in question remarkably easily, thanks to Rupert's skill as a driver and Mr Campion's natural charm with junior nurses and diplomacy when dealing with sterner ward sisters, even negotiating access to the patient outside normal visiting hours due to the fact that he was in a private room. In a quiet aside to Rupert, Mr Campion confessed that he did not know the BBC ran to providing private medical care for what he assumed would be a freelancer rather than a regular employee. Unfortunately, the patient in question was unable to enlighten them.

'I'm afraid Mr Chapman cannot talk to anyone,' said the white-coated doctor who had ambushed them in the corridor. 'In fact, he should not really be having visitors, he really is quite unwell. You are from the BBC, I presume.'

'Indirectly,' said Campion warily, noting that the doctor was holding his stethoscope in a clenched fist like a cosh. 'My name is Campion and I am in Dorchester at the request of the governors of the BBC.' Campion felt rather than saw Rupert's eyebrows shoot upwards. 'It seemed only decent to see how Mr Chapman was doing, given that he was taken ill in the line of duty, so to speak.'

'I'm Dr Gordon,' said the medic, betraying the ghost of a Highland accent, 'and I've been assigned to Mr Chapman because I have consulted for the local public health bodies, and the police here in Dorset, for many years.'

'So Don Chapman was poisoned,' said Campion in the tone of a fellow doctor agreeing on a diagnosis.

'There was an incidence of food poisoning,' said the real doctor, 'which is not quite the same thing.'

'Naturally you must be careful, Doctor, and of course you have patient confidentiality to consider, but I would be very grateful for any light you can shed on what happened to Mr Chapman, if only for purely selfish reasons in that we are staying at the same pub where he ate his thankfully non-fatal meal.'

'I know The King's Head,' said Gordon, 'and I've eaten there myself, but all I would say is you should avoid Roy Higgins's homemade curry. He did his National Service somewhere out East and brought the recipe back with him. I've eaten it in the past, even though he insists on serving it with chips, but I think it's off the menu at the moment.'

'We had the cottage pie,' Rupert contributed. 'It was very nice.'

'The ingredients, and the kitchen, were all checked and clear of noxious substances, I presume,' asked Campion.

'Of course!' snapped Dr Gordon, 'I know my job.'

Mr Campion struck a pose, as if considering a deep philosophical question. 'My first thought was something horticultural – a *Digitalis* or an aconite – but I could see no obvious source in Kingswalter.'

Dr Gordon was clearly impressed, but stifled the emotion as effectively as only a Scot could.

'An interesting conclusion.'

'It was just a passing thought, perhaps because I had it in mind to visit the old abbey and see if there were still any signs of the physic garden.'

'We have the same suspicious mind, Mr . . . Campion, was it? Campion as in *Silene dioica*, the woodland guardian?'

'That's us.' Mr Campion smiled.

'What is?' asked Rupert.

'Forgive my son, Doctor – he is an urbanite of the first order and I have clearly failed in my duties as a parent to educate him in the mythology of the red campion, whose pretty flowers are said to hide and protect woodland fairies and the secret honey stores of bees. It is also, as far as I am aware, completely harmless to man and beast, unlike some other plants.'

'Quite,' said Dr Gordon, clearly restraining himself from saying more.

'But your interest is in the dangerous aspects of Mother Nature, isn't it?' prompted Campion.

'It is my hobby and, you might say, my speciality, but I shouldn't really say any more before the toxicology results are in.'

'Could you tell me without breaking too much confidentiality what Don Chapman's symptoms were?'

The doctor cleared his throat, as if what he was about to say carried a bad taste. 'He was admitted with blurred vision, disorientation and dizziness, as well as stomach cramps, vomiting and diarrhoea – all fairly normal reactions to food poisoning.'

'Unpleasant, but treatable, surely?'

'Certainly, but there were complications – irregular and slow heartbeat, low blood pressure and then the onset of dysphagia.'

'What's dysphagia?' asked Rupert.

'Problems swallowing, plus he developed lockjaw.'

'An all-round bad reaction to something,' said Campion. 'Something he ate by accident?'

Dr Gordon shook his head slowly, then slapped the rubber tubes of his stethoscope into his open palm. 'Unlikely. We contacted his doctor in London for his medical records and there seems to be a history of heart problems, but I suppose he could have come into contact without knowing how dangerous it was.'

'How dangerous what was?'

'Well, we're still waiting for the test results, but I have seen a case like this before which involved oleander, but it supposedly tastes awful, so ingesting it accidentally would be unusual.'

'But not impossible,' said Campion, 'if, say, it was disguised in a curry?'

Dr Gordon shrugged his shoulders. 'On that I could not comment, but I would point out that in certain parts of south-east Asia, where I believe curries are popular, ingesting oleander is a very popular method of suicide.'

If Rupert had felt uneasy with the way his father had so confidently hinted that he was an official of the BBC in order to glean medical information, he was distinctly queasy at the prospect of the Campion charm falling flat on its angelically innocent face when it came up against a real, live employee of the corporation, for their next port of call was The Junction Hotel and a meeting with the producer, the high-flying Tamara Reams. But then he mentally pinched himself. He was a resting actor and he was meeting with a BBC producer who was known to be casting a film. This was not the time to feel queasy; this was an opportunity. It was time for deep breaths, putting shoulders back and best feet forward, with one's audition piece in the breech ready to fire, and confidence in your own ability to cry real tears on demand.

Primed and ready as Rupert was to meet the BBC's latest *wunderkind* producer (as his agent had described her, although fellow resting actors used the term 'hottest'), he had not rehearsed the scenario that confronted the Campions as they were going into

The Junction Hotel for, as they did, they ran into Tamara Reams and the male escorting her going out.

The pair were clearly leaving, as they carried luggage, and the expressions on their faces suggested that they would not take well to being delayed. Even Rupert realized this was probably not the best time to pitch his acting credentials.

Mr Campion, who had noticed a taxi pulling up to the hotel, as well as the head-down determination of what he guessed was his quarry following Rupert's excited whisper, 'That's her!', had no qualms about interrupting their progress, and in repeating his outrageously false credentials.

Flamboyantly removing his fedora and sweeping it in a Cavalier's arc until it covered his heart, Mr Campion confidently announced his presence.

'Miss Reams, I presume. Allow me to introduce myself; my name is Albert Campion and I have been asked to offer any assistance I can with your production of *The Moving Mosaic*.' At his side, Rupert coughed indiscreetly. 'And this is my son, Rupert.'

'I am sure I would be delighted to meet you, Mr Campion,' said Tamara Reams, 'at any other time. I am afraid I have been called back to London and we have a train to catch.'

'That is a pity,' said Campion, noting that the woman had made no attempt to introduce her male companion and that the man had instinctively moved behind her, as if using her as a shield.

Tamara Reams did not meet the specification of any BBC producer Mr Campion had met in the past; not that he had met many, and the ones he had were all middle-aged men in tweed suits, sometimes dinner jackets. She was young, probably of Rupert's generation and, noting her ring-less fingers, presumably unmarried. She wore a blue denim trouser suit, her black hair was tied back in a bun curl, and her face betrayed not a trace of make-up, giving her a slightly military look, certainly that of a general who does not take kindly to criticism of his strategy.

'How on earth are you able to offer me assistance, Mr Champion?'

'It's Campion, actually, and I come at the request of Alun Williamson, a BBC governor, and with the blessing of the Evadne Childe Society.'

'And what makes you think I need your help?'

Even as she spoke, Tamara Reams did not seem remotely

interested in an answer. She turned away from Mr Campion and spoke quietly to her male companion, who was still intent on sheltering behind her.

He had successfully avoided presenting a clear profile to the Campions, his face shaded by a green trilby with a multicoloured feather cockade, and the upturned collar of a tightly buttoned raincoat, despite the weather being far from inclement.

'I'm aware that *The Moving Mosaic* has been dogged by misfortune,' said Campion firmly, as if quite happy to conduct his business out on the pavement in full public view, 'or what one might call niggling acts of sabotage.'

Tamara Reams turned back to face him, but only after nudging the man behind her with an elbow, at which the man broke cover and scurried towards the waiting taxi, almost diving head-first into the back seat.

'I have no idea what you are talking about, so if you'll excuse me—'

'Please, Miss Reams, do not try and brush this off,' Campion challenged her. 'People have been hurt; in London your director of choice has been beaten up, and here in Dorset one of your associates has been poisoned – we've just come from the hospital. Someone is circulating salacious photographs, and your main filming location, the pastoral village of Kingswalter, has been invaded by what I would politely describe as a caravan of would-be psychics and mediums who are probably harmless, but will get in your way. All these things are connected and conspire to make life as difficult as possible for *The Moving Mosaic*.'

Now Mr Campion at least had her attention, though clearly not her confidence.

'You seem remarkably and rather wildly ill-informed, whoever you are, and I fail to see why you should be concerned. Are you a producer?'

'No.'

'A policeman?'

'Certainly not.'

'Then you must be a concerned citizen who has paid their television licence and therefore thinks they can poke their nose into aspects of production of which they have no knowledge or experience.'

'As it happens,' said Campion, remaining calm, 'I have paid my licence fee and I like to think of myself as a concerned citizen. Plus, I do have some slight experience of attempts to sabotage a dramatic production.'

'You do?' The woman's upper lip twisted in a cynical grin.

'It was before the war, so clearly before your time, and it was in the theatre rather than television. In fact, it was before television, if you can imagine such an era, and I witnessed some petty and rather cruel acts of vandalism aimed at sabotaging a West End show, one of the nastiest being the insertion of a pin in an actor's stick of greasepaint. Just the thought of that gives me the shivers to this day.'

Tamara Reams's response dripped with sarcasm.

'A fascinating anecdote – would that I had time to hear others. I fail to see its relevance, or what it – or you – have to do with the project I am currently working on. Now I really must go and catch my train.'

'Miss Reams,' Campion's voice suddenly had steel in it. 'I am here because I have been asked to help the Evadne Childe Society in any way I can in ensuring that your production is not derailed or delayed in any way. Perhaps we can talk when you are not in such a rush.'

'But I am in a rush, and if you really are a representative of the Evadne Childe Society, you will appreciate why I need to get back to London' – Miss Reams growled rather than spoke – '*without delay.*'

'I'm sorry, I'm not following you.'

Campion seemed genuinely at a loss and Rupert, unused to such a spectacle, experienced a twinge of apprehension.

'Tania Smith,' said Miss Reams, almost in triumph, but when Campion failed to respond, she continued as if to put him out of his misery. 'Or perhaps you haven't heard.'

'Heard what?'

'That Tania was found dead this morning and the police are involved. That's why I've been recalled to London. Now please, if you wouldn't mind, let me pass.'

Not waiting for a response, Tamara Reams swept past the Campions like a cartoon dust devil, the small pink suitcase she carried connecting, probably deliberately, with Rupert's left knee-cap. They watched in silence as she joined her companion in the back seat of the taxi and the car pulled away and disappeared around the corner.

Bending to rub his knee, Rupert said, 'Who the hell is Tania Smith?'

'I haven't the foggiest idea,' said his father, replacing his fedora and tugging down the brim. 'I am still trying to work out who the chap with Miss Reams was, the one she was determined not to introduce to us.'

'Oh, he's divine,' said Rupert dreamily.

'I beg your pardon?' Campion said sharply.

'That was Alec Devine, the film star. He clearly didn't want to be recognized.'

'Well, that's suspicious for a start,' said Mr Campion, recovering. 'For a film star, I mean.'

'Perhaps he thought we were autograph hunters.'

'Do I look like an autograph hunter?'

'Mother would have asked him for one. She finds him quite dishy, and of course, she's a huge Rex Troughton fan.'

'Are you telling me that this Alec Devine will play Rex Troughton in *The Moving Mosaic*?'

'That's the rumour, though it's not official yet. I think he'd be rather good. Why are you looking so worried? Did you have another actor in mind for the part, perhaps?'

Mr Campion chose to ignore the hopeful tone of his son's last question. 'I think somebody has very firm ideas on that particular piece of casting – firm and very dangerous.'

# THIRTEEN
## Death in the Square Mile

Another change of plan was called for, once again denying Mr Campion a daylight viewing of the Kingswalter mosaic, and much to the consternation of Tessa and Roy Higgins, who were genuinely upset to be losing their two guests, but clearly relieved that it was due to bad news from London and totally unconnected with the pub's catering.

The Campions had packed quickly, and Mr Campion had used The King's Head's telephone to make two trunk calls, for which he added a goodly sum to the bill he was presented with, and then Rupert had been told to point the Jaguar towards London and not to spare the horses whilst being briefed en route.

Mr Campion's first telephone call had been to Miss Prim at Gilpin's but in her capacity as a committee member of the Evadne Childe Society and it had been a rather tetchy one, Miss Prim clearly on the defensive for not having put Campion fully in the picture.

When the Society had been bequeathed the film rights to the Rex Troughton books by the late Mrs Hatherall and the BBC had taken an interest in them, the Society had decided, after numerous committee meetings, to take legal advice. The sums involved, especially if a long-running series was likely, were potentially huge for a literary fan club of modest means, and so Tania Smith, a lawyer who specialized in theatrical contracts, was recruited to the cause on a modest retainer. Her mandate was to make sure that in 'exercising' the rights to the Rex Troughton stories (hereafter, no doubt known by some legalistic term such as 'the property'), the BBC honoured the wishes of Mrs Hatherall and the Society, which were, of course, the same thing.

Neither Miss Prim nor Eric Rudd had thought to burden Mr Campion with such a detail, as his mandate was to investigate the negative factors threatening the filming of *The Moving Mosaic* and no one could be more positively on side than Miss Smith, who had already proved her dedication to the cause by demonstrating patience and diplomacy as well as a fine legal brain.

But sadly, it was a brain which no longer functioned, for Tania Smith had been found dead that morning, at the bottom of the stairs which led up to the room that served as her home and office. The matter was now in the hands of the police.

Some gentle probing by Mr Campion elicited the information that the location of this fatality was an address in St Michael's Alley, which was 'an easy place to miss' and so Miss Prim had helpfully added, 'behind St Michael's Church in Cornhill.'

She had, however, maintained a confused silence when Campion murmured down the line, 'That would mean the City Police', although Campion was clearly in no mood to elaborate as he ended the call abruptly, almost rudely.

Campion's second trunk call took longer to connect, but did, eventually, get through to its intended recipient, Commander Charles Luke of Scotland Yard, an old and distinguished friend of the Campion family who, thanks to Mr Campion, had become very familiar with the life and works of Evadne Childe in the years before her death. Had he been honest, and invariably he was, Charlie Luke would have said he had not thought about Evadne Childe since he had attended her funeral in Essex with Mr Campion. If pushed, he would have admitted to reading one of her detective stories since then, but as a professional policeman with an unblemished reputation for being both effective and honest, he had little inclination to read crime fiction.

But Luke was not one to disparage the maxim that it was not what one knew, but who, for he had gained as much from his friendship with Mr Campion as Campion had from knowing a high-flying member of the Metropolitan Police from his days, twenty years before, as a detective constable, through divisional detective inspector and up the ranks to his current position of almost serene authority.

The two men had a relationship based on trust, a fundamental element of which was the assumption that neither would waste the other's time, something Campion was particularly conscious of now that he was beyond retirement age, whereas Luke was at, or very near, the pinnacle of his career, with a great burden of responsibility. He therefore began his telephone call with minimum pleasantries and profuse apologies for disturbing a busy man, before mentioning that he had heard of a suspicious death in the City that morning.

'Being disturbed by murder is what I'm paid for, Albert,' came Luke's laconic reply.

'So it was murder?'

'I've only seen the initial report as it's City Police jurisdiction, so not my case, but it smells like murder to me. Middle-aged woman living alone in a bit of London Charles Dickens forgot about, tangles with an intruder in the night and falls, or more likely gets pushed, down a flight of stairs and breaks her neck.'

'A burglary gone wrong?'

'Could be. The City boys are trying to see if anything valuable is missing, but I said intruder not burglar. Maybe I should have said visitor.'

'You mean she let him in?'

'Looks like it. What's your interest? And where are you? You sound as if you're talking into a tin can on a string.'

'I'm down in the wilds of Dorset but heading back to town momentarily. It will take us a few hours even with a fair wind, but I will explain all on arrival. In the meantime, could you give me a character reference to whoever's running the investigation in the City Police? I may be able to help them fill in a few gaps.'

'And no doubt you'll expect a quid pro quo to help you with whatever you're up to.'

'My dear Charles, I am a gentleman of leisure and rarely up to anything these days.'

Luke's explosive laugh came down the line so clearly and forcefully that Campion held the receiver away from his ear, until the policeman had composed himself.

'Very well, Albert, I'll clear the path for you. How do I get a message to you?'

'Via Lugg, either at Brewers' Hall or at the Bottle Street flat.'

'Is Amanda with you? This isn't interrupting a romantic little holiday, is it?'

'Not at all. I'm with Rupert, actually.'

'Still resting, is he? Or are you training him up as an assistant detective?'

'I'm sure I don't know what you mean, Charlie, but Rupert, as always, is auditioning for one thing or another.'

As he piloted the Jaguar towards London, Rupert certainly gave the impression that he was rehearsing for a role as a police detective – perhaps somewhere between *An Inspector Calls* and *The Mousetrap* – judging by the number of questions he asked his father. Mr Campion could, and did, answer many of them; others he admitted he could not and some he deliberately avoided.

No, it was not essential that they should get back to London before the elusive Tamara Reams. It would not only be impossible for them to beat British Railways back to the capital, but it would not be advisable to confront Miss Reams until they had gathered more intelligence.

But she had acted strangely, hadn't she? Mr Campion preferred to give the woman the benefit of the doubt. She had, he presumed, just been told of the death of Tania Smith – though why that was significant he could not as yet say – and they had waylaid her on the street like obstreperous reporters from a Sunday scandal sheet.

Was there a hint of actual scandal? She was, after all, leaving a hotel with a male companion whose identity she was clearly determined to hide, or at least obfuscate. Mr Campion dismissed that idea as fanciful, as the man was clearly an actor and a well-known one, probably anxious to avoid autograph hunters. But, Rupert protested, it had been he who had recognized Alec Devine when his dear, out-of-touch father clearly had no idea who he was.

'That's a fair point,' Mr Campion had conceded, 'but I guessed he was an actor by his hat. No dashing young chap of his age wears a cockaded trilby these days, unless they're getting into character for the role of Rex Troughton, though I suppose that's still a bit of a secret.'

'Alec Devine as Rex Troughton!' Rupert had said with a low whistle. 'How did you work that out?'

'I told you: the hat. A trilby just like the one he was wearing was Rex Troughton's trademark. He always wore one when on an archaeological dig. You really must forget you're an actor for once and read a book right through, rather than skimming a script looking for your entrances and exits and counting your lines.'

Rupert took the jibe with good grace, although his right foot did weigh on the accelerator rather heavily as he asked where the late Miss Tania Smith, whoever she was, featured in the saga.

According to initial reports, Campion said formally, she was – or had been – a lawyer and, from the sound of it, one who specialized in contracts in acting and entertainment. He was unsure why the Evadne Childe Society had seen the need to retain a legal eagle, as they were keen to see *The Moving Mosaic* made and the BBC seemed keen to make it, unless, that is, there was a question over the provisions of Mrs Hatherall's will.

If Tania Smith had been killed, either deliberately or accidentally, it might be a fair assumption that it was to throw another spanner in the works of the production.

Rupert's knuckles whitened on the steering wheel when he asked if his father was sure it had been murder, to which Mr Campion

replied that Charlie Luke thought it highly likely, though technically the case came under the jurisdiction of the City Police, that
body of traditionally very tall (because of their height requirements
on recruits) officers who patrolled the square mile around the
Bank of England. Still, Luke had promised to pull a few strings
to allow him access to the investigating officers at the scene of
the crime behind St Michael's Church in Cornhill.

Campion agreed when Rupert suggested that it seemed a
curious address for the offices of an entertainment lawyer, which
one might have expected to find in Wardour Street in Soho or
near Chancery Lane tube station.

'I assumed it was her flat rather than an office, but still, it's a
curious place to live. Not many people do live in the City, it's all
offices and banks,' Campion had said, and then his face brightened.
'Perhaps I should drag Lugg along, he knows the Square Mile like
the back of his paw, from the depths of his murky past.'

'Crikey!' Rupert had exclaimed. 'Don't tell me Lugg tried to
rob the Bank of England!'

'No, but he certainly thought about it.'

Magersfontein Lugg, whose ears were probably burning, would
have defended his good name and reputation by pointing out that
his intimate knowledge of the warren of alleys in the triangle
formed by Cornhill and Gracechurch and Lombard streets, which
had the Bank of England at its apex, was due entirely to him
doing his civic duty in wartime. Being, to his everlasting disappointment, a few months too old to be conscripted into the
armed forces – surely their loss, for here was a sergeant major
ready formed if ever there was one – Lugg had decided that if
he could not fight for his country on the front line, he could at
least help the city of his birth survive the assault from the air,
which came soon enough.

When the Blitz hit the City with full force, on a Sunday evening
just after Christmas 1940, Lugg was an established member of a
Heavy Rescue brigade, working alongside the hard-pressed Fire
Service. He was not, he would say, one of the 'glory boys' who
helped save St Paul's Cathedral, as he was stationed in the heart
of the City where offices, locked for the weekend, had to be broken
into to check for human habitation, gas leaks and fire hazards, and
the skills acquired in Lugg's misspent youth had no doubt come

in handy. Had he never had the sneaking wish that a Luftwaffe bomb would make a direct hit on the Bank of England, freeing a snowstorm of five-pound notes or, even better, the glint of a gold bar or two? In answer to such a question Lugg would have growled that, in the heat of battle, he had been more concerned with the survival of the historic chophouses which could be found down the narrowest, dingiest alleyways; chophouses immortalized in *Pickwick Papers*, with menus that had not changed since. Some of them still did stewed cheese, which knocked your average Welsh Rarebit into a cocked hat. If a Barnsley chop or a steak-and-kidney pudding were not worth defending, what was the point of being an Englishman?

It was somehow fitting when he and Mr Campion discovered that Miss Tania Smith had lived in a small apartment above one of those chophouses, accessed through a faded red door to the side of a span of begrimed mullioned windows which protected the privacy of the diners inside.

Not that there were any diners present, as it was evening – and lunchtime service at the chophouses had long since finished – when Lugg and Campion picked their way over the uneven paving slabs and through the dark emptiness of St Michael's Alley. Not only was the alleyway empty, but so was the City, or at least the segment of Cornhill they had entered. Only the faint growl of a bus chugging up Bishopsgate hinted that normal life continued beyond the graveyard quiet of the buildings which cocooned them: some ancient, some very modern, some religious but others most distinctly secular.

'A good place for crime,' announced Lugg in philosophical mood. 'Not yer big stuff o'course. The really big stuff – the fraud, the embezzlement, the dodgy trading in shares not worth the paper their certificates are printed on – all that goes on in the boardrooms during office hours. That's almost legal, but if you've had a few and you're wandering through this rabbit run after dark, hang on to your wallet. The chophouses only do lunchtimes, and unless there's an Evensong on at one of the churches, there's nobody around come night-time. Get away with murder, you could.'

'Perhaps somebody did,' said Mr Campion, 'and I think that exceedingly tall constable who hopes we didn't see him put out a crafty fag just now, marks the spot.'

Mr Campion was in fact grateful for the presence of the uniformed policeman, who measured six feet eight inches from boot to helmet, on duty in the dingy doorway; otherwise he doubted he would have been able to locate Tania Smith's address, which he had been told was number 11½, but there were no helpful numerals on any of the doors in the alley as far as he could see.

The lofty constable on guard duty, who looked disgracefully young when Campion who, even at six foot, had to crick his neck to make out his face, reassured him that they were expected. He opened the door he was defending, allowing a rectangle of light to illuminate the alley.

Mr Campion took a moment for his eyes to adjust to the light as he peered up the staircase behind the door and discerned that the bulky figure at the top of the stairs was Charles Luke.

'Good evening, Charlie. Working overtime?'

'Just following your trail of breadcrumbs, Albert,' said Luke, taking a step back so that Lugg had room to manoeuvre his bulk up the stairs.

'Breadcrumbs? I certainly did not intend to tempt you into putting in a personal appearance here tonight. How did I manage it?'

'You didn't.' Luke nodded towards Lugg. 'He did.'

''Ow do you work that out then?' bridled the fat man.

'Word reached me that you had been making inquiries about a hit-and-run over in Ealing and when Magersfontein Lugg Esquire contacts a police station voluntarily instead of being hauled into one kicking and screaming, I take notice.'

'Blooming cheek!' muttered Lugg.

'You were enquiring,' continued Luke, clearly enjoying himself, 'after a party by the name of Peyton Spruce, and as it happens the desk sergeant is a bit of a film buff. He recognized the name and thought it worth mentioning because a person of interest to Mr Lugg was almost certainly a person of interest to Mr Campion.'

Campion gave a nod of admiration. 'Your network of intelligence-gatherers is impressive, Charlie.'

Luke shrugged his doorframe shoulders. 'We are the police; we have branches everywhere. I just put two and two together.'

'Well, I can see the first half of the equation – the first "two", as it were – but where is the other two to make the four?'

'Through here,' said Luke, all frivolity gone from voice and demeanour.

They had to take no more than two steps to reach the heart of the apartment, though to call it an apartment would require the rose-tinted spectacles of an optimistic estate agent. In the West End, on the top floor of an office building, it would have been called a service flat. Here in the City, down an alley above a chophouse, it would be simply 'rooms', and even then the use of the plural was being generous.

'This was her living room and her office by the looks of things,' said Luke, surveying the main, windowless room furnished with four fiddleback chairs with padded leather seats, one of them tipped on its side, surrounding a small, square pine table. There was a bookcase bulging with thick legal volumes, a card table on which sat a portable typewriter and, in one corner, a metal four-drawer filing cabinet with a telephone balanced on top of it. Luke indicated the door at the end of the room. 'There's a small kitchen-ette and a bit of a bathroom which would be comfortable if you were a contortionist. There's also a bedroom, though I've seen bigger, better-appointed cells and certainly not big enough for any hanky-panky, if that's what you're thinking.'

'I wasn't,' said Campion. 'I take it this is where it happened.'

The small table was covered with papers, grey cardboard files and photographs, which had clearly been disturbed, with several sheets scattered on the floor.

'The investigating officers think Mrs Smith knew her assailant, let him in and was showing him these papers when something happened and he attacked her. They struggled and it's only a step to the top of the stairs, then thirteen steps down and a broken neck.'

'You said "Mrs Smith",' said Campion. 'I thought she was a "Miss".'

'I'll come to that, but if you've got your reading specs on, take a look at those photographs.'

Campion carefully pushed aside sheets of Xerox copies with a forefinger to reveal a ten-by-eight black-and-white photograph. From the stark contrast, it looked like a recent reprint of an older, autographed portrait, the sort issued by film studios to ardent fans. He did not have to try and decipher the florid signature, for the subject was very clearly Peyton Spruce in his heyday. Even as he guessed the picture had been taken more than twenty years ago, he conceded that the old actor had aged well.

'The talented Mr Spruce,' Campion murmured.

'That was my two and two making four. Two people interested in Spruce – Lugg, and therefore you, and now Mrs Smith – in the same week, and one of them ends up dead . . .'

'Who found her?'

'Staff at the chophouse downstairs when they turned up for work first thing. The door to the alley was half open and they found her scrunched up behind it. When she went down the stairs, she would have bunged up the doorway, so her killer would have had to pull her away and step over her to make his exit.'

'There's no other exit?'

'No, which is probably illegal. One tiny window in the bathroom that a cat would have a struggle to get through.'

'Fingerprints?'

'Apart from hers, few clear ones. Whoever killed her almost certainly wore gloves.'

'And no witnesses?'

'No nosey neighbours round here,' said Lugg, 'not after dark.'

'He's right,' said Luke. 'Nobody actually *lives* here any more, they just make money, eat chops and devilled kidneys washed down with claret, and then go home to their big houses in Surrey or Sussex.'

'Miss Smith did,' Campion pointed out, 'and had her office here, though it's an unusual set of chambers for a lawyer. Perhaps she was an unusual lawyer, though she was perfectly placed to entertain a hungry client.'

Lugg's nostrils flared and his eyes closed as he loudly sniffed the air and thought blissful thoughts.

'I bet the smells that come up from the grill downstairs are *luverly* at lunchtimes.'

'Did she regularly see clients here?' Campion persisted.

'It seems so. Her diary shows regular appointments, including one for next week with a Tamara Reams of the BBC. Does that name mean anything to you?'

'It might,' said Campion vaguely. 'Was anything taken?'

'We're not sure yet. There's a chap called Eric Rudd coming in tomorrow to go through her papers. He claims Mrs Smith was working for him.'

'I think she was, though he quite definitely called her Miss Smith.'

Luke flipped back the wings of his raincoat, pushed his fists deep into trouser pockets and leaned back on his heels.

'Now therein lies a tale,' said Luke. 'Tania Smith styled herself "Miss" both professionally and socially as far as we know. She had business cards as "Miss Tania Smith, LLB, Specialist in Entertainment Law and Contracts", whatever that means, and all her letters were signed and addressed to Miss Smith, though when she was found, she was wearing a wedding ring.

'So we checked with the holders of the freehold here, which turns out to be a stockbroking firm of some repute. It turns out that Tania Smith was their tenant because this had been the grace-and-favour staff flat of one of their former partners, a certain Giles Smith.'

Luke waited expectantly. 'You don't remember the scandal?'

'Should I?' asked Campion innocently.

'It was about ten years ago, when all the bits of the Empire were being hived off and places that had previously been coloured pink in your school atlas were becoming independent countries with their own flags. Giles Smith claimed to have the inside track on a new bauxite mine coming on stream on a particular Caribbean island previously British, now going it alone. He was sure there would be rich pickings for investors, and cooked up a prospectus with the title "You Can't Have Enough Bauxite".'

'Catchy. Did it draw in the punters with spare funds?'

'Oh, yes.'

'But it was all a con, I presume.'

'Totally. It turns out Giles Smith wasn't very good at investments and had made some disastrous ones himself, leaving him with massive debts, and the bauxite mine scam was his last hope at clearing them. Fortunately, he was rumbled before it went too far. He was defrocked, or whatever it is they do to stockbrokers but, before he could face charges of fraud, he filled his pockets with butchers' weights and jumped into the Thames.'

'Leaving Tania a widow,' said Campion slowly and precisely, 'who ended up living alone in a grace-and-favour flat owned by Smith's firm. How did that happen?'

'As you can see, it's not much of a flat, but Smith used it occasionally rather than trek back late at night to the couple's house out in Staines. When the bauxite fraud collapsed, the house went to pay off Giles's debts, which were substantial.'

'Leaving a grieving and homeless widow?'

'I don't think there was much grieving involved. From what I hear, Tania was trapped in an angry marriage and her way out had been to sign up at university to do a law degree and, though she'd only just graduated when the bauxite scandal broke and she was facing ruin, she was savvy enough to make a deal with her husband's firm. When the inevitable Stock Exchange enquiry came round, she was a star witness, putting all the blame entirely on her husband – her late husband by then – who had acted alone without the collusion of anyone in the firm.'

'And the firm was naturally grateful.'

'Let her have these rooms on a peppercorn rent and didn't mind her practising law from here, even slipped her the odd bit of work occasionally, though mostly she did stuff in the entertainment world.'

Campion looked around the room. 'It's all a bit sparse, isn't it? Very few feminine touches and no clues as to any social life.'

'She was in her fifties,' said Luke casually.

'Doesn't mean she was past it!' snapped Lugg.

'I wasn't implying that,' countered Luke, 'but I think she'd opted for a quiet life, tucked away in this little nook and cranny of the City. I reckon she'd had enough of men. Giles Smith wasn't her first husband; he was her third.'

The policeman swayed on his heel again and then he nodded pointedly to the portrait photographs on the table. 'And I'll bet you can't guess who her first husband was,' he said with a wolfish gleam in his eyes only matched by a similar animal-like cunning flitting across Campion's face.

'I think I can, Charlie, and I can go one better and tell you who her second husband was as well.'

# FOURTEEN
## Everybody's Leading Man

M r Campion's meeting at the BBC the next morning was prefaced by a long telephone call to his wife which required all his diplomatic skill.

After apologizing yet again for delaying his return home, where he was sure the domestic tasks allocated to him were piling up, and then passing on greetings and best wishes from Charlie Luke, he made the fatal mistake of casually mentioning that he was due to be meeting with Alec Devine.

For a moment he could have sworn that Amanda had positively squealed with joy, and there was certainly no doubt at all about the girlish excitement in her voice. *The* Alec Devine? Mr Campion said he presumed so. The actor? Yes, that would be the one. The one who had played the dishy young doctor in that television thing set in a hospital in Leeds in the 1920s? Probably, and yes, he was also likely to be the same Alec Devine she had seen in that drama set during the war in the Channel Islands where he'd played the only nice Nazi and the same chap who had played the dodgy Russian defector in that spy film. And yes, he was quite handsome Mr Campion supposed, but pointedly stated he would not be asking for an autograph.

Amanda had teased him by asking if perhaps she could detect a hint of jealousy in her husband's manner, qualifying the accusation with the admission that she should be the jealous party if he was the one meeting the 'divine Mr Devine' – and why was he doing that anyway? Campion took a deep breath, explained that he had an inkling – no more than a vague suspicion – that Alec Devine was in line to play Rex Troughton in *The Moving Mosaic*, and waited for his wife's reaction.

Somewhat to his surprise she considered her response carefully before answering him and, when she did, all traces of the star-struck film fan had disappeared.

'Do you know, I think he'd be rather a good fit. He's handsome and young enough, whereas most archaeologists you see on the television are tweedy old professors wandering around dusty museums. He'd bring a certain muscular charm to the role and he can act a bit – well, not classical theatre perhaps, but he comes across on the small screen well enough. The camera must like him.'

'Would Evadne Childe approve?'

'I think she might have, though authors are always a bit funny about who play their characters. Miss Prim at Gilpin's will be pleased as it will do wonders for sales, especially if they can get a picture of Devine for the cover of the paperback.'

'I'll suggest it to her,' said Campion, 'and give her your regards, of course. I have to call in at Gilpin's to borrow something from her before I storm the BBC.'

'This meeting at the BBC . . .' Amanda began hesitantly, '. . . is it a proper meeting? I mean not just a hoped-for passing encounter where you stand around looking surprised to find yourself there.'

'Darling, you know my methods so well and yet still have so little faith in them but, I assure you, this is a formal meeting with the producer and has been arranged by your admirer, Alun Gwyn Williamson.'

'When you say formal, does that mean there will be lawyers present?'

'I do hope not, I was hoping to get away before teatime.'

'Are you taking Rupert with you?'

'Wild horses couldn't keep him away from a chance to get into the bowels of the BBC. I'll say he's my secretary or youthful sidekick.'

Campion waited for the inevitable request to advance their son's career.

'Good. Make sure he sits on your right.'

'Why?'

'Because that way he shows them his good side.'


If they were not actually in the bowels of the BBC, they were certainly in the intestines of Broadcasting House, deep down below ground in the rabbit warren of small radio recording rooms. The Campions had been escorted there by a chatty uniformed commissionaire who had at first welcomed them with a big smile, the customary English running commentary on the weather and a jovial enquiry as to whether the visitors were there to talk about Uganda and the dreadful Idi Amin or the cod war brewing with the bloody-minded Icelanders, as nobody seemed to want to talk about anything else on the radio these days.

When Mr Campion informed him they had absolutely nothing of import to say on those subjects and were not there to record a news item, but were meeting with one of the corporation's producers, Tamara Reams, the commissionaire's face fell and his snow-white moustache positively bristled. 'Oh, her,' he muttered, consulting the daily roster on his clipboard, and then showed them down a long grey corridor to Recording Studio 7B without another word.

The cramped studio offered two chairs around a central table, over which hovered fabric-covered boom microphones nodding down from the ceiling as if communing with the stand microphones on the table, creating an image of an alien, or at least robotic, life form. Beyond them, behind a glass screen, was the control box, which Campion was relieved to see was empty.

In lieu of any pleasantries or greetings, Tamara Reams explained that the studio may seem an odd choice of venue, but as it was not in use today, they would not be observed or disturbed and, following Campion's gaze into the control box, she could assure them they would not be overheard and certainly not recorded.

Dressed as she was in jeans, denim jacket and a pale blue man's shirt, Miss Reams may not have looked like the archetypal BBC executive, but her manner left no doubt that she would take the lead in the meeting. At her side, in a smart three-piece pinstripe suit, stood Alec Devine, exuding charisma, looking far more the part than she did.

Campion offered a hand and said, 'Mr Devine, we have not been formally introduced, but my name is Albert Campion and this is my son Rupert. I might add that his mother, my wife, is a huge fan of yours.'

Devine's facial muscles flexed and pouted to express the unworthiness of such a claim but, as he shook his hand, Mr Campion wondered, rather churlishly, if the star-struck Amanda realized how short Alec Devine was, perhaps no more than five foot three in a good light, which proved, if nothing else, that the camera could lie. For a moment he was distracted by stories he had heard about Hollywood stars who had been forced to stand on boxes in order to mount a horse in a cowboy 'oater' film, or have their leading lady stand in a trench so that they could kiss.

Even as Rupert was extending his own hand in order to touch stardust, and no doubt mentally forming a short speech, the nub of which was that he was an actor too, Tamara Reams sat down with a thud and placed her forearms on the desk between them, as if trying to steady the oars of a lifeboat in a choppy sea.

'Let me make it clear,' she announced, 'I have convened this meeting because, basically, I have been told to, in order to keep the Board of Governors happy. I have asked Alec to join us because the topic of our conversation may well concern his career.'

'And because I *insisted* on being present,' said Devine in a low, mellifluous voice which Campion knew (and knew that Devine knew) could set a female heart fluttering at twenty paces.

Miss Reams did not seem to be influenced at all by Devine's honeyed delivery, rather she was irritated by his presence but dared not object and risk offending her 'star', despite being the producer, as Campion understood it, and therefore at the apex of the command structure. He had learned from Rupert that whilst in the theatre, a play's director might be the nearest thing to an artistic Field Marshal Montgomery in film and television, the producer was the all-powerful supreme commander.

'Let me begin,' said Campion, 'by saying I am here in a completely unofficial capacity but with the blessing of one of the corporation's governors . . .'

'Of that we are well aware,' said Tamara Reams dryly.

'. . . and the Evadne Childe Society, not to mention,' Campion continued with some relish, 'New Scotland Yard. I hasten to add that I am not a policeman, but a frank and open discussion with me might save you an embarrassing official visit with the press in attendance . . .'

'But isn't all publicity good publicity?' asked Devine, showing his acting skills, as Campion could not determine whether his tongue was in his cheek or not.

'Not when we don't yet have a show to publicize,' snapped Miss Reams.

'Nor when the newshounds sniff a connection to a murder,' said Mr Campion.

Now he had their undivided attention.

'I believe you had made an appointment to meet with Tania Smith.' Tamara Reams nodded silently. 'Which of course cannot now be kept because of her untimely death, which the police are treating as highly suspicious. May I ask what would have been the object of that meeting?'

Tamara interlocked the fingers of her hands, not as in prayer but making one tense fist as if to block, or bat away, Campion's questions.

'It was to try and reach completion on the rights option to *The Moving Mosaic*, as per the stipulations in Pauline Hatherall's will, which the Childe Society were insisting on.'

'Would that be Eric Rudd?'

'He has been particularly stubborn on the matter. Tania Smith was a lawyer well versed in artistic contractual matters, and she would have seen the need for compromise.'

'Was it an issue over casting?' Rupert asked his father, for no other reason than it gave him the perfect opportunity to show his best profile the other side of the desk.

'It was a sticking point, which should not have been insurmountable,' Tamara admitted through gritted teeth.

'Could you be specific for my benefit, please?' Campion nodded towards Alec Devine. 'Sparing the blushes of those present, of course.'

Devine smiled a modest film-star smile and indicated that his producer should proceed, though she clearly did so with reluctance.

'When we first approached Pauline Hatherall over the rights to the Rex Troughton books, she stipulated that the first episode should be based on *The Moving Mosaic* as it was a personal favourite and had sentimental memories for her. This was not a problem; we had to start somewhere, and our writers were happy to adapt any of the books, as long as they got paid.'

'Writers are like that,' said Campion, drawing a nod of approval from Alec Devine.

'It's a decent enough story,' Tamara continued, 'with good, picturesque locations, and we were well into pre-production when

Mrs Hatherall died and the rights passed to the Childe Society, but with a particular stipulation in her will.'

'That Peyton Spruce played Rex Troughton,' Campion supplied.

Rupert immediately felt the need to show solidarity with a fellow actor.

'But you'd already been cast and you're perfect for the role!' he said to Devine, who brushed off the outrage with regal modesty.

'You're too kind. There was nothing definite, though I had auditioned and it seemed to go well, so I was hopeful.'

'Was it a legal codicil to her will?' asked Campion, anxious to disrupt the actors' drift into mutual admiration.

'Not technically, but it was a note witnessed by a solicitor,' said Tamara, 'though the point of argument is that it wasn't in the original contract we negotiated with Mrs Hatherall. Eric Rudd, who now has to sign off on the deal, is insisting that the old woman's last wishes must be taken into account.'

'I know little of such things, but I was not aware that even the writers of the original material could impose their casting suggestions on television or film adaptations, which is why so many go into deep depression when they view the result.'

'They can't and we actively discourage them from thinking they can. Novelists simply don't understand that books are books, but television is television. If they don't like what we do, they shouldn't take the money or shed crocodile tears when they sell more books due to the exposure we give their work. Can I be frank, Mr Campion?'

'My goodness, I thought you were being. Please, feel free.'

'I have no doubts in my mind, either legally or morally, that we do not have to abide by Mrs Hatherall's fantasies, or Mr Rudd's desire to see them fulfilled, but once the Childe Society engaged a lawyer, the BBC had to involve its legal department *after* the programme had effectively got the go-ahead. That does not reflect well on the producer who is supposed to be running things – me. It raises eyebrows upstairs in the corridors of power' – she pointed a forefinger to the ceiling – 'where there are certain people who are watching and waiting for a woman to fail.'

'I am sure you have no intention of failing, Miss Reams. You intend to make a fine programme and I am sure Eric Rudd and the Childe Society want the same thing.'

'So why set Tania Smith on us? She sent us some pretty strict letters saying we were morally obliged to accede to the dying wishes of the rights' holder.'

'She was a lawyer doing her job,' said Campion, 'though she might have had an ulterior motive.'

'Really?' Tamara leaned forward, as did Alec Devine, clearly keen to play the role of police detective on the verge of obtaining a confession.

'Were you not aware that Tania Smith's first husband was none other than Peyton Spruce?'

'Well, that's a conflict of interest for a start, and an undeclared one,' said Tamara, giving the desk a triumphal slap.

'Hang on,' said Devine, pressing his detective credentials, 'you said first husband, which means she was his ex-wife. I wasn't aware Spruce had ever married, but my point is that, in our business, ex-wives are not noted for doing favours for their former spouses.'

'The marriage ended many years ago,' said Campion, 'and Tania Smith's loyalties are certainly worth investigating, given what happened to her.'

'You are sure she was murdered?' asked Tamara, although Devine's expression showed he had no doubt on the matter.

'I am sure she was killed, but more importantly, so are the police. The question is why.'

'You can't possibly suspect Peyton Spruce,' said Devine, although Tamara Reams's expression suggested she would have been perfectly happy with the idea. 'If the Smith woman and the Childe Society got their way, he would have landed the comeback role of the century, doing a reprise of his role in the original film.'

'But he's *old*,' protested his producer. 'He was too old for the role in the film and that was twenty years ago. Now he must be at least seventy-two.'

'Which is only thirty-seven in actor years, so I'm told,' said Campion, who paused for a laugh which did not come and so pressed on regardless. 'Do you know Peyton Spruce, Mr Devine?'

'I know of him because his performance as Troughton was part of my homework for this part, but I've never met him.'

Campion turned to Rupert and asked for the large brown envelope that his son had been nursing on his knees under the desk. He took two large black-and-white photographs from it, kept one face down and laid the other, one of the autographed publicity stills from Tania Smith's flat, in front of Alec Devine.

'Recognize him?'

'Yes, that's Peyton Spruce.'

'How old would you say he was in that photograph?'

The actor studied the picture then looked at Campion with a flirtatious grin. 'What was your formula for an actor's years? Thirty-eight? Forty?'

'I'm guessing he was at least fifty-two when that was taken,' said Campion, 'and I can assure you that when I saw him less than a week ago, he did not look much different.'

Devine was suitably impressed. 'He's taken care of himself,' he conceded, 'or he's got a very good make-up artist on tap.'

'That, I think, he has.' Campion slid over the second print, face upwards, hiding the hostile inscription written on the back. 'Now is this the same man, in rather a different, more private, pose?'

It was the picture of the couple in skimpy swimming costumes, lying on a beach so closely entwined that it was almost as if they were defying the incoming tide to find room to squeeze between them.

Alec Devine looked at the photograph for all of three seconds before bursting into laughter.

'Of course that's Peyton Spruce! Though I can't remember the name of the blonde bimbo he's giving mouth-to-mouth resuscitation to.'

'Are you sure it's Spruce?' pressed Campion. 'There's not much of his face showing.'

'But plenty of everything else – and the girl, as I remember, was notoriously young, at least as far as the film censors here were concerned; not in France, of course.'

'You mean, this is a still from a film?' asked Rupert, catching on.

'Of course it is. A French film called *D'ici à là* from the Fifties. It was a New Wave satire on Hollywood but, being French, was only found funny in France, so it never got distribution abroad. I saw it at drama school and didn't get any of the jokes apart from that one.'

Before Rupert could ask the question forming on his lips, Mr Campion reasserted his authority on matters of show business.

'*D'ici à là* . . . from here . . . Of course, it's a spoof on *From*

*Here to Eternity* and the infamous beach scene with Burt Lancaster and Ava Gardner.'

'Deborah Kerr,' corrected Devine.

'I'm so sorry, you are quite right.'

'I told you I'd done my homework,' said the actor, turning to accept an accolade, if not a round of applause, from his producer, but Tamara Reams was stabbing the picture with a violence Campion imagined equal to that expressed by Caesar's assassins.

'Is this the pornographic picture that was sent to the higher-ups here to discredit my project?'

Campion turned the print over to show her the legend on the back implying that Peyton Spruce might not be suitable material for a heroic figure on prime-time television.

'I would hardly class it as pornography, but you are right about the intention, yet it doesn't make sense.'

'Why not? Seems a perfect example of sabotage to me,' said Miss Reams firmly.

'Think about it,' said Campion calmly. 'It was sent with the intention of putting the Black Spot against the casting of Peyton Spruce in your programme, but you never had any intention of doing so, did you? You had earmarked this handsome fellow' – he paused to allow Devine time to blush – 'to play Rex Troughton, so why should someone try and influence the BBC against Spruce when he was never in the running? The Evadne Childe Society, adhering to Mrs Hatherall's last will and testament, or at least her final wishes, are in the *pro*-Spruce camp, so would have no logical reason to defame him. Which leaves the question, who would?'

'Someone with a grudge who *didn't* want Spruce to resurrect his career, but was unaware we were not casting him in the first place.'

'The ex-wife! Who had a better grudge?' said Devine excitedly, betraying the fact that he had not yet played enough police detectives on the provincial repertory circuit.

'His ex-wife was Tania Smith,' Campion said patiently, 'who was actively trying to impose Spruce on the production, not disgrace him.'

Rupert leaned forward slightly, mouthing the word, 'But . . .' and then caught the warning glance and raised forefinger of his father, which made him close his mouth with a goldfish-like snap.

'Also,' Campion pressed on, 'I cannot believe that a respectable lawyer, and I do believe they exist, would or could orchestrate the arrival of a group of itinerant ghost-hunters in Kingswalter, the very location you intend to use for filming, nor organize a serious case of food poisoning suffered by one of your advance scouts, or an attack here in London, on the man chosen to direct the film. I'm sorry, but I don't know his name.'

'Jonathan Barlow,' supplied Tamara Reams. 'Are you saying these things are all connected?'

'They may be. It might be useful to speak to Mr Barlow at some point.'

'You're in luck,' smiled Alec Devine, showing almost all his highly photogenic teeth, though his smile buttered no parsnips with Miss Reams. 'Jonathan's an old mate, we've worked together before and now he's among the walking wounded we're meeting for a lunchtime snifter in the Langham round the corner in about . . .' he consulted a large, gold wristwatch, '. . . fifteen minutes, actually. You'd be welcome to join us, if you can put up with the gossip and shop-talk about the television business.'

'Delighted to,' said Rupert immediately, only to have his dreams swiftly curtailed.

'I will certainly take you up on the offer of an introduction,' said Campion, 'but I'm afraid Rupert here has an important errand to run.'

'I do?'

'Yes, you do. You are driving back down to Dorset this very afternoon, after booking another room at The King's Head. Once there, you will make contact with The Prophetics and persuade them to quit Kingswalter for ever and leave Miss Reams's film set alone.'

'He can do that?' Tamara's eyes widened, as if noticing Rupert in the room for the first time.

'Of course he can,' said Mr Campion, 'he's a very good actor.'

Tamara Reams could not join them as she had an office to go to, and Alec Devine had first to collect a script from another, so the Campions agreed to wait outside on Langham Place, which gave Rupert the chance to quiz his father.

'You didn't tell them about Tania Smith's *other* husband.'

'No, I did not, but you were going to.'

'I picked up on you flashing the warning sign, though I don't see why I'm being exiled to Dorset.'

'You're going there to impress Tamara Reams, the next great television producer, of course.'

'I am? How?'

'By acting. I want you to introduce yourself to Sally DeLuca, the leading light in The Prophetics. Get her on her own and spin her a yarn. You, being of her generation, were utterly appalled to discover that your father, being of an older and more distinguished generation, has used his not inconsiderable influence and reported The Prophetics to his high-powered chums at Scotland Yard for dealing drugs. You can hint at Freemasonry if it helps dramatically, but basically you thought this so unfair that you charged back to Kingswalter to warn them, and they ought to vacate the village within the next twenty-four hours before the Drug Squad complete with sniffer dogs descend on them.'

'Why would they believe me?'

'Because you'll act the part of a spoilt, rebellious child to perfection; and you'll have Lugg with you.'

'Are you expecting any rough stuff?'

'Not really, not from The Prophetics, and Lugg's rough-housing days are well in the past now, but he does have a certain intimidating aura, and that could come in useful with young Ranald Ward-Tetley.'

'How?'

'I want the lord of the manor to make The Prophetics as uncomfortable as possible, threaten to plough up their campsite, cut off their privileges at the pub, put sheep in among their vans, string barbed wire or dump sileage nearby; you know, the hundred and one things a landowner can do to make life unpleasant for innocent ramblers. Put Lugg in the bar of The King's Head together with that gamekeeper chappie and they'll cook up plenty of mischief.'

'And why should Ranald cooperate and lose his regular supply of hash?'

'Because he'll be getting a big cheque from the BBC *very soon*, as long as the coast is clear, and in the meantime, to tide him over if he cooperates, he'll be getting a small advance from me – well, Lugg actually, who will be in possession of my chequebook.'

'You trust Lugg with your chequebook?' Rupert did not need his acting skills to express shock and horror.

'I do, because I have seen his pathetic attempts to forge my signature and have no fears on that score, plus the fact that Lugg would add more gravitas to the situation. He will be there to impress upon Ranald that he will have great expectations, as in Dickens's novel, if he does as we suggest. He will play the mysterious benefactor; it's a role he was born for.'

'Not Miss Haversham, surely?'

'Good Lord no, I was thinking of Abel Magwitch.'

Mr Campion was glad to have Alec Devine there to make the introductions, but he would have had little trouble spotting Jonathan Barlow in the bar of the Langham Hotel, unless having your right arm in a sling, a three-inch-wide white bandage around one's head and sporting a black eye had become a popular fashion statement.

'Jonno!' Devine yelped as he moved, arms wide, to embrace the invalid, stopping a hair's breadth from his victim when he realized a full-strength bear hug might inflict yet more damage. He altered his line of attack and settled for a gentle two-handed squeeze on Barlow's still intact left arm. 'Good to see you; you look bloody awful!'

'Thank you, Alec,' Barlow said wearily. 'As I am currently unemployable, you do realize you will be buying lunch?'

Injuries aside, Campion felt that Barlow was a naturally weary sort of man, possibly one disillusioned by having to deal with actors on a daily basis. He was quietly spoken and dressed like an off-duty chemistry teacher: his trousers were short in the leg, revealing too much sock, and his brown wool jacket had the mandatory leather elbow patches. With one arm in a sling, a true thespian would have worn the jacket over his shoulders with flair, like a cape. Barlow had attempted to squeeze into it with his good arm and someone, possibly a caring wife, had fastened the bottom button under and around the sling. He, or the considerate wife, had wisely abandoned the idea of a tie and opted for a dark red cravat which may or may not have concealed another wound.

'Sure you can handle a knife and fork, m'dear?' said Devine with unnecessary cheerfulness. 'I suppose I could cut your meat up for you. This, by the way, is Albert Campion. He won't be lunching with us but he wanted to meet you.'

'And ask a few questions, if you'll permit me,' said Campion, gently shaking the offered left hand.

'Albert's helping us out on *The Moving Mosaic*,' explained Devine, 'helping to smooth the path, so to speak. We've just come from a meeting with Tamara, so Albert's here with her blessing.'

'I'm not sure I can be of much help, Mr Campion, I'm rather out of it thanks to . . .'

He shrugged his right shoulder and winced in pain.

'You can help me by telling me how that happened. I'm afraid I have not had a chance to read the police report yet.'

'That's the sort of thing you can do, is it? Access police reports. Are you . . .?'

'No, I am not a policeman, but I am usually on their side, and in this case we are co-operating fully. Could you tell me what happened to you?'

'There's not much to tell really. I was at an awards do in Soho, nothing big or fancy, just the presentation of a technical award to Bobby Ears. That's not his name, of course; it's Bobby Harris, but in the business he's known as Bobby Ears because he's a top-notch sound engineer who's done thirty years with the BBC's Outside Broadcasting Unit. He was noted for covering the Grand National and a documentary I directed on the Battersea Dogs' Home, so I was volunteered to present it.

'It happened in one of those small screening cinemas on Wardour Street, and after the speeches there were a few drinks laid on – not that anyone was plastered or anything like that. Some of the old hands wanted to carry on making a night of it round the Nellie Dean, but I left them to it and walked to Soho Square where I'd left my car. I was almost there when I heard somebody running behind me, and the next thing I knew I was being tenderized like a piece of rump steak.'

'Did you get a look at your attacker?' asked a genuinely concerned Campion.

'It was dark and he was wearing a balaclava. I got one quick look at what he was belting me with, put my arm up to block it, and then I must have blacked out. All I could tell the police, when I came round in hospital, was that he wore gloves and he wielded a cricket bat like he was the last man in a Test Match needing a six off every ball.'

'So he wasn't an Australian then?'

Barlow allowed himself a short snigger at that. 'Couldn't tell you, he never said a word, just battered me; didn't even bother robbing me.'

'You feel it was a deliberate attack on you personally?'

'Deliberate and unprovoked and – before you ask – I cannot think I have upset anyone enough in my career to warrant such a beating.'

'Who knew you would be there that night?'

'It was no secret. Everyone knew Bobby Ears was getting the award, it was in all the trades and *Ariel*, the BBC's house magazine.'

'And there was nothing you saw or heard which could identify your attacker?'

Barlow shook his bandaged head.

'It happened so fast and he didn't say a word. He came up in a rush, whacked me, and then charged off and jumped in a car. All I heard, or I think I did, was a car door slamming and the engine going as it shot away.'

'You definitely heard a car pull away?'

'Yes, just before I blacked out completely, I'm sure I did, because I remember thinking it made a hell of a racket. Bobby Ears, the sound man, could have identified it immediately. Sounded like a lawnmower going over a cattle grid.'

'Interesting,' said Mr Campion.

# FIFTEEN

## Collateral Damage

For Lugg, a trip to Dorset meant only one thing: Weymouth, a seaside resort with donkey rides, sandy beaches, candy floss, Knickerbocker Glories and, if wet, a brewery down on the harbour served by its own railway. What more could you want on a family holiday? *Now* could he pack his bucket and spade?

Crestfallen to hear that Weymouth was not to be on the itinerary, he cheered up immediately on hearing that he would be staying overnight in a fine country inn where the ale and the food were first-rate, though best to avoid the curry for reasons Campion promised to provide on completion of their mission, the background to which Rupert would explain on the journey down to Kingswalter. Once there, all Lugg had to do was wave a cheque under the nose of the impoverished lord of the manor and help him persuade a rather strange community of squatters to vacate the village. It would be a case of looking impervious and scowling a lot, so – in other words – no acting skills were required.

Mr Campion was in luck, Lugg had said haughtily, as his duties as the beadle of Brewers' Hall were unusually light that week, and he might well be able to spare a couple of days of his valuable time. Once that was clearly appreciated, he had asked if his having to chaperone Rupert had anything to do with the lawyer's death in the City.

'In a roundabout way, yes,' Campion had admitted, 'but what you will be doing is tying up some loose ends – no, not quite that, more like pruning some of the wayward shoots from the main branches of this mystery.'

'Well, that's clear as mud,' huffed Lugg. 'Did Charlie Luke hear anything from your old mate?'

'What old mate? I have colleagues, acquaintances, old and distinguished friends and connections to the nobility, but I am not sure I have "mates".'

'Don't come the airs and graces with me, chum, you know who I mean, the chap she was working for who was supposed to go through that poor woman's papers.'

'Actually, that's a very good point, old fruit. I must check, though I'm loath to pester Charles too much as the case really belongs to the City Police.'

'Oh, you'll pester him all right,' said Lugg with a grimace. 'You won't be able to help yourself, 'cos pestering is your middle name.'

Having armed Lugg with his chequebook – one cheque only bearing his signature – and wished the travellers *bon voyage*, Mr Campion did indeed succumb to pestering his old friend Charles Luke, justifying his action on the basis that if one did have an old friend in the higher echelons of New Scotland Yard and one was convinced that crime had been committed, then why not encroach on that friendship? The only curmudgeon who would complain that it wasn't what you knew but who was the curmudgeon who did not have any friends.

'At your beck and call as always, Albert,' said Luke when the telephone connection was eventually made.

'I hope I am not being a pest and interrupting anything important, Charlie.'

'If I said you were – and, by the way, you are – would it force you into wearing sackcloth and ashes?'

'Probably not, but I'd be a soft touch for tickets to the next policeman's ball, if you still have those things.'

'I'll remember that, Albert, but now please be quick. I can give you two minutes, no more, so what are you after?'

'It concerns the poor lady whose hideaway in the City we visited last night.'

'I thought it might, and because I knew you were interested, I made sure the City boys on the investigation kept me interested. Nothing much new to report, though, only an administrative problem as to what to do with the body – eventually.'

'No witnesses, leads?'

'Nothing. Mrs Smith had no neighbours to speak of, and all the businesses around there were locked up for the evening. Nobody saw nuffink, as Lugg might say.'

'Did anyone *hear* anything unusual?'

'Don't think so, there was just nobody around. If you wanted to pick somewhere to live out of sight of other people in London, Mrs Smith chose well. I doubt if even the local postman knew who lived at that address, and postmen are almost as nosey as you are.'

Mr Campion allowed the jibe to wash over him.

'You said there may be a problem with the body of the late Mrs Smith?'

'The problem is that we don't know her next of kin. We were hoping the chap from the Evadne Childe Society would help us out.'

'Eric Rudd?'

'That's the fellow. She was working for him, and they were clearly close, as she left him all her worldlies in her will.'

'Really?' exclaimed Campion.

'Don't jump the gun; there was no fortune involved, unless she had a Swiss bank account hidden away. From what we can see, she had a few hundred in shares and two thousand in the local Nat West.'

'My surprise is neither at the amount nor the beneficiary, Charlie, but the fact that you have the details so quickly.'

'No great detective work required on the part of the City boys, which is probably just as well, though never let on I said that. Mrs Smith's last will and wotsit was on her bedside table. It wasn't lodged with a lawyer because she was a lawyer, and it had been done properly, witnessed by a doctor and the rector of St Olave's Church on the other side of Leadenhall Market. The scene-of-crimes chaps were trying to find her next of kin.'

'And did they?'

'No, no clues as to who she might have named. She was a widow, of course, so it wouldn't have been the late Giles Smith, and she never had children as far as we know.'

'What about her previous husbands?'

'No mention of them, though clearly she knew of Peyton Spruce's whereabouts from the work she was doing for the Childe Society. Anyway, I'm not sure what the form is with previous spouses.'

'You say previous spouses like you would say previous convictions, Charlie. Surely you'll need one of them to identify your body.'

Down the line Luke sighed heavily. 'It's not *my* body, Albert, it's not my case.'

'I'm sorry, Charlie. You are busy and I am a pest.'

'I agree on both those things,' said Luke, 'though this is clearly *your* case, it seems, and so I will keep an ear open for you, but please don't ask me to get involved. As to identification, I'm sure City will do its job and get hold of birth certificates and so on, but as a stopgap, this Rudd chap is surely the best person to do the formal identification.'

'Has anyone broken the news to Peyton Spruce?'

'I doubt it. He could, of course, be a suspect.'

'Oh, I don't think that's likely.'

'Don't you be so quick to judge. You've been wrong before,

Albert. We'll know more when Eric Rudd helps City Police go through all her papers.'

'I thought he was doing that today.'

'He was, but he hasn't shown up, at least not yet. I'm sure City will be chasing him.'

'I have a couple of letters from him,' said Campion, combing his memory, 'with his address and phone number. He lives on Roman Road.'

'That's Bethnal Green, not the City, though it's near enough. The City boys will track him down; if not, they'll ask Bethnal Green police station to send a car round. Let them – let us – do the job we're paid for, Albert.'

'Of course, Charlie, have I ever done otherwise?'

'Always,' said Luke.

Mr Campion smiled as he hung up the telephone in Bottle Street, then he scrabbled through a pile of letters on the small desk until he found the letter from Eric Rudd inviting him to speak at the Evadne Childe Society's AGM, which bore his address and telephone number.

Campion dialled.

There was no answer.

As he had, too generously he now realized, allowed Rupert and Lugg to travel in comfort to Dorset in his Jaguar, he was without transport, and so resorted, with some trepidation, to telephoning the man Lugg referred to as his 'trusted lieutenant' in all matters, though it was unwise to leave alcohol or loose change unattended in his presence. Campion had met Donnie Diggle on several occasions but knew little about him beyond his nursery-rhyme name, which Lugg claimed was exactly what was on Mr Diggle's birth certificate. He appeared to prefer a number of part-time employments rather than a single job in a timekeeping, tax-paying establishment. These included: portering at Smithfield meat market, being a waiter at formal dinners for numerous livery companies, a bookies' runner on the Mile End Road, a relief doorman at Claridge's, and a delivery driver for an expensive car dealership on Grosvenor Square.

Campion had no idea where Diggle lived, but Lugg had entrusted Campion with a telephone number on which Diggle could be contacted at any time when the pubs were shut.

Contact was established and Campion had to suppress a giggle as he was reminded of the sound of Donnie's high-pitched, child-like voice. But Donnie, deferential as always, was only too pleased – nay, honoured – to be of assistance, and was prepared to do anything for a friend of Mr Lugg.

Yes, Y'r Honour, he did have access to a motor vehicle later that evening; in fact, several, did Mr Campion have any preference? Something small and nippy and inconspicuous? Yes, that was certainly possible, so he wouldn't be required to wear a chauffeur's uniform, then? Oh, so it wasn't formal, then? It had to be unobtrusive if that was a word. Yes, Donnie Diggle could do unobtrusive if need be. Bethnal Green? No problem, he knew it like the back of his hand. Could be a bit rough after dark, though. Would there be any need to take along a bit of protection? Well, if Mr Campion said not, fair enough. Mr Lugg always said Mr Campion's judgement was to be relied upon in delicate situations. And this was a delicate situation, wasn't it?

Mr Campion said he certainly hoped not.

When Donnie arrived, exactly at the agreed time, outside the Bottle Street flat (and the police station it rested on), it was clear that his idea of a small and inconspicuous transport was far removed from that of Campion. He was driving a dark blue Transit van, the sort of vehicle popular with small-business owners, market traders, bank robbers and, indeed, the police. Even as Campion was climbing into the front passenger seat, Donnie volunteered the information that the Transit had enjoyed an active previous life with the Metropolitan Police, which explained the blowing exhaust, the dents in the doors, the damaged front bumper and the cracks in the windscreen, and its bargain price when it had been sold off after a rapid respray to obliterate the word Police from its side panels. The air horns and flashing blue roof light had also been removed during its decommissioning, a source of much disappointment to Donnie and great relief to Campion.

'I thought I requested something unobtrusive,' he said as the Transit lurched away from the kerb suggesting that the clutch also needed work.

'We're going out East, ain't we, Mr C.? Nobody'll bat an eyelash at this little runner in Bethnal Green. Anybody asks, we're market traders. Plenty of them nipping around this time of night.'

Campion turned in his seat and surveyed the tinny emptiness of the back of the van from which everything that could be had been removed. 'We don't appear to have anything to take to market on board.'

'That's 'cos we're on our way *to* Smithfield or Spitalfields to pick stuff up. How do you think all that meat and potatoes gets fresh to the shops and stalls every day so Londoners can fill their faces? It's in vans like this during the wee hours of the night. I tell you, Mr C., where we're going we won't look out of place, whereas a top-range Bentley – what I could have got you for tonight – would have the curtains twitching, and if we parked up, the wheels would have been gone in a trice. A trice, Mr C.! An' I ain't exaggerating; I seen it done.'

'I bow to your superior knowledge, Donnie, so let us proceed on our mission in the hope the police don't want their van back.'

'No chance of that, guv'nor, and anyway, I've got a legitimate bill of sale in my pocket. The beauty of this old gal,' he slapped the steering wheel to emphasize his point, 'is that the number plate is well known to the boys in blue, and they know it used to be one of theirs. Only a right turnip would pull a job in one of their old vans.'

Mr Campion chuckled politely. 'Surely, no one could be stupid enough to do that?'

''Appens more often than you might think, Mr C.'

Mr Campion had not set out that evening with anything nefarious, and certainly not illegal, on his mind, yet as he found himself buzzing through the streets with surprising speed – Donnie being clearly a veteran London driver, giving way only to black cabs and buses – he felt a strange tingle of excitement, a youthful feeling of being up to no good. The atmosphere inside the cold, echoing Transit was given a further frisson whenever they passed under a streetlight and Donnie's face would be illuminated in profile for a second or two. There, under a flat peaked cap was a snub-nosed man-child who might have been described as impish by a kindly grandmother, but behind a steering wheel could only have been suspected of being a get-away driver, never a chauffeur. The baby face and the pre-pubescent voice might fool that compassionate granny, who at the very worst might think him a scallywag or a rapscallion, but to most policemen on the beat, he was a rogue at first sight and, in his heart, Mr Campion enjoyed the company of rogues; it helped keep him young.

When they reached Bethnal Green, Donnie appeared to navigate the van to the address Campion had given him by using numerous street-corner pubs as compass points, but seemed to know where he was going. Which was just as well, as Campion was busy being appalled at the brutalist architecture of the blocks of, thankfully, low-rise flats, which had rehoused the local population, courtesy of the Luftwaffe and an awful lot of concrete.

Eric Rudd's house had somehow survived the attentions of both a lucky strike by a V2 rocket and the attentions of the Greater London Council. It was the end house in a terrace of three Georgian villas flanked on either side by ribbons of apartment blocks, where above the ground floors, small balconies had hopefully replaced the loss of a front or back garden. At least most of the flats had lights on, indicating the residents were at home and, by the sound of it, all tuned in to the same television channel, unlike Rudd's house which was in total darkness.

Just in case he was being overlooked from the flats, though he saw no sign of a twitching curtain or raised blind, he approached the front door and knocked loudly. He was, after all, a smartly turned-out elderly gentleman calling on an old friend, another equally respectable elderly gentleman. Admittedly, it was rather late in the evening for a social call – local custom would surely have demanded a meeting in a local pub – and Campion had arrived in a vehicle not known for transporting well-dressed elderly gentlemen.

When there was no answer to his repeated knocking, Campion lowered his long, thin frame into a position he knew was a cliché, that of the nosey neighbour peering through the letterbox. Not that it brought any reward as the interior of the house was as dark and as silent as the exterior. Campion tried a forlorn 'Hello?' through the opening but there was not even an echo in return and, when he straightened up, his knees and thighs told him he was not as limber as he once was.

As he stared at the all too solid door which barred his entry

– and he did now feel that he needed to gain entry as a matter of some urgency – his heart-rate jumped several percentage points when a voice very close to his right ear broke his concentration.

'Can I 'elp you there, Mr C.?'

Diggle had disobeyed orders, left the Transit and sneaked up behind Campion without making a sound. It was, Campion thought, pure instinct at work, the instinct of someone who would not allow a locked door to inconvenience him, or his employer, especially after dark on what he regarded as his home turf.

'It seems no one is home,' said Campion, almost apologetically.

'But you'd still like to get inside, wouldn't yer?'

Campion thought it best to make no comment, but for Donnie noncommittal silence was as good as an order to advance.

'Allow me, sir,' he said, easing by Campion and producing a short, stubby piece of plastic from his jacket pocket and inserting it into the crack between the door jamb and the Yale lock. As he exerted pressure, the tongue of the Yale slid back into its housing and the door swung inwards.

'That's a handy implement you've got there,' said Campion.

Diggle held the piece of brown plastic up for inspection. 'Got it out of a Christmas cracker. Supposed to be a shoe-horn, but a bit of gentle melting on top of the gas oven turned it into something useful.' He paused, looked at Campion, then added: 'If you lose your keys, that is.'

'Of course,' said Campion with a smile. 'I hear these new plastic credit cards can perform the same trick.'

'Yeah,' sighed Donnie, 'but who's gonna give *me* one of them?'

The open door silently willed them to enter; but before doing so, Mr Campion considered two things. Firstly, the dead bolt function on the lock had not been engaged, as one might have expected at this time in the evening in a darkened house where an elderly gentleman lived alone. Therefore, the resident could well be out and due back at any moment, or, alternatively, someone had left, simply closing the door behind them. Secondly, he noticed that Donnie Diggle was wearing tight-fitting black leather driving gloves, although he was sure he had not when actually driving the Transit.

'You've done this before,' he said quietly.

'Possibly,' said Donnie.

In Campion's mind, a possibility became a certainty when Donnie produced, as if out of thin air, a long, slender torch, but before he could press the on-button, Campion's hand covered his.

'Let's find a light switch, shall we? Lights on in a house are far less suspicious than a torch beam flashing about.'

'Good thinking, Mr C.,' said Donnie, staring innocently into Campion's face, as if daring him to blink first. 'Leaving the lights on deters intruders, and I take it we don't want to be disturbed.'

'I am too old to go stumbling around a strange house in the dark, Mr Diggle, and I won't be disturbed by any other intruder, because you'll be out here sitting in the van keeping watch. Should any suspicious persons approach the house, two toots on the horn should be sufficient warning. If that doesn't scare them, you drive away and I'll telephone the police.'

'What if it's coppers who come snooping?'

'Policemen on patrol are not high on my hit parade of suspicious characters, Donnie, in fact I might welcome their presence.'

For the first time that evening Donnie Diggle was clearly confused, the expression on his face that of a schoolboy expecting to be tested on his multiplication tables, but having an algebra problem sprung on him instead.

'But I can still drive away, right?'

'If you strongly feel the need, please feel free to do so.'

'An' it won't be 'eld against me?'

'Absolutely not. You'll get your fee, as agreed, and I won't hold it against you.'

'Begging your pardon, Mr C., but I ain't worried too much about you, it's whether Mr Lugg would think badly of me. I'd 'ate to get on the wrong side of him.'

'I'm afraid that, my dear Donnie, is a cross we all have to bear.'

Campion made his way into the house, turning on lights as he went. In the small hallway which led directly to the staircase and the upper floor, he noted a small bamboo table on which rested a telephone and a row of hat pegs at head height, from which hung two well-used trilbies, one brown bowler in pristine condition, two raincoats and an assortment of scarves. Toes randomly placed to the wall were four pairs of shined shoes, two of them containing rolled-up balls of socks, a sure indication, thought Campion, that Eric Rudd lived a bachelor life.

An open door at the end of the hall showed an empty kitchen which Campion did not deem worthy of further investigation, which left two closed doors. He decided that the one nearest the kitchen was likely to be the dining room, and the other, which would have a window fronting the street, would be the living room, or possibly Rudd's office, as much of the work of the Childe Society emanated from his address. He would start there, but before committing, he stood at the bottom of the stairs and called out, 'Eric? Mr Rudd? Are you home?'

He let the silence of the house settle around him for a moment, then opened the door to the front room and fumbled to where the light switch should be, and fortunately was. As his eyes adjusted to the light from a high-wattage bulb hanging from a central fitting in a glass shade in the shape of a Georgian coaching lamp, he realized he had chosen wisely, for this was not only Eric Rudd's office, but also his library and indeed something of a shrine to Evadne Childe.

The floor-to-ceiling bookshelves contained box files – presumably the proceedings of the Society – and books, hardbacks and paperbacks, most bearing Evadne Childe's name on the spine. On a leather-topped desk against the far wall was an ancient portable typewriter, a pile of blank paper, more books, and a mahogany letter rack overflowing with correspondence. Flanking the Adler were framed black-and-white photographs: one a publicity portrait of Evadne Childe, as used on the dust jackets of her books; the other a still from the film version of *The Moving Mosaic*, showing Peyton Spruce, pipe clenched between teeth, trademark trilby on head, marching across an archaeological dig site as Rex Troughton.

He felt sure the desk would give him a clue as to the whereabouts of Eric Rudd, and if the desk drawers were locked, he could always summon the resourceful Mr Diggle to his aid. And he could do that fairly instantly, as Donnie would certainly be watching Mr Campion's progress through the brightly lit uncurtained window, possibly even giving him marks for stealth and efficiency.

Yet as he stepped around a large wing-back armchair – the only chair in the room apart from an industrial typist's chair by the desk – and over two piles of books knee-high on the floor, he knew he would not have to ransack the desk to find a clue to Eric Rudd's whereabouts; for Eric Rudd was sitting in the armchair, and Mr Campion realized that the dark stain under his feet was not part of the natural pattern of the carpet.

That he was dead was obvious, and Campion, being honest, was relieved that it was far too late to attempt any sort of medical intervention. Eric Rudd had been stabbed – several times, Campion guessed – in the neck, and a massive loss of blood had turned his white shirt front red.

The weapon which had inflicted his wounds appeared to be a small sabre, almost certainly some form of novelty letter-opener, judging by the handle sticking out from just above the victim's bloodstained shirt collar. Campion knew better than to touch it, and its removal would not have improved the condition of the very late Mr Rudd.

Campion moved to the window and closed the curtains, then carefully retraced his footsteps into the hall. He took a fountain pen from the inside pocket of his jacket and flipped the telephone receiver off its cradle so that it lay purring on the bamboo table. Kneeling down, he used the pen to dial 999 and spoke clearly and calmly into the mouthpiece, requesting immediate assistance and promising to remain in situ until it arrived.

As he got to his feet, ignoring his creaking knees, he thought that there was no reason why Donnie Diggle need be involved in the imminent official proceedings, which would probably be uncomfortable for him as his boyish innocence would butter no parsnips with hardened homicide detectives. The best thing was to tell him, in the nicest possible way, to get lost, and Campion made his way to the front door in order to do just that.

Donnie Diggle and the Transit van were no longer in the street outside and there was only the faintest whiff of exhaust fume and the distant sound of an engine disturbing the night air.

It was a good two minutes before he heard the siren and saw the flashing blue lights of an approaching police car.

# SIXTEEN
## Rural Rides

'Looks a snug enough little hole, can't see the sea though,' said Lugg, observing Kingswalter from the top of the hill on the Dorchester road. 'Pity, I fancied going for a paddle before dinner.'

'I thought you were told to leave your bucket and spade at home,' said Rupert, changing down a gear and concentrating on steering the Jaguar down the serpentine slope.

'I was given my instructions, as was you, but they didn't include anything about not taking the salty waters, for medicinal purposes o'course. Supposed to do wonders for yer feet, seawater is.'

The car negotiated another twist of the corkscrew, Rupert's foot tapping the brake and, as it slowed, Lugg leaned forward in the passenger seat so much that an extra sharp tap on the brake would certainly result in his nose colliding with the windscreen.

'That's it, i'n'it,' exclaimed the fat man with the excitement of a seven-year-old who actually had been the first to see the sea. 'That's The King's Head, down there. Scene of the famous Kingswalter Massacre.'

'Hardly famous,' said Rupert, 'as virtually nobody knows about it. It's been kept very quiet for nearly thirty years.'

'Enough people know about it, your pa included, to stir things up.' As he spoke, Lugg raised and twisted his head as the Jaguar took another bend, anxious not to lose sight of the pub; something Rupert put down to thirst and hunger rather than an interest in the local topography or his driver's navigational skills.

'I wouldn't mention the massacre to the landlord's wife,' Rupert advised. 'She doesn't like any suggestion there may be a ghost in the pub as a result of it.'

'Pity, could be a tourist attraction, and not just for them looney hippies – what do they call themselves?'

'The Prophetics; because they predict where ghosts are going to appear. The leading light is a woman called Sally DeLuca.'

'She'll be the one we have to serve the eviction notice on, then?'

'In a sense, but with delicacy and sensitivity.'

Keeping his eyes on the road, Rupert felt his passenger's eyes bore into him and heard the dismissive 'Pah!' sound which Lugg could make simply by vibrating his lips on a frequency only he knew.

They had made good time on the drive from London, stopping only once on the way for petrol for the car and a choc ice for Lugg, and they descended into Kingswalter as the afternoon sunshine began to dim.

It had never been necessary to check Lugg's internal clock against a wristwatch.

'At least the pub'll be open.'

'We'll be residents,' Rupert pointed out, 'which means licensing laws won't apply to us.'

Without looking at him, Rupert could sense that his passenger had cheered up immensely.

Tessa Higgins greeted Rupert as if he were a regular visitor on his annual holiday – one of the 'been coming here for years, always done us proud' brigade – rather than a resident returning to complete his cut-short booking. Her reaction to finding that Mr Campion had been replaced by Lugg was less enthusiastic, for although he seemed to be able to behave himself, was gruffly polite, and had quickly ingratiated himself with her husband Roy by saying how much he was looking forward to sampling the delights of the pub's beer cellar, he wasn't quite the gentleman Mr Campion was. In fact she suspected he wasn't a gentleman at all, and later, when confiding in her husband, voiced her doubts that he had even been a gentleman's gentleman.

However, Lugg's natural and sincere enthusiasm when Mrs Higgins relayed what would be on the menu for residents that night warmed her professional heart and allayed most of her initial doubts. She even managed a nervous laugh when Lugg took her by the shoulders and gently propelled her to the kitchen, saying that if he didn't get some 'decent Dorset grub' inside him soon, she'd have to take in his trousers.

Rupert dropped his overnight bag in his room and then went

next door to find Lugg unpacking his rather large suitcase and hanging a formal suit – black jacket and pinstripe trousers – on a coat-hanger. The outfit also came with a bowler hat, which Lugg blew on then wiped with his shirtsleeve. He could sense that Rupert was holding back from asking a question and pre-empted him by saying merely, 'I've had my instructions,' then, as an afterthought, 'but let's get some grub before we get down to business.'

'Of course,' said Rupert vaguely. 'I thought we should tackle Ranald Ward-Tetley first.'

'Fair enough, but not on an empty stomach, I might turn ugly.'

'Heaven forfend.'

'Cheek!' muttered Lugg. 'Now what was it we weren't supposed to try on the menu here?'

'The curry.'

'Pity, I likes a good, hot curry – spicier the better.'

'You could risk it. It's hardly likely a curry will strike twice in the same place, and it would have to be a powerful one to incapacitate such as you.'

'Again with the cheek, but you don't scare me. Come on, curry, let's be having you. Do yer worst.'

Lugg's carefree disregard for both his digestive system and waistline earned him the admiration of landlord Roy, who was delighted when the 'well-padded elderly gentleman' ordered his own-recipe mutton curry for an early dinner, despite his wife's apprehensive glances and eagle-eyed supervision of every aspect of its preparation. Such was her concern that her husband had to tell her to 'stop hovering' over him on several occasions, and to get on with cooking the cod and chips the young fellow had ordered.

As Rupert and Lugg were the first, and only, customers in the pub that evening, they had the place to themselves and the rapt attention of Mr and Mrs Higgins, who observed their every forkful from behind the bar whilst pretending to polish glasses and rearrange bottles. Their expressions of innocent curiosity only cracked, turning to scowls of concern and apprehension, when Lugg pushed aside an empty plate and demanded, in a voice which boomed around the empty pub, 'Who cooked this, then?'

Roy Higgins opened the bar hatch and stepped through. Behind him his wife appeared to be trying to wring the ink out of a printed, perfectly dry tea-towel.

'I do the curry,' said the landlord nervously. 'I like to think of it as a bespoke dish. Was anything wrong?'

'Yus!' Lugg was emphatic. 'This bespoke dish is empty! Any chance of seconds?'

From that moment on, Rupert knew that he might well be tolerated but Lugg would be treated royally at The King's Head, not just for the remainder of their stay, but possibly for ever. In the short term it earned him an extra-large portion of clotted-cream ice cream, with wings of ginger biscuits – Dorset biscuits, of course, from the factory in Morcombelake – for dessert from the landlady and a post-prandial barley wine from the landlord.

Rupert, who had been comparatively abstemious on both the food and drink fronts, suggested that they should walk up to the manor house whilst the light held, although it was a bit of a hill climb and if Lugg wasn't up to it, they could take the car.

With a weary shake of his giant bald head, which summed up his despair at the youth of today, Lugg said firmly but politely that he would not mind a stroll in the countryside, to stretch his legs and work up an appetite for a late supper.

To avoid the prospect of having to carry Lugg down the hill in the dark, should such a thing be physically possible, Rupert suggested they set off immediately and, to his surprise, Lugg slapped his ample thighs, sprang to his feet, and headed immediately for the bar counter, where he shook Roy Higgins by the hand, patted him on the shoulder, and spoke to him in a low, animated tone. The landlord appeared in turn horrified, surprised and then genuinely delighted, and finally, looking at his wife, incredibly smug.

Once outside and striding towards the lane leading up to the manor, Rupert asked what that had all been about.

'Complimenting 'im on 'is curry,' Lugg said innocently. 'Credit where it's due, and it never hurts to keep in with the man in charge of the beer pumps.' He sniffed the early evening air like a drowning man breaking the surface of deep water. 'Ahh, yer can't beat the countryside for fresh air and fun.'

'I thought that was supposed to be the seaside at Skegness.'

Lugg snorted loudly again. 'Well, the sea's not that far away, over the next hill I reckon.' Lugg held up a paw to shield his eyes from the sinking sun. 'All them sheep up there will have a good view of it,' he said, scanning the hilltops dotted with white snow-flake blobs above the treeline. 'Whose are they?'

'The sheep? I think they're Ward-Tetley's, but he can't sell them, otherwise they would have been lamb chops long before now to pay off his debts.'

'Now you've got me thinking.'

'About what?'

Lugg smacked his lips. 'Mint sauce.'

Once through the gates leading to the manor house, Rupert suggested a slight detour into the trees to view the Roman mosaic while the light held, thinking that the older man would appreciate a chance to catch his breath after climbing up the lane. To his surprise, and slight chagrin, Lugg seemed not to have broken sweat on the climb from the pub which, considering the slope, the sheer physical bulk he had to move up it and the curry he had consumed, was quite remarkable.

Daintily he extended a foot on to the mosaic, like a child would prod the ice of a frozen puddle, as if testing to see if it would take his weight, then took tentative, balletic steps until he was leaning over and peering down into the face in the centre of the design. For a moment two pairs of eyes locked across the centuries, and Rupert had the unsettling feeling that if this was a proper staring match, it was one that Lugg would win.

'So hoo's this fella then?'

'Pa thinks it could be a portrait of the chap who built the villa that the floor decorated. The villa fell down over time, but that in a way preserved the floor and when the real archaeologists dug down and moved the rubble, they found it almost intact.'

'Nice workmanship,' said Lugg. 'Got to admire the workman-ship. Late fourth century, you reckon?'

Rupert stepped back in amazement. 'You're an expert in Roman mosaics?'

'I saw my share during the Blitz, clearing up after the bombs had dropped. Found the remains of a Roman bathhouse near the Aldwych tube station after one raid. If you ask me, the Luftwaffe did more archaeology in London during the war than Mortimer Wheeler. This one, though,' he pointed to the design beneath his feet, 'I read about in Evadne Childe's book. Yer mother made me read it, said I needed improving. Can't think what she meant by that.'

'Me neither,' said Rupert diplomatically. 'Shall we go up to the manor? I'll warn you now, if Ranald offers you any refreshment, it won't be the sort you're used to.'

'Like that is it? Still, he ought to be pleased to see me as I bring tidings of comfort and great joy and he'd better be grateful. Come on, let's go sort out the little tyke.'

The little tyke in need of sorting out appeared very relaxed at the prospect when he opened the front door of the manor to his visitors; so relaxed, in fact, that only the edge of the door seemed to be holding him upright. Behind Ranald's head hung a faint, ethereal blue cloud, accompanied by a distinct herbal scent.

'Rupert, Rupert Campion,' Ranald's eyes were wide but unfocused, 'to what do I owe the pleasure of another visit so soon after the first in . . . how many years was it?'

'Good evening, Ranald. This is . . .'

That was as far as Rupert got as Lugg heaved past him, stretching out an arm until the palm of a meaty right hand made contact with Ranald's shirt front and pressure was exerted. Not that it took much effort on Lugg's part to propel the stumbling lord of the manor backwards into the house, at times grasping the material of Ranald's shirt to keep him upright as he pushed him along the hall, aiming for the open door to the kitchen.

'We don't need no formal introductions, young sir.' Lugg's voice boomed around the empty house. 'All you need to know is that if you pull yourself together, behave like a young gentleman should, do what you're told and, above all, give us no lip, then all your Christmases and one or two birthdays might come at once.'

Just how much of this proclamation Ranald Ward-Tetley took on board was, Rupert thought, debatable. As he was backed towards a kitchen chair, on to which he sank moments before his legs gave way, Ranald's face could have functioned as a recruiting poster for The Prophetics, for here was a man who had truly seen a ghost, or at least something frightening.

'What do you want?' Ranald managed to say, shaking his head to clear it whilst turning it nervously to follow the looming Lugg, who was pacing around the chair and kitchen table as if taking stock, or looking for a snack.

'We've come to help, to bring you good news,' said Rupert gently. 'From the BBC.'

'Really?' Now they had his full attention, or what was left of it.

'Not directly,' said Lugg, striding around the kitchen, scowling like a teacher forced to invigilate an exam. 'Your fairy godfather, Mr Albert Campion, has, for reasons best known to 'isself, intervened at the highest level to make sure that any ruffled feathers at the BBC can be smoothed and that filming around your mosaic can go ahead, which means a substantial fee for providing the location will be coming your way.'

If Lugg noticed Rupert's raised eyebrows and pursed lips, he made no sign, and Rupert knew better than to interrupt the big man in full flow.

''Owever,' declaimed Lugg, still pacing, his back to Ranald, who was fixed to his chair as if he had been tied to it, 'Mr Campion, in his wisdom, which is sometimes spread thin in my opinion, realizes that a body which calls itself a corporation isn't usually that swift in signing cheques.'

He turned on his heels to face Ranald, and with a flourish produced a Coutts Bank cheque from the top pocket of his jacket, and unfolded it with the delicacy of an origami master.

'So he has, out of the goodness of a wayward heart, instructed me to hand over his cheque for £500, which you are to accept as an advance – a subvention if you like – to help you out of your present difficulties.'

Ranald looked at the cheque, then at Rupert, then back at the cheque. When he returned his gaze up at Rupert, it was full of pathetic hope.

'This isn't some sort of joke, is it? A trick by my creditors?'

'Do I look like a bookies' runner?' boomed Lugg, startling the younger man, who had clearly believed that the huge apparition waltzing around the kitchen was a figment of his addled imagination.

'It's a genuine offer, Ranald,' soothed Rupert, 'to tide you over until the BBC come through.'

'It's an h'offer,' said Lugg, low and menacing, dancing the cheque before Ranald's eyes, 'you'd be very foolish to ignore, very foolish indeed.'

Ranald looked back to Rupert for support. 'That sounds like it comes with conditions.'

'Don't look at him, look at the cheque,' growled Lugg, snapping the rectangle of paper tight within an inch of Ranald's nose, 'and don't think of them as conditions so much as obligations.'

'Obligations?'

'You just have to do a few things to smooth the way for the BBC to come and film here,' Rupert said reasonably. 'The first thing is to get rid of your stash of marijuana, open all the windows and give the house a good airing.'

He was clearly being far too reasonable for Lugg.

'Don't come the innocent, chum, the place reeks of it. The Drugs Squad could park up down by the pub and wouldn't even have to let the sniffer dogs out the back of the van.'

'Drugs Squad?' he appealed to Rupert.

'I'm afraid my father works hand-in-glove with the police, and word has reached him that the local Drugs Squad may well be taking an interest in some of Kingswalter's temporary residents.'

'You mean The Prophetics?'

'Now you're getting it,' encouraged Lugg. 'Can't have the likes of them hanging around corrupting the nice ladies and gentlemen from the BBC, can we? The Sunday papers would have a field day, and the dear old BBC doesn't like scandal.'

'What can I do? They're not causing trouble and I'd need a lawyer and injunction to force them off that campsite.'

'Hold fire on hiring a lawyer,' said Rupert.

'Always sound advice,' echoed Lugg.

'Are they planning another midnight vigil tonight?'

'I guess so, they just wander up and sit outside the front door. Actually, I've got rather used to them.'

'Well, tonight, it's no more Mr Nice Guy. When they turn up, you go out there and tell them they're squatting on private land and they're not welcome any more. If you've got a radio or a record player, put some music on and make it loud – loud enough to scare off any ghosts they might be expecting.'

'Ever kept dogs?' asked Lugg. And when Ranald shook his head, added, 'Pity. You could chuck a bucket of water over them or use a garden hose; that always works on misbehavin' dogs.'

'But they're harmless—'

'They're a stumbling block to you and your mosaic becoming famous. Just think of the tourists after the programme goes out.' Rupert paused and held up a cautionary finger. 'And you have to stop buying your dope from them.'

'If I agree to that, can I have the cheque?'

'You also have to tell The King's Head not to serve The Prophetics any more.'

'That should do it,' agreed Lugg.

'The Higginses won't like that, they need the trade.'

'They'll get plenty of trade from the BBC film crew and then all those tourists. You own the pub – you can tell them whatever you like. Ring them right now and tell them.'

'I can't, my phone's cut off,' said Ranald sadly, as if he had been told a much-loved pet had died.

'We'll give them the good news when we get back there.' Lugg did a little soft-shoe shuffle so the cheque danced in front of his victim's eyes. 'If you're in agreement, that is.'

'If you're sure the BBC will come through . . .'

'Get rid of The Prophetics and clean up your act and they will,' Rupert reassured him.

'In that case . . .'

He reached a hand for the cheque quivering so close, only for Lugg to withdraw it just out of range.

'Two more things,' said the fat man, at which Ranald gave a loud sigh of defeat. 'First off, your gamekeeper chappie, Joe Lunn – where does he live?'

'In the village, but you'll find him in The King's Head. He's there every night.'

'Splendid.' Lugg allowed the cheque to be taken as gently as a communion wafer would be.

'What was the other thing?' Ranald asked suspiciously, though his attention remained entirely on the valuable paper between his fingertips.

'Are them your sheep on the hills?'

The light was beginning to fade as they left the manor, but less than halfway down the drive Rupert said he had forgotten something, and dashed back to hammer on the front door until a startled Ranald – clearly frightened that his precious cheque was to be recalled – let him in.

When Rupert reappeared and fell into step beside the fat man, he had a bound sheaf of papers tucked under one arm.

'That the script you were pining for?' said Lugg, marching on, eyes front.

'Ranald agreed to lend it to me,' answered Rupert meekly.

'He would have agreed to anything as long as you let him keep that cheque.'

'Can we keep this just between us? Pa doesn't have to know.'

'It was your dad who bet me fifty pence that you wouldn't leave the house without it. Thought I was on a winner for a minute.'

Near the bottom of the lane, where it joined the main street, they saw a group of eight or nine people leaving The King's Head, clutching bottles and packets of crisps.

'That's them,' said Rupert. 'The Prophetics off to their vigil with their supplies to sustain them in the night.'

'They don't know it's last orders for them,' muttered Lugg. 'Mebbe it's best we're not seen.'

They dodged into the side garden of the nearest cottage. Not for the first time, Rupert was impressed with how light on his feet Lugg could be (when he wanted to be) as he hopped and skipped over a well-tended vegetable patch and then sank down on his massive haunches as Rupert crouched down next to him.

The Prophetics went by, up the hill towards the manor, in a chinking of bottles and a low, rumbling murmur of expectation that tonight might indeed be the night.

Once the coast was clear, Rupert and Lugg marched briskly to the pub, where Lugg, magnanimously, allowed the younger man to reach the bar first.

'That's him, in the window,' he said, handing over a brimming pint of bitter and watching in awe as Lugg downed half of it in one gulp, a technique he referred to as 'taking the top off to avoid spillage'.

When he came up for air, Lugg spoke quietly so only Rupert could hear, 'Right, I'll deal with 'im, you go whisper sweet nothings to the landlord,' which made Rupert feel he had drawn the short straw, as having to tell a publican he was going to lose customers was never easy.

Lugg, on the other hand, seemed to be perfectly matched as he settled himself in the window seat across from Joe Lunn. The two of them could almost have been a pair of chess grand-masters, but for the fact that the only moveable pieces on the table between them were glasses of beer. True, Lunn was a dozen years younger and several stones lighter than Lugg, but in many ways they could have been bookends carved to represent two aspects – one urban, one very rural – of the same roguish character.

'Yes, I'm Mr Lunn, but everyone calls me Joe,' he had said as the fat man loomed over him.

'You can call me Mr Lugg. I've got a bit of employment for you.'

'Oh, have you now? What makes you think I'm looking for a job?'

'I know you've got a job; you work for young Ward-Tetley at the manor. Pays well, does it? Regular wage packet?'

Lurking at the bar, trying to have a quiet word with Roy Higgins in between him pulling pints and washing glasses, Rupert managed to keep half an eye on the two old men in the window. Although he could not hear their conversation, in demeanour it was clear they were not playing chess, but poker.

'Don't see that's any business of strangers from London,' said Joe Lunn, frowning into his almost empty glass.

'Not even strangers who buy the next round?'

'They wouldn't be strangers then.'

Even as Lugg levered himself out of his seat, Roy Higgins was pulling two fresh pints and had them standing to attention on the bar by the time Lugg got there.

'As I was saying,' began Lugg, once the ale had been sampled and not found wanting, 'I have a little job for you, Mr Lunn.'

'I told you, it's Joe to my friends.'

'That's as may be, but even if we're not strangers, it don't mean we're friends, so it's still Mr Lugg to you. Best to keep it formal while you're working for me.'

'I told you, I work for—'

'Yes, I know, but I reckon you do odd jobs for all and sundry if there's a bit of cash on offer. Out here in the country, that's what you do, isn't it?'

'We can turn our hands to many a thing,' conceded Mr Lunn.

'Would you have access to a lorry?'

Mr Lunn reacted as if he was asked that every day, along with how many sugars he took in his tea.

'I have my own tractor and trailer; no call for a lorry.'

'That sounds even better . . .' Lugg seemed deep in thought, '. . . more *agricultural* somehow.'

'Better for what?'

'The little job I have in mind, but first things first.' Lugg pulled open his jacket with a flourish and produced his wallet as if drawing a gun. He plucked out two ten-pound notes and dealt them like Tarot cards in front of Joe Lunn, guaranteeing that he had the man's full attention. 'That's a down-payment, a gesture of good faith if you like. There'll be the same again after the job's done.'

'You haven't said what the job is, or whether it's . . .' Lunn's voice dropped to a whisper, '. . . *legal.*'

'Do I look like a solicitor? No, don't answer that, just trust me. You work, so you say, for young Ranald Ward-Tetley.'

Lunn nodded slowly in agreement, though his eyes never left the notes on the table.

'Well, earlier this evening, Mr Ward-Tetley consulted me on certain matters concerning his financial future.' Lugg paused for refreshment. 'Of course I cannot go into details about that, but I can say he was very happy with the proposal I put to him and it has his full support, so in effect, you'd be working for him if you undertake this little job for me tomorrow.'

'You haven't told me what's involved.'

Lugg paused for more refreshment.

'Can you get your tractor and trailer hooked up and ready to go first thing tomorrow morning?'

'I can be up and out before you've even thought about what to have for breakfast.'

'I very much doubt that, but you might need an early start.'

'Why's that?'

'Depends how good you are at herding sheep.'

# SEVENTEEN
## The Biggest Fan

Mr Campion had left the front door ajar and retreated to sit on the bottom steps of the staircase to await the arrival of the police. The door was pushed open by the fingertips of a young, ginger-haired uniformed constable, who offered a plaintive 'Hello?' before stepping over the threshold and then froze like a statue when Campion replied, 'Do come in, Officer.'

A second policeman loomed up behind the first, and the two of them blocked the hallway just in case the thin, bespectacled pensioner, sitting on the stairs with his long legs stretched out before him, decided to bolt for the street and freedom. Not that the elderly gentleman seemed at all inclined to run away, nor did he look particularly dangerous, but these days you never knew, so they stuck to procedure.

When Campion volunteered the information that it was indeed he who had dialled 999 to report the body that was awaiting them in the front room, the red-headed constable pointed a finger at the door on his left as if requiring confirmation. Only after Campion had nodded, did he tell his colleague to 'take the gentleman's statement' and then, swallowing hard and taking a deep breath, did he enter. The second policeman was still reaching for the notebook in his tunic pocket and advancing on Mr Campion when the first burst from the front room, a hand over his mouth, and virtually threw himself out into the night.

'It's his first,' said the second constable with a shrug of his shoulders.

'Oh, the poor boy,' said Campion.

Reinforcements were swift to arrive. Plain-clothes detectives, with a senior investigating officer called Hornbeck in charge, then photographers and fingerprint technicians, a doctor to pronounce the obvious, and finally an ambulance, which arrived quietly and without fanfare, to take the body away.

The commotion produced in the street did not go unnoticed by the neighbouring residents of Bethnal Green and several decided that, although it was late, their dogs really did need walking. Naturally, they expressed curiosity as to what was going on, as did numerous pubgoers heading home after closing time, and the ginger-haired constable, who had been put on sentry duty in order to enjoy the fresh night air, listened to them all and, on discovering they did not know the deceased, invited them to move along.

Mr Campion had given statements to three different officers and offered a formal identification of Eric Rudd before he felt he was accepted, if not as an ally then at least neither a suspect or threat. Detective Inspector Hornbeck had been polite and efficient, making Campion wait in the kitchen while his scene-of-crime team went to work. He was genuinely grateful that Campion was able to identify the body for him, and seemed to believe Campion's reason for being on the premises, particularly the fact that the late Mr Rudd had failed to turn up to assist the City Police in their inquiries into another suspicious death.

How did Mr Campion know this? The inspector was curious, and it allowed Campion to drop the name of Charles Luke, of New Scotland Yard, who was taking a personal interest in that case and would certainly be interested in this one. In fact, a simple phone call and Commander Luke would not only be pleased to be brought up to speed, but he could also vouch for Mr Campion.

'It's after midnight,' Hornbeck had said. 'Mr Luke won't be in his office at this time of night.'

'I have his home phone number,' Campion had said helpfully.

All things considered, Charles Luke was in a remarkably good mood when he arrived in Bethnal Green and although unshaven and wearing a raincoat over casual trousers and a roll-neck sweater, the sheer force of his personality ensured that he had a clear path into the house, with every attending officer standing to attention and saluting him.

'This gentleman says he is known to you, sir,' said Hornbeck.

'I am afraid he speaks nothing but the truth,' said Luke. 'He has been a stone in my shoe for more years than I care to count.' He reached out and touched Campion on the shoulder. 'You are Albert Campion, and I claim my five pounds.'

'I'd call that a bargain, Charles, now how can I help?'

'Promise me that two murders in two days is your limit for the year, and that you've had your fill of London, because it's a much more restful place with you not in it.'

'Restful, but not so interesting.'

'That's your opinion, Albert. Now what's going on here?'

As succinctly as he could, Campion explained how he had attempted to contact Eric Rudd without success and had become increasingly worried when he heard that Rudd had not reported, as promised, to the City Police, to assist in their inquiries into the death of Tania Smith. On the spur of the moment, and as he had Mr Rudd's address, he had decided to come to Bethnal Green to see if he could locate him. Unfortunately he had, but far too late to help the poor man. Did he arrive by car? No, he got a lift with a friend of Lugg's who knew the area (a grey, if not white lie) who, lucky for him, had dropped him off and left for another appointment. At this, Charles Luke had muttered that if it was a friend of Lugg's, that convenient appointment would not have been at Evensong. He then gently raised the question of how Campion had gained entry, given that Mr Rudd was in no position to answer the door, at which point Campion avoided eye-contact and admitted that although the front door was on the latch, it was not deadlocked . . . perhaps had not been closed properly . . . and it had yielded to very slightest pressure . . .

Luke, hands on hips with the expression of a patient school-teacher, asked if that suggested anything to Campion, who replied that one could infer that Rudd had let his killer into the house and the killer had left, pulling the door closed on the latch. Further speculation, should speculation be called for, might suggest that the choice of murder weapon – the letter-opener in the shape of a sabre – pointed to an impetuous crime rather than one premeditated. The murderer got in the house, had an alter-cation with Rudd and grabbed the first weapon that came to hand.

That was certainly a credible scenario, Luke had admitted, but then there was the question of the time of the murder. Campion had naturally deferred to the opinion of the police surgeon on that matter, as he had strenuously avoided physically touching anything in the house, especially the late occupant. Luke had agreed that

that had been a wise move on Campion's part, particularly the trick with the telephone when he dialled 999.

Campion had acknowledged the compliment – for he took it as such – and asked if the telephone had any connection with the time of the murder. Luke said it may well have, as the doctor's estimate of the time of death – a rough-and-ready one, of course, at this stage – put it at closer to the death of Tania Smith in her flat in the City than to Campion's arrival.

After some arithmetical gymnastics, Mr Campion had said that was impossible, as Rudd had been contacted by the City Police investigating Mrs Smith's death and indeed had offered to cooperate with them. 'Contacted' was, Luke had suggested, the appropriate word, for it had been contact by telephone. No City Police officer had seen Eric Rudd in person; they had heard a voice on the phone offering full cooperation and had waited patiently, but in vain, for him to turn up in person.

A cold mist descended into the pit of Campion's stomach. Was Luke suggesting that Rudd's murderer was here in the house when the City Police rang and it was he or she (it was definitely a 'he', Luke insisted) who answered the call, pretending to be Eric Rudd? It was a theory. Had Campion touched the body? Of course not, so he would not have noticed that rigor mortis had been and gone, meaning that Rudd had been killed at least twenty-four hours before Campion found the body, possibly around the time the City detectives were attempting to contact him about the death of Tania Smith. The fact that the house telephone had been wiped spotlessly clean of fingerprints supported, in Luke's mind, the fact that the murderer had taken the call and bluffed it out. A cold-blooded joker like that, he predicted, would get what was coming to him and that was a promise.

Was it possible? Campion had asked, though he already suspected Luke's thinking was along the same lines and slightly ahead, that Eric Rudd's killer had come hotfoot from an altercation with Tania Smith to an equally violent confrontation in Bethnal Green? It was certainly a possibility which a post-mortem and the forensic reports might be able to prove, but if it was proved, it pointed to a very dangerous killer being on the loose, one capable of committing two murders, one after the other in rapid, frantic succession.

Even though they might have been unplanned, they had not been random acts. Something – something which had inspired a ferocious passion – had linked the violent demise of a middle-aged divorcée lawyer and a bachelor bibliophile, other than being three stops apart on the Underground, and Campion knew very well what that was.

Evadne Childe.

'I think,' said Mr Campion, 'that on a quiet night you can hear Evadne Childe spinning in her grave over the trouble her books have caused. I'm sure she never dreamt something like this could happen, and certainly not to her biggest fan.'

'I thought that was supposed to be Amanda, from what you've said over the years.'

'Oh, Amanda was a dedicated reader, an avid consumer you might say, of Evadne's books, but Eric Rudd was certainly her biggest fan, and that's fan with a capital F. As I understand it, the original idea for the Evadne Childe Society was his and he pitched it to Evadne some years before her death, but she refused to bless or sanction it until after she was gone.'

'That's odd, isn't it?' Luke was genuinely curious. 'What writer wouldn't want their own supporters' club?'

'A sensible one who never got above herself just because she had her name on the spine of a book. She was really quite a wise woman, and once told me that the biggest threats to a writer were alcohol and praise.'

'I take it she wasn't much of a drinker, then.'

'Not so you'd notice. She lived quite frugally, though her books made her, and her publisher, a good living. Not the having-to-move-to-Ireland-for-the-tax-benefits sort of living, but a very comfortable one nonetheless.'

'What happened to her money? Did the Society benefit from her will?'

'I don't think so . . . well, not directly,' said Campion. 'Evadne was widowed in 1939 and had no children. As we know, she must have wasted a lot of her income on psychics and séances and other mumbo-jumbo, trying to contact her late husband until . . .'

'You put her right. That would be ten years ago, wouldn't it, in '62?'

'That's rather brutal, Charles, but essentially correct. You know she dedicated her last novel to me?'

'I think you've mentioned it, but not more than six or seven times.'

'And she left me a complete set of signed first editions in her will. Amanda was quite jealous, even though she'd been collecting Evadne's books since she was a teenager.'

'So you got her out of a very tricky, not to say dangerous, situation and she remembers you with a pile of old books?'

'Spoken like the Philistine you often have to pretend to be, Charlie, but this is your Uncle Albert you're talking to. I take it you noted the "piles of old books" in Rudd's office.'

'Couldn't help tripping over them. Must be hundreds, if not a couple of thousand.'

'I'll bet you none are missing; they didn't even look disturbed to me, though I bet some of them are quite valuable. Which suggests to me we can rule out a burglar being disturbed.'

'I'm ahead of you there, Albert. I thought we'd established that Rudd let his killer in to the house and he wouldn't let in a friendly neighbourhood burglar. Goodness knows, there are enough of them around here. Therefore he must have known him, so who did Eric Rudd know?'

'Well, he knew Tania Smith for a start, though it was clearly not her who came calling. I am not familiar with Mr Rudd's social circle, but I suspect – and I may be doing him an injustice – it was limited to bibliophiles, book dealers, and anyone connected to Evadne Childe, and that would include her publishers, the people at the BBC involved in the present production of *The Missing Mosaic* and, of course, Peyton Spruce, who was in the 1952 film.'

Mr Campion removed his spectacles, flourished a handkerchief and gave the large round lenses an unnecessary polish.

'Your mention of wills though, Charles, there may be something in that. Eric Rudd certainly knew Pauline Hatherall, and she left the Childe Society something in her will: the film rights to Evadne's books.'

'Valuable?'

'Certainly, but not the sort of thing a random burglar could steal and take down the local pawn shop.'

'Hatherall . . .?' Luke savoured the word, an experience he clearly did not enjoy. 'That would be the mother of Veronica who was . . .'

'And Evadne never forgave herself, so she looked after Pauline as a sort of penance, paying her expenses for a nursing home down near Brighton. I shouldn't think Evadne ever thought Mrs Hatherall would outlive her, but she made provision for that in a most Christian way, and left her comfortably off and with the film rights as a bit of a nest egg. It is the film rights which have, I am convinced, precipitated all this nastiness.'

'Did Rudd get himself put in Mrs Hatherall's will? Any dubious goings-on there?'

'I doubt it. In my limited experience of him he seemed an upright and honest fellow, who would be appalled at such a slur. In any case, the will benefited the Childe Society, not Eric personally and, as far as I know, was not contested by anyone. But Rudd certainly visited Mrs Hatherall before she passed away.'

'And how do you know that?'

'From the lady who runs White Horses, the home she was in. A woman – I almost said a nun – called Mary Graham, who gave me a list of people who had visited Mrs Hatherall. Rudd was on that list, as were various BBC types, and Peyton Spruce, whose picture we found at Tania Smith's and indeed is present on Rudd's desk here.'

'You noticed that too? Thought you would. Was Tania Smith one of her visitors?'

'I don't think so. I think she was engaged only after Mrs Hatherall's death and the provisions of her will became known, particularly the casting of Spruce as Rex Troughton, which is the subject of some dispute.'

Luke took a deep, regretful breath. 'Part of my job, Albert, is to expect the worst of people, so is it possible that Mrs Hatherall was "got at" before she made her will?'

'By her visitors, you mean?'

'You seemed interested enough to get a list of them, so I'm guessing you had the same thought, though I know your natural bent is to look for the sweetness and light in everybody.'

Mr Campion feigned surprise, showing Luke a facial expression which suggested he had found a five-pound note which had slipped through the lining of a jacket pocket.

'I do not understand how you could say such a thing, Charles, being well aware of my long acquaintance with Magersfontein Lugg. As for Mrs Hatherall's visitors, well, she seemed to have no immediate family, so all her visitors were connected somehow with Evadne Childe. There was Rudd from the Society, Miss Prim from Gilpin's the publishing house, Peyton Spruce – she had a soft spot for him, that's for sure – along with some of his theatrical chums, and then Tamara Reams of the BBC. Plus, there was a name I didn't recognize until I met him, an actor who accompanied Tamara Reams, called Alec Devine, who turns out to be in the running to play Rex Troughton in the new production.'

'Really, Albert, you are out of touch. Even I know that Alec Devine is "the next big thing", as they say, and causes palpitations among the ladies – young and old – whenever he's on television. Where did you come across him?'

'Accidentally, down in Dorchester, and then more formally at the BBC this morning, though that seems an age ago.' Campion looked at his watch. 'Good grief! It *was* ages ago, well, yesterday to be precise. We're both losing beauty sleep, Charles, and at my age I can ill-afford that.'

'Well, there's nothing much either of us can do here, so I'll get one of the Bethnal Green cars to run you back to Bottle Street and you can get your head down.'

'Thank you, Charles, that's much appreciated, though I hope you don't think I roped you in tonight just to provide a taxi.'

'All part of the service, Albert, though it will cost you. I want your list of the people who visited Mrs Hatherall. On my desk please, by lunchtime tomorrow – I mean today – if possible.'

'Of course. I think you're right, Charles, Mrs Hatherall is the key to all this, or rather Mrs Hatherall's post-mortem wishes.'

'Because they involved Rudd, who then involved Tania Smith, who just happened to have once been the wife of this Spruce chap?'

There was an unexpected hesitancy in the policeman's voice, as if he was testing a theory which needed Campion's approval.

'Exactly, though I'm still unclear as to who benefits from the deaths of Tania Smith, whoever she used to be married to, and dear old Eric Rudd. All I can see that achieving is to confuse the issue.'

'Somebody must benefit,' said Luke, now the confident law officer. 'Somebody always does, if they get away with it.'

'To put it crudely, the only way I can rationalize this is that with Rudd and his lawyer out of the picture, there is no one pressing the case for Peyton Spruce to play Rex Troughton in the new film.'

'Well, there you have it,' said Luke resignedly. 'Take your pick of two suspects with very juicy motives.'

'Two?' asked Campion over the rims of his glasses.

'Number one is that matinee idol Spruce, who thought he was all set for his big comeback.'

'But Tania Smith and Eric Rudd were on his side, they were pushing for him to get the role.'

'Fair enough, but what if Spruce felt his ex-wife wasn't doing enough or maybe even sabotaging his chances? Actors are funny creatures and prone to emotional outbursts. I don't include Rupert in that, by the way.'

'No offence taken, Charlie, and believe me he can be emotional whenever there's a script in the wind and there might be a part in it for him. And who is your second prime suspect?'

'The younger, handsomer version the BBC want for their film, Alec Devine. If there's no one lobbying for the old guard, then the new boy gets the role.'

'The BBC are firmly set on having Alec Devine as far as I can see. They have plenty of lawyers far more highly paid than Tania Smith, I suspect, and do not seem unduly worried about the rights situation. Devine wouldn't have to resort to violence to get the part, the lawyers would do it for him.'

'Are you sure about that?'

'I'm no lawyer. My mother made me promise when I was a nipper not to become a lawyer or a politician or to take up Morris Dancing when I grew up, and I will keep that oath to the grave. However, I believe the point at issue is that Mrs Hatherall added the codicil about casting Peyton Spruce *after* the rights had been sold to the BBC.'

'Which brings us back to my suggestion that maybe Mrs

Hatherall was got at when she was in that nursing home. I think I really need to look at that list of visitors.'

'I've given it considerable thought, Charlie, and the obvious person on it who *might* have tried to influence Mrs Hatherall was Peyton Spruce himself, plus all his cronies from Curtains.'

'Curtains? What's that?'

'It's a house on Broughton Road in Ealing where Spruce lives with a rum mix of theatrical people. They used to go with him on his visits, I guess.'

'Ealing,' Luke murmured. 'That's where Lugg was sniffing around about a traffic accident involving your man Spruce. This Ealing mob, do they have anything to do with the Evadne Childe film?'

'I don't think so, they are just close chums of Peyton's, and one of them would have had to drive him down to Brighton because he doesn't drive himself.'

Campion got to his feet slowly, arching his back and stretching his long legs, having decided that sitting on the stairs in the home of a murder victim for the best part of two hours was bad for his posture. In the narrow hallway, he and Luke squared off against each other like boxers at a weigh-in, though an unbiased observer might have complained that they were clearly mismatched and from different weight divisions, as well as exhibiting little of the aggression or bombast normally expected at such encounters.

'There's something you should know about one of the names on that list, Charles.'

'I thought there might be, knowing you,' grinned Luke.

'One of Spruce's fellow residents and close friends is Brogan Bates.'

'Another actor?'

'Of a sort, more of a voice artist. You'll recognize the voice, not the face, from the radio and numerous commercials.'

'So what about him?'

'I told you I knew who Tania Smith's second husband was. After she was Mrs Spruce and before she was Mrs Smith, she was Mrs Brogan Bates.'

'And husband the first now lives in the same house as husband the second?' Campion nodded silently. 'Crikey! Talk about taking two at bedtime! That's a bit cosy, isn't it?'

'Don't jump to conclusions, Charles. I have no idea if she kept in touch with either of her exes.'

'But Rudd did?'

'I would guess so, but how does it benefit Spruce if his biggest fan and his lawyer are prevented from arguing on his behalf for a plum comeback acting job?'

Luke put on his most impressive policeman's frown.

'Spruce lives among actors, one of whom he shared a wife with, and you don't think that jealousy, pure and simple old-fashioned jealousy might not be a motive for the violence – the *passionate*, frenzied violence – on show here and in the City? Are you sure you've ever met an actor?'

By the time the police car delivered Mr Campion to the Bottle Street flat in the small hours, he was so tired that he almost tipped the constable driving him, who had asked if his passenger was feeling all right and would no doubt have offered to help him indoors had he not been reassured by the fact that the address was above a police station.

Once inside the flat, Campion headed directly for his bed, convincing himself – not that much convincing was needed – that he was far too old for such late nights spent at the scenes of violent crimes. To be honest, he was too old for late nights watching television, playing cribbage, knitting woollen mufflers or even reading improving books.

His pyjamas beckoned, almost seductively, but his brain told him there was something he had to do before he allowed his bed to engulf him.

At that hour, there was little he could manage practically, and so he found pen and paper and wrote himself an *aide-mémoire* to remind him to contact Miss Prim at Gilpin's, as she was now his main contact with the Evadne Childe Society.

In a cross between scribble and shorthand which only he could decipher, he made a note to remind him to ask her if she knew the next of kin of Tania Smith and Eric Rudd.

Even in his half-asleep state, he realized that the content of the note was somewhat grim, but it was not as forbidding as his final, scrawled reminder to himself: *Tell her not to be alone. She may be in danger.*

# EIGHTEEN
## Shepherding

'The country air seems to agree with your friend,' said Tessa Higgins, tying on an apron. 'It certainly gives him an appetite. I'll start your breakfast now.'

Rupert smiled politely, not thinking it worth informing the landlady that Lugg's appetite was a universal constant, unaffected by environmental differences.

'I'll have what he's having, please, but cut the portions in half,' he said, looking into the bar where the fat man was entrenched behind a pile of bacon, eggs and mushrooms, under which there was, presumably, a plate.

'You go and sit down, there's tea in the pot.'

'Any chance of coffee?' Rupert asked cheerfully.

'If you insist,' sniffed Mrs Higgins, returning with a flounce to the pub's kitchen, which left Rupert in no doubt that he had somehow blotted his copybook and that Lugg had now leap-frogged him into the position of Most Favoured Resident of The King's Head.

He sat opposite Lugg, defending a place setting in danger of being overwhelmed by the flotilla of plates, bread, butter, jams, cutlery and condiments which had been deemed necessary for the demolition of Lugg's breakfast. Observing him across that culinary battlefield, Rupert could only think of the word 'trencherman' and how Lugg could have been a model for a Hogarth caricature. His bulldog face, unshaven and covered in short white stubble sturdy enough to strike a match on, his open-necked collar-less shirt revealing the top of a taut string vest, and his braces hanging slackly over his shoulders, combined to form an image which would probably have persuaded other residents, had there been any, to take breakfast in their rooms.

Yet his clear appreciation of the repast set before him and the sheer guiltless gusto of the way he tackled it had clearly endeared

him to Mrs Higgins, who waited on him as though he were a
sickly child in need of building up.

'Good thing they don't have a dress code here,' Rupert said
after Mrs Higgins had firmly placed – not exactly slammed – two
jugs, one of coffee and one of hot milk, in front of him.

'Good grub, this.' Lugg smacked his lips and continued to dig
and shovel. 'Didn't want to get egg on my best gear. Egg is the
very devil to get off. You'd better think about smartening yerself
up too, after you've noshed o'course.'

'Oh really? Why?'

'Because you've gone up in the world, my lad. Yesterday you
was my driver, but today you've been promoted to chauffeur.'

If Tessa Higgins had developed a soft spot for the informal,
almost toddler-like Lugg who had demanded to be breakfasted,
it was the more formal and severe Lugg, descending from his
room an hour later, who impressed her husband Roy. So much
so that he stood ramrod straight, almost to attention, as Lugg
strode across the bar to the still-locked front door.

'Let me get that for you,' said Mr Higgins, gently shouldering
Rupert out of his way. 'We're still well short of legal opening time,
so we keep the door locked, otherwise the local chancers like Joe
Lunn would be standing at the bar with their tongues hanging out.'

The landlord stood to one side, holding the door open, as
respectful as one of the top-hatted doormen at The Savoy
welcoming a minor duke. Indeed, Lugg did cut an impressive
figure; a figure only a fool – and a drunken one at that – would
argue with. Bathed and shaved, Lugg had dressed in a fresh white
shirt with black tie, pinstripe trousers, grey waistcoat and tailed
morning coat. The bowler hat completed his uniform.

Lady Amanda would have said he was 'dressed to the nines',
and Mr Campion could not have resisted pointing out that in
medieval English the expression would have been 'to the eyne'
or 'to the eyes'. Lugg would have ignored them both. He was
dressed to intimidate.

'Don't you worry about Joe Lunn knocking your door down,'
he said as he glided out of the pub like a Dreadnought down
a slipway, 'he's working for me this morning, but we'll be in
for lunch, so you'd better get cracking on your special curry.'

The beaming smile on the publican's face followed them out to where the Jaguar was parked.

'Well, you certainly made his day,' said Rupert when they were out of earshot. 'It's not like you to leave a pub landlord so happy.'

'Some would say – though no names, no pack drill, but I mean your pa – that an innkeeper is *only* happy when I leave, but I reckon that's just rude.'

Lugg stood beside the Jaguar, clearly waiting for Rupert to open the rear door for him, and after ten seconds of looking innocently at the hillsides and softly whistling a jolly melody, Rupert succumbed to the pressure of Lugg's steely gaze and reached for the door handle.

'Where to, sir?'

'Through the village and up the hill. There's supposed to be a lay-by or parking spot on the left.'

'There is, we turned round there when I drove Pa.'

'And that's where we're meeting Joe Lunn.' Lugg pulled a half-hunter from a waistcoat pocket. 'We've plenty of time, though, so go slow passing the beatnik camp.'

The big man squeezed himself into the rear seat directly behind the driver, and stared imperiously straight ahead, not flinching when Rupert closed the car door with more force than was absolutely necessary.

The Jaguar purred through Kingswalter and Lugg had a perfect view of The Prophetics' encampment, though The Prophetics themselves did not seem to be up and about but still cocooned in their vehicles and tents.

'Looks like they're having a lie-in,' said Rupert over his shoulder.

'Late night,' grunted Lugg, 'and one with no ghosts to spot, thanks to the noise.'

'Noise?'

'Tessa at the pub told me' – Rupert noted the implied familiarity – 'the young fellow-me-lad up the manor started playing pop music around midnight. It was a racket loud enough to wake the dead, except it didn't. Mebbe the spirits didn't like Ranald's taste in music. Shouldn't think I would've if I'd 'eard it, but I didn't as I was sleeping the sleep of the just.'

Rupert bit his lip at that and concentrated on his driving, changing down a gear as the Jaguar began to climb out of the

village. As before, his fear on that narrow road was to meet
something big and agricultural coming the other way, and his
heart leapt towards his throat as he saw a tractor pulling a high-
sided trailer top the summit of the road ahead. He did a rapid
calculation to judge whether, if he accelerated, he could make
the lay-by up ahead, but then he was able to exhale as he
saw the tractor and its load turn to its right and enter the lay-by
itself.

'Pull in beside him,' said Lugg from the back seat. 'I need to
inspect me troops, then you can lead the convoy back down
the hill.'

As he did so, Rupert recognized the tractor driver, despite the
flat cap pulled low over his brow, as Joe Lunn, and also noted that
the tractor displayed neither a tax disc nor number plates. He
wondered if he would in fact be leading a convoy or driving a
getaway car.

He felt Lugg's knees nudge him in the small of the back through
his seat.

'Door!' came the command. 'Must keep up appearances.'

Rupert sprang into chauffeur mode. It was all good practice, as
he might one day land a role as a chauffeur in a television series
set around a country house in the Thirties, a proper country manor,
not like the one Ranald Ward-Tetley ran. The galling thing was
that Lugg was unlikely to appreciate his performance as he dived
out of the Jaguar and positively quivered to attention, allowing his
distinguished passenger to exit the car.

'Cor blimey!' Joe Lunn shouted as he turned off the tractor's
engine. 'Are you a bailiff or is you late for a funeral?'

Lugg drew himself up to his full width and sniffed loudly in
disdain. 'I'll take none of your lip, Joe Lunn. You done what you
said you would?'

Joe Lunn eased himself back on the tractor's metal seat, which
had been padded with folded hessian sacks, and jerked a thumb
back over his shoulder to the trailer behind him. 'Oh aye, I got
them,' he said, and now the tractor's engine was quiet, it was
possible to hear the constant bleating of Lugg's recently recruited
commandos, but whether they were anxious for battle or merely
annoyed at being plucked from their morning grazing on the hillside, it was impossible to tell.

What Lugg actually knew about sheep could probably have been written in broad brushstroke calligraphy on the back of a beer mat, but he gave a convincing performance – not that he had an audience which needed impressing – of a man who could be a connoisseur of livestock. Standing on the wheel arch of the trailer, keeping his morning suit well away from the muck and rust which coated it, he hauled himself up into a position where he could peer down into the trailer and inspect, or at least count, his troops.

He descended to ground level looking satisfied, passed money from his wallet into the open hands of Joe Lunn, and then went and stood by the Jaguar waiting for the door to be opened.

'What exactly is the plan?' Rupert asked once he was behind the wheel again.

'Down the 'ill and into that field where them hippies have parked, we're reclaiming the *passchewer* for its rightful owners.'

It took Rupert a moment to decipher the word 'pasture'.

'We're going to turn the sheep loose in there?'

'It's got grass, hasn't it? That's their natural 'abitat, not like them ghost-hunters. I reckon most of them will be townies and not used to the ways of us country folk.'

'Since when did you become a rustic son of the soil?'

Rupert looked in his driving mirror and saw that his passenger was genuinely indignant as he responded.

'I've always loved the countryside. There's hardly nothing you can't eat here.'

The Prophetics' camp was rudely awakened by the rumble of Joe Lunn's tractor, the rattle of its trailer, and the over-revving of the Jaguar's engine as Rupert negotiated the lumps and bumps of grass and offered a silent prayer that it had not rained recently so he would not have to suffer the indignity of being stuck in a muddy field under the disapproving glare of Lugg and the threat of the opprobrium of the car's owner.

From the tents and vehicles they emerged, wearing a vast assortment of clothing from conventional striped pyjamas accessorized by wellington boots, to one hardy soul who climbed with some difficulty out of the back of a Reliant Robin wearing at least three pullovers and an overcoat. They staggered around, confused and uncertain, like shell-shocked troops when a barrage has finally lifted or zombies in a Hammer horror film, and slowly they gravitated to the Jaguar, where Lugg in all his glory stood, legs apart, his ample buttocks resting on the side of the bonnet.

'May I have your attention!' he bellowed, frightening the sheep in the trailer into another chorus of loud bleating, which further distracted the stumbling Prophetics.

'What's going on?'

The door of a nearby camper van was flung open, and Miss Sally DeLuca hopped into the fray. Rupert, who had stayed in the car, shrank down behind the steering wheel, but wound his window down an inch or two so that he could hear.

'Are you the lady in charge of this gathering?' Lugg asked her in what he felt was the voice of a prosecuting barrister.

'I suppose so,' said Miss DeLuca, and her supporters nodded in agreement. 'Who are you? And whose are those sheep?'

'I am here representing the County Sheriff,' Lugg declaimed as if addressing a jury, as he thought this was the persona a County Sheriff would adopt, if Dorset had one and he was pretty sure it did, when faced with a rioting mob of farm labourers demanding the right to be in a union, but then Lugg's grasp of civic affairs outside London – and of history – was generally vague. 'And those fine animals are the new residents of this prime piece of bottom-valley grazing land.'

He was rather proud of the addition of 'bottom-valley'; although he had no idea what it meant, he was willing to bet that neither did The Prophetics.

'It's a car park!' wailed Sally, fists clenched at her side. Her outrage did not match her apparel as, although she had a grey-green anorak bearing West German army insignia draped around her shoulders, the effect was spoiled by the fact that she was wearing a set of pink nylon pyjamas with lace trimming around the Mary Jane collar, which did not fit well with the open-tongued, unlaced hobnail boots into which she had hurriedly thrust her feet. It was as if she had been posing for a fashion shoot for *Woman's Own* which had been interrupted by a military coup.

'I think you'll find that *legally*' – Lugg savoured the word – 'it's a field or, at a pinch, a paddock, though your solicitors are free to contest that before the local magistrates.'

He squinted suspiciously at Miss DeLuca, as if daring her to take up the challenge or at least admit she did not have legal representation.

'Thought not,' he said to himself, before getting back into pompous character. 'If you be the leader of this gathering, miss, then I'm afraid I must serve you due notice that this field will be returned to grazing land and advise you to vacate, taking any rubbish and litter with you in accordance with the county's policy of keeping Dorset tidy.'

The Prophetics began to congregate around Sally, confused and demanding to know what was going on, several of them prodding her or nudging her towards their nemesis, who remained implacable, arms crossed, jaw jutting.

'We have the permission of the landowner to remain here,' shouted Sally, her voice wavering, her hands tugging the edge of her anorak over the pink pyjamas.

'Not any more, darling. Mr Ward-Tetley has had a change of heart pending a visit from the authorities and all previous verbal permissions and . . . arrangements . . .' in the Jaguar, Rupert sank even lower in his seat, cringing at Lugg's attempts at subtlety, '. . . are hereby rescinded and revoked. Henceforth, the only thing parked here will be sheep.'

'You're evicting us?'

'I'm doing no such thing!' Lugg was indignant and clearly enjoying the experience. 'I'm merely giving you notice that the landowner's sheep are reclaiming their grazing rights.'

Miss DeLuca flung her arms out in supplication, revealing a considerable amount of pink nylon. 'When is this supposed to happen?'

'Right about now,' said Lugg reasonably, touching a forefinger to the rim of his bowler.

It was a signal which Joe Lunn picked up on immediately, as he jumped down from the tractor and scurried to the back of the trailer. He rapidly unhooked its rear gate, and heaved out a long wooden rectangle to serve as a disembarkation ramp for its complaining passengers.

Suspiciously at first, one adventurous animal clumped its way down the ramp, sniffing the air, no doubt seeking something fresh to nibble on. Then another and then two more followed, as seemed to be the way with sheep. Joe Lunn climbed halfway up the ramp and helped three more out by slapping them gently across the face with his flat cap, as though challenging them to a duel. By the time the last one had descended in something of a woollen heap thanks to Joe Lunn's boot, the first of the flock were gambolling through the camp, in between the vehicles and actually, in one case, into one of the tents, to a symphony of squeals and panicked shouting as The Prophetics ran to and fro to protect their property from the ovine invasion.

Lugg decided it was time to twist the knife, just as Sally DeLuca was aiming a kick at the rump of one inquisitive animal sampling the grass around her camper van.

'These sheep are thoroughbred and valuable livestock, and if any harm comes to a single one of them, there will be consequences,' he bellowed. 'The local laws of Dorset are strict, and sheep rustlers have always been treated severely, as the grandfathers of half the population of Australia will testify.'

Rupert shrank even further into his seat, although his embarrassment went totally unnoticed. The Prophetics were far too busy gathering their belongings and packing their cars and vans; some had even started their engines. Only Sally DeLuca had not run for cover, but had remained near her camper van, watching in disbelief as the sheep flocked by her, aiming for the lushest grass on the lower slopes of the hills at the far end of the field.

'Told you they were mostly townies,' said Lugg out of the corner of his mouth. 'Scared of a few woolly lambs! Now if we'd released a herd of pigs, they would've had to scarper for their lives. Pigs don't take prisoners.'

After delivering this homily, he eased his backside off the Jaguar's bonnet, which Rupert swore relaxed the car's suspension, and strode over to the distraught Sally DeLuca.

'There, there, miss,' soothed Lugg, 'I know you meant no harm, but you're in the wrong place at the wrong time.'

'What do you know?' asked Sally, determined not to let this self-important bully see her eyes moistening.

'I know there's no ghosts in Kingswalter and, no matter 'ow many midnight vigils you 'old, the ghost of Ivy Trimble isn't going to appear.'

The woman turned on her tormentor sharply. 'What do you know about Ivy Trimble?'

'I knows what happened to her, tragic as it was back in 1944, but she's never put in an appearance since, and your lot are only here because there *might* be the off-chance of a haunting.'

'What are you getting at?'

'Listen, love,' Lugg moved in gentle, grandfatherly mode, 'did it never occur to you that the whole Kingswalter Massacre story was handed to you on a plate to make you think that there must be a ghost here?'

'Are you saying I'm suggestible?'

'I'm not sure if that's proper, my dear lady, so I'm not committing myself. What I'm saying is why are you and your . . . followers . . . wasting your time trying to guess where ghosts *might* appear, when you could be investigating places where there's more known sightings than you could shake a stick at?'

'So you're not just a landowner's lackey or whatever it is you are, but you're an expert on psychic phenomenon?'

Lugg reacted as if shocked to the core. ''Ow many spirits have you actually seen, miss? And I don't mean in some fancy cocktail bar, 'cos I've seen at least two ghostly apparitions in what must be one of the most 'aunted places in England.'

'You have?' Lugg now had Miss DeLuca's full attention.

'Too right I have, and I've got testimonials to back me up, from people with loads of letters after their names. Verified sightings they were, shook me to the core.' He lifted his bowler to reveal his shiny bald pate. 'Resulted in sleepless nights and massive 'air loss.'

'And what form did these verified apparitions take?' asked a sceptical but clearly intrigued Miss DeLuca.

'One was what they call a woodland spirit, took the form of a goat standing on its hind legs so it looked nine feet tall. Scared a titled lady to death, a Lady Petherick, and now *she* haunts the place. You can look that up. There was a professor there at the time, Professor Cairey, who wrote it all up, but that's only half the story because the same place has an old tower where there's a secret room in which lives the worst of the spirits, who nobody's ever seen and lived to tell the tale, but many have felt its presence.'

Rupert, straining to hear Lugg's dramatic rendition, failed to see how anyone could be taken in by his blatant overacting, but it appeared that Miss DeLuca was hooked.

'Where is this place?'

'It's a village called Sanctuary up in Suffolk.'

'Never heard of it.'

'Not surprising, they keep themselves to themselves up there, what with all their secrets and ghostly goings-on. It's a sleepy little place on the surface, wiv a church an' a pub called The Three Drummers. Even got a public campsite called Pharisees' Clearing, a lovely spot in the woods.'

Not only hooked, thought Rupert, but being reeled in. Any minute now she'd get her *AA Book of the Road* out and be asking for directions.

It took a good hour for The Prophetics to pack up and drive out of the field, heading towards Dorchester in a ragged convoy. Sally's camper van was the last to leave, its driver hunched over the steering wheel, concentrating on the view through the windscreen. She never acknowledged Lugg's polite bow or Joe Lunn cheerily waving his cap in a circle around his head.

The sheep had made themselves at home and were slowly spreading over the hillside. Lunn took a toolbox and a coil of barbed wire from his tractor and said he would string a strand or two across the entrance to the field in case any of 'them daft beasts' had a mind to wander out on to the road, so Lugg had better move the Jaguar while he could.

Determined to play out his part to the maximum, Lugg moved to the driver's window and rapped on it twice with his knuckles.

Grimacing with weary annoyance, Rupert climbed out and opened the rear door for his distinguished passenger, who looked around the green and pleasant hills as if he was seeing them for the first, or possibly last, time.

'I loves the countryside,' said Mr Lugg, 'there's *nachure* everywhere you look. Blue skies, green grass, and them sheep up there on the hills like little fluffy clouds. Makes you appreciate the beauty of things.'

As he bent to squeeze himself into the car, it was as if he had remembered something important and he swivelled his huge head until he could see Joe Lunn.

'Joe! You'll be joining us at the pub for a spot of lunch, won't you? I've got a sudden hankering for mutton curry.'

They found that The King's Head was doing its best lunchtime trade for some time, which Rupert put down to the undercurrent of mutterings about 'now the weirds have gone', at the bar on which the locals leaned whilst exchanging pleasantries with a smiling Tessa Higgins.

Roy Higgins was also smiling as he greeted Lugg, clearly his most favoured customer, and showed him to a table with a small Reserved sign sandwiched between salt and pepper pots before hastily setting a third place for Joe Lunn. The locals at the bar, though, only had eyes for Lugg, resplendent in his uniform of – well, no one was quite sure. It was a form of dress many had not seen since the last televised state funeral, and though bowler hat and frock coat were not the usual dress code for rural Dorset, unless there was a hunt meeting, the ample figure inhabiting those clothes was clearly at home sitting in a captain's chair with a pint mug in his fist, being waited on hand and foot by mine host.

'I've cooked up a fresh curry this morning, Mr Lugg.'

'Mutton?'

'Of course.'

'Good, let's be having it; I've worked up quite an appetite. Trade's looking up.'

'It is indeed, Mr Lugg; let's hope it lasts.'

'I reckon you'll be seeing some new customers soon. Just remember what I told you.'

Roy Higgins gave him a piratical wink and tapped a forefinger to the side of his nose before hurrying back to the kitchen.

'What was that all about?' asked Rupert.

Conscious that he was still attracting stares and straining ears from the locals at the bar, Lugg leaned forward and spoke softly. 'I told him that whatever trade he might lose from a few off-sales to those hippies on their midnight vigils, he'd more than make up from the film crew who will soon be arriving. Could be an opportunity for some outside catering too, by special appointment to the BBC.'

'How can you possibly arrange that?'

'I can't, but I reckon your father can. If I know 'im, he'll make sure they owe him a few favours for getting them out of a scrape, and it'll be a case of the old "quid pro quo", as the lawyers might say.'

Joe Lunn, who had been listening intently, also leaned forward to join the conspiratorial huddle. 'Don't know if Roy will go along with that,' he said, folding his arms on the table. 'He don't get on with them BBC chaps, not since one of them went down with food poisoning from his kitchen.'

Lugg turned his steeliest glare on him.

'Piffle! That weren't his fault, and anyway, the bloke didn't die – well, not so's I've heard. There's nothing wrong with the land-lord's curry an' I'm living proof of that, and you will be too because I've ordered three servings.'

'Did you meet that BBC man who ended up in hospital, Joe?' asked Rupert casually.

'No, not I,' Lunn said quickly. 'I was over in Bridport at a darts match that night.'

'But you did meet one of the BBC's location scouts in the past, a couple of months ago, didn't you?'

Lunn considered his answer carefully, clearly more worried about Lugg's reaction than Rupert's. 'I met a chap. He was staying here. Not sure what he did, but he was interested in the manor and the old abbey gardens and he said he was on expenses, so we had a few beers together.'

'And you told him the story of the Kingswalter Massacre?'

Rupert noticed the look on Lugg's face – a mixture of curiosity and, dare he think it, admiration? Was he actually receiving Lugg's approval for asking the question his father would have?

'Probably I did,' said Lunn. 'He seemed interested in anything to do with the village.'

'And it kept him buying the drinks,' Lugg pointed out.

Joe Lunn did not deny it. 'I'm the village character, it's what I do, but he was a nice enough chap.'

'What was his name?' asked Rupert.

'Don't know I ever heard it.' Lunn shook his head. 'He was just a man in a pub.'

'Can you describe him?'

Lunn's head shook more violently. 'I told you, it was just a bloke, on his own, looking for a bit of company and some intelligent conversation.'

That drew a loud derisive snort from Lugg, which made Joe Lunn squirm.

'So nothing memorable about this chap from the BBC?' Rupert persisted.

'Nothing,' said Lunn, 'apart from his crappy motor.'

'What about it?'

'It was one of those rubbish French things.'

'You'll have to be more specific than that,' said Lugg, toying dangerously with a fork.

'You must know the story. After the war, the Americans left a load of lawnmower engines in France, and the Brits left a load of metal dustbins. The Frogs put them together and built a little van which was ugly and noisy but did the job, and then the French post office bought a ton of them and painted them yellow. You see 'em everywhere in Frogland, but you notice them in Dorset. Probably very fashionable in Ealing.'

'Ealing?' pounced Rupert.

'I just remembered,' said Lunn, pronouncing it remember-ed, as if citing Shakespeare. 'He mentioned he was from Ealing, up London way. Ealing, that's like in the Ealing Comedies, isn't it?'

# NINETEEN
## Take Two at Bedtime

'Are you sure this is something you should be involved in, Albert?' said Lady Amanda, sounding uncomfortably as if she was at her husband's shoulder and not over one hundred and twenty miles away down a telephone line. 'No, don't answer that; I don't know why I asked. You've made a career out of burrowing into other people's problems.'

'I do feel somewhat obligated, darling.'

'Because of Evadne Childe? She wouldn't thank you for trying to protect her legacy, if that's what you think you're doing. Evadne never wanted a fuss made about her books.'

'I'm not making a fuss, my dear, but a fuss is being made by someone and it is nasty, criminal and now murderous.'

'Which is why you should let the police handle it.'

'They are handling it, and I've even strong-armed Charlie Luke into taking an interest in the case.'

'I can't see Charles being bullied into anything by you, but if he's on the job with the entire Metropolitan Police at his disposal, what on Earth do you think you can do to help?' Mr Campion heard his wife sigh heavily into the telephone. 'Don't answer that either,' she said, 'I know you too well. You've already made your mind up that you are uniquely placed to sort out this mess and bring peace and justice to all concerned parties.'

'I would not go that far, but I do feel I can provide a particular service and one which should be done out of common decency if nothing else.'

'Explain yourself,' said his wife, but it was an invitation not an admonition.

'It concerns that poor woman, Tania Smith, who died the other day in the City. The police are having trouble tracing any next of kin, and it just so happens that I have discovered that two of her previous husbands—'

'Two?'

'She had three in total.'

'How energetic.'

'Well, we know the most recent one is deceased, but curiously, the first two now live in the same house in Ealing.'

Across the miles from Norfolk there was a heavy silence.

'You are joking.'

'My dear, I never joke about the monarchy, income tax or a lady's former spouses. That is the plural of spouse, isn't it? Or should that be spice?'

'Don't be inane, darling; after thirty years of marriage, I'm not taken in any more. Seriously, though, two ex-husbands living together in Ealing? Is this a story Lugg came up with after a night down the British Legion?'

'It most certainly is not and, anyway, the British Legion would never have Lugg as a member. It's absolutely true and really rather bizarre, but Tania Smith was married first to Peyton Spruce—'

'Good grief!'

'And then to Peyton's great friend, Brogan Bates. It's even rumoured that they were best man at each other's weddings. This, of course, was ages ago, back in the war years I think, when strange things happened.'

'Clearly. How the dickens did you find this out?'

'Oh, I didn't, it was Rupert. He did all the detective work.'

'Did he now?'

Mr Campion swore he could hear his wife's brain whirring and he knew what was coming. 'And this is all to do with a new detective series for the television . . .'

'Yes . . .' Campion agreed hesitantly.

'So he's really auditioning for a part, isn't he?'

Breaking bad news – the worst sort of news – to next of kin was a task Mr Campion avoided at all costs, and his heart went out to the policemen, and increasingly policewomen, who were charged with such an onerous duty. Yet in this case he felt it was a duty he had to perform, though he was not quite sure why. Amanda would have said it was out of a misplaced sense of obligation to the memory of Evadne Childe, for he had no connection with the deceased, Tania Smith; indeed, he had never met her, and surely it was a freakish coincidence that her two ex-husbands were living quietly in Curtains out in Ealing. Or perhaps not so quietly, as Peyton Spruce might be on the brink of a career revival, for which his ex-wife had appeared to be campaigning. And as all that revolved around the new version of *The Moving Mosaic*, Campion justified his intervention on the grounds that he should do whatever he could to ensure that Evadne Childe's work received the best treatment possible. It also seemed the only decent thing to do.

Deep in thought in the back of the taxi he had hailed at Hyde Park Corner, Campion came to the conclusion that all roads lead not to Rome but to Ealing, and specifically Curtains on Broughton Road.

Everything that had happened had that house or its inhabitants somewhere in the background. The late Mrs Hatherall, who had started *The Moving Mosaic* hare running, had been visited by its residents. Eric Rudd had actively encouraged Campion to go there to meet with Peyton Spruce. There he had found Brogan Bates (who, it turned out, shared more than a bathroom with Spruce), only one of an eccentric cast of housemates. There was Anastasia Tempest, known on the electoral roll as Alice Dubbs, and to Lugg and no doubt countless others of a certain vintage as the Clapham Cossack; a music hall comedian who did not look as if he had laughed in the last two decades; and the shy and retiring Sheila Kaye, a make-up artist who, Campion suspected, spent most of her waking hours in a labour of love keeping Peyton Spruce looking young enough to be ready for any full-screen close-up required.

He had toyed with the idea of telephoning ahead, but decided against it, as bad news, when it has to be delivered, is best done face to face, without announcing that it was en route and making the intended recipients suffer in agonized anticipation. That still left him with the challenge of telling not one man, but two, that their ex-wife had died in unpleasant circumstances.

He reflected on Luke's rather off-colour remark about 'taking two at bedtime' and dismissed it as unhelpful. He was not aware that Spruce and Bates had engaged in a *ménage à trois* with Mrs Spruce, or, for that matter, Mrs Bates as she became, but it was surely such an odd relationship that it might have raised an eyebrow even in France, where the actor and his friend had lived. Was there a motive in that relationship which had been festering for perhaps twenty years, and if so, a motive for what? When he had seen them together, Campion had detected a genuine bond of friendship, even though the characters of the two men were as different as chalk and cheese. Spruce struck him as vain, very conscious of his image, and unwilling to accept that his career had ended, but then he was an actor, whereas Bates was the loud, hail-fellow-well-met sort of man who was happy to live a semi-Bohemian existence as long as the house bar was well stocked and he had a stooge like 'Tommy Tuppence' he could bully.

Perhaps he was overthinking the problem and not seeing the wood for the trees. Charles Luke had been convinced that jealousy was at the root of it all, an emotion not uncommon in the world of the performing arts, and Campion recognized that all the residents of Curtains were, in their own way, 'artistes'. But which of them would be jealous of which other and why? If any of them resented the fact that Peyton Spruce might revive an old role and thus the dying embers of his career, it would explain the litany of misfortunes which had affected the new production of *The Moving Mosaic*, though that was such a widespread campaign of disruption, if all the incidents were connected, ranging from a hit-and-run road accident to an assault with a cricket bat on one BBC man and the food poisoning of another, to the disruption of the main filming location by The Prophetics and the violent deaths of two of Spruce's supporters. But was simple jealousy a sufficient motive for such a catalogue of orchestrated malice, even among theatricals? More to the point, they were *old* theatricals; all, like himself, well past pensionable age, who had lived together for some time, giving them ample opportunity to settle old scores, which could rule out revenge as a motive.

But when two principal players in his cast of characters, as Campion was beginning to think of them, shared an ex-wife, perhaps revenge came into the equation somewhere.

If nothing else, it left him with a conundrum: to which ex-husband should he first break the news that his former wife had died?

'Good afternoon, Mr Champion.'

'It's Campion, actually, as in the small but perfectly formed white or pink flower.'

'I prefer "Mr Champion". It would look so much better on the billing; a novelty turn perhaps, below the magician but above the comedy double-act.'

'That sounds about right, Miss Dubbs,' said Campion, doffing his fedora. 'May I come in?'

'Gentlemen Callers always welcome! Do you know, it once said that on the bottom of a theatre bill I was on! Hard to believe these days.'

'I hardly think stars of your calibre had the need to advertise in such an uncouth way.'

'That is most gallant of you, Mr Campion, and it would be even more gracious if you said you were here to see me, but I suspect you are not.'

'You are wise beyond your legendary persona as the Clapham Cossack, Miss Dubbs. I am here to see Peyton and probably Brogan Bates as well.'

'Probably?'

'I am afraid I bring sad news.'

'You mean there isn't a part for him in this *Moving Mosaic* thing?'

'About that I could not say. I'm afraid it's a more personal matter.'

'Then come on in, they're both here. Peyton's been going over his old script, so may be a bit sensitive, doing his lines with Brogan, though that hairy ape had far too much wine at lunchtime and probably thinks he's rehearsing *Hamlet*.'

Campion took a deep breath and followed those famous Clapham legs and hips, decorously covered by an ankle-length blue velvet dress drawn tight at the waist, into the house. She showed him the door to the front room – the Green Room, as they called it – and said she would put the kettle on for tea. Although Campion demurred politely, resistance was futile.

He entered without knocking to find Peyton Spruce in the middle of the room, down on one knee, scratching at the carpet with a garden trowel. He was wearing brown cord trousers, a tweed jacket with leather elbow patches and a battered trilby with a green feather cockade. When he glanced up as the door opened, Campion could see he was in full make-up.

'Don't mind Sprucey,' said Brogan Bates from behind the make-shift bar, 'he insists on getting fully into character.'

'Rex Troughton, out on an archaeological dig, complete with his trademark trilby,' said Campion. 'It looks just like the one in the film.'

'It is,' said Spruce, rising, with some stiffness, to his feet. 'I claimed it as a souvenir when the film wrapped.'

He looked down at the trowel he was holding and then at his tartan-slippered feet. 'Had to borrow this from Tommy Tuppence, though it's not the right sort of trowel, more for potting plants rather than archaeology, and I didn't dare wear my digging boots indoors. Alice would have had a fit. What can I do for you, Mr Campion?'

Brogan Bates thumped his forearms on the bar top, spilling red wine from the glass he was clutching. 'Of course he's here to see *you*, the star of the show,' he sneered. 'Why else would anyone call, if not to catch the main attraction?'

Campion decided it was not the time for discretion, nor to take into account Brogan's delicate feelings, for clearly the man had none worth considering. 'Actually, I am here to see you both,' said Campion, 'and I have some very personal questions to ask you, if I may interrupt your rehearsal.'

'Interrupt away, old chum!' said Bates, toasting Campion with his glass then draining it. 'This has been more of a dressing-up game than a rehearsal.'

Campion shot a glance towards Spruce to note how he took the slight, but it turned out not to have been an insult.

'Peyton is as word-perfect now as he was twenty years ago,' Bates continued, reaching for a new bottle and a corkscrew. 'Rex Troughton was always his favourite part, perhaps his best part. He was a natural for the role and still is. The bones might creak a bit, but the acting chops are still all there and Sheila, our make-up wizard – or should that be witch? – keeps him looking young, even if it does cost a fortune in Leichner powders and greasepaint.'

'Thank you, Brogan,' said Spruce, who then turned to Campion, 'and that, believe it or not, was what passes for a compliment from my old and distinguished friend Mr Bates.'

The two men exchanged a glance of affection which Campion recognized as a genuinely sincere exchange between two elderly male friends, or two very good actors.

'I think perhaps we should sit down,' said Campion. 'Miss Dubbs is making tea and I would like to get one or two things straight before she returns.'

'Sounds serious,' said Spruce.

'Sounds positively ripe if it can't be said in front of Alice,' said Bates, emerging from behind the bar, bottle in one hand, glass in the other.

'Well, that's rather up to you, I suppose. The two of you.'

'Come on then, let's have it,' challenged Bates. 'Me and Sprucey are old comrades, you're not going to shock us.'

That, thought Campion, remained to be seen.

'I must begin by asking you some personal questions, I'm afraid, just to get things straight in my head.'

'My dear sir, ask away.' Peyton leaned forward in the chair he had taken and pulled a pipe from his top jacket pocket. He sucked on it and tapped the stem on his teeth but made no attempt to light it. He was, Campion realized, still in character as Rex Troughton.

'It's about your wife, Tania. The wife of both of you.'

'Oh, that old thing!' spluttered Bates, then corrected himself. 'By which I don't mean sweet little Tania, I mean that old story, which they bring up at every blessed opportunity.'

'It is something we are used to being asked about,' said Spruce smoothly. 'I doubt very much you will shock us or cause offence, which I doubt is your purpose. What can we tell you?'

'Start with when you met and married Tania.'

'It was a wartime romance. I was a few years older than she was and she was an orphan of the Blitz, making ends meet as a hoofer – that's a dancer – in the chorus line, including The Windmill, which is where I met her at an after-show party.'

'An orphan of the Blitz?'

'Her family was bombed out down the East End, mother and father killed. Left her with nothing, absolutely nothing. She even had to get a replacement identity card. I remember that because we had to use it to get a marriage licence, though things were pretty lax during the war. It was 1942 and I was in uniform – only the Pay Corps, nothing heroic, but it counted.'

'And what was her maiden name?'

'Parsloe.' Spruce smiled sheepishly. 'We nicknamed her our little sprig of parsley, though she was never too keen on it.'

'How long did the marriage last?'

'Legally, about eighteen months, emotionally no more than three. There was an inevitability about it really: a chorus girl, a man in uniform, the blackout, the war. She was in London, I ended up in Catterick.'

'Without implying anything untoward,' Campion turned his innocently vacant stare on Brogan Bates, 'were you in London during the war?'

His face now pink, but probably due to wine rather than embarrassment, Brogan barked a laugh. 'Be as indelicate as you like, old chum! God knows, we've heard it all before. Yes, I was in London during the war, doing my bit on the BBC's French service, reading out those coded messages for the Resistance because I was a dab-hand at speaking Frog. No idea what the secret messages meant, of course, but I like to think what I did made a bit of a difference. Didn't get any thanks for it, just snipey little bits in the gossip columns about stepping out with an actor's wife. And yes, there was something untoward going on, as you put it. *Very* untoward. Tania was a sweet little thing and very energetic.'

Bates curbed the leer he was giving Campion and waved his glass towards Spruce, who was sitting relaxed and calm, his handsome features totally untroubled. 'Don't worry about Sprucey; he knows all this and he was very decent about it at the time, all things considered. Once the divorce came through in '45 I made an honest woman of little Tania and Mrs Spruce became Mrs Bates – for a while – and again the papers had a field day. One of them even said "greater love hath no man than that he lays down his wife for his friend" – damn cheek.'

'Have we shocked you, Mr Campion?' asked Spruce, as though genuinely concerned.

'No,' said Campion slowly, 'not shocked. Surprised, perhaps. So when did Mrs Bates became Mrs Smith?'

'Who?' said Spruce and Bates together.

Mr Campion had not been seeking a natural break in order to regroup his thoughts, but welcomed it when it came in the form of the noise of an unruly car engine grinding and clanking to a halt in the road outside.

Brogan Bates sat up with ears pricked. 'The old girl's back in one piece,' he said with a nod of satisfaction.

Campion, aware of car doors slamming and footsteps approaching the front door, got to his feet. 'Excuse me for one moment, gentlemen. I want to continue but I do not want us to be disturbed.'

He made it into the hallway just as the front door was opened by the short, somewhat harassed figure of Sheila Kaye, clutching a white paper bag with Boots printed on it to her chest, a door key in one hand and a set of car keys dangling from between clenched teeth.

'Oh hullo, Mr Campionth, were we exthpecting youth?' she asked before realizing the keys were restricting her diction.

'No, no one was. I dropped in to have a private word with Peyton and Brogan.'

Sheila Kaye misjudged Campion's look of concern. 'Don't mind me, I won't disturb you, I'll just put this lot in the bathroom.' She tilted her shopping so Campion could see it was crammed with boxes and tubes of make-up, the name Leichner very much in evidence. 'Then I'll stay out of your way.'

'That's kind of you, but you surprised me. I didn't know you could drive.'

The woman looked at him as if he was mad. 'I don't have a car, but I can drive. I have a licence. Do you need to see it?'

'No, of course not. It's just that I thought Brogan was the only driver in the house.'

'He's the only one with a vehicle, clapped-out old van though it be. We all use it; well, when I say all, I mean me and Tommy. Alice is too old and too grand to take a driving test at her age and Peyton, bless him, never learned. That's why you never saw him behind a wheel in his films, it was always a stuntman or a double. Tommy and I have the use of Brogan's van whenever he's over the limit, if you know what I mean, which is actually quite often these days.'

'I understand,' Campion said, moving aside to allow Sheila to squeeze by him. 'Did Tommy not go shopping with you today?'

'Tommy? Not likely. If it's not to buy plants or something for the garden, Tommy's not interested. He practically lives out in that shed of his but magically' – Sheila's gaze moved beyond Campion's face and down the hallway – 'he can hear a kettle being boiled even down at the bottom of the garden.'

Campion followed her gaze and saw Tommy 'Tuppence' Taylor through the open kitchen door. He was making no effort to help Miss Dubbs with her tea-making, rather stood there, dirt-soiled hands down by the sides of his dungarees, staring silent and unblinking directly at them.

'So neither of you knew that Tania had remarried and become Mrs Giles Smith?'

Spruce and Bates shook their heads in unison. As far as Campion could tell, they had not moved during his foray into the hall, though the level of red wine in Bates's glass had risen – perhaps more than once.

'Tania and I were divorced in 1952,' said Brogan, 'the year golden boy here starred in *The Moving Mosaic* the first time round.'

'Did you go on location for the filming?'

'What, down to Dorset? Yes, 'course I did. Had to support an old chum; that's what chums do.'

'Did Tania accompany you?'

'Good god, no, that would have been fodder for the film mags, wouldn't it? No, Tania and I had gone our separate ways by then. Never seen her since, as a matter of fact. Who did she get her claws into after me?'

'Brogan!' hissed Spruce. 'There's no need for that.'

'A chap in the City called Giles Smith, but that marriage didn't last either,' said Campion carefully.

'And this was when?'

'I think it would be around 1957 or '58.'

'By which time we were living the low life in France, making wine, *eh, mon vieux ami*?' Bates flapped a hand to slap Spruce's thigh, and the actor smiled as a fond memory returned.

'And films, I understand,' observed Campion.

Spruce smiled his most charming *Photoplay* smile. 'Some bloody awful films, but thankfully no one over here got to see them. I rarely knew what was going on with those French directors and I always blamed Brogan for reading all those bad scripts for me.'

'There was one which I think was called *D'ici à là . . .*'

Bates burst into loud guffaws of laughter. 'That was a corker! You remember the beach scene with that young French girl and you trying to look like Burt Lancaster? If the tide hadn't come in quicker than expected, that could have been really steamy and you'd have only seen it in one of those peep shows down in Soho.'

'I'm surprised you've heard of it, Mr Campion,' said Spruce with a self-deprecating smile. 'Don't tell me you've actually seen it.'

'No, no,' said Campion rather too quickly, 'but stills from it, showing that particular beach scene, were sent to the BBC and others in an attempt to discredit you. Any idea where someone might acquire such things?'

'Apart from my bedroom,' said Bates gruffly, 'no bloody idea.'

'Your bedroom? Here at Curtains?'

'It's the only one I have! I've got a few souvenirs from the old days that I saved from the rag-and-bone man. Got a few movie posters and a stack of old stills.' He grinned lewdly at Spruce. 'But only the raunchiest ones. You're welcome to go through them. They're in a pile on a shelf held down by a cricket bat.'

'A cricket bat?' Campion was all ears.

'Oh, I don't play, I pinched it from the BBC's sound effects department years ago. Makes a useful paperweight.'

'Mr Campion, what has all this got to do with our ex-wife?'

asked Spruce. 'I feel you are avoiding getting to the point. Let me assure you, there is nothing you can say about Tania which would shock or disturb either of us.'

'That remains to be seen.' Campion leaned forward and concentrated on the faces of both men. 'You say you didn't know Tania as Tania Smith, who was a lawyer employed by Eric Rudd and the Evadne Childe Society in dealings with the BBC on the new film of *The Moving Mosaic*.'

'Tania? Little Parsley, a lawyer?' scoffed Bates in disbelief, while Spruce shook his head slowly.

'I am assured she was, and I am afraid I have to use the past tense. Tania Smith, the former wife of both of you, died violently the other night and the police, quite correctly in my opinion, suspect murder.'

The crash of a dropped tray packed with plates, cups, jugs, spoons and two teapots which exploded on impact was spectacular.

Mr Campion mentally kicked himself. He had been watching so closely for a reaction from the two divorcés that he had totally missed the fact that the door to the room had been quietly opened by Tommy Taylor so that Miss Dubbs could make her entrance bearing refreshments.

Perhaps he was getting old, he thought, old and careless, but he would worry about that later.

In the instance, he sprang out of his chair to assist Miss Dubbs, who had collapsed like a marionette into a pile of broken crockery and steaming liquid, and who was wailing like a banshee.

# TWENTY
## Ealing Black Comedy

'Tania was my daughter. No one here knew. Even she didn't know.'

Alice Dubbs had been placed in the chair vacated by Peyton Spruce and examined for cuts, bruises and scalds by Sheila Kaye, who had hurtled downstairs when she heard the commotion. A white-faced, visibly shocked Tommy Taylor had produced a dustpan and brush from somewhere and was kneeling on the carpet, scooping up the wreckage of the tea service, whilst Brogan Bates had, with remarkable agility, gone behind the bar and poured a large measure of brandy into a sherry glass and, after a moment's thought, offered it to Miss Dubbs before returning to the bar to pour himself one.

Mr Campion had allowed the room to settle and then drawn his chair up to Alice's so that their knees were almost touching. Spruce and Bates stood either side of her, a hand on each shoulder, like two Chinthes, the lion-like mythical beasts which guarded the entrance to Burmese temples.

Despite the disruption and hysteria, Miss Dubbs's dramatic declaration had commanded the attention of the entire room, as it would have on stage on an opening night, or it did for about thirty seconds, and then all hell broke loose and everyone spoke at once. Or almost everyone. Mr Campion remained silent and noticed that so too did Tommy Taylor. Eventually he called for order.

'Please can we all calm down! This is an afternoon of shocks for this household and I fear there may be more to come. Unless anyone has a strong objection, I intend to declare myself umpire or chairman of this conclave and I promise you will all get a chance to have your say, but only after I have established some facts which I think it best you all hear.'

He clasped his hands in prayer and dipped them towards Miss Dubbs.

'Alice, this is your house. May I proceed?'

Miss Dubbs took a deep breath and pushed her shoulders back as if about to go on stage. 'Please take charge, Mr Campion. I am assuming you can tell me what happened to my daughter.'

'I will try, though I cannot provide any comfort.' Campion looked around the crowded room and saw he was the sole focus of attention. Even Brogan Bates had put his glass down.

'I came here today to break the sad news to Peyton and Brogan that their former wife was deceased, for the simple reason that the police had been unable to trace a next of kin for the woman. Neither I nor the police had any idea that I would find myself in the house of her mother.'

'We had no idea either,' said Spruce, with Bates nodding in agreement.

'I was twenty-seven when I had her,' said Miss Dubbs, loudly and clearly. 'Old enough to know better, but I didn't. I was unmarried and making good money on the music halls.' Her voice dropped. 'The father was a wastrel, a musician, who was long gone before Tania appeared, so I gave her away. Yes, gave her away. It was the best I could do for her. She went to a family called Parsloe who couldn't have children of their own. They were neighbours from back in my Clapham days and they looked after her and brought her up proper. I can't say I was pleased when I heard she had decided to go on the stage, but at least I could keep an eye on her and put in a good word with some producers. She was a lively, cheerful thing but, like her mother, not over-blessed with talent. I used to send money from time to time, anonymously of course, but then the war came and the Parsloes were bombed out.

'I went frantic trying to find what had happened to her, and for two years didn't have a clue. Then I saw a paragraph in the paper. Forthcoming weddings: Peyton Spruce and Tania Parsloe. I had given her the name Tania because it was uncommon, so it had to be her, and from then on I followed Peyton's career with interest. And then, of course, Brogan's, and when *they* got married, there were pictures in the papers and magazines, so I knew it was her.'

'Did you know of her subsequent marriage to Giles Smith?' Campion asked.

'Of course, and I knew he was a bad 'un from the off. I shed no tears for him.'

Spruce's hand squeezed Alice's shoulder. 'But you took in Brogan and me. Why?'

'You needed somewhere to live and I thought I might learn something of my daughter's life by having you under the same roof. But you never gave much away except that' – she turned her head and smiled at the two men in turn – 'you both cared about her in your own peculiar way. I think Tania had the misfortune to come between two fascinating men who had a friendship so complete, there was no room for a wife.'

She raised a hand and gently patted the two male hands on her shoulders. It was, Campion thought, one of the most touching gestures he had ever seen.

'Were you aware Tania was studying for the law?' Campion asked her.

'It was mentioned when that pig Giles Smith did the decent thing and topped himself. I almost tried to get in touch with her then, but I held back. She didn't need me in her life then. I don't think she ever had.'

'But you did try and help her in her legal career, didn't you?' Campion spoke softly. 'By recommending her to Eric Rudd and the Evadne Childe Society.'

Alice Dubbs fixed Campion with a pair of pale blue, very moist eyes. 'How did you know that?'

'An educated guess. Eric Rudd tracked down Peyton to this house, so I assume you met him and recommended a good show-business lawyer, without disclosing the family connection.'

'I found him a charming man and he only seemed to have Peyton's best intentions at heart. I had no idea whether Tania was any good as a lawyer, but I thought that if a nice man like Mr Rudd was getting involved with actors and film people, he could probably do with some legal help.'

'Hang on,' said Brogan Bates, expelling air through pink, inflated cheeks. 'Does that mean that little old Tania was helping Sprucey get the part in the new film?'

'She was certainly on his side, as was Eric Rudd.'

'After all this time . . .' Spruce whispered dreamily, then his eyes flashed to Campion. 'Wait; you said "was". Has something happened to Eric?'

'I'm afraid it has,' said Campion soberly. 'Eric Rudd has, like Tania, died violently, and the police have no doubt this time it was murder.'

'Are the deaths connected?' asked Alice Dubbs, automatically reaching to pat Spruce's hand on her shoulder.

'Almost certainly, and almost certainly the police will want to talk to everyone in this house.'

'Why?' Bates blustered. 'Surely our only concern is whether Sprucey's going to get the part now.'

'Oh, put a sock in it, Brogan. Don't be a pig for once.' This shrill outburst came from Sheila Kaye, who was wringing her hands together as if trying to thaw them out.

Campion stretched out his arms, as a referee would separate two boxers. 'Actually, Brogan, you have almost answered your own question,' he said. 'Two deaths, one quickly following the other, of people working together lobbying for Peyton to get the role of Rex Troughton.'

'But he so deserves it!' wailed Sheila.

'Sheila, please . . .' Spruce tried to deflect the woman's adoration. Was it genuine modesty, or good acting? When he turned to Campion, he was in another role, perhaps that of a barrister.

'Are you suggesting that two *deaths* are connected to *The Moving Mosaic*?'

'I am, along with numerous other incidents. The photographs from that French film sent to the BBC and Evadne Childe's publisher, a wilful disruption of the location down in Kingswalter and the food poisoning of a BBC scout down there, plus an attack on Jonathan Barlow, the designated director, in Soho, with a cricket bat, and, of course, the hit-and-run attempt on yourself.'

Mr Campion had concentrated on Brogan Bates when he said 'cricket bat', and was rewarded with a dropped jaw and wide-eyed reaction, but before he could exploit that, Peyton Spruce had a bombshell to drop.

'About that,' he said after clearing his throat. 'It wasn't a hit-and-run. No car was involved. It was an argument which turned into a fight, and I came off very much second best.'

Alice Dubbs glared up at Brogan Bates and slapped his hand away from her shoulder. 'Brogan! You thug!'

'It wasn't me!' exclaimed Bates, reacting as if stung.

'It wasn't Brogan, Alice,' said Spruce. 'It was . . . where's Tommy?'

Where Tommy 'Tuppence' Taylor had been kneeling in the doorway, there was a dustpan filled with broken crockery and a hand brush. Of the lugubrious comedian there was no sign.

'He was just here . . .' Sheila Kaye floundered as if startled by a magician's trick.

'He'll be in his shed,' said Alice Dubbs forcefully. 'He always goes there when he's upset.'

Campion attempted to reassert his authority as umpire. 'Could you explain things, Peyton?'

'I was out for my evening stroll and suddenly Tommy jumped out and started to berate me, demanding that I turn down the role of Rex Troughton. I thought he was being insanely jealous and I told him so. Things got heated, we tussled, and punches were thrown. He turned out to be a better puncher than me.'

'You always were a softy, Sprucey,' grinned Bates, only to be silenced by icy glares from Alice and Sheila.

'But you let everybody think it was a traffic accident,' said Campion.

The actor dropped his chin to his chest and concentrated on the carpet under his feet.

'Tommy helped me up and apologized for hitting me. I think he was more upset than I was and he started crying. I calmed him down and suggested we come back to Curtains separately and not say anything about our quarrel, and I would make up the story of a road accident.'

'There's something else, isn't there, Peyton?' Campion probed as Spruce's voice tailed off.

'Jonathan Barlow. The man who was appointed director for *The Moving Mosaic*. I told Tommy he'd been offered the job and I even mentioned that Jonathan would be at that awards ceremony in Soho.'

'He was the one clouted with a cricket bat!' Brogan Bates began to bluster. 'That's why you were grilling me about it! Well, it's no secret I've got one, but anyone in this house could have borrowed it without me noticing. Tommy could have lifted it easily.'

'Then we'd better find Tommy,' said Campion. 'Peyton, come with me, Brogan, phone the police and don't have another drink until you have.'

They paused at the back door. Campion had opened it but stretched out an arm to block Spruce's progress. At the bottom of the long rectangular garden with its neat, raised beds and geometric planting, was a clump of fruit trees and a small wooden shed painted green with a roof covered in black roofing felt. Campion had seen Wendy houses built for spoiled children which were bigger, but the absence of windows made it clear this was a utilitarian shed.

'Is there any way out of the garden?'

'There's a thumping great wall beyond the apple trees, but I doubt Tommy could get over that without a ladder. He's our age, you know.'

'Don't remind me,' said Campion. 'I came to terms with the fact that I could no longer leap high buildings years ago. I do not see any wires from the house.'

'I'm sorry?'

'Is there electricity laid on to the shed?'

'No, he has an old kerosene lantern in there. Is that important?'

'Anything else?'

Campion read the puzzlement on his companion's handsome face, which was so close to his own that he could see the faded 'tide mark' of his make-up. 'Does he have anything dangerous in there?'

'He has a little camping gas burner,' said Spruce, 'with which we always thought he would blow himself up, but that's just for boiling a kettle to sterilize plant pots or whatever it is he does when he takes cuttings and does his planting.'

'But no weapons?'

The actor did not have to act; he was genuinely shocked at the thought, and doubly so when he realized he was still holding the garden trowel he had been using as a rehearsal prop.

'Good Lord, no! Well, shears and pruning saws. I suppose they qualify as sharp objects. Oh, and a scythe, but that's a bit Grim Reaper-ish, isn't it?'

Campion responded with a completely straight face.

'Let's be careful out there and, Peyton, I want you to stay absolutely quiet. I mean that. Whatever happens, you don't say a word, not a word. Got it?'

Spruce nodded, but Campion knew he was asking the impossible of an actor about to take to the stage, for there was no doubt they were now playing out a drama.

'I mean it, Peyton. You must keep absolutely silent unless I introduce you. Wait for your cue, understand?'

Peyton nodded again, more enthusiastically than before, then followed Campion out of the doorway and into the garden.

Although he could see there were no windows in the shed at the bottom of the garden, and had been assured that Taylor was unarmed, Campion automatically shrank his torso into a stooped crouch which Spruce copied immediately behind him. With an almost comical Marx Brothers gait, Campion stepped quickly but lightly down the gravel path between the raised beds and pots, planted or arranged in neat geometric shapes.

His eyes flicked from side to side and, though he did not slow his pace, he felt as if his long legs had turned to lead. Although the flower beds looked neat at first glance, they contained many unkempt and unusual plants. Campion spotted the big finger-shaped leaves and red stem of a castor oil plant, water hemlock growing as a weed in one bed, giant hogweed and deadly nightshade snuggling between flowers in another, and along the south-facing wall, in between trained peach trees, oleanders in terracotta pots. As they closed on the shed, he saw, almost with resigned satisfaction, that the apple trees beyond were sprouting mistletoe, and they formed a fitting boundary to what Campion was mentally thinking of as a poisoner's paradise.

A yard from the shed, Campion sank down on one knee, Spruce doing the same at his side like a fellow penitent, and stared at the wood-panelled door. A rusty metal hasp, which slotted over a staple, seemed to be the locking mechanism and one usually secured by a padlock, but the hasp hung open and the padlock was missing.

Carefully, Campion leaned forward and hooked his fingertips under the bottom lip of the door and gently tested its resistance, then he looked at Spruce and shook his head. Spruce immediately mimed loading a bolt-action rifle and pointed a finger to the top of the door, at which Campion raised a thumb to indicate he had understood, then placed a finger to his lips, reminding him of his vow of silence.

'Tommy, this is Albert Campion. I know you're in there and we really need to talk. I am not the police, Tommy, but they are on their way. You do not know me and I certainly cannot say I am your friend, but I am a sympathetic ear and I think you could do with someone to listen to without judging you.'

His appeal was met with total silence.

'Mr Taylor,' Campion tried again, 'I am sure you can hear me and I think I know the reason you are ashamed to show your face. You did not know Tania Smith was Alice's daughter, did you? How

could you? No one did. How did you even know she existed? I
presume you were present when Alice recommended her to Eric
Rudd – and him you knew thanks to your visits to the late Mrs
Hatherall down in Brighton and your interest in *The Moving Mosaic*.'

Still there was no response and Campion, feeling old age
creeping up on him, stood up and stretched, then lowered himself
on to his other knee. Spruce could not help but notice that Campion
was concentrating intently on the actual wooden door rather than
what might be behind it.

'You see, I was very stupid, Tommy, or perhaps simply slow,
a legacy of advancing age. I got it into my feeble brain that Brogan,
with his really quite ugly van, was the only driver in the house,
but the police now have a list of visitors to Mrs Hatherall and you
are on it and that noisy little van was also spotted down in Dorset,
the filming location, on more than one occasion.'

Campion now stood up to his full height and stepped close to
the shed door, extending his fingers so that the tips traced the
outline of the wooden slats, feeling for places where the door did
not fit flush to the frame.

'You've been actively trying to sabotage the remake of *The
Moving Mosaic* for some time, haven't you, Tommy? What I can't
understand is why, and if you won't tell me, perhaps you'll tell
Alice Dubbs. I think you owe her an explanation.'

'No!'

At last, a reaction.

'Not Alice. I can't see Alice – not now, not ever.'

'I can understand that, Tommy. How about Peyton?'

Campion and Spruce exchanged glances, Campion hoping that
the actor would stick to his vow of silence.

'No, not him! I can't face him. It was all for him, but I can't
face him either.'

Behind him, Campion heard Spruce's sharp intake of breath.

'You've known him for quite a while, haven't you?' he said,
his fingers still exploring the edges of the door.

'On the set of *The Moving Mosaic*, twenty years ago.' The voice
from inside the shed was fainter, softer. 'I was just an extra in a
scene in the pub in Kingswalter. It was just one scene and I didn't
have any lines; it was my first and last experience of being an
actor.'

'And that's where you met?' Campion's fingers had reached the bottom of the door edge and had begun their spidery climb upwards.

'He didn't even notice me at the time, though he said he remembered me when we met again in London when he came back from France with Brogan. He was broke and down on his luck and I couldn't stand to see him like that, so I suggested to Alice that he moved in to Curtains.' There was a pause and a sigh. 'And Brogan had to come too. I had no idea they had both been married to Alice's daughter, but now I see that Alice relished the idea of being able to keep an eye on both of them because, mad as it sounds, she's very fond of them.'

Campion thought that was not the maddest thing he had heard recently, but kept it to himself. He realized that Peyton's face was quivering, there was no other word for it, as he struggled to contain – if not control – his emotions.

'An unusual set-up to be sure,' said Campion, suddenly intrigued by a section of the door near the top where he guessed the bolt was fixed on the interior, 'but one which seemed to work; and all concerned seemed to get on well enough until the prospect of a remake of *The Moving Mosaic* cropped up. Would I be right in assuming that?'

'That bloody film!' The voice from the shed was weak, but there was a genuine anger in it. 'And that stupid woman trying to insist on casting privileges! She just wouldn't listen.'

Campion froze and stopped his examination of the door. 'Tommy, you didn't do anything to Mrs Hatherall when you visited her, did you?'

Next to him, Spruce leaned forward, anxious to catch the answer. 'No, I didn't, though I was tempted.' The reply came punctuated with a bout of coughing. 'She said she was Peyton's biggest fan. Hah! To say that to me! I could have killed her, but I didn't, and when she died I thought it was over until Rudd got involved.'

'And things escalated,' Campion said calmly, the fingertips of his right hand definitely finding purchase in a gap between the edge of the door and the frame where it did not lie flush, 'although I am terribly confused still. Surely it was Peyton's big chance for a comeback, reprising his most famous role. Why would you want to sabotage that?'

He was answered by a throat-rattling cough and a thumping noise, as if someone had sat down heavily or fallen to the floor.

'Tommy? Mr Taylor? Are you all right?'

Campion put his fingers flat against Spruce's lips to stifle the actor's urge to break silence and tried, with his eyes, to tell him to restrain himself. As he did so he noticed that Spruce was still holding, in fact gripping tightly, the gardening trowel he had been rehearsing with.

They were both distracted by a bout of sustained coughing from the shed and they had to strain to hear Tommy Taylor's next words.

'It wasn't right, it wouldn't have been right. Peyton was too old to play Rex Troughton again, no matter what that stupid old woman thought, no matter how good the make-up. He would have shown himself up.' More coughing and a gagging sound. 'He would have been pilloried by the critics.' Now an audible gasp. 'He would have been laughed at. I wasn't going to have that as a memory.'

'Tommy!' yelled Spruce, unable to contain himself any longer. 'That was never your decision to make. You had no right!'

'Peyton? Is that you?'

The voice was now very weak, a faint radio signal struggling out of the ether.

'I had to save you . . . from yourself.'

There was another loud thump from inside the shed, followed by the unmistakable sound of breaking glass.

Campion ripped the trowel from Spruce's hand and inserted the curved tongue into the minute gap he had located between door and frame. It was far from the ideal tool for breaking and entering. A proper triangular archaeologist's trowel with a point would have been better, as would a chisel or a knife; instead, he had only an outsize dessert spoon to work with. Yet, by hitting the handle with the palm of his hand, he pushed the metal a half-inch into the gap and twisted. It was enough. The wooden slats of the door were old and the edges friable and the bolt holding it on the inside was hanging by a thread.

Campion used the trowel as a lever and an inch-wide strip of wood snapped off with a loud crack. He dropped the trowel and thrust the fingers of both hands into the gap and heaved. The door creaked and swung outwards, bolt and all.

As Campion staggered backwards still holding the edges of the door, Spruce took a step towards the entrance then stopped dead in his tracks.

'Jesus, Tommy! What have you done?'

Without ceremony, and possibly with some relish, Campion pushed the actor to one side, lowered his head and looked inside.

In the statement he was later to give to the police, Mr Campion described the scene which greeted him as 'the immediate aftermath of a hand grenade'. The interior of the shed, lit by a single paraffin lamp, which had somehow remained intact hanging from a hook in the roof, was an incoherent jumble of broken plant pots, crushed plants, sacks of compost which seemed to have exploded and shelves containing glass jars and bottles, which had all been pulled from their supporting brackets. There was a table of sorts, with a saucepan on a gas-ring burner and a smell of something having been cooked in it.

Try as he might, Campion could not identify the smell, though he could detect aromas of fruit, possibly tobacco, and something akin to burnt liquorice.

The table and the saucepan were covered with a frosting of broken glass, leaves and twigs, from the kitchen cabinet of jars which Taylor had brought crashing down upon himself as he had blundered around the shed. That he had done so whilst in considerable agony was clear, for Tommy Taylor now lay on his back on a pile of broken plant pots, crushed plants and smashed bottles, clutching a Kilner jar containing a black liquid to his chest. There was vomit on his chest and his face was disfigured by a rictus grin.

'Amazingly,' said Commander Charles Luke, 'he's going to survive, though whether he'll be fit to go to trial is another matter.'

The police had arrived at Curtains along with an ambulance, which had carried Tommy Taylor off to hospital under guard. Alice Dubbs's doctor had been summoned to treat her for shock, despite Brogan Bates's assertion that she could be put back on her dancing feet with a large brandy. It was decided that she should go to hospital for a thorough check-up, though not, of course, in the same ambulance as Tommy Taylor. Sheila Kaye went with her, touching up her make-up as she lay on a stretcher so that she would look her best for the doctors.

After telephoning Charles Luke, Mr Campion had returned to the garden to keep the uniformed constable placed on guard duty on the shed company, whilst statements were taken from the residents. He was wandering idly around the raised beds when Luke arrived and joined him.

'One way or another, Charles, it has been a good clear-up day for you chaps,' Campion said, his mood melancholy. 'Crimes in the City, in Bethnal Green, here in Ealing and down in Dorset can all be laid at Taylor's door.'

'Dorset?' queried Luke.

'There's a BBC man called Don Chapman in hospital in Dorchester. I am ninety per cent sure he was poisoned by Taylor, using that.' Campion pointed out the evergreen shrubs growing in pots along the garden's south wall. 'Oleander. Looks pretty, but can be very nasty, like so much in our world. Best tell your chaps not to touch anything without gloves on, especially in the shed.'

'You reckon that's what he tried to do himself away with?'

'The doctors will tell us, but he certainly seems to have brewed up some horrible concoctions in there in case he needed them and, once the game was up, he headed straight for his shed with no intention of coming out.'

'And what was his motive?' Luke studied his shoes, idly kicking the gravel in the path.

'You had it right all along, Charles,' said Campion, 'or *almost* right.'

'Would you say ninety-nine per cent right?' asked Luke with a sly grin.

'Perhaps eighty per cent. It was a crime – or crimes – of passion, as you thought, but the passion in question was never jealousy. It was love.'

# TWENTY-ONE
## Mr Campion, Producer

'I don't think we could have done this without you, Mr Campion,' said Tamara Reams, 'and if all was fair in the world, you'd deserve a credit as a producer, but this is television and it isn't fair, so you won't be getting one.'

'I really do not mind staying out of the limelight, I am just happy that things seem to be going to plan at last.'

Campion was sitting on a folding camping chair trying to enjoy a plastic cup of milky tea, in the middle of the driveway leading to Kingswalter Manor. He had positioned the chair not so that he could see downhill and the village below, or up the drive to the manor house, but rather off to the left of the drive where the copse of trees and a tangle of brambles, now cleared away, had previously hidden the remains of the Roman villa and its infamous mosaic floor.

It was a scene of bustling activity, with cameras, battery-powered spotlights, assistant cameramen holding up large paper discs to prevent or cause shadows (Campion did not know which and was reluctant to ask), sound technicians wearing headphones and waving long, prehensile boom microphones, and a dozen or more young people, the majority girls, criss-crossing the site clutching clipboards, scripts, make-up bags and mirrors or more plastic cups and vacuum flasks of the sweet milky tea Campion was trying to surreptitiously dispose of.

It was nearly three months since the real drama in Ealing had cleared the air for the fictional drama to begin production, and the decision had been taken to begin filming the 'exteriors' on location before autumn arrived in earnest. There was already an autumnal nip to the air, which had divided all those involved, in that the technical crew, including the platoon of younger 'runners' (Campion had been told the American equivalent was 'gophers' but he thought this undignified) were warmly covered in anoraks or duffel coats, whereas the actors who were to be filmed as if it was high summer looked distinctly unhappy in short-sleeved shirts and shorts.

Mr Campion, in the sole chair allowed on the 'set', as he was learning to call it, had been approached by a nervous teenage girl 'runner' who had asked if he would like a blanket around his knees. He had declined the offer politely, pointing out that he was quite toasty in his shooting jacket, which had been recommended by friends at Holland & Holland, and that he hoped he didn't look like an invalid.

Secretly he hoped he looked like an eccentric Hollywood director, especially with his fedora pulled down over his eyes, observing proceedings with a critical eye. In truth, no one apart from Tamara Reams had paid him much attention, and he was regretting his dismissal of Amanda's rather caustic suggestion that he should dress in jodhpurs and jackboots, sport a monocle and carry a megaphone. That would have got him noticed, but almost certainly to the dismay of his son Rupert, who had accepted an offer of gainful employment as an extra – one of the archaeologist diggers working for Rex Troughton – though without any lines of dialogue.

From his vantage point, Campion could see Rupert taking his position on the mosaic with the other extras under direction from Jonathan Barlow, who had recovered completely from his battering – as he liked to call it – by Tommy Taylor. The scene involved the archaeologists carefully trowelling away at the sand and soil which had been supplied by the props department (in wheel-barrows probably leased from Joe Lunn), in order to 'reveal' the mosaic for the first time, or at least a portion of it in close-up. It was a carefully staged scene, lacking only one thing, the arrival of the star of the show, Rex Troughton.

The manor house itself had been commandeered as the main production office, Ranald Ward-Tetley having negotiated a favour-able rental agreement which included the reinstatement of a working telephone line. The principal actors had been allocated dressing rooms there, but the nearest the extras – who were expected to change in a large and rickety caravan imported from a campsite at Lyme Regis – got to the manor was the catering truck parked in front of it. Referred to as the 'chuck wagon' by the veteran BBC technicians, the long, flat-back lorry with drop sides dispensed free hot drinks, soups and snacks seemingly during all the hours of daylight.

It was clearly popular with the young 'runners' and the extras, not to mention the two uniformed Dorset constabulary constables, who were officially in charge of traffic and crowd control and were stationed by the drive gates.

'It is going to plan, isn't it?' Campion asked Tamara Reams when she tried to press him to another cup of tea. 'It seems all rather chaotic to the uninitiated, but at least it looks like organized chaos.'

'I suppose it does, but somehow it all comes out right in the end.'

'I am sure this will be a triumph for you, even though you have had to make compromises.'

Tamara allowed herself a wry smile.

'In this business, little compromises are necessary to get to the day of principal shooting. Once that is achieved, things tend to go smoother because too much has been invested to turn back.'

Mr Campion knew, because Amanda had insisted he kept track of developments, that Tamara Reams had been forced into one major compromise by her lords and masters high up at the BBC. Fearing the taint of bad publicity when – if – Tommy Taylor came to trial, the executive decision had been taken that Tamara's vision for a two-hour film of *The Moving Mosaic* be cut to a much more 'manageable' (BBC code for cheaper) one-hour drama, with the distant promise of a series if the pilot film proved popular. This had meant considerable pruning of the story and the script and the loss of many carefully chosen locations which would have added to the nostalgic 1950 setting.

From the script Rupert had purloined from Ward-Tetley, and which Amanda had devoured and memorized, he knew that key scenes of a car chase involving Wolseley police cars and a recreation of the departure lounge in the Europa Building at London Airport, as it was then known, had been axed. Still, he reasoned, that meant the story should move along quicker, and the few scenes which were being filmed on location, and not in a BBC sound studio, would be more memorable and eye-catching, especially the ones in Kingswalter which, after all, featured a real Roman mosaic, the beautiful Dorset countryside and, of course, Rupert Campion, surely a magnetic presence, even without lines of dialogue.

Rupert was certainly taking his role seriously, and from his picnic-chair throne, Mr Campion watched with approval as his son engaged with the director, determined to follow every instruction to the letter as to where he should stand, or rather kneel, as if busy clearing the mosaic. He was one of half a dozen extras, all male, all dressed as young men would have been for a summer digging on an archaeological site in 1950, in collarless ex-army shirts, too-long khaki shorts rolled up above the knee, dark socks and black plimsolls. Given the chilliness of the incoming sea breeze, Campion thought Rupert was controlling the goosebumps and shivers admirably.

'Here comes our star,' said Tamara at his shoulder, and Campion immediately turned his head to see Alec Devine marching down the drive, flanked by two girls, one holding a clipboard, the other armed with a blusher brush and a compact of powder, occasionally stabbing at the actor's valuable cheekbones with the accuracy of an Olympic fencer.

Apart from a long woollen overcoat hanging loose over his shoulders, Devine was dressed for the part in a check countryman's shirt and sober blue tie, tweed trousers held up with bright red braces (which were to become a trademark, Campion had been told) and brown brogues. In his right hand he held a trilby with a green feather cockade identical, Campion thought, to the one Peyton Spruce had liberated from the set of the original film, which he used to flap ineffectively at the make-up girl when she became too intrusive, as if swatting away an attack of midges.

As he approached, Devine waved away the two girls and gave an exaggerated shrug so that the overcoat slipped off his shoulders. It was an impressive, practised move; the girl with the clipboard had been expecting it and caught the coat with aplomb before it hit the gravel.

'Mr Campion, we are honoured,' he declaimed in Shakespearean tones, as if aiming for the rear stalls. 'I hope you're being looked after.'

Campion levered himself out of his chair to greet Devine's

arrival. 'It is an honour to be present as the magic of television is created,' he said, 'and Tamara here has looked after me splendidly, though I suspect she has far more important things to do.'

'As a matter of fact, I do,' Tamara agreed, 'so if you'll excuse me, I'll leave you to watch Alec's scene. If you stay here, you won't be in shot, and I needn't remind you to keep absolutely quiet.'

'If you insist,' Campion smiled, 'but I had fully intended to jump up and down and shout "Yoo-hoo" when my son is on camera.'

'Please don't,' said Tamara as she hurried off.

'Your son?' asked Devine.

'Rupert, you met him briefly in Dorchester. He's a big fan of yours and he's wangled a job as an extra. He's one of Rex Troughton's loyal diggers.'

'Does he have an Equity card?'

'Oh yes, he's a fully qualified, by which I mean mostly unemployed, actor.'

Devine chuckled politely, though Campion had the feeling he was not laughing with his eyes and indeed looked at Campion with something akin to suspicion. It was as if he could not comprehend why this clearly well-connected elderly gentleman, who obviously had influence with the BBC, was not in thrall to actors and programme-makers and seemed to regard the whole thing as no more than an excuse for a stroll in the country, blissfully unaware of the vast amount of talent and creative energy assembled on that Dorset hillside, dedicated to the production of perhaps five minutes' worth of priceless television.

Neither did he seem impressed when a mechanical voice crackled through a loudhailer with the announcement: 'First positions, please. Mr Devine, please take your mark. Quiet on set, we'll be going for a take.'

'Break a leg,' said Mr Campion cheerfully, 'if that's what one says. Good luck anyway.'

Devine gave him a simpering look of thanks, as if indicating that luck was not really in it for an actor of his calibre, and strode over to the edge of the mosaic, jamming the trilby on his head as he walked.

'Mark!' said the loudhailer from over by the camera position, and Devine stopped, turning his head to the left to make sure the camera had his best side.

'Hold positions please. Wardrobe! Check on Mr Devine's hat, please!'

'What the . . .?' Devine reached up and fumbled his trilby, as if to make it fit better, then pulled it off completely and glared at it.

'Sorry, Jonathan, the girl gave me the wrong one,' he shouted across the mosaic, then he turned back towards Campion and grinned sheepishly, twirling the trilby on one finger around the rim. 'The idiots in wardrobe always get them mixed up. We have several for continuity purposes. This one's the small size and is a static prop, not one for wearing. I thought it felt a bit odd.'

Campion leaned back in his chair and crossed one long leg over the other and watched with amusement as one of the young 'runners' actually fulfilled her job description and began running up the drive to the manor to fetch a replacement.

'There will be a short delay in proceedings,' said Devine grumpily.

Taking advantage of the hiatus in filming, Campion acknow-ledged a wave from a kneeling, trowel-wielding Rupert by raising his fedora.

'In my day, every young man knew his hat size,' he said inno-cently, then raised his fedora again. 'I don't suppose my titfer would be of any use in the meantime?'

Devine looked at him with a mixture of amazement and distaste.

'That would be out of character for my character,' said Devine, 'and whoever heard of an archaeologist wearing a fedora?'


Lady Amanda was being far more deferential in the presence of a noted thespian than her husband, so much so that Lugg had muttered the words 'star-struck' under his breath more than once.

Campion himself had suggested that Tamara Reams, Jonathan Barlow and, of course, Alec Devine, should lodge at The King's Head, which would be good public relations for the village as a whole, and a vote of confidence by senior BBC people in the pub's catering. As an added bonus, Tessa Higgins had declared herself a fan of the dashingly handsome Alec Devine and had vowed to treat him royally.

Rupert, along with the other extras, had been put up in one of the bed-and-breakfast establishments which had mysteriously sprung up almost overnight in Kingswalter, which meant that the Campions and Lugg, who would not be left behind in London, had booked rooms in a Dorchester hotel, where to Amanda's surprise, though not her husband's, a fellow guest turned out to be Peyton Spruce. What did take Campion slightly by surprise was the fact that Peyton was accompanied, naturally in separate rooms, by Sheila Kaye.

Amanda volunteered enthusiastically to act as a chauffeur for Peyton and Sheila, in fact she insisted on it, dismissing the local taxi pre-ordered by the BBC, and because Peyton was not required to report for duty until mid-afternoon, she grasped the opportunity to have lunch with her fictional hero, Rex Troughton.

Except it was not Rex Troughton that she sat down with in the hotel dining room. It was not even the Peyton Spruce who had played him in the original film. The same chiselled features were there, but there were lines on that matinee idol face and the hair, though still luxurious, was now unkempt and shockingly white. A pair of wire-framed glasses had completed the transformation, or rather the ageing, of Peyton Spruce. For once, Peyton Spruce not only looked his age, but actually older, and certainly older than her husband.

'Can I confess,' Amanda said over oxtail soup served with a small schooner of dry sherry (it was a rather pretentious hotel), 'that I always fantasized about having lunch with Rex Troughton, ever since I read my first Evadne Childe novel.'

'I am so sorry to disappoint you, Lady Amanda, and while I can no longer appear as your favourite archaeologist detective, I hope you find the presence of Professor Chenery, his disapproving former tutor at Cambridge, equally engaging.'

'I am delighted to meet you, Professor Chenery,' said Amanda, graciously playing along. 'To be honest, I was unaware of your existence until now.'

The elderly academic looked suitably embarrassed.

'I'm afraid I do not feature in the novels of Evadne Childe.'

'I know, I would have remembered as I am something of an expert on them, though according to my husband that is "expert" pronounced "bore".'

'Surely not. Mr Campion is well aware of your love of the books, and hoped you would not mind the introduction of a new character in this latest adaptation and appreciate that it is a fond nod to tradition and continuity.'

Amanda thought about this as the soup plates were cleared away. 'Well, that certainly sounds like my husband. Are you saying that Albert had something to do with the creation of Professor Chenery?'

A waiter hovered with a bottle of red wine and poured out four glasses, before Peyton requested water instead as he was performing that afternoon. Lugg muttered 'I'm not' and slid Peyton's glass towards his own.

'Mr Campion had everything to do with my creation,' said Spruce, peering at Amanda over the tops of his clear-glass spectacles, as a professor might address an enthusiastic but rather dim student. 'He suggested it to our producer, Tamara. Rex Troughton's old tutor could fill in something of his backstory for people who haven't read any of the books – and I can tell from your face that's a heretical thought – and to give me a cameo role would be a nice touch for fans of the first film. It might also help with a bit of publicity, if anyone remembers me, that is.'

'Oh, I'm sure they do,' gushed Amanda. 'You'll always be Rex Troughton for the true fan.'

'With bit of luck, Alec Devine will now be Rex Troughton and hopefully for a long-running series to come.'

'That means more work for you, don't it?' Lugg asked, tucking into a plate of gammon and chips, having carefully pushed the pineapple ring to one side for dessert.

'Fingers crossed, it might. I only have two scenes, so I have to make a good impression as Alec's – I mean Rex's – older, wiser mentor so he becomes a regular, indispensable character.'

'Well, you certainly look old and wise,' said Amanda. Then hurriedly added: 'With all that excellent make-up.'

'That's down to Sheila here.' Spruce laid down his fork and patted the back of Sheila Kaye's hand. 'She's spent the last few years at Curtains making me look younger, but making me look my age took a matter of minutes.'

Sheila Kaye smiled and blushed endearingly.

'How are things at Curtains? Albert told me all about his adventures there.'

'And, no doubt, the crazy theatricals who lived there, but we're really not a bad bunch. Not even poor Tommy Taylor.'

'If you don't count 'im as one of a bad bunch,' growled Lugg, 'then I wish you'd been a magistrate when I 'ad to do my act before the bench.'

'You're right to pull me up on that, Mr Lugg,' said Spruce, who did not know quite who or what Lugg was, other than a person not to annoy. 'What I should have said was that Tommy was disturbed and not really responsible for his actions, and his actions were, of course, reprehensible. Oddly enough, his crimes have brought two of the residents of Curtains closer together. A touch of comedy out of the tragedy, you might say.'

'Really?' Amanda was immediately alert as this was the sort of intelligence Albert never reported back on.

'It involves my good friend Brogan, who has been down on his luck for some time. He and I had the same wife – not at the same time, of course. Tania, the daughter of Alice Dubbs, though we did not know that until recent events. With Tania's death, Brogan inherited her estate, what there was of it, as her nearest next of kin. It was a few hundred pounds, but it has cheered Brogan up no end, plus he is spending it with Alice Dubbs. In fact, he's quite enjoying having a mother-in-law.'

'But you was married to this Tania as well,' Lugg pointed out.

'Yes, but Tania and I were divorced and then she married Brogan after me.'

'So,' Lugg said ponderously, 'it isn't who the first husband was that matters, only who's the most recent . . .'

He raised his eyebrows and treated Amanda to a leer ripe with mischief.

'You should keep that in mind, Lady A.'

'Dr Troughton, Professor Chenery's here to see you.'

'Rupert has dialogue!'

'Cut!'

'Lady Amanda, you really must be quiet while we're filming,' admonished Tamara Reams.

'I am so sorry; it was just such a surprise that my son had lines to say. It won't happen again; I promise to control myself.'

'Please see that she does,' Tamara said quietly, but she said it to Lugg as she had already identified him as the one who would stand for no nonsense.

The viewing gallery at the mosaic had expanded to four camping chairs, occupied by Sheila Kaye, as Spruce's personal make-up artist, Amanda and Campion and, the chair straining and creaking under his weight, Lugg.

After Amanda's involuntary exclamation had interrupted proceedings, filming was halted until the principal actors, now including Peyton Spruce, and the extras resumed their original positions and, in the case of the 'diggers', scraped back the soil and sand they had excavated from the surface of the mosaic.

Lugg, ruminating on a full stomach, but already looking forward to a dinner of mutton curry at The King's Head, remained unimpressed at seeing the wonders of television unfolding before him. He leaned in to Campion until their shoulders touched and spoke out of the corner of his mouth.

'If they was to make a film of your life and all your adventures, who would you fancy to play you?'

Mr Campion appeared to consider the question seriously. 'It is pointless to speculate,' he said, 'as, to ensure box-office success, any film of my adventures would be sure to omit the character of Albert Campion all together.'

Lugg considered Mr Campion's reply for a full half-minute before responding. 'But there'd be a part in it for me, wouldn't there?'

# Author's Note

The location of the house 'Curtains' is a homage to Margery Allingham, who was born at 5 Broughton Road, Ealing in 1904, although the actual house was destroyed by bombing during World War II. Each year, on or near 20 May, the Margery Allingham Society holds a birthday lunch in her honour, with a guest speaker and, of course, a cake. I am grateful to Sheila Mitchell for allowing the name of her late husband Harry Keating to be taken in vain.

The rather acidic put-down 'but you are well known', attributed here to Brogan Bates, was inspired, *almost* verbatim, by a lively exchange between the artists Dennis Wirth-Miller and Francis Bacon in The Black Buoy, Wivenhoe, Essex, in 1979. Those were the days.

The radio horror story Campion remembers in chapter five was almost certainly *The Thorns Are Vicious* by Philip Youngman Carter, first published in *Argosy* in 1946 and later collected in *Tales on the Off-Beat* (Ostara Publishing, 2015). It was never, to my knowledge, adapted for radio.

The 'Kingswalter Massacre' was inspired by a real-life incident which took place in October 1944 at The Crown Inn, Kingsclere, in Hampshire. I have appropriated certain details of that shocking case, which was kept very quiet for many years after the war. It was brought to my attention by a group of 'ghost-hunters' (the inspiration for 'The Prophetics') after the story was told in an article in *The Mail on Sunday* in June 1988 and again in the *Hampshire Gazette* in 1996, at which time the pub was closed and boarded up. Further information was supplied to me by Ms Laura Stuart of Hampshire County Libraries, for which I am grateful, but attempts to trace the fortunes of those convicted through US military records proved fruitless. The Crown, under new ownership, is today a thriving pub-restaurant and, if it is not haunted, perhaps it should be.

The Burgess Meredith film *Welcome to Britain* was made in 1943, and the scene dealing with segregation, or the lack of it in Britain, is particularly toe-curling.

The idea of making a television crime drama with location filming and episodes lasting two hours was probably unthinkable in 1972. It was not until January 1987 that *Inspector Morse* broke the mould with 'The Dead of Jericho', after much internal debate and lobbying with ITV by producer Kenny McBain, scriptwriter Anthony Minghella and the series producer, my old chum Ted Childs OBE, who allowed me to ransack his memories.

The advice 'books are books, but television is television', attributed here to Tamara Reams, was guidance often given to young crime writers by Colin Dexter.

Anyone familiar with the beautiful county of Dorset will easily recognize Abbotsbury and its famous swannery as the inspiration for Kingswalter, with apologies for all liberties taken.

The mosaic found in the grounds of Kingswalter Manor was inspired by the mosaic, dating from around AD 350, found in a Roman villa at Hinton St Mary in Dorset, which is illustrated in Peter Salway's *Oxford Illustrated History of Roman Britain* (1993). I am also indebted in many ways to research by Anne Lambert, who made the byways of southern England that much more interesting. The ancient Roman method of moving a mosaic floor featured in the novel *Murder on the Appian Way* by Kenneth Benton (1974), which was inspired by Cicero's defence of the gladiator Milo (*Pro Milone*).

Lugg's fanciful description of supernatural goings-on in the Suffolk village of Sanctuary in chapter eighteen is taken, somewhat frivolously, from Margery Allingham's 1931 novel *Look to the Lady*.

During Margery Allingham's lifetime, only one of her Albert Campion books was filmed, the 1956 version of *The Tiger in the Smoke*. The character Albert Campion was completely omitted.